D1808922

Sins of the People

Andrew D Malloy

PNEUMA SPRINGS PUBLISHING UK

First Published in 2022 by:
Pneuma Springs Publishing

Sins of the People
Copyright © 2022   Andrew D Malloy
ISBN13: 9781782284833

Andrew D Malloy has asserted his right under the Copyright, Designs and
Patents Act, 1988, to be identified as Author of this Work

British Library Cataloguing in Publication Data. A catalogue record for
this book is available from the British Library.

Pneuma Springs Publishing
A Subsidiary of Pneuma Springs Ltd.
7 Groveherst Road, Dartford Kent, DA1 5JD.
E: admin@pneumasprings.co.uk
W: www.pneumasprings.co.uk

'Success depends almost entirely on how effectively you learn to manage the game's two ultimate adversaries: the course and yourself.'

Jack Nicklaus

Acknowledgements

This book is dedicated to my amazing family – Sue, Dani, Stephen and Ollie the Collie.

Apologies to the good people of Tel Aviv, Zurich, Washington DC. and Las Vegas for mixing the fake with the facts as regards street names, buildings and landmarks. And please don't worry, Washington DC., the iconic Joan of Arc statue is still there in the middle of Meridian Hill Park!

And finally, my heartfelt thanks to Vivian and her team at Pneuma Springs for their sterling work in transforming my ramblings into something special and dear to my heart.

THE CATALYST

CHICAGO, USA

'Third and last call, it's over to you! Breakfast's on the table!' The father stands at the bottom of the stairs. Hands on hips. Exasperated. Shakes his head. 'I swear to God-'

A muffled cry. Her bedroom door creaks open. In a state of semi-consciousness, the daughter shuffles into the bathroom. Twirls the shower knob. Checks the time. 'Sonovab-! Dad, I have to be out in fifteen minutes, why didn't you call me?'

'Don't even go there, Maddie. And please, mind your language!'

'*Sorry.*'

Ten minutes later she is sitting at the kitchen table, pulling a brush through her wet hair with one hand and spooning cereal into her mouth with the other.

Troy Williams leans back against the stove, folds his arms and shakes his head, again. 'Why don't you run the after-school arrangements past me one more time, just so I have it clear in my mind,' he says, his eyes narrowing.

She stuffs the brush in her bag and grabs a mouthful of milk as she stands. 'Dad, I told you already. I really do not have time for this. Look, I'll send you a text.'

'No, no texts. Tell me again. I'll walk you to the door.'

'Whatever.' Sighing heavily, she throws the bag over her shoulder, heads along the hall to freedom. Pausing at the front door, she sighs again, says, 'Okay, Alison, Suzy, Georgia and me are all going back to Dani's to do some study work ahead of the test on Friday. You know the one I told you about the other day, the English test?'

'Okay, and how're you getting home?' he asks.

'I told you this as well. Dani's mom is going to drop me off around seven-thirty.' Her voice cuts a frustrated tone as she huffily pulls open the door.

'I hope this is an all-girl arrangement, Maddie,' he calls after her. 'I wouldn't like to hear later that that punk kid, Declan, is it, is going to be tagging along as well?'

'It's Damien, and no, he isn't going to be there.' She turns to face him, still walking, but backwards. 'And even if he was, what are you gonna do, shoot him?' She turns around again when the school bus arrives. Good timing.

'Yeah, I just might at that.'

The bus ride to school consists of twenty minutes of chatting with a friend about boys, the latest fashions, make-up, reality tv shows, everything bar school work. And exchanging daggers with arch-enemy, Megan Dance, the source of their angst, some cute boy that both she and Maddie liked.

A creature of habit, Maddie disembarks at the little corner shop close to the school to pick up her daily fix of carbonated water and twiglets. As she hurries out of the shop preparing to run the two minutes to the school gate, she is unaware of the dirty white van pulling up behind her.

The whole thing takes barely thirty seconds: the side door of the van slides open; two hooded men jump out; one of the men grabs the startled girl from behind, clamps his hand over her mouth; the second man catches her legs before she falls into unconsciousness; seconds later, the door slides back into position before the van rolls inconspicuously past the entrance to the school.

Thirty seconds.

No witnesses.

It was as if Maddie Williams had never existed.

PROLOGUE

Faceless mourners huddle near a black marble coffin. There is no sunshine at this funeral. No consoling hugs, sweet smelling flowers, or lovingly prepared eulogy. Instead, black clouds, angry clouds. And low, barely audible murmurings from hooded phantoms, their bony hands folded in prayer.

Giant ravens darken the barren branches of a dead tree. And indistinguishable shapes close in. Animal shapes, dog-like, but with cloven hooves. Not of this Earth.

He is standing beside the coffin. It is open, but no matter how hard he tries, he cannot see inside. Although shrouded in mist, he senses she is there. Cold hands pull at his arms, his shoulders, trying to tug him away. Long, gnarled nails spear into his skin.

And he is always naked in the dreams; vulnerable, helpless, ashamed.

A silent scream.

Fighting back gathering nausea, he again tries to scream. As before, no sound.

Then, he is released. He reaches for her. The tips of his fingers freeze at the mere touch of the cold marble. The sensation takes his breath away. Indescribable pain seeps through his bones, threatening to overwhelm him.

The mist begins to clear. He sees her face for the first time, pale and serene, as if she were asleep. He reaches in, strokes her cheek with the back of a hand. Her skin is always glacier cold at first, then warm...hot...burning.

She opens her eyes, smiles at him. His heart lifting, again he reaches for her, recoils when he feels the bubbling liquid sear his fingers.

Blood...Rising...Rising.

The red sea cascades over her shoulders, neck, face. She screams. Again, he can hear no sound.

Quickly, she is engulfed.

The dream always ends the same; heart slamming, head pounding, lungs gasping for air.

I am a dutiful follower of Lord Voldemort, the chosen one. Only the other day he'd overheard his daughter tell a friend on the phone. Before this, nightmare. *I must have the only Harry Potter-hating-child living on the planet,* he'd joked with the guys at the golf club. Not only that, she had gone and dyed her gorgeous white-blonde hair the blackest colour imaginable. Her eyelashes were now heavy with mascara. Lips glossed blood-red. Skin powdered white as Alaskan wastes. Wholesome candy kid, Hannah Montana, had left the building, in her place an extra from The Evil Dead.

She's twelve, it's a phase. It was the general consensus.

Troy Williams had made light of the change. And with good reason. He knew his daughter better than anyone. He knew his Maddie was a good kid with a good heart. He and his wife had done an excellent job. Everyone said so.

The trouble was, Williams didn't exactly feel much like parent of the year, especially under the circumstances. What he did feel was culpable for the breakdown of his marriage to Corinne. And in a perverse way it felt worse to him that none of the usual suspects could be blamed; no workplace indiscretions, irreconcilable differences, no violence or mental cruelty. *The job. The damned job.* Had it already cost him his marriage? And was it now to take away his main reason for living?

Five days ago, on her way to school, Maddie Williams had vanished. The phone call had come within the hour, before Williams was even aware his daughter was missing.

The training had automatically kicked in the moment he heard the strange voice. Before the voice had reached the end of its opening salvo, Williams had ripped a page from a notebook, begun to scribble - *male, middle-Eastern, well educated, thirties/forties, slight wheeze. Asthmatic?*

In the end the message was stark and clear, the instructions simple.

We have your daughter. If you want to see her alive again you will listen very carefully and do exactly as I say. The next flight to Tel Aviv from Chicago is today at 1700 hours. Book it. When you get there, take a cab to The Hotel Meridian. Check into Room 226, pre-booked under the name, George Wesley. You will wait there until I contact you again. You must not breathe a word of this to another living soul or the girl dies. If we see or hear from any of your colleagues from the CIA, the police, or the FBI, the girl dies. Be assured, we are watching every move you make. If we do not like what we see, the girl will die and you will never hear from me again. It is very simple; all you have to do to save her, Mr. Williams, is the right thing.

Troy Williams was back in the present, holed up in yet another hotel room, this time half-way across the world. Courtesy of his daughter's abductors, he was studying a live CNN news feed on a laptop.

El Al Airlines: flight EA3492, touches down bang on time and taxis to a quiet corner of an otherwise vacant runway. Soon afterwards, the steps are rolled into place before the door near the front of the aircraft slides open. Four Mossad agents are first to appear. Dark suits, sunglasses, whispering into sleeves. Two of the agents pause at the top as the others take the steps, one continuing onto the tarmac to greet the driver of a black limo arriving on the scene.

A quick conversation. More whisperings.

All clear.

At the top of the steps, the target emerges into the Tel Aviv sunshine. Troy Williams' eyes narrow in concentration. He glances down at a type-written note placed on the desk in front of him.

Israeli Foreign Minister, Menahem Liebermann, age 45.

Family - wife Elena, 42, daughter Maria, 14, son Ira, 12.

Williams' gaze lands on a glossy photograph pinned at the corner of the note.

'Target identified and confirmed,' he growls into a phone.

Williams watches as father and mother briefly kiss at the bottom of the steps before the family hold hands in a chain on the way to the limo. He exhales deeply, recalling similar tradition within his own family during happier times.

All safely aboard, the agents disperse and the limousine departs the scene.

Williams' hands wash over his face. It had been almost a week since he received the telephone call that would change his life forever. For the zillionth time he replays the conversation in his head, the last sentence burning brighter than the rest for obvious reasons; *all you have to do to save her, Mr. Williams, is the right thing.*

CHAPTER ONE

'I hope you are well this morning.' A familiar voice opened proceedings.

'My daughter, put her on, now!' Still feeling the after-effects of that morning's nightmare - headache and all - Williams snapped back. *If I could just squeeze my hand through the phone...*

'In time, Mr. Williams, in time. First, I have to be sure that you are familiar with our objectives?'

Williams bit his lip hard. 'I know all about your objectives.'

'Very well,' the voice continued, 'As I said before, you must complete the assignment. Do this and it will be over soon. Your daughter will be returned unharmed. I promise you that.'

'Maddie?' Williams could feel his temper rising.

'One moment.'

Muffled sounds. Voices drawing closer.

'Daddy? Dad, I-is that you?' The voice was a few tones higher than normal and slightly hesitant, but it definitely belonged to Maddie. *His* Maddie. She was still alive. Instantly, the imaginary anvil was lifted from his shoulders.

'Maddie honey, it won't be long now. I promise. Just a little while longer, baby. Are you alright?'

'I-I guess so. Daddy, where are you?'

'Enough!' the voice cut in. 'Your daughter is alive. To keep her that way you know what is expected of you. I am sure you will do the right thing.'

'No, wait! Don't hang up!' Williams' heart sank to the soles of his feet as the call dropped out. Bang! He slammed the flat of his hand down on the bedside cabinet. Angrily prodding his mobile, he rose to walk over to the window, only just resisting the urge to drive his boot through it. He stared out across a waking Tel Aviv. Today it was bathed in crystal clear sunshine. Though he tried hard to banish it, at that moment one thought kept flashing into Williams' brain, making him want to vomit. His mind rewound to seemingly endless missions spent fighting for his life and the lives of his comrades, against all odds. In Iraq, in Kuwait, in Afghanistan. The thought that became a go-to statement among the guys as they watched the sun rise every morning: *At least it was a good day to die.*

It was supposed to help. To make the situation a little more bearable. Today, it most certainly was not helping.

Holding a small device against the speaker in his phone, Williams hit record. The phone replayed the last conversation. Afterwards, he set the ring tone on silent – *The Star-Spangled Banner* kicking off in the middle of a delicate operation would surely not work out too well for all concerned.

Williams cleared everything from his mind as best he could and closed his eyes in deep concentration. Selecting the final part of the recording for special treatment, he jerked the device's controls backwards and forwards, backwards and forwards, backwards and forwards...

I am sure you will do the right thing.

I am sure you will do the right thing.

I am sure you will do the right thing.

I am sure you will do the right thing.

And another couple or three times, for good measure.

CHAPTER TWO

Williams pulled the car over close to the target location and flipped open the laptop. CNN flashed up again, showing images of Menahem Liebermann happily waving to gathering crowds on Begin Road, en-route to Tel Aviv's Azrieli Center.

Staring blankly at the screen, Williams allowed his thoughts to drift away from his daughter - for a few moments at least - to run through his planned activities for the coming hours.

Faced with a difficult mission, CIA operatives are trained to follow protocol to the letter. Williams was no different. He had done a full number on his mark prior to the mission, all the way down to establishing Liebermann's favourite breakfast cereal. *Unroasted and unsweetened Muesli served with clusters of red and black berries and chunks of banana. Seriously?*

Williams concluded that, whilst the Israeli definitely had his supporters in government, he came across to most people as a bit of a wet fish, not well liked by the man in the street. Now being unpopular among his own people was bad enough, but it was nothing compared to what the neighbouring Palestinians thought of Menahem Liebermann. A raft of random chemical weapon strikes on civilian targets on the Gaza Strip a few years back were directly linked to him, despite Israeli spin suggesting otherwise. Since then, the men in grey suits had immediately doubled the minister's security detail. And with the Israeli elections right around the corner, the detail had been trebled. Troy William's mission was going to be difficult. Difficult, but not impossible.

As a kid, Liebermann hadn't had it easy - far from it - but as often happens with people from disadvantaged backgrounds, they'd be prepared to scrap like dirty dogs in the street to hit the top of the pile. To be the alpha-dog. The Israeli would never win any popularity contest, that was clear, but also unimportant, to him at least. He was successful at manipulating the system to make money, for others as well as himself, and people with such skills were in short supply in this modern world. Whilst most of his financial dealings were, shall we say, *questionable*, this was irrelevant to the pocket-liners. Liebermann was box office, no doubt about it, but being box office would not be enough to save him. This time he had overstepped the mark, and, as a result the remainder of his life would be measured in hours.

Williams scanned Liebermann's entourage. Straight off he identified three bodyguards working close, and envisaged at least another three scattered around the periphery. The camera began to pan out the moment the Foreign Secretary reached the Azrieli Center complex, perfectly framing the three impressive Hashalom Towers in the background. The circus then disappeared into the huge shopping area.

Liebermann's eventual destination for the visit – The Circular Tower – was the tallest of the skyscrapers and, due to its curiously named Code Zee security rating, considered a huge no-no for any would-be terrorist organisation planning a surprise attack.

St Peter's Church, a seventeenth-century construction set in the ancient city of Jaffa, near Tel Aviv, was a different matter. Different, but still far from the perfect choice as the sea locked it in on one side, whilst on the other, the main plaza was big and open, and not nearly busy enough to expect a comfortable getaway.

The structure itself could best be described as a reverberating hulk, amplifying the slightest noise over a hundred times. Even the insignificant pop of a gun's suppressor would in all probability be clearly heard in most areas of the church. Not that there would be an available precedent in this particular Lord's house. At least, not yet.

Despite any concerns the blackmailers may have had regarding the eventual success of the mission, they did hold one all-important trump card: Maddie Williams.

Earlier, Troy Williams had taken out the contents of an envelope he'd found pushed under his door - plans detailing how Liebermann's final day on this Earth would play out – and splayed them across the car's steering wheel. Although the papers were poor copies of the originals, Williams could still make out a ghostly imprint of the Israeli government's official crest at the corner of one. Somewhere close, he assumed, lurked a traitor. He didn't dwell on the thought. He had enough on his plate. He had a job to do, a daughter's life to save.

Wiping sweat from his forehead, he again speed-read the documents before running through some final checks in his head.

1.35pm: Williams reached into the back seat for his holdall. Sitting it on his knee, he unzipped it and rummaged inside for a small towel tucked in the corner before spending five minutes or so wiping down the hired car for prints.

Satisfied he was leaving a clean vehicle, Williams slung the holdall over his shoulder and glanced up and down the street. So far, so good. The car's central locking system chirped. Orange lights flashed twice.

Williams' instructions included a very short stay at another hotel close to the church. Half a mile up the road from said hotel, he dropped the car keys down a street drain, making sure they disappeared into the silt.

He checked in quickly at the hotel, taking care to avoid eye contact with the desk clerk, then took the stairs to his first-floor room. *Treat elevators like the plague during a mission* - it was one of the CIA's golden rules, all to do with *unpredictable timings.*

Williams clicked the door shut behind him and tossed the bag on the bed. He walked over to the window and peered down at the street, taking care to stay out of sight. In the distance, the tall white tower attached to the church speared into the afternoon sky.

Easing down into a soft chair by the window, Williams nervously rubbed sweaty palms back and forth along the arms.

His mind began to race through the events of the past few days. He frowned deeply as that one question kept coming back at him again and again. He tried to banish it, but couldn't. *Maddie, what's going to happen to her?*

He knew the answer. He knew the type of people he was dealing with. And he knew there wasn't a hope in hell these people were going to just hand over his daughter after he'd done as they'd asked.

The only positive Troy Williams could draw from the whole crappy situation was that he'd been underestimated before. He hoped for more of the same.

Williams started at a sudden banging noise coming from the bathroom. It sounded to him like nothing more than a pressure build up in the water pipes, but he was in no mood to leave anything to chance.

Stay focused.

Balling his fists, he pushed open the bathroom door. Relieved to find the room empty, he walked over to the wash hand basin and splashed a little water over his face. As he dabbed himself dry with a towel, he bent to check behind the basin as per his instructions. In a small area hidden from view, he noticed the end of what looked like a piece of grey tape. He slipped his hand behind the tape and tugged down sharply. A plastic bag tore away from the wall, its contents clattering to the floor at his feet. He swore a couple of times before gathering up the items. They appeared undamaged. He'd been lucky. Studying the weapon closely he smiled at once again coming face-to-face with an old friend, though he conceded the circumstances could have been better. Williams was holding a prime example of the CIA's premier weapon of choice: a German-made Walther PPK, 9mm, semi-automatic; seven rounds per clip, stainless steel barrel, black grip; small and light and easy to conceal, with a kick like a wrecking ball hurtling through a plate glass window. A spare clip, which, if required would mean the operation wasn't going too well, and a top-rated Brausch suppressor, completed the haul.

2.20pm: Williams laid the stuff down beside him on the bed. His mind drifted off to some of the more enjoyable days he'd spent with his family in the recent past, the days before his marriage began to fall apart. At that moment he felt as if he'd been awake for weeks, and as such, he didn't find it too difficult to ease back and close his eyes.

***

3.40pm: The limousine purred into a coned-off parking space in the grounds of St Peter's church. Three Mossad agents appeared from nowhere as the car drew to a halt. The agents looked calm and relaxed, smiles exchanging among them before they allowed Liebermann to get out and take the short walk to a service entrance door in the corner of the grounds.

A special Mass hosted by St Peter's was next on the minister's agenda. With its Roman Catholic affiliation, the church had been specifically chosen to present the image of an impartial Israel to the watching world. Before St Peter's had received final official confirmation of the visit, there had been some loose talk doing the rounds regarding the possibility of some kind of Muslim ceremony getting the nod. Unsurprisingly, this suggestion was quickly booted into touch. Even in a modern Israel, such a thing would be seen by the majority as a step too far. In any case, it was generally felt by the Israeli public that the whole *exercise* was no more than a charade - a pantomime - played out to improve the West's perception of the country, presumably to help stimulate overseas trade or whatever.

The order of the day was to present a relaxed, low-key Catholic service to the watching world. *Engineered* press releases described the event as *potential PR heaven*. The reality would be somewhat different.

Inside the church, a couple of hundred people were waiting for the Mass to begin. Specially selected guests from all walks of life, all religions, packed into the small auditorium.

Liebermann's remit for the visit was simple. An hour or so out of his day to partake in some good old-fashioned handshaking, hearty hugging and baby kissing. It all sounded innocent enough but without realising it, Liebermann's advisers had got themselves so wrapped up in trying to improve his image, along the way they'd also compromised his safety.

A local children's choir was stretching its collective vocal chords in one of the ante-rooms as the entourage passed by. Liebermann smiled at a small boy, presumably late for practice, scurrying along the narrow corridor towards them. Everyone stood aside to allow the breathless child to pass. The guards felt for their weapons at the sound of heavier footsteps, then stood down as a red-faced priest, his ceremonial robes flowing in his wake, dashed towards them.

'I'm sorry, I'm so sorry!' the priest called out before they again gave way. Everyone smirked as they watched him disappear into the toilet at the top end of the corridor, then sniggered at the sound of a cubicle door banging shut.

'Bad curry,' one whispered, provoking muted laughter.

Liebermann took up pole position in the front row nearest the altar, his protection detail filing in behind. The rest of the congregation took their seats.

A side door opened and the choir slipped quietly in, heads bowed, the youngsters' impeccable decorum delighting their families, drawing proud smiles all round.

Liebermann cast his gaze around the auditorium. Whilst the church could never be described as huge, its domed ceilings, beautiful stained-glass windows, ornate carvings, breath-taking paintings and stunning artefacts, donated over the years from all four corners of the world, more than compensated for its lack of size. Expensive renovations had taken place soon after the end of the Second World War, resulting in the Catholic community of ancient Jaffa growing steadily, though unfortunately to the detriment of the less glamorous surrounding parishes.

Liebermann spotted the little boy who had earlier passed them in the corridor. The boy's face flushed at the attention. He smiled uncomfortably, lowered his eyes and began studying his shoes. The Israeli minister leaned to his right to share the joke with an aide. As he straightened his hand slipped on something greasy smeared on the wooden pew in front. An observant lady sitting in the row two behind fumbled around in her bag before reaching over between heads to pass him a small pack of wet wipes. Thanking her, he forced a smile as he ripped a couple of sheets from the pack. His smile quickly vanished when the lanolin only served to turn his hands into a smeary mess. Worse, the minister then discovered grease had transferred to his trousers, staining the expensive material. Shaking his head in frustration, he barked an instruction to his aide before storming off to the rest room.

One of the lackeys appeared from nowhere, slip-streaming his charge before taking up an arms-folded position outside the door.

The Mossad agent smiled as he heard the unmistakeable pump of a suppressed bullet coming from behind him. Two seconds later, another.

'Tell them it is done,' he whispered into a mobile.

CHAPTER THREE

Alarm bells were ringing like runaway fire engines in Troy Williams' head. He'd ditched the fake priest's robes in a rubbish bin before slipping out the rest room window. A ten-foot drop to the courtyard was followed by a short burst across the main plaza. Williams paused at the top of stone steps leading to a tiny quayside with half a dozen mooring rings set into the ancient flag stones. In the distance he could see the power boat tied to the end ring. *The White Lady* was inscribed along the hull and the boat tamely listed in the sea's gentle ebb and flow. Williams pulled the Walther before ploughing down the steps, through a dark underpass, and into a mini-vennel set between outbuildings. Stepping out gun-first onto the quayside, he stood for a few seconds to steady his nerves. A gentle breeze ruffled his dark hair. Soon, he would be on his way out to sea heading for the neighbouring bay. He would have taken that scenario ten times out of ten. No doubt. But this was almost too good to be true. There were no agents on patrol, no civilians, and no other boats to be seen in the bay. *Hell, there wasn't even a gull in the sky.*

Williams holstered the gun, crouched and ran. He tugged the boat free from its mooring, jumped aboard. The St Martin F-15 dipped as the seventy horse-power Tohatsu engine's prop dug into the water. A sixteen-foot projectile, *The White Lady* hurtled into open water and in no time was a dot in the distance.

Inside the church, the congregation was getting restless. The organist, in the middle of his warm-up, was lost somewhere in the music and most of the members of the kids' choir were fidgeting nervously in anticipation, giggling and waving at their families in the audience. Garbled conversation rose, echoing around the auditorium.

Liebermann's aide beckoned to one of the agents. The pair spoke briefly, the aide staring into the impassive agent's eyes the whole time, repeatedly tapping the face of his wristwatch. To him it was all about punctuality, about keeping appointments and sticking to the programme. Overruns or last-minute curve balls worried such people, even if they occurred through no fault of theirs. To them it was personal, always personal. As if *they* had failed.

Suitably chastised, the agent cursed the aide under his breath before going to check on Liebermann. By the time he'd got halfway along the corridor, he was reaching for his gun. He'd expected to see his colleague on guard outside the rest room door. The guy was nowhere to be seen. Grasping the weapon tightly in both hands, the agent crashed in the door with his boot. The sudden noise could be easily heard in the auditorium, and in no time back-up in the shape of another Mossad agent was at his partner's side. Both stood just inside the doorway, sweeping their guns over the area.

The agents' attention was drawn to an open window at one end, bumping softly in the breeze. They shot each other a quick glance, as if recognising the signs. The scene reeked of assassination.

The only occupied cubicle at the far end, near the window, was duly crashed in. At the same time the top hinge flew off the door, the sudden weight shift causing the bottom hinge to also pop its screws. The unrestrained door thumped down on top of a gagged Menahem Liebermann, knocking him out cold. Bizarrely, he was still sitting on the toilet, though the fact that he was gaffer taped to it perhaps had something to do with it. The agents holstered their guns and lifted the door off the stricken official.

'Cut him loose,' ordered the third man, the senior agent. The second man pulled his knife and bent to slice the tape spread across Liebermann's chest. The knife crashed to the floor as the third agent expertly snapped his colleague's neck with a sickening twist. He then rested the gun's suppressor against Liebermann's forehead. The Foreign Minister's eyes sprang open at the touch of the cold steel before they were closed for good. Before exiting the scene, the double agent fingered the two bullet holes Troy Williams had earlier fired into the cubicle wall. Shaking his head, he smiled before pulling his phone to call in the deception.

Williams eased back on the throttle and swept around a rocky cape into a quiet stretch of water. The adjacent bay was only minutes away at most, with the keys for a blue BMW waiting for him under the mat in the driver's footwell. At least that was what he had been told.

He cut the engine and reached for his mobile. Hitting the on button, he waited for international roaming to pick up the signal. The little boat bobbed and lurched in the choppy water, but Williams could hear or feel nothing. He was aware only of the phone's display, such was his concentration. Eventually the name of the local network fizzed up on the screen. Maximum signal bars rose in the corner. He checked his watch: almost time. Williams' heart drummed loudly as he waited. Never before had he felt so helpless.

'Come on, Danny, I'm counting on you, pal,' he whispered, closing his eyes. The sea, tide, waves – all were deathly silent to his ears.

A text message arrived, the display reading *Danny Foster*. As he read the message, Williams raised a clenched fist. The thought of what might have been making him a little light-headed, he grasped the side of the boat with both hands to try to steady himself. The tiniest of beeping sounds coming from close by soon did the trick. Stuffing the phone in his pocket, he stooped to look along under the boat's fascia. Another beep from directly behind made him wheel around.

''Oh no!' he gasped when he saw the size of the device taped under the steering wheel.

The blast could be heard back on the quayside near the church. The Mossad agent who had watched Williams' escape raised his mobile to his ear.

'Now it is done,' he said, smiling smugly.

CHAPTER FOUR

Ten minutes previously

The dingy bedroom had been her prison since she'd come round, five days ago. *Or was it four?* She couldn't be sure.

Maddie Williams recalled walking out of the shop near her school. That's when it got a bit fuzzy: a white van with sliding side door; two men – both tall, wearing hoods; a strong hand covering her face; a handkerchief; a sweet, sickly smell, then...blackness.

She had woken up in this room with no recollection of how long she had been there. She had no idea if she was still in the country, let alone Chicago. Every morning she had scratched another notch on the wall next to the bed with the edge of a nail she'd found in the bedside cabinet drawer.

Five notches. Definitely five days.

The bedroom boasted one window, or at least that's what Maddie assumed it was. Much as she tried, she had not been able to prise open the wooden shutters covering it. A cat-flap – her only contact with the outside world and set as normal in the bottom half of the door - was opened twice a day when trays of food were passed through. Basic stuff; milk, toast, eggs, fries, burgers, yogurt.

Twice, a man had burst into the room brandishing a phone and had hauled her roughly to her feet. Understandably alarmed and terrified, the sheer relief she'd felt when she heard her father's voice was indescribable. Although each *conversation* lasted mere seconds, it mattered not a jot to her. Her dad was on the case. It was all she needed to know. To Maddie, he was the toughest, yet kindest and most loyal man in the world. If he told her not to worry, that he would make things right, she knew it was only a matter of time before he delivered.

There had been heightened activity in the house earlier today with endless phone calls, a whole different set of voices, and cars coming and going outside the window. Something was in the air. Maybe Maddie had inherited some of her old man's grit and guile, for as harrowing as the experience had been, she had refused to buckle, unwilling to shed even a single tear.

The plucky twelve-year-old had spent her time in captivity formulating an escape plan of her own. Maybe she would surprise her father by getting out of there under her own steam. It would be a long shot, but it was still a plan, nevertheless.

Six months ago, Maddie watched her best friend suffer a seizure in the middle of the night during a sleepover at the Williams' house. She'd kept a cool head, making her friend comfortable before calmly alerting her parents when it was all over. A few weeks later, mom and dad looked on as proud as punch as their daughter appeared before the press to be presented with a special bravery award at one of those *heroes in the community* functions at the local city hall. The news had then gone viral on social media, so-much-so, that at one time the matter was being touted as a possible subject for Oprah. As expected, Williams' bosses at the CIA, determined he maintain his anonymity, hit that one on the head straight away.

'What about the girl?'

'Make it quick. Join us back at the house when it is done.' One man left and the other unlocked the door. Gun drawn, he stepped inside the room.

Make it quick.

Maddie was lying on the floor by the bed. Her eyes were rolling and flicking, the whites clear and bright. Her body was twitching, her head lolling. Saliva dribbled from the corner of her mouth. She gurgled, choked, panted between long, slow inhalations.

The man looked puzzled at first, then he grinned as he prepared to finish the job. The gun barrel nestled against Maddie's head. The trigger mechanism creaked.

Maddie swung a hand from behind her back. The knife that had gone missing the day before, somewhere between the kitchen and her prison, speared into the man's lower gut. He screamed in agony and hit out, striking her cheek with the back of his hand. She fell to the floor, hitting her head in the process, knocking her out cold.

The man stumbled into the middle of the room. He yelled again in pain and frustration as he carefully pulled out the knife and dropped it on the floor. Stemming the blood flow as best he could with the inside of his arm, he again raised the gun.

'Say goodnight, bitch,' he said through clenched teeth.

'Goodnight, bitch.' The strange voice came from behind him.

Before the injured man could react, the bullet ripped into the back of his skull and exploded through his forehead, popping tamely against the wall at the other side of the room. He dropped to his knees, drawing a couple of final shuddering breaths before slamming face-first into the floor.

'Maddie, honey. Come on, we have to go now.' The rescuer was at her side, gently stroking her face. Maddie Williams peered up at him through the fog of semi-consciousness, his familiar voice guiding her back among the living.

CHAPTER FIVE

Glasgow, Scotland

He never switched off his mobile phone. He couldn't. Not in *his* line of work. *Silent vibrate* was a compromise.

'Doesn't even make sense,' he'd said to her. *'It's the damn thing vibrating you hear. How can that be silent?'*

She'd replied, deadpan: *'No, you hear it. I sleep.'* She'd then pulled the duvet across her shoulders and switched off her bedside lamp. Rhythmic breathing had quickly followed.

He'd laid down his book, smirked when he considered the neat and tidy order that was his wife's life.

This morning only served to prove his point about *silent vibrate,* the mobile edging across the glass-topped dresser like a demented bee on speed.

He opened an eye at the first buzz, worked out who and where he was at the next. Switching on the lamp, he checked his sleeping beauty. Didn't even break stride.

'All right, hold your horses,' he whispered. He reached across to pick up the phone, at the same time swinging his legs off the bed. Blinking his eyes, he squinted hard at the display. It wasn't the usual secure MI6 number he'd expected. Right away, he recognised the United States international dialling code. Then he glanced at the clock by the bed: 3.33am.

'Who the hell-?' Realising he was raising his voice, he stopped mid-sentence, although he really needn't have worried. He often formed a mental picture of his wife, dead to the world, in the middle of a brass band in full swing, marching up and down at the end of their bed.

'Hello,' he said quietly as he backed into their en-suite. Gently easing the door close behind him, he stretched his bare feet across the cold tiles, hoping to accelerate the waking-up process.

'I-I'm looking for Ryan Taylor.' The small, vulnerable voice on the other end was female, and familiar.

Taylor sat on the toilet and backed against the cistern, the shock of the cold ceramic on his skin apparently helping to jolt the caller's name into his brain.

'Corinne, is that you?' he said, unable to be certain due to her tone.

'Oh Ryan, thank God I got hold of you. S-something terrible's happened. And Maddie...I-I'm sorry, I can't-.' Her voice trailed off.

'Okay, wait. Give me a minute.'

Taylor stood. He stared at his half-awake reflection in the mirror, laid down the phone on top of the cistern. Grappling with the cold tap, he splashed some water over his face before grabbing a towel to dab himself dry. Picked up the phone.

'All right, Corinne. Now just take it slow. Tell me what's going on.'

'Th-they said Troy did a terrible thing. Said he killed somebody. And now my baby. She's gone. And I don't know where...' She broke down, sobbing.

Taylor lowered the phone and slipped his hand over the receiver. Rhythmically tilting his head from side to side, he blew out a couple of long breaths.

Think!

Finally: 'Corinne. I want you to take some deep breaths for me, can you do that?'

She didn't answer. No matter, he could hear her trying to do as he'd asked.

A short silence.

'I'm sorry,' she said. 'I know it's really early over there. I just had to talk to somebody.'

'Don't worry about that,' he said, 'I'm with you. Now I want you to go back, start again.'

'Troy and I...' She hesitated. 'We separated. Two, no three months back.'

'I'm so sorry, I didn't know.'

'No, it's fine. How could you know? We were trying to work things out. Troy moved into a friend's house. He said we needed some space.' She gulped between sentences. 'We took turns with Maddie. Y'know, two weeks on, two weeks off, that kind of thing?'

'Maddie? What's happened to her? Is she ok?' Taylor sounded concerned and it wasn't an act. He genuinely liked the kid.

'I-I don't know,' her voice quivered. 'She was supposed to come to mine last Monday. She never appeared. A-And when I called Troy...'

'Corinne?'

She sniffed. 'When I called him, he didn't answer. I think he switched his phone off. And then when I saw the news...'

'News?'

'The minister who was killed. I-In Israel. I-I can't remember his name.'

'Liebermann?' Taylor said.

'Yes, Liebermann.'

'Troy had something to do with that? I don't understand,' Taylor said, bemused.

'Neither do I. It was all over the news tonight. The phone's been ringing off the hook. It was newspaper reporters the first three times. I didn't answer after that.'

'Corinne, are you calling from home?' he asked, now fully awake.

'Y-Yeah, why?'

'Listen.' He looked at his watch. 'We have to get off this line. I'll call you back in exactly an hour.'

'I understand.'

The phone went dead.

Ryan Taylor left a scrawled note for April, dressed, and was out the door in ten minutes. He hoped the short drive to the office would give him time to figure out the next step.

Taylor acknowledged Larry, the night security man, on his way to the lift. As the doors closed over, he reflected on the earlier call from Corinne Williams.

His job meant it was his business to know about the Liebermann incident. Details coming out of the East had been sketchy and the information Taylor's department had so far received amounted to not a great deal more than general bog-standard press releases. Things had obviously changed, but for a man such as Troy Williams to be implicated? Taylor shook his head. *Not a chance! Unless...*

One thought kept coming back to him. The man he knew was American to the core and extremely proud of it. Taylor was convinced unerring patriot, Troy Williams, cut open, would bleed red, white and blue. But then, when your own flesh and blood is involved...

Apart from a baby-sitting mission in Switzerland last year, it had been some time since their paths had crossed in a professional capacity.

Williams and Taylor first met in late 2006, sharing a dusty foxhole on the outskirts of Kabul during the hunt for Bin Laden. The pair had immediately hit it off and with their families growing close, Troy and Corinne had agreed to be godparents to Ryan and April's son, Jake, now aged three. Only in the last few months had the lines of communication broken down. Right off, Taylor had put that down to the job. Corinne Williams had confirmed as much with her phone call.

The lift doors sucked open at the fourth floor. Taylor flashed his key fob at the sensor and the door to the office at the end of the corridor unlocked.

Mathie, Gilfillan and Robb was a rather unusual solicitors' practice. Unusual, in that it was client-free, and with not a lawyer in sight. Utopia, some might say. A cheery, middle-aged female receptionist and a couple of front office *admin staff* would be at their posts in a few hours, completing the deception.

Taylor made himself a coffee before entering an office behind the sign: *William Gilfillan LLB*. The fake Mr. Gilfillan sat at his desk and flipped open his laptop. Tapping in his personal verification code, he wired straight through British Intelligence to a restricted CIA site, and watched on in horror as images unfolded before his eyes. Recent photographs of Liebermann and Williams flashed up on screen, side by side; victim and murderer.

What soon became clear to Taylor was that the agency was hanging Williams out to dry. As far as the CIA – or someone in power there - was concerned, Menahem Liebermann had been killed by a rogue operative. According to the site, there had also been unconfirmed reports of an explosion on board a small boat around the coastline from the church where Liebermann had been killed, but so far there had been no established connection between the two incidents.

Ryan Taylor eased back in his chair and sipped at his coffee. He noted the time of the last update to the site – six hours ago - and blew out his cheeks with relief. No movements were good. No news really was good news in this case. However, as Taylor had expected, an official CIA kill-order directive was already in place.

The process had begun.

Taylor looked at the clock on the wall. It was almost an hour since he'd hung up the phone on Corinne Williams. A nauseous feeling curdled his gut as he tapped out her number using his untraceable *office* phone. By the time she answered, Taylor had already made up his mind on how he would play it.

I promise I'll do everything in my power to find out what's going on. Well, it did sound infinitely more palatable than: *I think Maddie has been kidnapped and used as a bargaining tool to force Troy to kill Liebermann. If that's the case, and as Liebermann is now dead, chances are she is as well.*

CHAPTER SIX

'You got a coffee through there?'

'Just poured another one.'

'Another one? How long you been in?'

'Since around four.'

'Four? You're a sad man, Ryan Taylor, you know that?' Brian Ricker took a quick sip from his cup before stuffing a ginger biscuit in his mouth.

The unit chief picked up his thin briefcase from the worktop and slipped it under his arm before limping through to *Gilfillan's* office.

Ricker was a tall man, six-four, mid-forties, with a shock of prematurely greying hair. Eight years ago, he'd taken a bullet for Queen and country during a special ops mission in Iraq. Doctors found the bullet nudging his spinal cord and had advised against an operation. A pronounced limp and daily pain in his lower back was considered a lucky outcome, given the circumstances. Sometimes Ricker didn't feel quite so lucky, especially when the painkillers had little effect, but he was alive and fairly mobile. *Could be a lot worse*, he would usually comment when asked after his health.

Not only did Taylor have a lot of time for Ricker, he had plenty of respect for him as well. They had never served together in the field, but according to colleagues of Taylor the big guy could be relied upon in a tight spot.

Ricker winced in pain by habit as he stooped to lay the laptop on the desk, and eased down into a chair. Snapping off half of the biscuit, he dunked it in his coffee before turning to face Taylor.

'What's up?' Ricker said. He'd caught the serious expression on Taylor's face and stopped mid-dunk. A piece of the soggy biscuit broke off and plopped into the cup. 'Damn!' he said, before pushing the cup to one side.

'You remember Troy Williams?' Taylor said.

'The CIA man. Aren't you two friends?'

Taylor nodded. 'Haven't heard from him for a while. Turns out he's separated from his wife.'

'Really? That's too bad.'

'I take it you haven't heard the news then?' Taylor said.

Ricker shook his head. 'That's why I employ you guys.' He smiled. Taylor wasn't smiling, so Ricker knew to tone it down a bit before continuing. 'Jill and I have been away for the weekend. We have an *understanding*. No laptop for her, no telly for me. Our technology-free weekend. Why, what's happened?' Ricker shifted uncomfortably.

'Corinne, Troy's wife, called me just after three this morning. She's in some state. Her daughter's missing and Troy's carrying the can for the Liebermann assassination.'

Ricker looked puzzled, said, 'But Williams is no rogue agent.'

'I know that. I think somebody snatched his daughter,' Taylor said.

A short silence.

'Kidnap the daughter and blackmail the father.' Ricker was on the scent.

'I think so.'

'Then he *has* done it. Has to be him. He's killed Liebermann to save her. He had no choice.'

Taylor nodded.

'If we know this then the CIA know it as well,' Ricker said. 'I take it Williams has gone to ground?'

'Gone to ground, already dead, who knows?' Taylor shrugged. 'I know there are no guarantees, but as there's a kill order in place and there's been no update, I assume he's still missing.'

'There's another thing to consider,' Ricker said.

'I know.' Taylor pulled in a long breath, said, 'Maddie's probably dead by now.'

'I'd say there's a fair chance of it. What did you say to Troy's wife, Corinne, is it?'

'What could I say? I told her not to worry. That I'd see what I could find out.' Taylor stared at his boss, looking for a reaction. He didn't have to wait long to get one.

'I was afraid you'd say that. Come on, Ryan, I can't sanction something like this. You know how much they cut the budget this year?'

'Brian, the guy's a good friend. He's Jake's godfather.'

'Look, you know the rules. We can't muscle in on this. We can only collaborate when the subject concerns both sides or we receive a request. Right now, this has nothing to do with MI6. I'm sorry.'

Taylor rose and walked over towards a window at the far end of the office. He pulled the blinds open and looked out across Glasgow. A stiff gust blew a blanket of rain onto the glass. He trailed a raindrop with his finger all the way down to the sill. Resting his forehead against the cold surface of the glass, he took a deep breath before turning to face Ricker.

'You know you were right,' Taylor said.

'About what?' Ricker looked puzzled.

'Last week you said I should take a holiday. That I looked tired. I'm only saying I think you were right.'

Ricker shook his head, exhaled slowly, his gaze firmly fixed on Taylor. He rubbed his forehead, raked his fingers back through his hair. At that moment the look of determination he saw etched on Taylor's face reminded him of one he'd seen many times before, staring back at him from a mirror. He knew resistance was futile.

Ricker reached across the desk and tore out a sheet of paper from a notepad. Scribbling something on the paper, he folded it over before sliding it in front of Taylor.

'What's this?' Taylor asked, holding up the note.

'When you get to Tel Aviv, call this number and ask for Mehdi. He'll help you get anything you need. The guy's rock solid.'

'One of *your* old field contacts, Brian? You getting all soft in your old age?' Taylor smirked.

Ricker ignored the comment, his mood darkening. 'And for God's sake,' he said, 'Don't get yourself arrested. The Israelis will throw away the key and MI6 will deny all knowledge. What's the word? Ah yes, disavow. We'll leave you high and dry. As far as we're concerned the party line will be: you're working alone, helping an old friend.'

'Fair enough,' Taylor said, his smile vanishing. Again, he held up the note. 'Thanks Brian, I owe you one. I'll be back as soon as I can.' He headed for the door.

'Ryan, wait. Take this.' Ricker tossed his mobile across the room. Taylor plucked it out of the air as Ricker continued, 'It's a scrambler. Call the secure line here if you need anything. And if you call out of hours, I'll make sure it's on divert. It'll come direct to me. Off the record, of course. Okay?'

Taylor lifted the mobile up in front of his face, nodded.

As he walked to the lift, Taylor began working on the story he would need to spin for his wife. He hated deceiving her, but under the circumstances felt he had no choice.

It came with the territory.

CHAPTER SEVEN

Taylor arrived at Ben Gurion Airport on the outskirts of Tel Aviv and checked in under the name: Neville Longden.

It had been a while since he was last in Israel. Three years to be exact, but not nearly long enough in MI6 parlance. Taylor had been part of a covert operation investigating the emergence of so-called Israeli death squads, set up to cause havoc in Palestine. Although the mission had been successful in snuffing out the units, things had turned messy when a handful of secret service men, including Taylor, found their identities compromised. Mugshots did the rounds every few months. Taylor knew he was taking one hell of a chance. He could easily be identified by some eagle-eyed member of the Israeli security force, especially at a heavily-fortified facility such as Ben Gurion. Hell, they could even have his photograph pinned up right now. So, when the hatchet-faced flight officer glanced between Neville Longden and his passport photo too many times for comfort, you could perhaps forgive the MI6 agent for feeling a little uneasy.

'Business or pleasure?' the man growled.

'Visiting a sick uncle.'

A nod and a grunt from the man as he slipped the passport back under the glass.

Taylor began to breathe a little easier when he walked out of there and into the night air. In no time he managed to hail a taxi for the short run to Jaffa.

A quick check of the watch signified it had been more than twenty hours since Corinne Williams' telephone call disrupted his day. A hearty dinner and a few hours' sleep would fit just fine. He would take up Troy Williams' trail in the morning, after he picked up some essentials from Brian Ricker's contact in Tel Aviv.

Taylor knew time was of the essence. The CIA assassin would be closing in. He prayed he wouldn't be too late.

***

Taylor opened his eyes and, only for a few seconds, found himself in that place between different worlds. The place he could control, where nothing bad could happen. For that short time, he imagined himself in Glasgow, tucked up in his own bed with April lying beside him, and little Jake sleeping soundly next door. It happened almost every time at the beginning of a mission. A kind of last look at normality. And this certainly was no normal mission. This time there would be little, if any back-up, though Taylor was sure Brian Ricker would pull through for him. He would soon find out through the quality of contact Ricker had given up.

Taylor enjoyed a hot shower and a little breakfast, body swerving a few broken-English questions from the well-meaning boss of the little hotel at which he had chosen to spend the night.

When he got back to his room, he dug out the scrawled note and pulled Ricker's mobile from his pocket. Tapping in the number, he heard three purrs.

'Hello,' the voice said.

'Mehdi?'

'Who wants to speak with him?'

'A mutual friend suggests he may be able to help me.'

Long pause.

'Are you visiting a sick uncle?' the voice asked.

'That's right.'

'He said you would be in touch.'

'So can you help me?'

Another pause, then, 'Take a cab to 431 Hayarkin Street. Eleven o'clock. Be on time.'

The call disconnected.

***

10.52am: The cab rolled up outside 431 Hayarkin Street. Taylor paid the driver and stepped out into the Tel Aviv sunshine. He dragged his sunglasses to the end of his nose, lowered his head to peer over the top of them.

Number 431 looked like a general store. It sat slap-bang in the middle of a short row of dilapidated shops. Ancient advertisements for newspapers, cigarettes, groceries and alcohol plastered the windows. Most of the other shops were boarded up, with the exception of a run-down, *greasy-spoon* type café at one end.

A couple of down and outs were sitting in front of the café, around a rusty old barrel that doubled as a makeshift table. Both smiled, flashing mouthfuls of rotten teeth at the stranger. Taylor acknowledged them as they lifted their wine bottles in unison. I *could be in any one of a dozen areas in Glasgow*, he mused.

Taylor walked to the front door of the shop. Patted his breast pocket. No gun. He felt naked. He pushed his way inside. A little bell rang. It was typical of the feel of the place, as if the shop had been stuck in a time-warp. Waxed paper lined the wooden shelves that were laden with tins of produce arranged in mini-pyramids, coconut shy style. The lighting was low, the walls painted green above and brown below a high-set dado rail. As Taylor walked towards the counter, the dusty floorboards creaked and heaved under his feet. And no fancy high-security, modern cash register either. Instead, simple fortified drawers with tarnished brass locks. On the counter top lay a sharp pencil, an eraser, a red marker pen and a packet of notepads, all containing off-white, tissue-thin paper.

A short, balding man of around sixty, wearing wire-rimmed glasses with lenses that seemed to make his eyes appear the size of golf balls, emerged between chocolate brown curtains, presumably from the back shop.

'Mehdi?' Taylor asked.

'Yes, one moment, please.' He brushed past Taylor on his way to the door, rising on tiptoes to look both ways along the street through small glass panels at the top. Locking the door, he then carefully tugged the roller blinds down, continuing to peer out until they completely covered the glass.

As he watched Mehdi turn and back against the door, Taylor sensed a movement behind him. Before he could react, he saw something flash in front of his face. Bony knuckles quickly drilled into the back of his neck, the man's knee pressing hard into the small of his back.

The wire tightened.

His mind already dulled through lack of oxygen, Taylor flailed his arms around him, elbows flying, fists thrusting behind his head. He tried to dig his nails under the wire, but it was in too deep. The attacker pulled tighter, forcing his knee further into Taylor's back. In a few seconds Taylor knew it would be all over.

Close to unconsciousness, Taylor realised he had only one card to play. He feigned one way, lurched the other. The ploy worked, the man's centre of gravity quickly shifting, catching him off balance. His grip lessened for a few seconds, allowing Taylor enough time to catch his breath.

His head clearing, Taylor lurched again before both men fell heavily against the counter. Taylor reached across to his right. Objects flew across the room, clattering on the floor. Taylor's hand settled on the thing he had been searching for. His thumb flicking across the point, he firmed up his grip before jerking his head to one side, opening up the target.

One firm jab was all that was required. There was a muted whimper. The wire loosened as the man behind him slumped to the floor, the sharp end of a pencil sticking through his right eye, piercing his brain.

Taylor dropped to his knees, fighting to pull oxygen into his lungs. Gathering up the wire, he flung it angrily across the floor and got to his feet.

'Do not move,' Mehdi said, still backed against the door, but now with a gun for company.

'Not exactly the welcome I expected,' Taylor said, still panting heavily. He rubbed at his neck. 'What now?' he asked.

Mehdi said nothing. Raised the gun.

One of the drunks Taylor had acknowledged earlier stumbled past the window and began hammering the locked door with his fists. By the time the startled Israeli had gathered his senses, he was clutching at the handle of the steak knife that had been speared into his neck. Taylor hadn't been completely naked when he entered the shop. Ordering the medium-rare last night had been a good idea after all.

As he watched the man fall to the floor, the life slipping out of him, Taylor thanked God for shop opening times and cheap wine.

He felt he had pushed enough of his luck for one day. Although it wasn't exactly Rodeo Drive, at some point more people were going to wonder why their local shop was still closed.

He cleaned and pocketed the knife used to kill Mehdi, and the gun - a Walther – that had almost put paid to his own future prospects.

A quick search through the back shop produced three spare Walther magazines, a basic kit for producing fake passports, and what looked to Taylor like some kind of black book contact list which MI6 intelligence might find interesting...if he were fortunate enough to make it back.

As he slipped out a rear exit door, Taylor was considering his next move. One question kept gnawing away at him. The visit to Brian Ricker's *rock-solid* contact had almost cost him his life. What was Ricker's involvement in all of this? Taylor aimed to find out. But for now, at least, he had no need of his boss. The next part of the mission he would have to complete on his own.

CHAPTER EIGHT

Neville Longden signed the agreement at the Eldan car rental office in Tel Aviv and accepted the keys to the most insignificant vehicle he had ever seen, let alone driven. The 1.2 litre engine of the little mint-green Chevvy Spark burst into life before joining the mainstream traffic.

A couple of miles along the road, Taylor became aware of a car slipping in and out of the line behind him, about four back. He made a point of throwing in a couple of random moves on the way back to his hotel. The silver Toyota followed.

Great, just great. Adjusting the back of his seat to a more upright position, he gripped the wheel tightly.

Up ahead, traffic lights at a busy junction hit amber as Taylor approached. He took his chance, flooring the pedal as the lights changed to red. The little car responded immediately, zipping across the junction and into a long straight section of road before the waiting traffic could move.

Tearing into the distance, Taylor checked his mirror for the reaction. The Toyota pulled out of the short queue and scraped along the side of a couple of cars. Horns blared as it edged forward, somehow finding a small gap in the flow crossing the junction. The car didn't quite come through the manoeuvre unscathed, clipping the back wheel of a motor bike as it passed. The force of the impact spun the bike around, slamming it into the side of the Toyota. The rider flew across the roof and landed in a heap on the other side. The car following then struck the mangled bike, screeching to a halt an inch short of the stricken rider's head.

As Taylor rounded the corner at the end of the straight, he knew he had a decision to make. Heading back to the hotel was obviously not an option. If he really wanted to outrun this guy, he would need to fashion a change of car as a matter of urgency.

Taylor watched the Toyota break out of the corner he'd negotiated moments before. As the driver hit the pedal, the sudden power rush caused the back end to swing across the road, narrowly missing a truck travelling the other way. Very quickly, the driver wrestled the car back into a good position. Taylor realised at that point he wasn't dealing with an amateur.

The Toyota danced around a couple of slow movers to close in fast. The Chevvy stood no chance in a straight race against its more powerful counterpart, and in no time, Taylor found himself staring into his mirror at the whites of the driver's eyes. Bumper against bumper. A nudge, a more pronounced thump, then a full-blooded rear-ender almost tore off the Chevvy's entire back section.

Taylor lifted his foot to coast into a left turn before again hitting the power coming out of the bend. The car's exhaust system had been damaged so badly the engine couldn't respond in the way he needed. Mortally wounded, the Chevvy spluttered and shuddered, the engine gamely trying to deliver. Taylor had little choice but to try and sideswipe the Toyota as it cruised alongside.

A gun, torn from the passenger's grasp by the move, scuttled between both cars and disappeared into the distance.

Taylor was now staring down the barrel of the driver's weapon. He jerked back against his seat as the bullet zipped in front of his face, shattering the passenger window on its way. Now a sitting duck, Taylor knew he had to act fast. He glanced briefly to his right then jumped on the brakes. The Toyota carried on for a further twenty yards, smoking brakes finally bringing it to a halt. By the time the driver had performed the perfect handbrake turn, the abandoned Chevvy was breathing its last. The driver's door was lying wide open with the driver nowhere to be seen.

Taylor heard the squeal of the Toyota's tyres not far behind as he legged it up a side street. Arms pumping, he sprinted towards his target – a metallic blue 318i BMW with twin exhaust, alloys, and an open door. Even better, he heard the low purr of the engine as he closed in. The shouts from the Beemer owner standing at the top of the steps of his house holding a television set, fell on deaf ears. Taylor pushed the back door shut, wrenched open the front. A quick glance over his shoulder told him the Toyota was only yards away.

Taylor's frame immediately moulded into the plush leather seat. He drove the gear stick home, hit the pedal hard. In seconds, the BMW was putting distance between them.

'Bloody hell!' he gasped when he looked in the mirror.

CHAPTER NINE

'Okay, don't panic. I'm not going to hurt you. Do you speak English?'

No response. Taylor's gaze flitted between mirrors and road. 'Do you have your seat belt on?'

The girl sitting in the back seat still didn't answer. He looked over his shoulder. She seemed to stare right through him. He looked again, noticed her belt was clipped in place and blew out his cheeks with relief. He shook his head, cursing his luck under his breath.

Taylor checked her out again. He decided she couldn't be any older than eight, maybe pushing nine. She reminded him a little of his niece, but not quite. There was something different about her. But what?

Swinging around a couple of slow movers, Taylor was forced to hit the brakes to avoid a car nosing out of a side road. The sudden braking made the car slew sideways, slamming the kerb hard. As Taylor squared it up and the car gently shimmied through the camber of the road, he heard an unexpected sound coming from behind him: *Laughter.*

He noted the Toyota's position. The Beemer's extra power had already put seventy yards between them. Flooring it again, Taylor overtook a bus, almost colliding with a small family saloon travelling in the opposite direction. He was close enough to see the look of terror in the driver's eyes.

More laughing.

He stole another glance over his shoulder. There was a huge grin on the girl's face. Taylor reached behind him and waved his free hand in front of her eyes.

No response.

He waved again, closer to her face.

Still no response.

He rocked the wheel from side to side, a trick Taylor's own father had often used to amuse his young son.

More laughter.

This just keeps getting better and better, he mused. *I'm in the middle of a high-speed car chase in Tel Aviv, with a blind kid as a passenger!*

'What's your name?' Taylor asked, leaning forward to peel himself from the expensive leather seat, the feel of the damp sweat heavy on the back of his shirt making him uncomfortable.

'Anna,' she giggled.

'All right, Anna. I don't want you to worry.'

'I am not worried. I like going fast!'

Dropping a gear, Taylor sped past a couple of cars before swerving to avoid a pick-up truck by the width of a coat of paint. The Toyota waltzed in and out of the traffic not far behind them.

Damn, this guy is good! Taylor mused, his mood darkening.

The main routes around the city centre were starting to clog up.

'Christ!' he hissed. Banks of brake lights were flashing up all around them. The BMW was rapidly heading for the back of the queue, but Taylor was in no mind to slow down.

As if by instinct, Anna seemed to brace for the impact a split second before the Beemer swerved away from the car in front.

'Wooooooo!' she shrieked as the BMW clipped the kerb and flew into the air over the central reservation. The chassis hit the tarmac on the other carriageway so hard it sprayed a shower of sparks in all directions. After a few seconds, Taylor felt a little traction return, enough to spin the tyres into life. He was now firmly in the line of fire, dozens of vehicles braking, swaying and swerving to avoid the madman going the wrong way on the wrong carriageway.

Taylor planted his foot, cut one way, then the other, expertly finding gaps in the flow. Anna whooped with every manoeuvre. 'Ole!' she shouted, throwing both arms in the air. Other drivers, panicked into over-braking, slid from side to side, struggling to control their vehicles. Cars were bouncing around like ball bearings in a giant pinball machine.

Taylor had temporarily lost sight of the Toyota among the heavy traffic. Not that he could concentrate much on what was happening behind him. He had enough on his plate coping with what was coming. Lights and horns were going crazy, with drivers frantically trying to protect themselves and their passengers from the out-of-control idiot speeding towards them.

Taylor spotted a tunnel in the distance around two hundred yards away. Big problem! Only two lanes were emerging from this claustrophobic looking hole in the side of a hill, and he was struggling to hold it together on three. And he was running out of road...fast.

'Anna, it's going to get a little rough now!' Taylor barked at his passenger. Before she could respond, he was yanking the steering wheel to the right, at the same time pulling up firmly on the handbrake. Anna shrieked as the car swung around, nosing the front of a small pick-up before careering across all three lanes. Taylor braced for impact, the car broad-siding into a Sunday driver, ironically hugging the inside lane for safety.

Taylor shook his head clear, metaphorically at least. Now facing the correct way, he dropped the handbrake and hit the pedal, hoping to minimise the effect of the inevitable shunt. A little white goods van left a trail of steaming rubber on the road before it smashed into the back of the BMW. The force of the impact catapulted the car forward, straight into the back of the car in front. Taylor watched as the passengers' heads snapped back due to the force of the impact.

Grappling with the wheel, he backed up then sped into a tiny space opening up on the right. As he headed for free road, a flash of silver at his shoulder instinctively made him turn away.

He heard the familiar crack of a bullet passing through his window, again exiting the passenger's side. Taylor checked on the girl. She wasn't laughing anymore. She was cowering in her seat, her hands clamped over her face.

'Stay down!' Taylor shouted. He sideswiped the Toyota once, twice, three times, eventually pinning the car against the boundary wall. The driver's gun flew from his hand as both cars careered wildly, side by side, hugging stone.

Showers of sparks and rocks spewed in their wake. Mixed debris fired in every direction, like shells under pressure.

Hammering the butt of the Walther against the window, Taylor cleared the broken glass with his arm and took aim.

The driver grasped his shoulder when the first bullet hit home. Bullets two and three entered through the ear and the left cheek respectively. The driver's limp body fell against the passenger, pinning him against his door. Worse, the shock of instant death had stiffened the driver's leg, his foot jerking down hard on the accelerator. The sudden injection of speed wrested the Toyota free of the Beemer's attention, but sent it out of control and hurtling towards a huge concrete bridge support.

The passenger could see from fifty yards away what was coming. He screamed in terror as the car struck the support full on, the impact turning it into a fireball. Taylor sped past, shielding his eyes from the blinding flash.

'Are you okay?' Taylor asked.

No reply.

He tried again. 'Are you hurt?'

When it did come, the voice was small and pathetic. 'I want to go home now.'

CHAPTER TEN

Taylor could see flashing blue lights coming his way. The scream of the sirens was calling to him from a distance, growing louder and louder, the lights drawing ever closer.

A roadside sign indicated two kilometres to the next exit. Powering on, the engine roared back at him, as if screaming for mercy. Huge palls of smoke billowed from the exhaust. Taylor winced at the sound of the grinding and rattling of bent and twisted pistons and valves in the heart of the engine. The BMW was dying, and with three police cars looming large, he would need to act fast.

Taylor knew surrender was not an option. Back home, Brian Ricker had told him the British Government would disavow all knowledge of unofficial military operations in Israel. Taylor would be hung out to dry. This was purely protocol and nothing personal and he knew that, but he was determined to make sure he wasn't going to end up in front of a firing squad, or rot away in some Israeli prison for the rest of his life.

He was almost at the exit. The leading police car was now maybe five hundred yards away, and closing. The Beemer's engine was on its last legs. Finally, release came via an earth-shattering bang.

Coasting off on the exit, the car swept silently down the ramp into a busy street.

Pulling up, Taylor reached into the back seat and gathered Mehdi's bag, at the same time checking on his passenger. She looked a little shaken, but otherwise fine.

'Anna, you'll be okay,' he said. 'It's been a blast, but I have to go now. The police will take you home.'

'Thanks for the ride,' she said, her smile returning.

Taylor strode out into the middle of the road, drew his gun and pointed it at the face of the driver of a blue Honda heading straight for him. Taylor stood firm, unblinking, steely-blue eyes staring at the man, daring him to drive on.

The car screeched to a halt about a foot from Taylor's legs. He was at the driver's door in a split-second, hauling it open and manhandling the poor guy out onto the road. At least the driver had the good sense to stay where he fell, allowing Taylor to jump in and speed away in the nick of time.

The police cars were now almost on his bumper. Taylor watched them as they weaved from side to side, crossing over again and again. He covered the width of the road, cutting them off as they tried to move in front of him. He was too long in the tooth to become the meat in anybody's sandwich.

Up ahead, Taylor spotted a slow mover in the fast lane and sped for its bumper, swerving across into the adjoining lane a second before impact. The cop in the car directly behind was not so lucky. He saw the slowcoach too late and couldn't avoid the collision. Clipping the edge of its bumper, the cop car spun a one eighty before careering off the road and rear-ending a fire hydrant. As if straight from a scene in some low budget Hollywood movie, the car stopped dead in its tracks, sending water from the hydrant spiralling skywards in a giant plume.

The Honda was now blazing a trail through the traffic, leaving everything in its wake. Everything, except the two remaining police cars, their light bars flooding the sky, ear-splitting sirens still blaring. The unbearable noise from behind seemed to clear the way ahead, ironically making it easier for Taylor to access free road.

Not for long, he cursed. A hundred yards away, a huge truck was lumbering out into the road from a loading bay behind a supermarket. A man standing at the rear was carefully guiding the truck out with one hand, flagging the approaching traffic down with the other. He froze when he spotted the entourage heading his way.

Taylor had already decided he could make the gap between the truck and the perimeter wall before it closed in front of him. The responsive Honda engine would deliver the goods. The rest was in the lap of the gods.

The guide was stuck out in the middle of the road, flailing his arms at both Taylor and the truck driver. The car was streaking towards an ever-diminishing space between truck and wall. Shoe-horning into the gap, it barely touched the wall before scuttling out the other side.

The first police car arrived closely behind, the driver also going for it, bouncing between wall and vehicle before emerging slightly narrower, but relatively unscathed. To be fair, the truck driver had helped him out by slamming on his brakes when he realised what was happening.

The final chaser had already decided he could not make the gap and was tugging desperately on the steering wheel, pushing the brake pedal through the floor. The severity of the manoeuvre made the car broadside towards the truck. The guide closed his eyes as the vehicle screeched to a halt with barely a millimetre to spare.

Two down, one to go.

A mile up ahead, the two cars exploded onto a stretch of free road. They were now leaving the centre of town, hitting the outskirts of Tel Aviv. The traffic there was much lighter and the superior Honda was beginning to streak away from the police car. Taylor was glad that cops on the continent tended to drive around in ordinary *Joe Public* cars and not the highly rated models their UK counterparts enjoyed.

Taylor glanced in his mirror. He estimated maybe half a mile of breathing space between them, the cop car's lights and siren still going strong.

'Persistent bastard!' Taylor spat. He shook his head slowly as he watched his pursuer. 'Whatever they're paying you, it ain't enough, pal.' Taylor almost admired the man, but knew he must bring the game to an end soon, one way or another.

A small village came into view about half a mile away. Taylor confirmed his position as he raced towards it. He reckoned he was now at least three quarters of a mile to the good. Gripping the wheel tightly, he swung the Honda into a long stretch of about four hundred yards which led to the edge of town. Taylor hammered the car there in seconds. Braking hard and dropping gears, he managed to retain control before expertly sliding into a sharp left some fifty yards in.

Spotting a small narrow driveway on the right on his way out of the bend, he turned sharply into it, jumping on the brakes as he did so. The smoking tyres lost it for a second in the shifting gravel and a shower of dirt and stones flew all around him as the car screeched to a halt.

An old man, stripped to the waist, was at the side of the house working in his garden. He nearly dropped his spade along with his jaw as the dust settled all around him.

Taylor, ignoring the startled man, didn't divert his attention from his rear-view mirror.

The sound of the police siren grew louder by the second. Taylor drew in slow breaths, steadying his nerves.

The siren now deafening, Taylor slammed the gear lever into reverse. Hitting the accelerator hard, the car shot out of the drive, digging two huge craters into the gravel as it left.

There was no way the police car could avoid the collision, the Honda catching it full force, just behind the front wheel, knocking it up onto its side. The cop car perched there for a few seconds before toppling all the way over onto its roof.

Taylor rammed the stick into first. He checked his mirror as he sped away, watching as the cop - suspended upside down but still very much alive - struggled to unclip his seatbelt.

CHAPTER ELEVEN

Taylor made his way back to the outskirts of Jaffa before ditching the Honda in a side street.

He sat down to coffee and sandwiches - bordering on the stale - in a quiet corner of a small, run-down diner. It was now almost 4pm, and as he watched customers come and go, Taylor decided on a slight, but necessary, deviation from his original plan.

He pulled Brian Ricker's mobile from his pocket, switched it on. He hit the secure number.

Ricker answered on the second ring. 'Ryan, what the hell is going on over there? My phone's been lighting up like a Christmas tree!'

'I don't know, Brian. What's being reported?' Taylor was choosing his words carefully.

'Christ, you're all over the news! They're saying you killed two men and kidnapped a little girl!'

'Gotta go. Can't talk now. Call you back.'

Short and sweet.

Imagining his hands locking together around Brian Ricker's throat, Taylor gripped the phone a bit too tightly for comfort, cracking the screen. He swigged the last of his coffee and tucked a couple of notes under the cup before heading for the door. A metal charity box hung on the wall near the exit. He dropped the mobile through the slot in the top of the box on the way out.

In less than fifteen minutes, the diner was playing host to some heavy hitters. Half a dozen cars squealed to a halt out front. In no time the place was awash with police officers and guns.

Taylor sat grim-faced near the front window of an internet cafe along the street. As he watched the officers frogmarch a handful of people out of the diner to waiting wagons, he took the chance to check out the seriousness of his situation. Tapping a few keys, he accessed the rolling Reuters news site. There it was: murder, kidnapping, car theft. The colour left Taylor's face when he saw an image of himself appear on the screen. Closing the lid on the laptop, he glanced around the cafe. It seemed nobody had recognised him, although surely it was only a matter of time. He reckoned it would be unwise to hang around to find out. Pulling up the collar of his jacket, he slipped out to mingle among the gathering crowd on the street.

Alone, betrayed and apparently public enemy number one in a hostile environment, for the first time since he'd picked up Corinne Williams' call, Taylor wished he hadn't answered.

One plus point - if there could ever be such a thing in his predicament - it was exactly the type of situation Ryan Taylor had trained for.

CHAPTER TWELVE

'April?'

'Ryan, I've been so worried. You're all over the news. People have been calling and asking for you. What is going on?'

April Taylor's normally calm voice had raised a level or two. No tears, but Taylor sensed they weren't a million miles away.

'I need you to listen. Don't talk, just listen. Okay?'

'Okay.'

'You know me, April. You know I would never do anything to harm you or Jake. The stuff they're saying about me. It's not true. It's the job. It's just the job, okay?'

'Yes.'

'I'm fine and I'll be home soon. I'll call you again in a couple of days. Give Jake a hug for me. Love you.'

Taylor hung up the phone. He felt sick at first, then guilty at the length of conversation. It was the way it had to be. He rested his forehead against the payphone as the coins dropped into the hold. Difficult task out of the way, Taylor should find the next somewhat easier. All he had to do was track down a copy of the most famous telephone directory in the world.

'Excuse me, do you have the Yellow Pages?' Taylor asked of the pretty receptionist at The Hilton. He figured if a place such as The Hilton didn't have the Yellow Pages, nobody would.

'Not yellow, sir, they're called *Golden* Pages in Israel.' She laughed before stooping to pluck the directory from a shelf below the counter.

Taylor found a phone kiosk off the main corridor. He stepped inside, flicked the pages until he reached 'H' for *Hotels*.

Trailing a finger down the page, he counted to fifteen. He whispered the name and phone number of that entry a couple of times, then checked both ways along the corridor before dialling.

'Thank you for calling the Hotel Indigo. And how may I help you today?' the cheery voice asked.

'I'd like to leave a message for a guest?'

'Yes, sir. If you give me the name, I'll see what I can do.'

'Thank you. It's for a Mr. Walter Coogan.'

'One minute,' the voice said. Taylor now wanted confirmation. He didn't have to wait long: 'Yes sir, and the message?'

'Tell him Mr. Callaghan is expecting him on the first tee at the arranged time. And tell him to bring along his spare putter.'

'All right sir, I'll make sure Mr. Coogan gets the message,' the voice said. 'Enjoy the game.'

Taylor decided to take the bus as he'd read that the service in the country tended to be regular and busy; both ideal for moving around undetected.

As the bus neared his stop, he took a moment to check out the people in the vicinity; a couple of backpacking tourists, an elderly man jogging past in shorts and singlet, and a young woman walking her dog. No obvious cause for concern.

Taylor picked up his bag and stepped off the bus. There were a couple of cars parked out in front of the hotel and another three around thirty yards away on the other side of the road.

Taylor noticed a figure in the driver's seat of the car nearest to him. The window was down and an arm was dangling out, fingers drumming on the door panel. As he walked towards the hotel, Taylor caught the man staring at him in the wing mirror. His senses tingled and he felt for his gun when the man snatched his arm inside. The door began to swing open as

Taylor reached the back of the car. A foot shot out, planting itself on the ground. Taylor managed to catch the door before it opened fully, flicking it back against the man's leg as he made to get out. The man squealed in pain. Heavy footsteps hit the road behind Taylor and he wheeled around. He stopped short of pulling his gun when he saw a teenage girl in front of him, a horrified look on her face.

'I'm sorry,' Taylor said. He held up his hands. 'Please, forgive me.'

By the time Taylor had smoothed things over with father and daughter, the incident had attracted two or three interested onlookers. Unwanted attention was not good and he was glad to get out of there before the police became involved.

Taylor sat for a few minutes in the foyer of the Hotel Indigo. He didn't have long to wait before one of the staff approached him.

'Mr. Callaghan?' she asked.

'Yes.'

'There is a call for you at the desk.' She indicated over her shoulder.

'Thanks.' He walked over to the desk and picked up the receiver.

'Hello.'

'Callaghan?'

'Yes.'

'What kept you?'

'Been a little busy. You okay?'

'I've been better. Take the back exit. It's next to the stairs. I'll meet you there.'

The call disconnected.

Taylor stepped into the stairwell area, pausing for a few seconds to check in case he'd attracted any interested parties.

Satisfied he hadn't, he walked to the exit door and glanced out into a back yard. Wheeled rubbish bins and tubs of discarded grease and used cooking oil sat near the door serving the kitchens. Beside them, a familiar face caught his gaze. Taylor pushed his way out into the yard.

'Never thought I'd be so happy to see your ugly ass,' Troy Williams quipped. The pair clasped hands, briefly hugged. 'You remembered the arrangement?'

'Yellow pages. Look up hotels and call number fifteen on the list. You're Coogan and I'm Callaghan. Clint Eastwood characters from the movies.'

'I knew you'd come, man. Thanks,' Williams said.

'You'd do the same for me,' Taylor said, smiling. His mood changed quickly as he considered matters at hand. 'What's going on, Troy? Where's Maddie?'

'She's okay. Danny Foster's looking after her.'

'Thank God,' Taylor said, blowing out his cheeks. 'But Foster? I thought he'd packed it in.'

'You never get out of this game, Ryan, you know that. Danny was the only man I could trust.' He paused to nod at Taylor. 'Barring present company, of course. I owe Danny, big time. He rescued Maddie.'

'The CIA is saying you killed Liebermann.'

'He was alive when I left him, Ryan, I swear.' Williams leaned in closer. 'They took Maddie.'

'I kind of figured out what had happened when Corinne called me,' Taylor said.

'Corinne called you?' Williams perked up.

'Yes. Listen, I'm sorry to hear about...you know.'

'It's cool, Ryan,' Williams said. 'We'll work things out.'

'Any idea who might be behind this?' Taylor said, changing the subject.

Williams shook his head. 'I got the call to come here and take out Liebermann or they'd kill Maddie. One of the techs owed Danny a favour. The guy began to monitor every call. Eventually we got lucky and he picked up a signal from one of their cell phones. Danny got there in the nick of time. My girl's fine, thank God.' He smiled broadly.

Taylor wasn't smiling. 'They would've killed her, Troy. You know that?'

'Yeah, I know it. Almost got both of us,' he said, ruefully. 'They had a speed boat moored in the bay next to the church. After the hit I was to take the boat around to the next bay and pick up a car. Maddie was supposed to be in the car, tied up in the trunk. Somebody had other ideas. The boat was rigged. I only just managed to get off.'

'Where's Danny now?' Taylor asked.

'He and Maddie are hiding out somewhere south of Tel Aviv,' Williams said, frowning. 'I want to keep as far away from her as I can right now.'

'Good plan,' Taylor said, nodding.

'I hear you're having some problems of your own?'

'One or two. Should've had a routine pick-up from an established contact. Didn't exactly work out that way.'

'Your contact?'

Taylor shook his head. 'Brian Ricker's.'

'Ricker? But I thought he was a good guy?'

'So did I,' Taylor said, shaking his head. 'The whole thing stinks, Troy. After I got clear I called Ricker from a cafe on a so-called secure mobile he'd given me. As soon as I hung up, I got out of there. Left the mobile behind. Five minutes later, the place was swarming.'

Williams shook his head. 'Looks like both of us are being set up. Sorry for getting you into this, Ryan.'

'It's not your fault. As I said, you'd have done exactly the s-, what?' Taylor caught the look on Williams' face.

Williams was staring at him, blankly. 'A five-year-old could've escaped from that church. At the time I couldn't help thinking it was far too easy.'

'What are you thinking?' Taylor asked.

'After Maddie was taken. After I got the phone call... when I got my head round what was happening, actually thought it through...'

'Go on.'

'Well, at first I was convinced I'd been picked at random. Vulnerable kid. Great leverage. Y'know, that kind of thing? But I think it was more than that. There's a reason for all this. And someone in the CIA is going along with it. And now you're in up to your neck. And MI6 are involved. The whole thing's a set-up. We're missing something here.'

'But what?'

Williams shrugged. 'We'll work it out as we go along. There is one thing I'm certain of.'

'What's that?'

'Neither of us is a traitor.'

Taylor felt a knot in his gut. 'So where do we go from here?' he said.

Williams paused for a moment. 'Liebermann. Or rather, his chief aide.'

CHAPTER THIRTEEN

'Did I not make myself clear?' the man snapped. He swivelled around in his executive chair in his executive office and stared out at the gathering dusk casting long shadows over central London.

Brian Ricker squirmed in his non-executive chair, purposely set lower. Unfortunately for Ricker his height meant he still sat higher, a fact not lost on Leo Mannheim or his fiery temper.

'Sir, I'm taking care of it as we speak,' Ricker said.

'Which is what you told me yesterday.' Mannheim swung back to face Ricker. 'And now what do we have? No wait, I'll tell *you*, shall I? Two double agents on the loose on foreign soil. Two potentially catastrophic, walking, talking breaches of national security. Who knows, they might even be working together already...*as we speak*.'

Mannheim was short, fat and bald. Early fifties and single, he was only six months into the job as Head of MI6. His background was not in the field, but in admin and number crunching. Already, he had built up a reputation as a man not to be messed with; a man with little regard for human feelings and sentiment; a man without a conscience, capable of almost anything; a man who detested everything that lived, breathed and crawled. Or so he liked people to think. In six months, he'd assumed the persona of a man who lived only for his job and the security of his country. Some might say Mannheim had all the qualities and pre-requisites of the perfect Head of MI6.

During the past few months, sources for the CIA had unearthed sensitive information regarding the *extra curricular* activities of one of their top agents. By all accounts, Troy Williams was selling secrets to anyone willing to listen, or rather to anyone willing to pay top dollar for them. The best part of a hundred thousand of them had been lodged in offshore accounts in Williams' name. It was as cut and dried as it gets. Not only that, but it transpired that one of MI6's most experienced field agents – ironically a close friend of Williams' – had also been randomly supplying and receiving to all and sundry for similar reward.

Brian Ricker had thought Ryan Taylor's indiscretions incredibly stupid, and entirely unbelievable. Clearly, something stank up the place as far as Ricker was concerned. He felt bad, yes, for what he had done and what he still had to do, but for the moment he was courting self-preservation. And orders were orders.

'I want these bastards zipped into body bags by the end of the week.' Mannheim was as straight-talking as ever. 'Now can you achieve this for me? Or do I have to hire someone who will actually do as I ask?'

'Consider it done, sir,' Ricker whispered.

Brian Ricker knew nothing about the assassin hired by the CIA to settle the US issues. Hell, he knew next to nothing about the individual he had reluctantly set up to take care of Ryan Taylor. All he had was an assurance that the job would get done.

And a name: *Federici.*

CHAPTER FOURTEEN

'Danny, when can I go see my dad?'

'Won't be long now, kiddo. Your dad has one or two things to clear up first. And did I not tell you that already?'

Maddie Williams and Danny Foster were holed-up in a flea-infested bedsit in a run-down suburb of Tel Aviv. *The more run-down the better*, Troy Williams had insisted. He figured his daughter would be a whole lot safer in such a place than in a more up-market part of town. Williams considered it natural to assume that people who wanted to disappear off the radar for a while would tend to do so in comfortable surroundings. And just to be extra sure, he made Foster promise he'd move them around the ghettos every three days until this thing was over. Three days were up.

'Gather up your stuff, kiddo. Time to go,' Foster said.

'I need to shower first,' Maddie said, hunching her shoulders. 'Wash this stinking place off me, okay?'

'Twenty minutes,' Foster said. He smiled as he tapped his watch. He hardly knew Maddie Williams, but had quickly taken a shine to the kid. 'I'm going to take a look around before we leave. And remember-'

'Yeah, I know,' she cut in, 'Don't open the door to anybody.'

'That's my girl. We'll make an agent of you yet.' He made a pretend pistol sign with his fingers.

Foster waited until she had gone into the bathroom before he left, locking the door behind him. He headed along the narrow alleyway towards the main street at the top of the road.

When he reached the main street, he glanced back along the alleyway. All clear. Turning west, he made a point of checking out every shop on both sides of the road, casually observing people going about their business. About fifty yards along the street, he picked up a dog-eared newspaper abandoned on a table outside a cafe. He ordered a coffee and sat staring at the newspaper, not taking in any of what he was reading. Eventually, with no alarm bells going off in his head, he decided enough was enough.

'Kiddo, we ready to go? You got your stuff together?' Foster was back at the safe house. He paused inside the main door, key in hand. 'Maddie?' His eyes narrowed as he listened for movements. Nothing. He pocketed the key and took out his gun, flicking off the safety. His breathing quickened. Continuing silence, save the ever-quickening thump of his heart. The tiny squeak of a floorboard near the bathroom door tightened his finger on the trigger.

The girl emerged in the doorway. She was stiff, rigid even, and visibly trembling. At her neck the cold steel of a gun barrel confirmed Danny Foster's worst fears.

'I-I'm sorry, Danny. He said my dad was in trouble and he needed to take me to him,' she said, her voice wavering.

'It's all right, honey,' Foster said as he stepped into the middle of the room, both hands on the gun, arms ram-rod straight, leaning to try to get an angle on the intruder.

Maddie felt a push on the barrel and stepped forward into the room.

'Holy f-?' Foster spat. He could hardly believe his eyes as the stranger came into full view. He relaxed his grip on the gun for a few seconds, at least until the element of surprise had waned. 'Fontaine? What the hell are you doing here?'

'Following orders, Foster. You know how it is.'

CIA assassin, Blake Fontaine, pushed Maddie Williams all the way into the room, making sure he kept her between himself and Foster.

Foster cursed his luck. There he was, gun-drawn in an Israeli ghetto, responsible for the welfare of his friend's daughter. And worse, going toe-to-toe with the agency's number one *shit-shoveller*.

Fontaine worked alone, always alone. He was the JFK killer, if you believed the conspiracy theories; the guy who would bring down a plane full of aid workers to take out a single target; the guy who would cut his mother's throat for a muddy dollar; the guy the CIA would never admit to having in its employ.

Foster knew Troy Williams had been in some dodo when he took the call from him. He didn't realise exactly how deep that dodo was, until now. He would have to think...and fast.

'Let the girl go, Fontaine. This has nothing to do with her.' Foster shifted position again as he spoke. His trigger finger twitched as he kept trying to work that angle.

'You know I can't do that, Danny,' Fontaine said as he edged back behind her.

'I know where Williams is. I'll take you to him. Let her go. You don't need her. She's a kid.'

'Don't insult my intelligence.' Fontaine pointed the gun at Foster for a second, then back to Maddie. 'Now drop the gun or I shoot this pretty little girl in the head.' Maddie froze as he jammed the barrel hard into the base of her skull.

'Danny!' Maddie shouted. She closed her eyes tightly.

'Okay! Okay, don't shoot!' Foster held up both hands. He stepped forward to lay the gun on a low table before straightening.

Fontaine paused. He drew Foster a look of disgust – his reward for cowardice and weakness – and picked out a spot between his eyes. Foster swallowed hard. One final glance down the barrel.

Maddie formed a strong fist and swung it behind her with all her might into Fontaine's groin. As Fontaine doubled over Foster leapt forward, grabbing his arm. The two men grappled for the gun.

'Run, Maddie!' Foster shouted as both men wrestled on the floor.

She bolted through the open door into the hall and down the stairs to the alleyway. Hesitating for a split-second, she heard a shot ring out above her. Seconds later, another. Before she knew it, she was at the top of the road, chest heaving.

Fifty yards away, on the other side of the street, some people were standing in a short queue. A bus trundled past her, heading east, and stopped beside the queue.

Moments later, Maddie was on board. Clenching and unclenching both hands on the metal grab rail on top of the seat in front, she glared at the driver who was stealing some final drags on his cigarette before he continued on his journey. Peering over his shades, he was laboriously checking information pinned to a little clipboard at his side.

Come on, mister. Please. Drive. Please... Maddie kept looking over her shoulder.

Eventually, the driver tossed the clipboard behind his seat, flicked the cigarette butt out the window, and crunched home the gear lever. The bus shuddered into life.

Relief.

Maddie closed her eyes, exhaled carefully. She leaned back in her seat, her mind racing as she tried to figure out her next move.

A flash of light startled her, the streaming sun bouncing Blake Fontaine's reflection onto the glass cover of an information poster in front of her. He was running alongside the departing bus, trying to catch a look inside. Spotting Maddie, he rattled a flat hand on one of the side panels again and again, shouting at the driver to stop.

Bang! Bang! Bang!

Maddie closed her eyes, jumping with fright at each strike. She prayed bus drivers in Israel were exactly like the ones she was used to back home. That school bus back in Chicago. Now that would do fine.

She wouldn't have to wait long to find out. Another quick glance over his sunglasses into the mirror. A smirk, a shrug, a wink for the pretty kid...and a foot, heavy on the gas.

CHAPTER FIFTEEN

Williams and Taylor were in the former's hotel room. They had spent the last hour or so exchanging information. Taylor had asked the American to burn him a copy of his telephone conversation with one of the kidnappers, in case he should encounter the man on his travels. Williams smiled as he watched his friend and colleague go through exactly the same routine as he had done following the call. *Play, rewind, play, rewind, play, rewind...*

Troy Williams' mobile rang. He brightened when he read the name in the display. 'Danny, I was expecting you to call.'

'I-I'm sorry, Troy,' Foster gasped.

Williams stared at Taylor. He could hardly believe his ears as he listened to Danny Foster break into a throaty cough. One of Fontaine's bullets had split an artery close to his heart. The rest of his life would be measured in moments.

'What's happened, Danny? Maddie, is she okay?' Williams said, catching his breath. Taylor watched as the colour left his friend's face.

'Danny, please, speak to me,' Williams said slowly.

'It was F-Fontaine!' Foster spluttered.

Williams shivered at the mere mention of the name. 'Where's Maddie?' he asked again, swallowing hard.

'She ran. Maddie ran, Troy.' Foster's voice was growing weak.

'What's your location, Danny?' Williams said, 'I need to get you help.'

'It's too late...' Foster spat out the words before lapsing into one final gurgling fit. Then a sudden sharp blow pumped through the ear-piece, the sound of Danny Foster's phone hitting the floor.

Then, silence.

'Danny! Danny, can you hear me?' Williams shouted.

The signal had dropped out.

Williams closed his eyes. He placed the phone face-down on the table next to him. Every sinew and muscle in his hands and arms stretched and cracked and clenched and unclenched, the rage within him searching for a release. The mobile careered off the table and shot across the floor as Williams hammered both fists down next to it before slumping back in the chair.

'I'm sorry, Troy,' Taylor said quietly. 'I know you and Foster go way back.'

Taylor bent to scoop up the mobile. He turned it around a couple of times, checking the sides for damage. It looked to be undamaged. Signal bars pumped up in the display.

'It was Fontaine,' Williams said, staring ahead at nothing in particular.

Taylor didn't reply. He'd never heard the name.

'Blake Fontaine,' Williams continued. 'He's Agency, a real bad ass. Ryan, *what the hell's going on?*'

Taylor shook his head. 'Maddie?'

'She ran. She got away.'

'Don't worry, we'll find her,' Taylor said.

An imaginary switch flicked on in Williams' head. 'We should carry on with the plan, Ryan,' he said.

'Are you serious? We're talking about Maddie here.'

'Trust me, she'll be fine. My girl will know exactly what to do.'

CHAPTER SIXTEEN

The Shaar Zion Beil Ariela Public Library, Shaul Hamelech Boulevard, Tel Aviv.

It had been almost twenty-four hours since a dying Danny Foster had made that fateful telephone call to his friend, Troy Williams.

In the hope that the CIA was GPS tracking it, Williams' mobile phone was now on its way north, wedged into the battery compartment of a long-distance truck.

Williams was standing at the entrance to the somewhat preposterous looking, boxy-grey concrete structure that was Tel Aviv's biggest library: one hundred thousand square feet and home to half a million books, photographs, archive videos, newspaper clippings and audio music files. With a museum, an opera house, and a theatre all situated on prime real estate and on the same plaza as the library, one might assume that the city was well catered for on the arts front.

Right then, Troy Williams couldn't have given a stuff about the arty-farty set and their cultural likes and dislikes. He'd spent most of the last few hours praying that Maddie had not only escaped the clutches of Blake Fontaine, but that she had also possessed the presence of mind, given the circumstances, to follow her father's special emergency *procedures: make your way to the town's biggest library and wait for me.*

Williams figured that people tended to interact less and generally mind their own business in public libraries. He was ninety-nine percent certain that his daughter was inside that library, thumbing through some of her favourite gothic horror novels. It was contemplation of the other one percent that terrified him.

Climbing the final few steps to *Fiction*, Williams took a couple of long breaths to steady the nerves. He pushed through the glass door into the giant auditorium. The door floated back into place behind him.

Silence – as one might have expected.

To Williams' left sat the archetypal, middle-aged librarian assistant, complete with horn-rimmed glasses, frumpy dress made out of linen or similar, and permanent sour expression for everyone who dared enter. She looked Williams up and down, disapprovingly.

To his right, row upon row *of towering shelves* scraped the ceiling, providing a myriad of small, quiet study corners with private tables, two chairs at each. *Good cover. Excellent.*

His gaze was drawn to the information plaques attached to the top of each row: *Fantasy: Crime: Thriller: Mystery: Legal: Western: Science Fiction: Romance.* Eventually, *Horror.*

Maddie fought back tears as she watched her father appear before her eyes. As he walked along the narrow aisle towards her, smiling, she so wanted to leap from her chair and run into his arms. But she knew she mustn't. *Don't draw attention. No public shows of emotion.* Her father's advice did make perfect sense, as always, but sometimes she would feel like a child unable to behave like one.

All of this was lost in the moment when Williams broke protocol, lifting his girl off her feet and hugging her as though he hadn't seen her for ten years.

'Dad, I was so scared. Danny...and, and that...man, he had a gun. And Danny-'

'Danny's okay, honey,' Williams lied. The truth would keep. He didn't see the point in causing her further distress. 'Now I need you to stay calm for me, be my brave girl for a little while longer. Okay?' His voice cracked as he sensed the vulnerability shine right out of her.

'Uh-huh,' she said, nervously tucking wisps of hair behind her ears.

Williams selected three random books from the nearest shelf and sat, pulling his chair in close to her. He opened up one of the books and began idly leafing through the pages as he spoke. 'Honey, we haven't got much time so I want you to listen, okay?'

'Okay.'

'You remember Willie Pastorchek?'

'Mm-hmm. He was a cop.'

'That's right. You used to go over to his place when you were little.'

'Yeah, he had a dog.' She smiled, nervously rubbing her palms on her jeans.

'You remember how much you loved that dog, Popcorn, was it?'

'Popper.'

'Popper. Yeah, that was it. Anyway, you liked Willie and his family, right?'

'Mm-hmm, I guess so. His son *was* kinda geeky.' She blushed as she recalled how much of a crush she had on the older lad.

'I guess he was at that, honey.' Williams tenderly stroked her cheek.

'What's this about, dad?' Maddie had always been quick on the uptake.

Williams steeled himself. 'Willie and his family moved out here after he retired from the force. His wife's Jewish and she wanted to move here to be near her parents. They run a small farm in the north of the country.'

'No, absolutely not! I'm staying with you!' Maddie leaned back in her chair, folded her arms. Petulantly, she began tapping the leg of the table with her foot.

'It's not safe here, honey. I have to get you as far away from me as possible. Surely you-'

'But that man,' she said, interrupting him. 'He had a gun. And you weren't there. He was going to kill *me*-'

'He wouldn't have harmed you, honey. He was going to use you to get to me. That's why you'll be safe if we stayed apart. It'll just be for a little while. Till I get this thing sorted. Okay?'

More foot tapping on the table leg.

'C'mon, Maddie. You imagine what your mom would say if I let anything happen to you? A few days, that's all. I promise.'

Eventually: 'I guess so.'

'That's my girl. Okay, here's how we're going to do this.' Williams moved closer. 'There's a cab waiting outside. We go to the train station. It's about five minutes from here. You take the train to Haifa. It's in the north. Now I've called Willie already. He's going to meet you at the station there, okay?'

'I guess. But you owe me, big-time,' she said, pointing an angry finger at her dad.

'Absolutely. Cross my heart, as soon as this is over, we're taking a vacation. Anywhere you want.'

'Anywhere?'

'Anywhere.'

'Dad?'

'Yeah?'

'Can mom come too?'

A smile formed on Troy Williams' face. 'Yeah, mom can come too.'

Maddie Williams' own smile was so infectious it seemed to light up the whole place.

CHAPTER SEVENTEEN

Hashalom Railway Station, Tel Aviv

'This is a note of Willie's address and cell number. Remember he'll *be* waiting at the station,' Williams said as happily as his breaking heart would allow. Sending her away again was the last thing he felt like doing, but with a dangerous scumbag like Blake Fontaine on their case he knew it was the only option.

Willie Pastorchek's farm was located in the kibbutz of Ein Hamifratz, a little to the north of Haifa. Pastorchek was another within Williams' small circle of friends, worthy of his complete trust. The big Chicago ex-cop had been Williams' partner during his five years on the force, before the lure of the CIA became too strong for Williams to resist. Their lifelong friendship was cemented the day Williams stepped up to save Pastorchek's skin during a delicate hostage situation, when a botched bank robbery went tragically wrong. Four hostages had already lost their lives to a deranged gunman before Williams took the guy out with a clean head shot. It was typical of big-hearted Willie Pastorchek, in the bank voluntarily as a straight-swap for a pregnant woman the gunman had agreed to release during a lucid moment. Willie was about to become dead hostage number five until Troy Williams' timely intervention.

Earlier, during their brief telephone conversation, Williams had no cause to mention to Pastorchek about the precarious *situation* in which he and Ryan Taylor found themselves. Not that it would have made any difference to the big guy. Willie would lay down his life for Troy and his family, no questions asked.

Williams handed his daughter some currency and a small food bag he had prepared earlier for the journey. She stuffed the notes in a pocket and clutched the bag tightly to her. They hugged one final time on the platform before Maddie broke away and quickly boarded the train. She stood inside the doors looking out at her father, her hands pressed against the glass as she tried her darndest to muster a smile.

The train shuddered into life and began to slip away from the platform. Troy Williams noted the look of horror on Maddie's face. By the time he turned around, it was too late.

CHAPTER EIGHTEEN

Dusk was gathering fast as Taylor crept into the courtyard at the back of the house. He ducked for cover behind a tall conifer in the garden when a light from one of the downstairs rooms lit up the yard. A woman of around sixty, wearing one of those wrap-around aprons that screamed *servant*, tugged the drapes closed.

Taylor blew out his cheeks. *Close call.*

The house looked almost as impressive from the back as it had done from the front. Taylor didn't profess to know a whole lot about house prices in Israel. He didn't know a whole lot more about house prices in Scotland either, for that matter, but reckoned this Israeli minister would have been fortunate to recover much change out of a million for a gaff like this in the middle of a posh suburb in Taylor's home city of Glasgow.

His train of thought naturally puffed along to ministers' salaries and the like. Again, he couldn't be a hundred percent sure, but he would be willing to bet any money that there was no way on this Earth an aide – chief or not – could possibly afford such a place.

Setting aside the paranoia, Taylor noted the time: 7.30pm. He couldn't be sure when people in Israel normally sat down to dinner, but assuming similar arrangements to back home in Britain, it could be anytime between five and seven thirty. This assumption would appear to be on the money when Taylor saw the light in the downstairs kitchen illuminate, signifying that the hired help had cooked and served the meal and was now ready to wash up and, hopefully, leave for the night.

Taylor had already scanned the yard; no trampolines or bikes, and no football goals, basketball nets or play houses, equals no children.

Smiling at his good fortune – kids were an obvious distraction - Taylor decided to wait a few minutes to allow the cook time to clear up and get the hell out of there.

7.42pm: a door opened from what looked like a utility area next to the kitchen and the cook stepped out. Barking what Taylor assumed was a brief farewell, she pulled the door over behind her and took off down some steps to the courtyard, the heels of her shoes sparking on the ground, echoing into the distance.

Again, Taylor couldn't believe his luck when he tried the back door and found it unlocked. No security alarms, controlled entry systems, guard dogs, warning sirens or lights, and no need to even pick a lock.

Inside the house was quiet, save for some faint sounds in the distance. *Music?*

As Taylor drew closer to the source, he realised somebody was watching the TV show, *Friends,* the unmistakeable theme tune giving the game away. He thought of his wife, April, back home in Glasgow. He could take it or leave it, but she was a big fan of the sitcom, had watched the devil out of a boxed set he'd given her the previous Christmas.

Taylor drew his gun and pushed the door open a few inches. The living room was surprisingly small, given the size of the house, and dimly lit, with most of the space being taken up by a couple of leather sofas. Flickering images from a television set in the corner danced across the faces of a man and a woman, sitting huddled together on one of the sofas. Taylor aged them early thirties.

Unaware they had company, both laughed in time with the live *Friends* audience until Taylor flicked a switch inside the door and the main centre light kicked in.

The woman reacted first, stifling a scream before grasping the man's arm tightly. The man's eyes grew wide as the intruder raised his gun.

Taylor flipped the gun at the TV. 'Turn it off,' he said.

No reaction.

'The TV. Turn it off,' Taylor said again, louder.

The man found the stand-by button on the remote control. The TV died.

'Is there anyone else in the house?' Taylor directed the question at him. Past experience told him whimpering women and information gathering didn't always mix well.

The man shook his head, said nothing.

'Okay, here's how it'll go,' Taylor said. 'I ask the questions, you answer them, and we'll get along just fine. Do you mind?' He pointed towards the other sofa.

'No, please...'

'Thank you,' Taylor said, sitting.

'What is it you want?' the man asked, pulling in a short gasp as he completed the sentence. It did not go unnoticed.

'Let's not over-complicate things, shall we?' Taylor said. 'I'll say it again. I *ask* and *you* answer. Yes?'

Another nod.

'Are you Moshi Rabinowitz?'

No reaction, except maybe a little tightening of the woman's grip on the man's arm. The man lowered his gaze, quickly lifting it again when Taylor raised his gun.

'Yes! Yes, please do not hurt us!' Rabinowitz held up both hands, spitting out the words as if fighting to breathe.

Taylor nodded. 'Better. Now you both do exactly as I say and this will be over soon. Got it?'

Another nod.

'You were chief aide to Foreign Minister, Menahem Liebermann?'

'Yes.'

'How long?'

'Five years.'

'And what was Liebermann involved in that led to his assassination?'

'I don't understand. How would I know this?'

'Come on, you were his chief aide. You must have known him better than anybody. What stuff was he making money from? Drugs, prostitution, gambling?' Taylor stood to try and further intimidate Rabinowitz. He reckoned it was worth a shot.

'No, I-I do not know. I have no idea what you are talking about,' Rabinowitz gasped. He pulled his arm away from wife Lola, used it to steady himself on the sofa.

'Then maybe this will help you remember,' Taylor said, lowering his voice. He bent towards Rabinowitz, hovering the gun an inch from his forehead. Rabinowitz closed his eyes tightly, began to visibly shake.

'Please do not hurt my husband!' the woman cried.

Rabinowitz's face seemed to literally explode with sweat. In seconds his shirt was stained dark with it. Hands digging deep into the sofa, his breathing pattern ramped up quickly to hard and fast like a steam train climbing a steep gradient. He fidgeted and twitched, coughed and spluttered. Sprawling a hand over his chest, he pitched forward in his seat, his face morphing in seconds from pink to crimson, then a shade of purple.

'What's wrong with him?' Taylor snapped.

'He has severe asthma!' the woman said, her voice trembling. 'It is worse when he gets agitated. He has medication. I-'

'Get it!' Taylor cut in, stepping aside to let her pass.

Rabinowitz lost consciousness, falling back onto the sofa.

Taylor reckoned the Israeli was close to checking out. He leaned across to open a couple of his shirt buttons at the neck. The wife scurried back into the room armed with a handful of pills and inhalers.

Taylor watched as she went through what he assumed was a well rehearsed routine. Steroid inhaler to open the airwaves, little magic pills to ensure they stayed open, and an electrically powered nebuliser with clear face mask to complete the process.

After a couple of minutes Rabinowitz was breathing normally, giving a weak thumbs-up to his wife. She sat beside her man, patting the back of his hand as if she'd done so a thousand times before.

'My husband does not speak of his work,' she said, her voice gaining strength. She turned towards Taylor. His gun was tucked away well out of sight, for now.

'You don't discuss anything at all with your husband concerning work?' Taylor asked.

'No.'

'What about you? Do *you* work, Mrs Rabinowitz?'

'No. Moshi does not approve.' She turned to smile at her husband, continued patting his hand.

'Did you know Liebermann?' Taylor watched for the reaction.

'No. Well, not really.'

'You've met him?'

'Yes...once...briefly.' She hesitated, her smile fading.

Taylor picked up on it. 'You didn't like him?'

She lowered her eyes. 'No.'

'Why not?'

Rabinowitz switched off the nebulizer and tugged off the mask to answer. 'Menahem's language is, was, colourful at times,' he wheezed. 'My wife does not understand the need for people to use bad language.'

'Was he abusive to you?' Taylor asked.

'No. Well, at least not *physically*,' Rabinowitz said, swallowing hard.

Taylor watched the Israeli's demeanour change before his eyes, hitting an imaginary self-relax button if such a thing were possible. Taylor put it down to the pills kicking in.

'I know who you are,' Rabinowitz continued. 'You are Taylor, the British Secret Service agent the authorities are looking for. But why would you come here to Israel?'

'I'm helping out an old friend.'

'Williams, the American? But he killed Liebermann.'

Rabinowitz stopped when Taylor raised his hand. He turned to face the woman. 'You have a nice house, Mrs Rabinowitz,' he said quietly. He knew Troy Williams was innocent. End of story. Arguing the point with this man was going to get him nowhere fast.

The woman's gaze switched between the two men before she replied. 'Thank you, it was my father's. We lived with him until he died, three years ago.'

That explains the house, Taylor mused. He began to think that maybe Moshi Rabinowitz *was* telling the truth. Brow-beaten, put-upon, scumbag for a boss. Par for the course for a lot of people.

Taylor stole a glance at his watch, remembering he'd scheduled to hook up with Williams back at the hotel in around half an hour. After the American had made sure Maddie was safely aboard a train heading north.

'I apologise for the intrusion,' Taylor said, backing towards the door.

'Mr. Taylor?' Rabinowitz said. Taylor didn't answer. He turned to face the Israeli. 'I do hope you resolve your issues,' Rabinowitz continued. 'I am sure you will do the right thing.'

Williams' recording still fresh in his mind, Taylor stopped dead in his tracks. 'What did you say?' he asked.

Rabinowitz shifted in the sofa, glancing uneasily at his wife. 'I-I said I hope you manage to resolve your-'

'No, after that.'

'I said I am sure you will do the right thing.' A puzzled look crossed Rabinowitz's face as he repeated the sentence.

Taylor took a small device out of his pocket and sat it on a coffee table in front of the sofa. 'Ok, now we have a problem,' he said.

'I don't understand. What do you mean? What is that thing?' Rabinowitz said. He made to stand.

'Sit down,' Taylor commanded.

The Israeli did as he was told. He held out his hands to his wife, shrugged.

Taylor pressed play on the digital device Troy Williams had used to record his last telephone conversation with the mysterious caller involved in the abduction of his daughter. He watched Moshi Raboniwitz's face turn various shades of grey as a few seconds of dialogue passed.

'Moshi, what is this? Why-' Lola Rabinowitz paused at exactly the right moment. She pulled in a sharp breath as she heard the words...

I am sure you will do the right thing.

Taylor hit rewind. Replayed the sentence.

The look on Lola's face merely served to confirm Taylor's diagnosis.

'Yes, let's clear this up, shall we?' Taylor said. 'Why don't I play the last part again? Maybe you can explain to your wife exactly what is going on.'

'Moshi? What is he talking about? Wh-what have you done?' Lola said.

'You don't understand my love.' He clasped her hands inside his. She snatched them away. Again, he reached out to her, pleading. 'I was threatened, blackmailed if I did not do as they asked.'

'Speaking of blackmail, why don't I take you to see Troy Williams right now?' Taylor asked. 'Why don't I let you explain to him how you almost got his daughter killed?'

'What is he saying? This cannot be true, can it, Moshi?' she asked.

'Let me fill in the blanks for you, Mrs. Rabinowitz,' Taylor said. 'Your husband's buddies kidnapped my friend's twelve-year-old daughter and threatened to murder her if he did not come to Israel to kill Liebermann.'

'Is this true?' Lola asked. Taylor noted how calm she had become. As if she had spent her life trying to be strong in the face of adversity.

'It was not like that,' Rabinowitz said, turning to Taylor. 'I had no choice. They threatened to kill Lola if I did not co-operate.'

'How dare you. That poor man...and his daughter?' Lola looked at Taylor. Her eyes asked the question.

'She's safe, at least for the moment,' Taylor said.

'Thank God.' Lola looked to the heavens.

'What are you going to do?' Rabinowitz said.

'That depends on you,' Taylor said.

'Please do not kill me. I can give you money. We have money.' Rabinowitz stared at his wife, seeking reassurances. None came.

'I've no intention of killing you, Mr. Rabinowitz,' Taylor said. 'And I have no need for your money. And even if I did, how do you suppose I'm going to live long enough to spend it? No, what I want you to do is tell me everything.'

'But I cannot. They will kill me...kill us.'

Taylor observed him for a few seconds. 'Looks to me as if you have little choice.'

'What do you mean?'

'If you refuse to tell me everything, and I mean everything, I'm going to take this little guy on a trip.' He picked up the recorder, holding it between two fingers. 'First, we'll visit the biggest daily newspaper in Israel. Then, just for good measure, we'll drop into government headquarters. The way I see it, it'll be a toss-up who gets to you first, your blackmailing friends, or the hangman's noose. I can only imagine the Israeli attitude towards treason.'

The mere mention of the word *treason* seemed to drain the very life out of Moshi Rabinowitz. He buried his face in his hands before rising to walk over to the window. Still wheezing, he turned to face Taylor. 'All right, Mr. Taylor. As you say, either way, I have no choice. I will tell you all I know.'

The first bullet made a *plinking* sound as it passed neatly through the window. Rabinowitz dropped to his knees. Clutching at his neck, blood oozed from the corner of his mouth. Panic stricken, his gaze darted between Taylor and Lola.

Plink. The second bullet caught him high on the back of his skull, tearing off part of his forehead as it exited. He was dead before he hit the floor.

'Get down!' Taylor shouted.

Wriggling from Taylor's grasp, Lola rose to try and catch her husband as he fell.

Plink. Her lifeless body landed at his feet, a gaping hole in its head.

The gunman flicked to automatic mode and sprayed the room, tearing the place to pieces in thirty seconds.

Shredded curtains hung like rags on what was left of the shattered windows. Portraits and pictures swung back and forth by their corners before crashing, one-by-one, to the floor along with chunks of crumbling plaster gouged out of the walls by the onslaught. The TV set, still connected to the electricity supply, smouldered as it lay face down in the corner, billowing wispy trails of white smoke up and across the ceiling. A solitary bulb within the centre light assembly was still intact. As the atmosphere in the room began to clear, the motion of the bulb swinging gently on the end of its short cable might just as well have painted a giant cross on Taylor's back.

Taylor had to assume the pause meant the gunman was reloading. He took his chance, shaking remnants of the ceiling from his hair and covering his eyes as he took aim to shoot out the bulb. The room was plunged into darkness. Taylor kept low as he crawled out into the hall. Hearing footsteps outside the hall window, he backed against a wall, his finger poised on the trigger. Then, out of the corner of an eye, he noticed something glint across the hall. On the floor, a foot inside the open door to a store cupboard, was a brass-coloured metal ring.

It was a handle, and it looked very much as if it could be connected to a trap door.

CHAPTER NINETEEN

Willie Pastorchek stopped his old truck in front of the barn. As the engine shuddered to a halt, he looked over his shoulder towards the short dirt track along which they had just travelled. Apart from the settling dust and the gently flowing breeze that stirred the trees, there were no obvious movements, no causes for concern. Half a mile away in the distance, the main road traffic looked to be flowing naturally for the time of day.

Willie lowered his head, his sadness at the loss of a good friend threatening to overwhelm him. As an ex-cop it was a feeling he'd experienced from time to time, a feeling he had to snap out of, and quickly. But he'd been in farmer mode for so long that he wondered if he had lost his edge. If he could be the man to cope with this situation. And if he could ever get back the desire, the hunger that made him want to be a cop in the first place.

Assessing the situation as things unravelled, Willie had concluded he would need to grow back that desire and hunger in spades to be able to keep his promise to Troy Williams.

He'd begun well, remaining calm enough to call his wife from the train station. He'd gently urged her to pack a few clothes. To take their son for that much talked about break in order to attend the soccer school the lad had banged on and on about. If there was a positive thing to be had from this, it would be the timing. The course was due to start the day after next. Willie had initially bombed out the idea, citing the huge amount of work that needed doing on the farm. Now, with the threat of imminent danger devastating the family unit, he had turned full circle.

He's a good kid, doesn't ask for much. And I've been giving it a lot of thought lately. Willie had said exactly the right things in exactly the right way. He had convinced her to immediately leave with their son. *Take a few days break. See how he likes it*, he'd said, silently thanking God when she agreed.

'Honey, you need to tell me everything. I know it's tough, but I promised your daddy I'd look after you and that's exactly what I intend to do.' Pastorchek turned to face his distraught passenger.

Maddie shook her head. Every few seconds she would sniff and shudder, like a two-year-old following a major temper tantrum. Her pretty face was puffy almost beyond recognition, and shaded and dirty with dried tear stains.

Willie felt her pain. He made a strong fist, bumping his knee with his knuckles as he contemplated how unfair life could be.

Forty years ago, at the age of only ten, Willie had witnessed the sudden death of his father. One minute Willie Pastorchek Snr. had been walking, talking, laughing, breathing, and the next flat on his back, his life over, gone forever. The finality of it all still made Willie break into a cold sweat at times.

As he tried to compare his experience to that of Maddie Williams, he considered that, in most ways, her loss was even worse. This poor girl had seen her father killed in front of her eyes. Not a massive heart attack like Willie Pastorchek Snr., or a stroke. Dead, but not due to something fancy like a cerebral haemorrhage, aneurism or thrombosis. It could be argued that it was simply Willie's father's time. That his fate had been written in tablets of stone the moment he was born - if one believes in that sort of thing. But a bullet in the brain was another thing. Same outcome, different journey.

'Let's go inside for a while, okay? It's not safe out here,' Willie said. He got out and walked around the front of the truck, all the time glancing back and forth towards the road.

Tugging open the passenger door, he helped Maddie to her feet, supporting her as she walked. Near the steps to the front door of the house, and without warning, her legs gave way. She stumbled into Willie's arms, sobbing, her shoulders rising and falling with the effort.

He held the girl close. Reaching down to lift her off her feet, he brushed open the door and carried her inside.

***

Pastorchek tugged back the curtain for the millionth time. He studied the traffic in the distance for the millionth time. He checked his watch for the millionth time.

Almost an hour had passed since he'd laid the sleeping girl down on his couch and covered her with a light throw. He'd sat close to her, watching the nightmares contort her face, while he turned his options over in his mind, again and again.

From what Maddie had told him before she'd drifted off to sleep, and from the rest of the story he'd pieced together, he figured that this killer may not be done just yet. His instincts were telling him the assassin's remit might be to clear away any loose ends.

Maddie Williams was an obvious loose end. And now she wasn't the only one.

A combination of the gathering gloom outside, stress and sheer exhaustion tugged at Willie Pastorchek's senses as he fought to stay awake.

CHAPTER TWENTY

Taylor thanked the waitress for his coffee. He caught her staring at him as if he had horns. Eventually, she felt the need to point.

'Do-it-yourself. It'll be the death of mankind,' he joked, untangling a little chunk of plaster from his hair.

'You have another.' She motioned again.

'Thanks.' He rubbed his head then dragged both hands through his hair. 'Still a novice. I prefer to leave it to the experts. It's the wife. You know how it is.'

'Not really,' she said. 'My husband can hardly tie his shoelaces. I'm beginning to think he's either very useless, or very clever.'

Taylor smiled politely as she turned to prepare a table.

His mood changed in an instant when he glanced at his watch. Troy Williams was never late.

Something's wrong.

Taylor sipped at the hot coffee. Inwardly, he cursed his luck. Rabinowitz had been about to sing like a canary. He'd seen it before. He'd seen up close the effect blind fear can have on a man. Most people would probably assume that a man would die for his family without thinking. Most men would. But there was a percentage, albeit a small one, willing to do or say anything to save their skins. At any cost. Taylor had witnessed the phenomenon first hand. He'd been among the queuing traffic following an accident when a lorry driver lost control on black ice in the middle of Glasgow's Kingston Bridge. The hulk had been heading for the barrier and a fifty-foot drop to the River Clyde when the driver took the decision to jump out, abandoning his nine-year-old son in the passenger seat. The man had made that decision on the spur of the moment to save himself and leave his own flesh and blood behind to perish. Certain death. But fate double-dealt the man when the lorry flipped onto its side the moment he leapt out, crushing him flat between the barrier and the road. The son escaped without a scratch, belted into his seat as the lorry came to rest on the edge of disaster. Rabinowitz had been the lorry driver of the story. *Blind fear.* Taylor was certain of it.

Another check of the watch.

Something's wrong.

His attention was drawn to a TV set at the end of the counter. Some news programme. A woman reporter was talking about a shooting. Taylor didn't pay much heed at first. He reckoned shootings were ten-a-penny in a place like Tel Aviv. He'd some experience of it.

His ears pricked when he heard reference to a train station: *Hashalom Train Station.*

The reporter continued: 'The man, believed to be American and in his thirties, was killed inside the station. Witnesses told reporters of hearing gunshots.

In other news...'

CHAPTER TWENTY-ONE

Willie Pastorchek woke with a start. By the time all of his senses had kicked in and he'd figured out what day and time it was, he was reaching for the key to his private cabinet.

Maddie was still sleeping soundly next to him on the sofa. He eased himself up, careful not to disturb her. Walked to the front door. Flicked off the latch. Slid the bolt across. Pulled the door open six inches.

Traffic on the main road was sporadic, not unusual for 6am.

Willie stared across the landscape for a full two minutes; same as every morning, nothing much out of the ordinary except a few rabbits, squirrels and birds. He squinted as the rising sun hit the level, throwing spears of blinding light into his eyes.

Willie eased the door closed. Re-latched it and slid over the heavy bolt. He easily picked his way across the squeaky board minefield to the den, barely making a sound. He reckoned he could do it blindfolded. Closing the living room door behind him, Willie dragged a heavy chair across the room and climbed onto it. The chair groaned under his 18-stone frame. He used the key to unlock a horizontally-set, wall-mounted cabinet. Rifle size. The door lifted up, propping open on side supports.

After he'd set up, he opened the door on the other side of the house leading out of the den. It led directly to the back exit into a smaller yard. He unlatched and unbolted the door to the smaller yard. Didn't open it. Instead, walked back into the den. Spun the heavy chair to face the door. Quick check of the equipment.

Willie's hands shook. He reached across to slide open the top drawer of a small unit. A pack of cigarettes he'd planted when he quit three years before was still there, along with a solitary match (for one cigarette, to be smoked only when under extreme pressure - his rule. He figured this qualified) and a silver hip flask full of his beloved scotch.

He sparked the match. Lit up. Inhaled. Long, slow pulls. The tremors subsided. He felt calmed. Unscrewed the flask lid. Closed his eyes as soon as the smooth elixir crossed his lips, burning its way down his throat, leaving that heavenly glow in his chest he so craved.

He laid the flask down and waited.

***

Pastorchek held his breath as he watched the door handle dip. The door edged open and a gun entered, followed by a hand. Willie identified the weapon straight away. It was a Smith and Wesson, his choice of hand-gun as a Chicago cop. The door opened further allowing an arm and a leg inside.

'Okay, buddy,' Willie said. The limbs froze. 'Let's do this nice and easy. No sudden movements. I got you covered. Now you keep comin' on in here? Nice 'n slow now. An' keep the piece in the air.'

The man stepped all the way in, hands aloft.

It became obvious from Willie's expression he didn't know this man from Adam. The man said nothing. He didn't seem fazed by the sight of the elephant gun on a stand facing him.

'This here's a Rigby 450 Nitro Express. It ain't been fired in a while, granted, but are you willing to take the chance? I sure as hell wouldn't. Only need to point this baby in your general direction. Now let's have the gun on the floor. Kick it over. Nice 'n' slow.'

Ryan Taylor put down his gun before the door behind Pastorchek burst open.

'Ryan!' Maddie Williams screamed. She bolted towards Taylor, throwing herself into his open arms. Taylor held the girl close to him as she again proceeded to let it all out.

CHAPTER TWENTY-TWO

Taylor and Pastorchek were sitting in the living room. The door into the kitchen/den was propped open so they could keep an eye on Maddie. She was leaning on the breakfast bar, sipping orange juice and nibbling at a half slice of toast. She looked exhausted, barely able to raise the stirrings of a smile when her gaze met one or both of the men.

'Poor kid,' said Pastorchek. He walked over to his front window, looking out for the hundredth time that morning. Nervously scratching his nails into his jeans and then wringing his hands together, he stood at one side of the window like a nosey neighbour, scanning the front yard, the bushes, the grassland, and the road beyond.

Taylor had been studying Willie Pastorchek's behaviour since he'd arrived on the scene. Pastorchek's growing irritability and nervousness worried him. But then, he thought, the man *was* really only a beat cop, used to, for the most part, handing out parking tickets and directions for tourists.

Troy Williams had briefed Taylor on the situation at the bank when Pastorchek had been pulled in as a hostage after offering himself up in place of a pregnant woman. Very noble. Very brave, thought Taylor. *And incredibly stupid*. The cemeteries are full of nobles and braves...and stupids!

Of course, Taylor knew all about protocol and *police* protocol simply dictates that the professionals remain on the outside of such situations at all times, coordinating, negotiating, in charge. That was how it was supposed to go. And, in ninety-nine times out of a hundred cases the thing simply fizzles out in the end anyway, and the perp or perps are persuaded to give themselves up. Okay, this particular case had resulted in the loss of lives. But who had remained calm and professional enough to take the guy out when push came to shove? *Troy Williams*. And where was Willie Pastorchek when this was happening? That's right – in the bank, on his knees, preparing to take a bullet in the head.

Taylor had arrived at the house a few minutes before dawn. He'd parked the car just off the road, out of sight. He'd crossed a few acres of parkland and in no time at all was close to the front of the house. Twice, he had seen Pastorchek at the window and once in the doorway. He could have taken the American out each time. Easily.

Taylor had heard the front door latch come down, the bolt slide across. He knew he was being directed towards the back entrance. He knew Pastorchek would be waiting for him, just inside the door. Taylor had played along, pretending to sneak in.

Had he been playing for real Taylor would have created a diversion at the front of the house. Maddie, being in the front room, meant Pastorchek would have been forced to compromise his position to save her. Taylor would have entered via the back door and shot Willie Pastorchek in the head as he stood confused in the middle of his living room.

Even when Taylor had laid his life on a plate, Pastorchek, as expected, had opted for the police route. Had the roles been reversed, Taylor would have used the scatter gun to blast Willie Pastorchek to kingdom come as soon as he laid a foot on the back doorstep.

Looking at things in the cold light of day, Taylor really wanted to know if the big American was going to be useful to him given their situation. In his mind, it was a question of whether or not Pastorchek was more likely to get them all killed. That was the main issue.

Willie turned to face Taylor. 'This guy's comin' for her, for us, isn't he?'

'I'd say it was a fair bet. And he won't be the only one,' Taylor said. He knew at least two had already been deployed.

And there could be more.

'But why? What possible harm could a little girl-?'

'It's all about tidying things up, Willie,' Taylor cut in. 'These people don't take chances.'

'But she's a kid for chrissake!'

'Doesn't make a difference. They'll kill us all, knock off and then drive their kids to *Dunkin' Do'nuts*.'

'Why? Why is this happening?'

Taylor shook his head. 'That's what I aim to find out.'

'So, what do we do now? Will they know where we are?' Pastorchek asked.

'I'd say, yes. It's an easy connection to make. You and Troy were cops on the same force. You left and moved here. Troy was on a mission in Tel Aviv. He runs into trouble, where does he go?' Taylor shrugged.

'Then we have to leave. Now!' Pastorchek threw on a jacket. 'Come on, Maddie, we have to go.'

Maddie pushed her plate and cup into the middle of the breakfast bar. She slipped down from the stool and gathered her bag at her feet.

'Okay, let's cool it a minute,' Taylor said. 'You can't just up and leave. You have to have a plan.'

'We can work it out as we go along.'

'Look, Willie-'

'Don't you *look Willie* me!' Pastorchek interjected, his voice resonating. 'The way I see it, we have to get the hell away from here.'

More scratching of jeans and wringing of hands. Taylor took note. His mind was now made up. 'Look. You're not a cop anymore. You're a farmer. Go back to that. You've done your bit. What you did took guts, but you've a family to protect.'

As he spoke the last few words, for an instant Ryan Taylor's thoughts flashed to April and Jake. He felt such a hypocrite.

'But I promised Troy I'd look after Maddie,' Pastorchek protested, though his protestations were even weaker than Taylor had expected.

'I'll take over from here, Willie.' Taylor rose, putting his hand on the big guy's shoulder. 'This is my thing, not yours. I'll get Maddie to safety. You take care of your family. I'd lock up the house and stay out of it for a few days. Long enough to give me time to take the heat off you.'

'What do you mean?'

'Once we get away from here, they're going to be looking to see where I turn up next. When that happens, their focus will shift. Means you and your family will be safe. You can go back to your lives.'

'Where are you going to go?' Pastorchek asked.

'Best I don't say. Good luck.' Taylor extended a hand. They shook. He glanced over his shoulder. 'Maddie, you ready?'

CHAPTER TWENTY-THREE

Taylor flicked the indicator and swept down the off-ramp into a small service station somewhere in the far north of the country.

The car was running on fumes. Taylor and Maddie had been on the road for a full eight hours, pure adrenalin keeping him in the game, forcing the last vestiges of energy from his body.

Willie Pastorchek had dropped them at Haifa train station that morning. Taylor had assumed that the car he had used to get to Pastorchek's home would have been reported stolen by the time they set out, so he decided to ditch it.

He'd selected a Volkswagen Golf at the train station. One, it had a full tank, and two, it was running a week's ticket. Taylor figured he had at least three days use of the car before the posse saddled up.

As he drew up to the pump, Taylor handed Maddie some cash. He directed her towards the little cafe area attached to the service station shop. Asked her to have a look at the menu to see what was on offer. He told her he'd be there in a few minutes, and that it would need to be a take-away.

After he'd filled up, Taylor paid the guy on the till. *Head down. Straight-forward. No chit-chat. Avoid giving anybody anything to remember.*

He then walked over to a single phone booth near the door into the cafe. He popped in a few coins, lifted the receiver and began dialling. As he hit the last number, he almost chickened out. He stood there filled with dread, as the connection kicked in.

'Hello.' Her voice was even smaller and more vulnerable than usual.

'Corinne, is that you?' Taylor asked tentatively.

Silence.

'Corinne?'

'Who is this?' A man's voice took over. It sounded annoyed.

Taylor hung up, immediately. His mind raced into overtime. *Cops? FBI? CIA? The agencies would definitely have urged Corinne to try and keep me on the line. No, it was most likely a male relative, there to comfort Corinne Williams. She'd have been inundated with calls following Troy's death.*

Taylor felt bad at being relieved he had been let off the hook. He wouldn't need to stand there and listen to Corinne Williams sob her heart out. At least he could have tipped the balance by telling her Maddie was with him, safe, for the moment at least.

Taylor easily overcame the urge to call April. He was certain somebody at MI6 would be keeping her informed of any developments. She'd know he was still alive. Surely that was all that mattered.

Maddie was standing at the servery when Taylor entered the cafe. She was picking her way through a menu that was sellotaped to the counter. As she turned to greet him, Taylor noticed her attention switch to something outside. He watched her face turn ashen. Her eyes grew wide as she froze on the spot, unable to speak. She was staring out into the car park area. Taylor glanced over his shoulder in time to see a man step from his car.

'Where's the rest room?' Taylor asked a passing waitress as he moved quickly to catch the girl before she slipped to the floor. 'It's my daughter, she feels a little faint.'

'Over in the corner,' the waitress said, pointing. 'Can I get you some water?'

Taylor didn't answer. He had to act fast. He half-walked, half-dragged Maddie into the toilet. The door snapped shut as the traveller walked into the cafe.

'Maddie, listen to me,' Taylor whispered, lightly tapping her face. 'The man in the car park. Is it him? Fontaine?'

She nodded frantically, unable to speak. The poor girl's whole body was shuddering through pure unadulterated fear.

'I want you to listen to me, okay?'

She kept nodding, shaking.

'I won't let anything happen to you. You have to trust me.'

More nodding.

'That's my girl.'

Taylor scanned the toilet. Four cubicles. Slim window near the ceiling, but too small for even a skinny twelve-year-old to get through. He walked her over to the furthest away cubicle, said: 'Stay in here, lock the door and try not to make a sound.'

She dropped the lid and sat cross-legged on the toilet, pulling in deep breaths, and still nodding. Taylor bent to kiss her forehead, swept her hair from her eyes. She forced a smile.

He raced back to the door, opened it an inch and peered into the cafe. Fontaine was speaking to the assistant behind the counter. Taylor watched as Fontaine produced a couple of photographs. He had expected it. It wouldn't be long before the hitman was walking towards him.

Taylor shut the door. Rushed into the first cubicle. Counted to ten before flushing. Stepped out and jammed the door shut from the outside with a little cardboard from the inside of a toilet roll. Slipped in behind the main door as it swung open.

Fontaine stepped in and drew his gun when he heard the flushing toilet. He grinned as he took aim.

Pop! Pop! Pop!

The door splintered and cracked as the bullets passed through and bounced around the cramped area.

From the other cubicle, Maddie let out a muffled scream. She clamped her hands over her ears.

As Fontaine turned towards her, Taylor grabbed the door with both hands and slammed it hard into Fontaine's back. The gun flew into the corner of the room as Fontaine crashed head-first through the door into the first cubicle.

Maddie sat whimpering as the two men fought for their lives.

After what seemed like an eternity, she heard one of them yell out and then exhale for the final time. The sound of the other breathing heavily drew closer. She held her breath as she watched his shadow creep under the door. Hot tears welled in her eyes, cascading down her cheeks as she blinked.

'Maddie. Come on kid, time to go.' Taylor's voice was unmistakeable.

Shrieking with relief, she wrenched open the door, but on seeing the blood her expression changed. 'You're hurt,' she said, her voice barely a whisper.

Taylor pulled his jacket over his injured arm, joked, 'I've had worse looking after Jake for a couple of hours. Come on, let's go.'

Taylor managed to get her to the door without mentally scarring her further with the sight of a dead Blake Fontaine lying face down on the floor, the handle of a hunting knife protruding from his neck.

As Taylor pushed his way out into the car park, a familiar face stopped him dead in his tracks.

His first instinct was to lash out.

CHAPTER TWENTY-FOUR

Brian Ricker dragged himself back to his feet, only for Taylor to again punch him to the ground. This time Ricker fell backwards, tripping over the edge of a step. The fall knocked him out cold when his head cracked off the bumper of a nearby car.

Taylor turned to see a man inside the cafe, presumably the owner, on the phone calling the police, or so he assumed. He reckoned fatal stabbings and wanton violence was a little out of the ordinary for this guy. He didn't look the type.

As if harnessing a sudden rush of *Hulk*-like fury, Taylor grabbed the unconscious Ricker by his jacket lapels and hauled him across the car park to the Volkswagen.

Maddie pulled open the back door and Taylor bundled his boss inside. They sped out of the car park, heading north.

Taylor didn't utter a word for the next thirty minutes. All he could think about was Brian Ricker's part in this whole mess. Taylor felt betrayed. Simmering anger distorting his thought processes, every glance towards the pale child in the seat next to him cranked it up another notch.

Taylor reached for his gun when he heard Ricker stir behind him.

'He's waking up,' Maddie said, looking over her shoulder.

'Perfect,' he said, checking in his rear-view mirror as Ricker tried to sit up.

Up ahead, Taylor spotted a little rest area. As he swung the car in and hit the brakes, the wheels locked up, showering dirt and stones all around. The car shuddered to a halt.

Taylor was out the driver's side in a split-second, wrenching open the rear door. He drew his gun, poked it roughly into Ricker's chest. The action snapped Ricker to his senses.

Taylor's breathing quickened, his concentration only broken by the presence of Maddie Williams. He relaxed his grip on the gun. Ironic perhaps, but she had just saved Brian Ricker's life.

'Look, Ryan. Hear me out,' Ricker gasped, clutching his injured nose. 'I swear to God I'm here to help.'

'I think I've had just about enough of *your* help,' Taylor hissed through clenched teeth. 'Tell me why I shouldn't blow your brains out right now?'

'I've been following orders. That's all. You know how it works. You know what Mannheim's like. Everything's black and white with him.'

'Then what are you doing here? You here to finish us off?'

'Something just didn't sit right.' Ricker shifted position in an attempt to ease the excruciating pain in his back.

'Oh, ya think?'

Taylor's attention was drawn to the front seat where Maddie Williams was once again sobbing her heart out.

'You want to do the right thing?' Taylor said. He motioned towards the girl. 'Then why don't you explain to that little girl why her father was shot dead in front of her eyes?'

Ricker shot her a pained expression. 'Maddie, I'm sorry. You have to believe me when I say I had nothing to do with what happened to your father.'

'Then who did, Mr. Ricker? And why?' Maddie said, mid-gulp.

'I'm going to help Ryan here find out. And I promise you we will. But the first thing we have to do is get you somewhere safe,' Ricker said.

'The thought *had* crossed my mind,' Taylor admitted.

'No, I want to stay with Ryan. Anyway, why should we trust *him*?' Maddie snapped.

'He's right, Maddie,' Taylor said. 'This is no place-.'

'Then I want to go home to my mom,' she said, interrupting him.

Both men looked at each other. Taylor knew from Ricker's reaction that Maddie Williams' request was not an option. Rational thoughts taking over, Taylor began to consider the fact that maybe Brian Ricker really was telling the truth. If he were lying, why was he there, in Israel, putting himself in the firing line? He must have expected the explosive reaction from Taylor. However, on the other hand, it had been touch-and-go at one time. Ricker would know that Taylor wouldn't kill him in front of the girl. *Was it a case of playing along for now, reserving judgement?*

'Maddie, Mr. Ricker and I have to talk. We'll just be over there.' Taylor jerked his thumb over his shoulder. He pulled open the door, turned and walked the few yards to a wooden picnic bench. He perched on the edge waiting for his colleague. Ricker gently lowered himself onto the bench, his face straining with the discomfort.

'All right, Brian. Cards on the table,' Taylor said, jabbing a finger at him. 'Let's say you're telling the truth. I need to know what you know.'

'Fair enough, though I'm not sure it'll help much.'

'Let me be the judge of that,' Taylor snapped. 'How many of these bastards are after me?'

'Truth is, I don't know for sure. The Americans sent somebody to take out Troy Williams. I've no details on him.'

'His name's Blake Fontaine.'

'He killed Williams?'

'That's right.'

'And you think Maddie's in danger as well?'

'Not anymore. At least, not from Fontaine.'

'He's dead?'

'Back at the café, just before you appeared,' Taylor said. 'What about my guy?'

'All I have is a name: Federici. I don't know anything else,' Ricker said before cursing under his breath. He was feeling a little nauseous at having made the call to Federici in the first place. 'Has he made a move yet?'

'Back in Tel-Aviv,' Taylor said.

'Did you get a look at him?'

Taylor shook his head. 'Liebermann's chief aide was about to spill his guts when this guy, Federici, you say, shot him. Bad enough, but his wife took a bullet as well. I managed to escape into the basement and out a side exit.'

'He'll be back. He's the worst kind, a gun for hire who'll work for anybody. Nobody knows anything about him. Not even Mannheim,' Ricker said.

'Don't suppose you can call him off?' Taylor already knew the answer before he asked the question. Ricker confirmed it with a slight shake of the head. 'I know how it works,' Taylor continued. 'If he fails, they'll send another, then another, until it's done.'

'Pretty much.'

'I'm hoping the CIA will call off the hounds now that Troy's dead. I'd love to tell Maddie she's going home.'

'You can't take that chance.'

'No, I won't.'

'What do you have planned for her?' Ricker asked.

'I'm open to suggestions.'

'I've a contact in Holland, outside Amsterdam. She'd be safe there and the guy owes me one. I've already cleared it with him.'

'I remember your last contact. Almost got me killed,' Taylor said.

'Sorry about that. Mehdi was a good call. He'd obviously been bought. I'd no way of knowing.'

'Aye,' Taylor said ruefully, rubbing at the remnants of the mark the cord had made on his neck. 'But, as I'm out of options...okay, arrange it for Maddie to go there. Though I'll tell you this. Anything untoward happens to her, I *will* kill you.'

Taylor still didn't trust Brian Ricker. How could he? But he felt he had no choice. He was backed into a corner. His only experience with the man known as Federici had not ended well for the people in his vicinity. Taylor would hate to have a twelve-year-old in tow when the assassin next locked in.

Ricker had ably demonstrated that he was essentially a follower of orders, but Taylor knew, deep down, that his boss could not just stand back and allow a child to be put in a dangerous position and not try and do something to help.

Ricker's reply to Taylor's threat was short. 'Noted. This chief aide, do you think he knew anything?'

'I guess we'll never find out now, will we?'

'I guess not,' Ricker said. He paused, as if choosing the moment. 'Ryan, at a meeting I attended in London, Leo Mannheim mentioned something about cash deposited in offshore accounts for you and Williams?'

'Cash, what cash?' Taylor looked puzzled.

'A hundred grand. Each.'

Taylor swore under his breath.

'Just as I thought,' Ricker said, glancing skywards.

Taylor swore again, louder this time.

'So where do you go from here?' Ricker asked.

Taylor didn't respond right away. He rubbed his face. Looked towards Maddie who was standing quietly next to the car, then scanned the surrounding countryside. Huffed out a long breath. 'Right now,' he said, 'I need to take a shower and try and get some sleep. I'll figure out the next move in the morning. Always been able to think better then.'

'Makes sense. I'll make a call...if that's ok? I'll find us a couple of rooms,' Ricker said. 'The girl can bunk in with you tonight. I'll organise her passage to Holland in the morning.'

'You had a car,' Taylor said, 'Back at the cafe.'

Ricker shrugged. 'Yeah, but it's fine. False plates. It's untraceable.'

'It's as well, the place will be swarming with cops by now,' Taylor said. He turned to Ricker. 'I take it Mannheim doesn't know anything about your little *defection*?'

Ricker shook his head. 'I told him I was coming to Israel to smooth things over with their top brass, apologise for the behaviour of MI6's rogue British agent.' He shrugged. 'Now they'll be expecting me to turn up dead.'

'When they piece together what happened back at the cafe?' Taylor said.

'Exactly. We'll need to get going again. They're bound to be setting up road blocks as we speak.'

'Sorry about the nose,' Taylor said as he got to his feet.

'I don't blame you. I'd have done the same.'

'One thing.'

'What's that?'

'I know I've said it already, but if you're lying, I'll put a bullet between your eyes.'

CHAPTER TWENTY-FIVE

There was a knock at the door.

Taylor reached for his gun. He glanced at the sleeping girl, then at the clock on the wall: 5.35am. He undid the chain, opened the door a crack and lowered the gun when he saw it was Brian Ricker.

'You sleep ok?' Ricker asked, pushing his way in.

Taylor laid the gun down on the table next to him. He shrugged. 'I dozed off in the chair. Got enough, I suppose.'

'What about Maddie?'

'Didn't see her move.'

'That's good. You had time to think?'

'Aye, some. Though it's not done much good, so far.'

'I've been speaking to my contact in Amsterdam. He has a daughter around the same age as Maddie. Says it wouldn't be a problem for her to stay a while.'

'At least that would be one thing off my mind.'

'This is no place for her,' Ricker said. 'By the way, I've got extra detail keeping an eye on April and Jake. Figured it was the least I could do.'

'Thanks, I haven't called...'

'And don't,' Ricker cut in. 'The geeks are tapping the phone. But I guess you'd have expected that?'

Taylor nodded.

Ricker picked up a small complimentary packet of shortbread biscuits from a tray next to him. Biscuits, kettle, two cups, spoons and saucers and a dish with various types of tea-bags, pots of UHT milk, coffee (normal and de-caf) and packs of sugar (brown and white). All part of the bog standard, B&B tea-making facilities. From Bogotá to Burnley, Tahiti to Tor-na-coille.

Ricker tore open the packet and began nibbling one of the biscuits.

'D'you mind?' he said as he pushed the button on the kettle.

'Carry on,' Taylor said.

Maddie stirred at the sudden rush of the water heating. She turned over a couple of times before settling down again.

'You and Williams,' Ricker said, breaking off a little piece of the second biscuit. 'When and where did you last work together?'

'Geneva. The UN summit, about four, five months ago, why?'

'How did it go?'

'Same as it always does at these things. I've seen more life in a pair of pants.'

'The US President was there, wasn't he?' Ricker asked.

'Because of him security was tighter than a duck's arse, but

the whole thing went like clockwork. Why, what are you thinking?' Taylor asked. He reached across to turn over a couple of cups.

'Not sure,' Ricker said, furrowing his brow. 'Can you remember the hotel where everybody was staying?'

Taylor nodded. 'The Pelican Beach.'

'You sure?'

'I remember the bath towels had these big red-and-white pelicans embroidered into them. I blagged a couple for the house. Jake loves them.'

The kettle rumbled for a moment and clicked off, puffs of steam clouding the corner of a mirror next to it. Ricker set down two cups of strong coffee.

'What's on your mind?' Taylor asked. He winced as the hot coffee burned his lips.

'Whatever's happening, it's got something to do with you and Troy Williams. And the last time you worked together was on that summit. It's worth looking into. You don't remember anything at all out of the ordinary when you were there?'

Taylor thought for a few seconds. 'No, nothing,' he said.

'Okay, but it's worth a phone call. Threlfall was in charge for us there, wasn't he?'

'That he was. Arsehole!'

Ricker chuckled as he lifted the phone and dialled reception. The call was answered on the first ring. 'Hello, do you have wi-fi network here?'

'Yes, sir,' the voice confirmed.

'Do I need a password?'

'No, sir. You can access our system directly.'

'Thanks.'

Ricker pulled out his mobile and began typing. After a few seconds, he was writing down the phone number for The Pelican Beach Hotel in Geneva, Switzerland. Taylor shook his head as Ricker prepared to deliver his finest Colonel David Montgomery Threlfall impression. *Insidious and obnoxious.* Perfect for the occasion.

'The Pelican Beach Hotel. How may I help you?' A male voice was on the line.

'You speak English?' Ricker asked.

'Yes, sir. Would you like to make a reservation?'

'Make a reservation? Are you being serious?'

'Sir?'

'Get me the manager.'

'One moment.'

Then: 'Guillaume Bavard, manager, how may I help you?'

'I certainly do not want to make a reservation, that's for sure.'

'Then why are you calling, sir? Do you require information about the hotel?'

'You could say that.'

'Sir, I am not following you.'

'You don't remember me, do you?'

Silence.

'This is Colonel David Threlfall of British Secret Service,' Ricker continued. He made a face at Taylor as he slipped into character. Luckily, Threlfall was the *Sean Connery* in every impressionist's repertoire. He had a distinctive voice, a voice easily mimicked. And not only that, Threlfall had garnered a reputation as MI6's biggest twat as well as holding a black belt in intimidation. Ricker was about to use both traits to full advantage. 'I am referring to the unfortunate incident that took place at your hotel during the United Nations summit some months ago.'

'I-I do apologize, Colonel Threlfall,' the voice stammered. 'I do, of course, remember you. How have you been, sir? Well, I hope.'

'Sir, my health is not in question. Now I demand to know if there has been any progress with the investigation. The Prime Minister himself has ordered me to look into the matter and report back personally. He will not be a happy man if we are no further forward with this.'

'You know I wish to help-'

'Then get on with it, man.' Ricker interjected. 'I haven't got all day.'

'The-the unfortunate young lady who died that night. She was a local prostitute.'

CHAPTER TWENTY-SIX

The secretary poked her head round the door. 'Sir, I have Chief of Staff McMichaels on the line for you.'

Leo Mannheim made a face. 'Have we heard from Brian Ricker yet?'

'No, sir.'

'Call him again, now. If you can't get a hold of him, send him another message. Tell him to get in touch as soon as he receives it. Got that?' Mannheim barked. He lifted the receiver, slipped his hand over the mouthpiece as he waited for her response.

'Yes sir, right away.' Arching an eyebrow, she made a face as she backed out the door, careful not to let him see her.

Mannheim waited for the door to close before prodding the line button. 'Walter. How've you been?'

'I hope you have some news for me, Leo.' Walter McMichaels opened the conversation in typical style. He was a straight-to-the-point, more polished, slightly more polite version of his British counterpart.

'I'm waiting for an update. When I know, you'll know.' Mannheim could also get to the point.

'Don't bullshit me. You know this should have been taken care of by now. We've kept our end of the bargain. Williams' body is zipped in a bag, already on its way home.'

'Yes, good work there, Walter. Killed in front of his daughter, I hear.'

'Unfortunate, but unavoidable,' McMichaels conceded.

'I assume you've provided safe passage back to the States for the girl?'

A moment's silence, then, 'Madeleine Williams has disappeared. And I believe your agent, Ryan Taylor, has something to do with it.'

'Are you saying Taylor has disposed of her?' Mannheim growled.

'Let's face it, Taylor's no more than a mercenary. And he's on the run. Do you think he needs the hassle of a twelve-year-old girl tagging along? There's no doubt he's killed her.'

'My God, Walter,' Mannheim said, leaning back in his seat. He sighed. 'Is this what we've become? Child murderers?'

'It's the business we're in, Leo. *National Security* is everything. The girl's death is simply collateral damage, no more,' McMichaels snapped back.

'You bastard!'

'Come again?'

'You heard. I didn't join MI6 to get involved in something like this. If Taylor is guilty, he'll receive just punishment. But I can guarantee you one thing - there's no way he's killed that girl.'

'Let's hope you're right. She's bound to slow him down, make it easier to take him out. Call me.'

The call disconnected before Mannheim could respond.

'Holy f-!' Mannheim found release by hurling a glass against the wall. It smashed into a thousand pieces.

There was a tentative tap on the door.

'Go away,' Mannheim hissed.

'Sir, Brian Ricker on line two,' replied the muffled voice.

CHAPTER TWENTY-SEVEN

'Ricker, what the hell have you been doing? I thought I said I wanted regular updates. You do know what bloody regular means?' Leo Mannheim's rage knew no bounds.

'Apologies, sir. There've been some *developments*.' Brian Ricker chose his words carefully.

'And Taylor?'

'I caught up with him. The American agent's daughter is with him.'

'He's dead?'

'No, sir.'

'He got away then?'

'Not exactly.'

'So help me, son, you'd better start explaining yourself.' Mannheim spat out the words.

'I tracked them to a café in the north of Israel,' Ricker said.

'Then the girl *is* still alive.' Mannheim said, smiling.

'Sir?'

'Never mind, go on.'

'They were coming out of the cafe. Taylor had, literally, just taken out the American assassin.'

'What? Taylor tracked him down?'

'No, sir. It was the other way round.'

'But why would he go after Taylor? His remit was for Williams only.'

'I think he was there for the girl.'

Mannheim shook his head. 'Collateral damage, my arse,' he muttered.

'Sir?'

'Never mind, it's nothing. And how did Taylor react to seeing you?'

'How d'you think?'

'Eh?'

'Sorry, sir. Let's just say, he wasn't best pleased.'

'That's the understatement of the year. Why didn't he kill you?'

'I think he would've if the girl hadn't been there.'

'I thought you were going there to smooth things over with the Israelis? For God's sake, I don't remember telling you to make contact with the target.'

Ricker steeled himself. 'Sir, I'm certain Taylor's being framed.'

'Really? Then how do you explain a hundred thousand pounds in an offshore account in his name.'

'I confronted him directly about that. Sir, I could tell by his reaction. There's no way he knew anything about the money.'

A moment's silence.

'Sir?'

Mannheim sighed. 'I think you're right. I don't believe Taylor knew about the money either,' he said.

'But I don't understand. You just said-'

'It's called playing devil's advocate,' Mannheim cut in. He puffed out his cheeks, eased back in his chair. 'We've a real mess now, though, haven't we?'

'It sure looks that way, sir. Can you do anything for us?' Ricker knew what the company line would be. He hoped for a little more.

'Officially, no. Damn US/British relations. I can't recall this agent, Federici, you know that?'

'I know, sir. He's already tried to kill Taylor. Back in Tel Aviv.'

'Then, by all accounts, Taylor's a lucky boy. Let's hope his luck – all of your luck - holds out, son. What about the girl?' Mannheim sat forward in his chair. 'No, wait, don't answer that. We've had a few problems with this line. You know what I'm saying?'

Mannheim's gaze roamed around the room. He'd been assured by the techs that there were no prying eyes, or ears, in his office, but then again...

'Listen,' Mannheim said, 'I have your number. I'll send you a message via my private scrambler. We'll use that for any future *discussions*, alright?'

'Yes, sir. Got that,' Ricker said quietly. His tone must have conveyed a trace of disappointment if Mannheim's next sentence was anything to go by.

'I'll do what I can for you, son. Good luck.' Leo Mannheim sighed heavily and rose to walk over to the window. In the distance he could see a storm rolling in; low growls and rumbles through the soles of his feet; the dimming of lights; bruised, purple clouds providing a perfect back drop for a couple of blinding forks of electricity.

Mannheim's attention was drawn to half a dozen cars, one SUV and two vans parked outside in the street. Inside one of the vans, a man continued to observe Mannheim on his monitor.

The man took a sip from his Starbucks, removed his headphones, and switched off the recording device.

CHAPTER TWENTY-EIGHT

Taylor and Ricker were back in Taylor's hotel room, preparing to leave for the long journey to Geneva. They'd agreed that flying directly from Ben Gurion International Airport to Switzerland would be folly in the extreme. Bus and train travel were infinitely slower but a whole lot more difficult to track, so while they were anxious to find out exactly what awaited them in Geneva, they reckoned it would keep for another couple of days.

The plan was to travel further north into Lebanon, through Syria, and on into Turkey. The final leg would find them boarding a plane at Larnaca International Airport, near Limassol, for the three-and-a-half hour journey to Geneva.

Thanks to Ricker, Maddie Williams had been issued with a new passport and identity and booked on a plane leaving Ben Gurion, heading for cover in Amsterdam as fourteen-year-old Letitia Reynolds. As airports around the world would not allow a twelve-year-old to travel alone, she'd had to grow up fast. It was felt by the British pair that, as CIA agent Fontaine was now out of the picture, Maddie would have to be relocated quickly before the agency had time to deploy a replacement. Taylor began to breathe a great deal more easily as he watched her plane taxi towards the runway.

'So, Liebermann did attend the Geneva summit?' Taylor asked.

Ricker nodded. 'Mannheim called me back to confirm it.'

'That's it. That's our link. Has to be. What did Mannheim have to say?'

'What do *you* think? He's sympathetic, but it's always the company line, Ryan, you know that.'

'Great, we're up to our neck in it, Mannheim knows the whole thing's a fit-up, and he's going to do sod all about it?' Taylor wasn't taking Ricker's news too well.

'I'm not defending Mannheim, but look at it from his end,' Ricker said. 'There's overwhelming evidence against you and Williams. Whether or not Williams was coerced to take on the hit on Liebermann is neither here nor there. And there's the money. How do you even begin to explain that? No, we need proof. And concrete proof at that.'

Taylor formed a fist and turned to swing a punch. His hand disappeared through the drywall.

Ricker shook his head. 'Perfect, now we're going to get tossed out for vandalism. God knows how much that'll cost? It's on my credit card.'

'Been worse if it'd been brick.' Taylor's foul mood softened. He even managed to force a smile.

'Wish it had been,' Ricker said, ruefully.

'Y'know Brian, I was going to kill you yesterday,' Taylor said, his smile disappearing.

'I did get that impression.'

'What I'm trying to say is, *I'm sorry*. I know you didn't have to come out here. I guess it must be true what they say.'

'What's that?'

'That you must be even stupider than you look.' Taylor was smiling again.

'Cheers, Ryan. Now we'd better get going before I change my mind.'

CHAPTER TWENTY-NINE

Geneva, Switzerland

The taxi pulled up at the kerb. Light rain peppered the windscreen as Ryan Taylor surveyed the grey building before him. He paid the driver before stepping out, hunching his shoulders against the rain and pulling up the lapels of his jacket.

Still feeling the effects of the interminable trip from Israel, Taylor somehow managed to summon enough energy to climb the twenty-five steps to the front door of the city morgue.

Soon after they completed the last leg of their journey and landed at the airport in Geneva, Taylor had suggested that, as it was still only early afternoon, they spend the next few hours productively, gathering information. He'd also suggested any enquiries be as discreet as possible. Not such a hard task they'd agreed, given the low-profile circumstances surrounding the young woman's death. It was obvious by Ricker's conversation with the hotel manager that her unfortunate demise had not exactly hit the headlines. Taylor's main aim for the afternoon would be to find out if there had been any reports of her death, and if not, why not. If he could also find out who the girl was and how she had died, now that would be a great few hours' work.

As Taylor had been on duty at The Pelican during the summit, and as such at greater risk of being recognised, it made sense that he took the morgue detail. That would leave hotel duties for Brian Ricker, after he'd managed to secure them two guns with spare clips. Taylor didn't even ask where he had obtained them.

Ricker's remit was to sniff around the staff at the hotel, but discreetly. He was heartened by the fact that the manager had opened up to him under very little pressure, albeit when faced with deceptive measures. Ricker was certain the man would spill his guts at the sight of a raised eyebrow, but he'd decided to poke around the subordinates a bit first and try and keep things under the radar. No point, he thought, in alerting either British Secret Service or the CIA to their current position. *It may be too late already*, Ricker mused as he felt a shiver trace all the way up his backbone to the nape of his neck. Every night recently, just before he'd managed to grab a little sleep, he'd begun to half expect the faceless Federici to be standing over him when he woke up. Shrugging off the notion, he took a good look around the plush reception area as he walked through the front entrance of the hotel.

***

Taylor swung open the heavy door at the entrance to the morgue and stepped inside. Stark white walls met him, with smooth grey floors, shiny at the edges, their walkways dulled by endless processions of gurneys carrying the dead. A strong smell of disinfectant. And cold. *Always cold,* he imagined. And bright. And impersonal, as such a place should be.

Taylor blew into his hands, then vigorously rubbed his arms. He'd had some experience of morgues and imagined all of them to be the same, wherever they were in the world. He shook away the shivers before pushing the bell next to a sign marked: *ATTENTION.* He heard a garbled ring coming from somewhere close by.

The attendant appeared from a side room. Right away, Taylor noticed how bleary eyed he looked. The place looked dead. Maybe death itself was becoming a rare occurrence in Switzerland. *How could anybody take a nap in a place like this?* he mused.

'You speak English?' Taylor asked, flashing one of Brian Ricker's fake identity badges - so fake that Taylor barely allowed the still groggy man to look at it.

'Yes, sir,' the attendant said, rubbing his eyes. 'Can I help you?'

'I hope so. I'm looking for some information on a young woman brought here some six months or so ago.'

'Are you a relative, sir?'

'No.'

'Are you working for the press or other media?' The attendant had clearly not had time to digest the information on the fake card.

'I'm an officer for the ICIU.' Taylor said, without hesitation. He'd recently read a novel by a new thriller writer a friend had recommended. In the story the ICIU was portrayed as a covert organisation...and fictional. Taylor figured it was worth a shot.

'I'm sorry, who?'

Maybe not.

'The International Crime Investigation Unit. The unit is affiliated to Interpol.'

In for a penny...

'Sir, these records are confidential. Only the police are allowed to access them, and only with special permission.' The attendant reached across his desk, protectively flicking off his computer's monitor.

'Look, I don't think you understand,' Taylor said, going into his back pocket. 'I'll show you my badge again.'

'Without at least prior written permission, sir, I'm afraid-.' The attendant stopped mid-sentence. To be fair the introduction of Taylor's gun into the proceedings had instantly changed the situation.

'Ok, let's do this the hard way,' Taylor said. Pointing the gun at the man's face, Taylor moved around the desk. 'Now switch the screen back on.'

The man turned ashen. He didn't have to think for too long before doing as he was told. Maybe he didn't fancy the thought of ending up in one of his own freezing cold drawers.

'Wh-what would you like to know?' he said.

CHAPTER THIRTY

'You are English?'

'Half-English. My mother's from Scotland. I was born there.'

'I'm sorry, I should have recognised your accent. I have a Scottish grandfather.'

'Really? That would explain your lovely red hair.' Brian Ricker openly flirted with the pretty hotel receptionist. 'Your grandfather, where does he live?'

She returned the smile, sweeping wisps of said hair away from her face, behind her ears. 'Thank you. He was born in Fife, on the east coast. Do you know it?'

'I do indeed. I spent many a family holiday in St. Andrews. Have you been there?'

'No, but I've seen it on TV.' She locked her hands together, pretending to swing a golf club. 'Papa lives not far from there, in Ockter-' she hesitated.

'Auchtermuchty?'

'Yes!' She said, beaming another toothy smile.

'Birthplace of the great Jimmy Shand,' Ricker said.

She wrinkled her brow. 'I'm sorry?'

Conversation stopper. He shrugged. 'Never mind. Before your time, I guess.'

'Do you have a reservation, Mr...?'

'Reynolds,' he said. 'And no, so can I book a room for a couple of nights?'

'Let me see...yes, we have a room on the second floor. Would you like breakfast?'

'That would be good.'

She began tapping away at her computer. 'Are you here on business, Mr Reynolds?'

'Mm, maybe, I suppose. Haven't made up my mind yet.'

'Sir?'

He leaned in close. 'I'm a writer. Shhhh,' he said in a faint whisper, putting his forefinger to his lips, winking at her.

'Really? What do you write about?' she asked excitedly, enthusiastically even.

Ricker glanced over both shoulders, then put his finger back to his lips for a second. 'Fiction, crime, action thrillers. That sort of thing.'

'And they pay you very well for that, yes?'

'Not as well as I'd like, unfortunately.'

'I've never met a real-life author before. It must be a really exciting life.'

'Far from it. It can be an extremely lonely existence. That's why I think writers are strange, solitary creatures. They hate crowds and fuss. They're actually very ordinary and straightforward, most of them.'

'This is why you lowered your voice?'

'Exactly. People are usually very nice, but writers get really fed up getting asked what they are working on at the moment. Especially if they're, *taking a break.*' He made little bunny ears with his fingers. He glanced at her, laughed. 'You're dying to ask me what I'm working on right now, aren't you?'

She made a face. 'Sorry, is it so obvious?'

'A little. Oh, okay then, seeing it's you.' He leaned in again, pausing for a few seconds. More bunny ears... 'I'm *taking a break.*'

She made a face before sliding the room key out of the pigeon hole behind her. 'Can you complete this for me?' she said, plucking a hotel questionnaire form from the printer feed tray next to her. She laid both form and key down in front of him. 'You said you hadn't made up your mind, does that mean you may do some writing here?' she asked, shielding her mouth as a couple of guests walked past.

Ricker picked up the pen and flicked it back and forth between his fingers. 'That's why I decided to stay here,' he said. 'Sometimes a story just presents itself. And if I do sniff out something I speak to as many people and carry out as much research as I can. I sort out a framework for the plot before I start fleshing it out.'

Do writers actually speak like that?

'Sorry, I do not follow,' she said, staring blankly.

Obviously not!

'Okay, let me give you an example. The incident here with the girl during the recent summit interests me. I'm sure I can work a great story around that.' Ricker studied her face as he reached the end of the sentence. He reckoned she was either a great actor, or she really didn't have an earthly. If he were a betting man, he'd bet on the latter. Her response would confirm it.

'I do not know of a girl-'

'Forget it, I must be mistaken,' he cut in.

'No, it's just that...I was not here when the summit took place. In fact, I doubt that any of the current staff were working in the hotel at that time. Except maybe one or two of the chefs. And the manager, Mr. Bavard.'

Ricker looked puzzled. 'Really? And how many staff would a place like this employ at any one time?'

She glanced left and right, checked over her shoulder before answering, as if she'd been warned against discussing such things. 'I think maybe around seventy, when you count the maids and cleaners.'

'And they moved everybody on? Why?'

'Money went missing during the summit.' Again, she cupped her hands over her mouth. Her eyes grew wide. 'A lot of money, by all accounts.'

'And management couldn't pin the blame on any one person, so they shipped everybody out.'

'Yes, that is correct.'

'But surely the workers have some rights over here. I know this wouldn't happen back home,' Ricker said, puzzled.

'No, you misunderstand. People did not lose their jobs. They were moved to other hotels in Geneva, within the same group.'

'I see,' Ricker said. He passed his completed questionnaire to her and picked up the key, preparing to go to his room.

She spoke as he turned to head for the lift. 'As I've said, every person was given another position, apart from the manager and the chefs...oh, and the two girls who were involved in the accident.'

'Accident?' Ricker stopped and turned back to face her.

'It was really sad. Two of the maids were walking home one evening, not long after the summit, when a car struck them. Both were killed instantly.'

'Did the police track down the driver?' Ricker asked.

'No, I'm afraid not.'

'That's too bad.'

'I heard the families received some money. Pity it cannot bring their loved ones back.' She frowned. 'Enjoy your stay, Mr Reynolds.' She returned to her computer screen.

'The hotel has a compensation scheme?' a surprised Brian Ricker asked. His knowledge of all things financial was pretty limited, but even he knew it was unlikely that anybody in such a low paid job would see his or her family benefit from some expensive death-in-service arrangement.

'No, the money did not come from the hotel.' She looked at Ricker as if he had grown horns. Again, she covered her mouth, indicating that what she was about to say was not for sharing. 'It is said that the American government paid-'. She cut the conversation short when a small, weasel-faced man with slicked down hair, a pencil moustache and horn-rimmed glasses appeared at her side. Ricker assumed he was the one he'd chewed out as Threlfall on the telephone - hotel manager, Guillaume Bavard.

Looking like a minor character straight out of a Dickens classic, Bavard eyed Ricker up and down, and up again, before nodding a half-hearted acknowledgement.

Dressed head-to-toe in grey pin-stripe and smelling faintly of toilet water, Bavard whispered something in the receptionist's ear, then vanished into a small office behind the desk. Whatever it was he'd said to her had had the desired effect as she blanked Ricker before following her boss into the office and closing the door behind her.

CHAPTER THIRTY-ONE

'He is here in the hotel.'

'You're sure?'

'Yes, I have the photograph in front of me.'

'Is Taylor with him?'

'I don't know...no, I don't think so. My receptionist said only Mr. Ricker checked in, under the name...eh, Reynolds,' he said.

'Alright, just take it easy. Your receptionist, does she know anything?'

'No, but people are talking. They are saying that your government sent money to the families of the women who were killed.'

US Chief of Staff, Walter McMichaels, tried to remain calm on the telephone. What Guillaume Bavard could not see, however, was a frustrated McMichaels quietly crushing a full pack of cigarettes to death in his free hand. A more than useful baseball pitcher in his youth, he hurled the unfortunate pack against the opposite wall, a trail of loose tobacco dropping in its wake like fallout from a comet. McMichaels cursed his country's *bloody conscience* for the umpteenth time.

'Mr McMichaels, are you still there?' Bavard asked.

'Yeah, I'm still here. And please, no names.' McMichaels got rid of the rest of his frustration by backhanding a small table-top calendar onto his plush, White House blue carpet. The calendar tumbled across the presidential seal, coming to rest right over the eagle's head.

'I'm sorry, I...I don't know what to do. Maybe I should contact the police here. I-'

'Listen,' McMichaels stopped him mid-sentence, 'I don't think you've quite grasped the seriousness of the situation.

What exactly would you say to the police? Would you tell them that you must have overlooked the fact that a woman was killed in your hotel? And that you stood by and did nothing while her body was taken away and disposed of?'

'But *you* told me what to do, how to deal with it.'

'And you have proof of this, where?'

Silence.

'Okay, here's what you'll do. If Ricker talks to you, asks you about the two women or the money paid, you'll say this: *The US party was dismayed and saddened to hear of the untimely deaths of the young women following the summit. Both had been assigned to look after the American delegation and had performed their duties in such a sterling manner, it was felt that a little financial aid for the bereaved families would be in order.* I don't wish to alarm you, but you saw what happened to these women. And all because they couldn't keep their mouths shut. This is serious business and, be aware that we will use every method, and I mean every method, in our power to ensure that the integrity and reputation of the United States is not compromised. Now do I make myself clear?'

'Very clear. I shall take care of it.'

'Thank you.'

'I have also assured Commander Threlfall of my best attention at all times,' Bavard said.

'What are you talking about?'

'He called me some days ago enquiring about the investigation into the young lady's death. He said the British Prime Minister himself had asked how the case was progressing.'

Although McMichaels could hardly believe what he was hearing, he managed to retain enough composure to end the telephone conversation calmly and in control.

Then he was again dialling. A voice responded on the first ring.

'Open up your inbox,' McMichaels growled. 'Your next assignment will be arriving very soon. Usual terms.'

CHAPTER THIRTY-TWO

Taylor was sitting in front of his laptop when Ricker walked in.

Taylor had earlier checked in to a small hotel, only a short walk from The Pelican. The room was tiny and tired looking, but clean and tidy. He had eyed the bed as soon as he opened the door; crisp white sheets and pillows, plump duvet invitingly turned down, it was all he could do not to succumb to the overwhelming urge to sleep. His watch signified 23 hours and counting since he'd last had the pleasure.

'You had something to eat?' Ricker asked as he slumped down on the bed, hands clasped behind his head.

'Grabbed some coffee and a sandwich earlier. You?'

'I wanted to hang around the hotel and poke about a bit so I had a meal there. Nothing great. Boy, you look absolutely done in.'

'I'll live,' Taylor grunted as he swigged a mouthful out of a cup of coffee he'd made half an hour earlier. No milk or sugar for maximum caffeine overload, he grimaced as the bitter, tepid liquid assaulted his taste buds. 'Help yourself.'

'No, you're alright. That stuff'll kill you.'

'It'd have to get in line,' Taylor said, forcing a wry smile. 'How'd it go?'

'I was having a nice cosy chat with the hotel receptionist until the manager appeared. She clammed up as soon as she saw him.'

'Bavard?'

'Yip.'

'What did you find out?'

'That only a handful of the current staff were actually working at The Pelican during the summit.'

'Eh?'

'She said some money, or rather a large sum of money went missing.'

'And they turfed them all out because they couldn't pin the theft on anybody?'

'Exactly.'

'Perfect!' Taylor pushed his laptop away in disgust.

'I did find out something interesting,' Ricker said. He sat up, swung his legs off the bed. 'Two chambermaids working for the Americans during the summit were killed by a hit and run driver. The driver was never found.'

'All very sad, but this helps us, how?' Taylor asked, irritated through a combination of frustration and lack of sleep.

'Apparently the US government sent money to the girls' families.'

Taylor thought for a moment. 'But why would they do that?'

Ricker shrugged.

'We have to find out who these girls were, speak to the parents. We'll take one each,' Taylor said.

'We'll get on it in the morning.' Ricker rose to leave. 'What about you? How did it go at the morgue?'

'It didn't. I tried the week of the summit, the week after, even the week before. Nothing.'

'Could the girl have been taken somewhere else, maybe to another morgue?'

'I asked that. The guy said everybody in this part of Geneva eventually ends up on one of his slabs. No, they must have got rid of the body.'

'If there ever was a body. I'm beginning to think-'

'Don't think there's any doubt about it, Brian,' Taylor interjected. He swivelled the laptop towards Ricker and stood to click on the kettle, planning a caffeine refill.

Ricker pushed the top back a little as the harsh centre-light was reflecting off the screen, dazzling him. 'What's this? *The*

Local, an English-speaking account of Swiss affairs.' He read the header page slowly, squinting at the small print, stubborn pride preventing him from getting his eyesight tested. *'Local woman, Stephanie Renner, 23, was reported missing earlier today. She hasn't been seen since last Monday morning when her family say she left for work as normal. The police are appealing for information as to Stephanie's whereabouts and have issued a recent photograph to help with the investigation.'* He scrolled down the page to reveal said image of the pretty blonde girl, then turned the laptop back to face Taylor. 'The date on the piece means it was written the week after the summit.'

Taylor pointed at the photograph. 'It has to be her.'

CHAPTER THIRTY-THREE

Taylor asked the taxi driver to drop him at the end of the street. He wanted to get a feel of the neighbourhood during the short walk to the Renner house.

All of the houses on the street were detached. Most were four or five bedrooms, Taylor guessed. Gardens neat and tidy, yards swept clear, clean cars in private driveways. Not too shabby. Not rich, but fairly well off. Parents in their fifties, mortgage-free, or as near as damn it. Kids in their twenties, an odd teenager. A typical Swiss suburb.

Number 45, Rue de La Maison, was one of the better houses on the estate. Taylor noted a Volvo saloon car parked in the drive. Ten to twelve years old. Red, or rather, faded red.

If you're in the habit of keeping your cars a long time, never buy red. Taylor smiled at the thought. His late car mechanic father had died tragically some ten years ago in his own garage, pinned under a faulty hydraulic ramp. Since then, life's triggers paved the way for some of the old man's random pearls of wisdom to enter Taylor's head. Taylor being Taylor had listened to his father's advice when his time came for learning to drive and contemplating what first car he should buy. The trouble was, that's all Ryan Taylor would do – *listen*. He'd sorted out a loan at his local bank before buying himself a second-hand Volvo for eight hundred quid. And it was red. He smiled again when he recalled his father standing, arms folded, at the front door.

Volvos are great cars, son, no doubt, but they're too heavy on the juice and, anyway, what would a boy like you want with a big car like that? Why not a Mini, or a Ford Fiesta? And what did I tell you about red? After a few years it looks like crap! It's the weather in Scotland. It's too severe. But, as always, you'll do what you want anyway.

Taylor looked to the heavens. *Sorry, dad,* he mouthed before stepping up to the front door.

If one could imagine what actual pandemonium sounded like, it must surely have come close to what Taylor heard when he pressed the bell: dogs barking, kids screaming, adults shouting, all baked in a pie with a high-pitched, blood curdling whoop-whoop noise coming from God-knows-what or where.

The noise rose when a man slid open the inside porch door, and fell when it sucked back into place. Taylor studied the man through one of the two slim glass panels fitted into the top half of the door. He was certain he saw him pause for a moment, as if composing himself prior to answering the door.

Taylor estimated the man to be mid-sixties. He had short grey hair with a neatly trimmed moustache and a pale complexion Taylor blamed on his being somewhat underweight. He was wearing a pale lemon sweater, an open neck white t-shirt with dark grey slacks, and a pair of black patent leather shoes.

The outfit screamed *golf* and Taylor confirmed it when he noticed a Dunlop bag with white golf shoes lying next to it, propped against the wall on the left-hand side of the porch.

There was a short period of uneasy silence as the two men came face to face.

Taylor went first. 'Mr. Renner?'

'Yes.'

'My name is William Fraser. I work within a special unit linked to the police force.' He flashed another fake badge. 'The unit deals with cases where people have gone missing long term and the local police have exhausted all lines of enquiry.'

Frank Renner closed his eyes for a couple of seconds. Taylor could almost feel the strength, the very life, seep out of the man, like soft sand in an egg timer.

'Stephanie?' Renner said, almost in a whisper.

'Yes.'

'Please, come in.' Renner stepped back and beckoned Taylor inside. Taylor's first welcoming committee nosed their way out of another door as he stepped into the hall.

A couple of Labrador dogs - chocolate and yellow - bounded towards him. 'Bloch! Huber! In deckung!' Renner scolded.

The dogs obeyed immediately, hunkering down and shuffling across the floor on their bellies towards Taylor.

'I am sorry. My dogs are very lovely, but excitable.' Renner bent to stroke their heads.

'It's fine. I love dogs,' Taylor said, getting down to their level. The dogs responded to his touch, rolling over to get their tummies tickled. 'We have a Cocker Spaniel called Brambles. He's only six months old.'

'Many years ago, my family used to keep Cocker Spaniels,' Renner said. 'It is a fine breed.' He watched the dogs vie for Taylor's attention. 'They like you. They don't often respond well to strangers.'

'You called them Bloch and Huber? Is that after Ernest and Hans?'

Renner inhaled sharply, his face lighting up. 'Yes, you have heard of them?'

'My mother loved opera,' Taylor said. 'I spent my childhood listening to it. I hated it at first, then it kind of stuck with me. I know that Bloch and Huber were among my mother's favourites. Were they Swiss?'

'Yes...well, Ernest Bloch was born here but brought up as an American. Hans Huber was Swiss. Please, excuse me for a moment.' Renner poked his head round the door into the room from which the dogs had escaped. A brief exchange of words took place before he turned to direct Taylor to a small conservatory at the back of the house.

'My grandchildren are much more difficult to control than my dogs,' Renner laughed. 'We will not be disturbed in here. Please, sit down. Would you like a drink? Tea, coffee?'

Taylor sank down into the plump cushion of a little basket weave chair. The dogs lay on the floor at his feet. 'No, thank you. I don't want to take up too much of your time.'

'WHOOP! WHOOP!' The sudden noise made Taylor reach for his gun. It was an instant reaction, years in the making. He cursed inwardly when he realised Renner had caught the move.

Taylor settled back down in his chair as Renner pulled back the cage cover to reveal a very big African Grey parrot, capable of making very big noises. Taylor and the bird eyeballed each other.

'My apologies. Oscar is almost as old as I am. He is such a show-off. I think he is trying to say, *hear me, I am not too old to play!*'

'You've had him a long time?' Taylor asked.

'My father won him in a card game over forty-five years ago. My mother went crazy at first. She had been terrified of birds since being attacked by nesting seagulls as a child. Oscar charmed his way into her heart and he's been with us ever since.' He hesitated, then said, 'Stephanie was fascinated with the bird. When she was a young child, she would sit for hours just looking at him.' His voice grew small. He bowed his head, unable to speak.

'Mr. Renner-'

'You are here to tell me my Stephanie is dead, Mr. Fraser?' Renner interrupted, as if not quite ready to hear the news.

Taylor sighed. 'The honest truth is, I don't know. I came to find out as much information about your daughter as I can. I'm here to help.'

Renner stood and made an excuse to leave the conservatory. To compose himself, or so Taylor assumed.

More eyeballing with the bird. Taylor felt a lot safer outside of the cage.

When Renner came back into the conservatory, he wasn't alone. He'd brought along a Glock for company, and it was aimed straight at his guest. Taylor made to rise.

'Please, stay there.' Renner's friendly expression had been replaced with one of steely determination.

Taylor did as he was told.

Renner stood over his visitor, said, 'I was a member of my country's secret service for many years, and, yes, when the occasion called for it, I was expected to kill people as part of my duties. I never regretted it. It was something I was ordered to do.'

'Mr. Renner. If you'll let me explain-'

'Please, I will finish.' Renner re-affirmed his grip on the gun.

Taylor's training compelled him to constantly re-evaluate a situation, minute by minute, even second by second. He'd already come to the conclusion that any rash move to draw his gun would probably not end well. The other man was calm and in control, and obviously used to handling guns.

Renner continued: 'You will tell me who you are, who you work for, and what your interest is in finding my daughter.'

'Look...'

Renner raised the gun. 'I will count to three. One...'

'If you kill me, you will probably never see your daughter again.'

'Two...'

'Okay, alright. Stop! My name is Ryan Taylor. I work for the British Secret Service.'

'And my daughter?'

A short pause: 'It's complicated.'

'Do not push me, Mr. Taylor. You know I *will* kill you.'

Taylor's mind was racing. 'I don't know exactly how, or why, but Stephanie appears to be in some way linked to an incident that happened during the UN summit a few months ago.'

'Yes, that is when she disappeared. You think my daughter is dead, don't you? And please, do not lie to me.'

Taylor stared down the barrel of the gun. 'I'm sorry, sir. Yes, I do.'

Renner slumped down in a chair, allowing the gun to dangle from his fingers. Again, Taylor assessed his chances. Again, he decided to leave his gun where it was.

'I think I always knew,' Renner said quietly. 'The first night she did not return home, I knew then. If she was staying over at a friend's house she would always call.'

Taylor watched as Renner placed the Glock on the arm of the chair.

He estimated his chances had hiked well over 50-50. Only now he did not feel under threat.

'I have cancer of the pancreas, Mr. Taylor. The doctors say I do not have long to live. Six, maybe nine months.'

'I'm sorry, sir.' Taylor did genuinely feel for him. At that moment his only interest was in grabbing the manager of The Pelican Beach Hotel by the neck and shaking the information out of him. It may still come to that, Taylor mused, as a last resort.

'Stephanie was a good girl, but too trusting. She was easily led. I think she did things that, well...they were not of her choosing, if you know what I mean?'

Taylor knew exactly what Renner was talking about. 'Can you give me the names of any of her friends, associates?' He stopped short of saying *pimps*. 'Anybody you can think of. Somebody must know something.'

'Yes, I will do this for you. Please, Mr. Taylor, find out what happened to my little girl. I have to know...before I die.'

CHAPTER THIRTY-FOUR

Brian Ricker had never before visited Switzerland. The ridiculous images he had in his head of the country were of streets populated with tax-dodging celebrities and stiff-shirted bankers, timorous watchmakers and yodelling pop stars; of glamorous people dressed in chunky knitted sweaters, drinking warm cider in front of sparking log fires, looking out at more glamorous people showing off their athletic prowess on the ski slopes.

Flying into Geneva, Ricker and Taylor had witnessed the breathtaking beauty of the mountains; on disembarking, they had drunk in the crystal clear, invigorating, squeaky clean atmosphere everyone associated with the country. If one could imagine waking up every morning in the most perfect place on Earth...

So, when Ricker stepped off the bus at the end of the street in one of the less affluent areas of the city, he could perhaps have been excused for thinking he'd travelled all the way into the next country.

Middle-of-the-road cars, two-up, two-down accommodation, flat roofs, waste bins next to front doors; community housing.

Ricker pulled the scribbled note from his pocket, unravelled it, and confirmed the street name. Confident he'd arrived at the correct address, he folded the note, stuck it back in his pocket, and headed up the street. He stopped outside the Heydrich house at number 179.

Last night, after Bavard had finished with his receptionist, Ricker had conjured up an excuse to again approach her. This time he'd applied a little more pressure than before, played some hardball and managed to not only get both dead girls' names out of her, but their address details as well. He'd stressed to her how important it was that the resultant information from any research work to support a writer's story be as authentic as possible. As with anything, you feed crap in, you invariably get crap back out, he'd explained. Ricker had finally sealed the deal when he promised to name one of the main characters in his next book after her. Chantelle De La Croix does have a ring to it. Maybe he'd email the name to Ian Rankin; no charge!

Ricker stared up at the tired little house at the top of a set of eroding concrete steps: skewed tiles, rusting gutters, decaying window frames and crumbling brickwork; in front, weeds as thick and strong as young trees and grass so long it could conceal an elephant.

Ricker hit the top step as the front door opened. A heavy set, balding man of around forty stepped out. He seemed to be in a hurry. Wearing a bright red, white and blue tracksuit and black Nike trainers, he reached back inside the door to lift out an orange suitcase displaying the *Easyjet* logo. The way he struggled to haul the case over the threshold suggested to Ricker that this man had just killed his wife and four kids, stuffed pieces of them inside, and was about to dispose of the dismembered parts in some disused quarry on the outskirts of the city. Wherever he was going it was for the long haul.

'Mr. Heydrich?' Ricker said, not loud enough to startle, or so he assumed.

The man instantly froze. He let go of the suitcase and backed up against the wall next to the door.

Ricker had seen the startled expression a few times in the past during operations in war zones across the world, usually while standing behind a rifle, about to send some terrorist into oblivion.

'Sorry, I didn't mean to startle you,' Ricker said. 'I'm looking for Fleur Heydrich's family.'

'She lived here,' the man said. 'Who wants to know?'

Ricker identified the accent right off. 'You're English?' he said, dodging the question.

'What do you want?' the man snapped.

'I need to speak to Fleur's next of kin. Are you her father?' Ricker said.

'And I'm asking, who wants to know?'

'Okay, listen,' Ricker said, 'The sooner we stop answering questions with questions, the sooner we'll get somewhere. Are you Mr. Heydrich?'

'No, he's dead. I'm her stepfather. Now who are you, and what the hell do you want?' He bent to pick up the suitcase.

Ricker ripped the case from the man's grasp, tossed it aside. Jamming his forearm hard into his throat, he pinned the man against the wall. Instinctively, the man threw his arms back to try and soften the impact. He yelped like an injured dog as the back of his head crunched into the wall, dislodging a chunk of loose render. Ricker stiffened his arm, pushing even harder.

'I can't...breathe. I...' The man stammered between short gasps. Ricker relaxed his grip a little, just enough to keep him from blacking out.

'Now let's start again,' Ricker was in no mood for any more delays. 'I'll ask the question. I'll loosen off long enough for you to answer. Then I'll ask another. You'll answer. And so on. I'm sure you'll catch on. And if I feel you're telling me porkies, it's gonna hurt. Nod if you understood all that.'

He nodded.

'Your name?'

'Ch-Christopher Halliday,' he gasped.

'Better. And where are you off to in such a hurry, Chris?' He motioned towards the case.

'I'm late. I'm going to miss my flight.' Halliday's gaze roamed the street behind Ricker as he spoke. Ricker realised his instincts had been right about this man expecting a visitor. And not with the express intention to swap golf stories. It was time to crank it up.

'Off on holiday to spend all that money?' Ricker asked.

'Wh-what money?' Halliday's eyes bulged, his breathing quickening.

Ricker pushed hard. Halliday screamed in pain. 'Ok! Ok, look, I'll give the money back!'

Ricker grabbed him by the shoulder and spun him round to face the door. 'Inside, now!'

'No! Please, you take the money. Just let me go.'

Ricker turned the handle, kicked the door wide open. It crashed against the internal wall, dislodging a tall mirror halfway along a short corridor. The mirror smashed into pieces as it hit the floor. Halliday was next. He tripped across the threshold as he was bundled inside, then hit his head on a small table as he fell, knocking him out cold.

'Great job, Brian.' Ricker shook his head as he stepped over the unconscious man.

'Hello!' He went to push another door. He had heard faint voices coming from inside. The door only travelled a couple of feet before hitting something solid.

Ricker pulled his gun. He craned his neck to take a look inside. The door stop turned out to be a dead dog with a huge bullet hole in the top of its skull. A dark, two-foot circle of blood framed the head. He pushed the body back a few inches and stepped inside, pausing until his eyes became accustomed to the gloomy surroundings.

The lights were out, curtains pulled shut. The TV was on in the corner, on low volume, playing some daytime soap, or so Ricker assumed. He could hear a swooshing noise coming from the adjoining room; the kitchen? *Could be a dishwasher or washing machine?*

Ricker switched on the light. The place was fairly clean and the carpet looked to have been recently vacuumed. A pile of clothes had been left lying on a chair and an open newspaper and a couple of magazines were pushed untidily up against the skirting board near the kitchen door.

Ricker's finger hovered over the trigger. 'Hello,' he said again. Again, no response.

The door creaked open. Again, it travelled only a few inches. Again, it edged against something solid. Another dead body was acting as a door stop, this time a woman's body. She looked to be late thirties, small, dark-haired. Fleur Heydrich's mother. A crimson river of blood, lots of it, pooled across the floor near her head. Ricker knew from the arc and pattern of the blood spatter that she had been on her knees at the time of her death. The scene screamed: *professional hit*.

Within moments, Ricker had pieced things together; the mother had been reading. Daytime TV was on in the background when the killer had entered. The dog had reacted first and taken a bullet for his troubles. The woman had run into the kitchen. The killer had told her to stop, to kneel and face him and then he'd calmly shot her in the head. Chris Halliday had been out at the time of her death. He'd arrived home not long afterwards, discovered the dog, then progressed to the kitchen. He'd found his wife's body, freaked, then packed a case, discarding a few unwanted items on to the chair. Ricker had arrived at the moment he was preparing to bail out. *No wonder he'd been spooked.*

Ricker's thought processes continued: The *killer could still be...*

'Dammit!' Gun still in hand, he bolted into the living room and back along the corridor to the front door as Halliday was getting to his feet. Halliday was groggy, but lucid enough to realise that a man brandishing a gun was heading straight for him and that he would have to move smartly to survive. He was not about to suffer the same fate as his poor wife.

'No, wait!' Ricker shouted.

Halliday ran out into the sunlight. He barely reached the top step before the bullet tore through the top of his head, ripping off most of the back of the skull as it exited his brain. The force of the impact jolted the body back through the door and it fell, face-up, at Ricker's feet. Like a snap-shot frozen in time, the eyes were wide open, glassy, distant.

Ricker knew it was futile, but bent down anyway to check for a pulse.

CHAPTER THIRTY-FIVE

Taylor's short taxi ride from Frank Renner's house to Valerie Giroud's parents' home had given him some unwanted thinking time.

No matter how hard he tried, he just couldn't get the image of the bereaved father's face out of his head. Taylor reckoned that if he'd burst through Renner's front door and buried an axe in his skull, the result would have been much less painful for the Swiss.

Renner had known from the start his daughter was dead. He had even said as much. And though Taylor felt guilty for wrecking any harbouring doubts the old man may have had with his message of closure, the situation unexpectedly turned in Taylor's favour when grief and anger combined to squeeze every last morsel of information from Renner's mouth. A few long-term school pals, a couple of ex-boyfriends and an 'associate,' known locally as Javier, were mentioned.

Renner didn't say as much, but Taylor got the message loud and clear. Javier was Stephanie Renner's pimp. Renner had found some scribbled notes at the bottom of his daughter's handbag. He'd then travelled into town and made one or two discreet enquiries on the pretence of picking up medicines to relieve his condition. At least that was the story he'd spun for his wife.

The upshot was that Taylor left the Renner house armed with a contact number for Javier, along with the name of the hotel where most of his high-class girls, including Stephanie, regularly plied their trade: *The Reigart Hotel*, on the west side. Things were beginning to slot into place.

It turned out Frank Renner had been in and about the latter stages of a plan designed to exact as much pain and suffering as possible on this weasel, Javier, when Ryan Taylor knocked on his door. Taylor's solemn promise to 'retire the scumbag for good' in return for information had swung the deal. The younger, stronger and fitter man was better equipped, no doubt, and, as time was of the essence, Taylor had made up his mind to head straight for go and track down the pimp, after he'd looked up the Giroud family.

Taylor paid the taxi driver and stepped out onto the pavement directly in front of the house. A name plaque on the wall next to the door confirmed he was at the right place. As he walked up the path, Taylor's spider senses began to tingle.

About ten feet or so from the door he realised it was open, maybe an inch or two. Drawing closer, he knew something was wrong. A familiar smell seeped through the small gap in the door. An unmistakeable smell. And Taylor should know. He had spent a decade in its midst. There was no mistaking the smell of death.

Taylor drew his gun as he slipped inside.

The first body, female, lay half way up the hall, face-down. Shot in the back, twice. Blood had leaked from both wounds, trailing across the floor, congealing against the bottom of a door. It was darker at the edges, almost black. He could see from the colour and consistency of the blood, feel from her cold, lifeless skin, that this killing had taken place at least two or three hours beforehand.

With the killer now long gone, Taylor holstered his gun before kneeling beside the body to look for clues. Judging by the flecks of grey in her hair and the fine lines and wrinkles on her neck and cheek, he aged the woman mid to late forties; *Valerie Giroud's mother?*

He pulled up her blouse and studied the bullet wounds. *9mm.* He glanced back towards the front door. From the position of the body, it must have been where the killer had stood when he fired the shots.

Taylor got to his feet, scanned the area just inside the door for bullet casings. None.

He had no way of knowing what horrors awaited him beyond the hall, but he was willing to bet that neither he, nor anybody for that matter, would be able to find a single trace of the killer anywhere in the house.

Another two bodies, both men, and again no bullet casings, were waiting for Taylor in the living room. The younger man, presumably the father, was lying the right way up behind a couch near the door. The bullet had blown part of his head clean off. Blood, hair and fragments of skull and brain matter peppered the wall behind the body, as well as the floor and the back of the couch.

The other man was older. *Grandfather?* He had bought it while still sitting in his chair, one neat, bruised red hole just below the hairline. Taylor noticed a gnarled walking stick sitting next to the chair. This man couldn't have reacted quickly even if he'd wanted to.

Taylor's mind was doing overtime working out the version of events. The woman had answered the door to the gunman. She'd turned and run only to be plugged in the back. Hearing the commotion, the husband had raced to the door. He was cut down before he got there when the gunman stepped into the living room. The old man would have been an easy target.

Taylor picked his way across the room, careful not to disturb the crime scene. He had no idea what kind of police force or forensics department Geneva possessed, but he would give them every chance to do their jobs, though he reckoned it would make little difference as it was unlikely there was anything to find. For once, Taylor hoped he was wrong.

Kitchen and conservatory, clear. Utility room, nothing.

He sneaked a look out into the street before heading upstairs. He didn't much fancy the prospect of going head-to-head with a couple of eager young policemen, checking out a concerned neighbour's random phone call.

A quick check of the upstairs rooms thankfully yielded no more corpses and Taylor was getting ready to exit the house via the back door when he stopped at the top of the stairs and turned to face the first bedroom he had entered, the one at the end of the corridor. The house had three bedrooms; one must be the parents', another remained a spooky shrine to a dead daughter – perfectly made bed, dozens of polished photographs, unopened birthday presents, clothes hanging in the wardrobe, pyjamas under the pillow.

Taylor pushed his way back into the third bedroom. This time he wasn't looking for dead bodies on the floor. Pictures of action heroes adorned the walls; Spiderman, Superman, The Hulk, Captain America.

A small pair of black trainers sat neatly under a footstool. Taylor opened a couple of drawers, pulled out a pair of jeans and held them up in front of him. He estimated the lad to be about ten years old. *It's Saturday*, he mused. No school. Where was this boy? He's only ten. Could he be sleeping over at a friend's house? What if he were to arrive home now? Something like this could scar him for life.

Taylor pulled his mobile preparing to call the police before making himself scarce, when he heard a faint noise behind him. In a split second he'd cocked his gun and was sweeping it across the room. The noise grew louder, like the drone of a washing machine on spin cycle, or maybe a model aircraft. It seemed to be coming from the other side of the room. Down low sat a footlocker against the wall next to a small wardrobe. Taylor crouched on hands and knees and crept towards the locker as the noise stopped for a couple of seconds, then restarted, ever so slightly louder than before. Another ten or fifteen seconds and it stopped again, then restarted.

Taylor put his gun away and reached across to lift the lid.

The boy leapt out of the locker like a jack-in-the-box, screaming at the top of his voice. Taylor grabbed him by the arm to stop him tumbling to the floor, taking a bite on the hand for his trouble.

'Ow! Okay! Okay! Calm down!' he said as he fought to restrain the boy.

'No! No! No! Don't touch me! No!' the boy cried, flailing his arms over his head and pulling and pushing at Taylor as he desperately tried to hang on to him.

'You're okay. I'm not going to hurt you.' Taylor reined in the boy's arms, held him in close until he began to calm. His breathing had been choppy and short at first as he struggled to break free.

Taylor was taken aback by the lad's strength. As he held him tightly, he suspected for the first time that something was far wrong. His suspicions turned out to be well founded when the boy suddenly stopped struggling. His breathing was returning to normal, slow and controlled, and his body became limp and unresponsive. Taylor felt him rock against his arms. Immediately, it reminded him of his own son. But then Jake *was* only two...

The lad continued to sway back and forth in Taylor's arms, his head snuggling into his chest. The monotonous drone began again, only pausing for short breaths.

This kid is autistic, Taylor thought. In a non-warped kind of way, he was relieved. Chances are the boy would be unaware of the horrors that awaited him downstairs.

'What's your name?' Taylor asked, releasing his grip ever so slightly.

No response. Shaking of the head. Humming volume increasing.

He lifted a hand, nodding at the boy for approval. 'Okay?' He reached into his pocket and produced a box of mint tic-tacs. Flicking the lid, he dropped a couple of mints into the boy's palm, offering them to him. He snatched them up, sniffed them a couple of times like a suspicious monkey, and popped them in his mouth.

'Thank you,' the boy said, smiling.

'You're very welcome.' Taylor shook the box a couple of times before pressing it into the boy's hand.

'Thank you.' He snatched the box, immediately burying it under folded arms.

Taylor smiled. 'You're very polite.'

'Mother says please and thank you are nice words. And it is much better to say nice words than bad words. Bad words make everybody sad.'

'Very good advice,' Taylor said, nodding. 'Do you want to tell me your name?'

The boy shook his head firmly then frowned. 'Mother says I shouldn't talk to strangers.'

'And that is also very good advice. But I'm not a stranger.'

'I don't know who...mother says I shouldn't talk to strangers.'

'I know your sister.' Taylor said, pausing for a reaction.

'N-no! I...you...mother says I-'

'And your mother is right. But I'm a friend. I know Valerie.'

'No!' the boy barked. In seconds, his breathing was again ramping up. 'Valerie does not know you. You're wrong. She tells me everything!' He began to rock back and forth, violently, clenching and unclenching his fists.

Again, Taylor tightened his grip. The contact seemed to soothe the lad, as if he were used to being calmed in this way.

'Alright, okay, I'm sorry. You're right, I don't know Valerie. Listen, maybe you could tell me about her.' Taylor made sure he didn't use the past tense. It was obvious to him that the boy did not yet know what had happened to his sister.

Silence.

'Mother says I shouldn't talk-'

'-to strangers, yes, I know.'

'I want my mother,' the boy said, his voice fading away to a tiny croak. Tears brimmed his eyes and he blinked hard, sending them tumbling down his cheeks.

Taylor frowned. He had a problem. He couldn't possibly dream of leaving this boy alone in the house. God knows what would happen to him should he wander downstairs. The shock may silence him forever. And he couldn't exactly stroll in to the nearest police station with him, hand-in-hand. He pondered how that would go: *excuse me officer, can you look after this child? I happened to be in the neighbourhood and walked in on his family. Oh, and by the way, they've all had their brains blown out.*

'I'm Luke.' The voice was still small, but different. More confident.

'Very pleased to meet you, Luke. I'm Ryan.' Taylor, noting the change, offered his hand.

Luke stuck the tic-tacs in his pocket before shaking hands. Taylor smiled when he felt the lad's strong grip.

'I like you, Ryan. You can be my friend. Do you want to be my friend?'

'Very much. But first I have to talk to you about another friend of mine.'

Taylor had read about different types of autism after a friend's son was diagnosed with the condition. The son experienced days when his moods changed like the wind. According to Taylor's limited knowledge on the subject, he may only have a small window in which to find out exactly what was going on in the boy's head, before the next phase kicked in. Taylor wasn't proud of what he was about to do, but as the stakes were so high, he felt he had no choice.

'What friend?'

'A girl.'

'Your girlfriend?' Luke asked shyly.

'Her name is Stephanie,' Taylor said, dodging the question.

Silence. Barriers up.

Oh no, thought Taylor. *I've lost him.*

Checking his watch, he thought again about what he should do with the boy. Time was moving on and he still had Javier to track down. He wondered how Brian Ricker was faring at the Heydrich's.

Then: 'Stephanie was *my* girlfriend.'

Taylor noted the past tense. 'Stephanie Renner?' he said.

No response.

Taylor continued. 'She was Valerie's friend as well?'

A brief nod. Tight lips.

Oh no, don't clam up, thought Taylor. 'What was Stephanie like? Was she pretty?'

Luke blushed. His chin landed on his chest. 'She was very pretty. She liked me. She said she was going to marry me when I grow up.'

'What happened to her, Luke?' It was time to cut to the chase.

More tears. 'Valerie said...'

'What did Valerie tell you?'

'Valerie said Stephanie had to go away.'

'Where?'

'To heaven. Stephanie is happy in heaven. Valerie told me that. She said I shouldn't be too sad because Stephanie is happy.' He beamed a huge smile.

'What else did Valerie tell you?'

Luke's smile vanished. 'She told me that one of the bad men hurt Stephanie.'

Taylor sat forward, eye-to-eye with him. 'Can you tell me about the man?'

'No! Valerie said no one was to know. She said the bad men would come and hurt me, hurt everybody if I told.'

'I'm your friend, Luke, remember? I promise I won't let anything happen to you.'

Taylor could almost sense the thought processes working away in the boy's brain. 'Luke?'

Nothing. Barriers up.

Taylor was distracted by a sudden noise downstairs.

Then: 'Police!' The voice was shrill and sharp, for reasons probably to do with the dead body lying in the hall.

Taylor leapt to his feet, edged along the wall to a window looking down on the street. He tugged the curtain back a sliver to see a concerned neighbour looking back up at him, arms-folded, standing beside an empty police car.

'Bloody hell!'

Hearing footsteps on the stairs, Luke bolted into his footlocker hideaway and snapped the lid shut. Taylor grabbed a chair and slipped it under the door handle, kicking the back legs in tight against the floor as the handle dipped.

'Luke, I know you can hear me,' Taylor whispered at the footlocker. 'These men are here to help you. They are friends. I have to go now, but I promise you I'll find the man who hurt Stephanie. You trust me, Luke, don't you?'

'I trust you, Ryan.'

By the time the policemen bludgeoned their way into the room, Taylor had slipped out the window to the back yard.

CHAPTER THIRTY-SIX

Taylor ran flat out for a couple of hundred yards, only slowing when he saw the inevitable flashing lights in the distance. He ducked into a shop doorway as the screaming siren sped past.

As he watched the car take the turn into the street, Taylor genuinely felt for the occupants. He'd heard one of the cops call it in back at the house as he was scrambling through the window. The guy's voice was panicky, yet hesitant, as if he had no clue as to what he should do faced with the situation. Taylor could tell the guy had never before been there. He recalled his first time, during a covert operation on the outskirts of Moscow. Two babysitting MI6 agents, along with their charge, a defecting lieutenant of one of the Russian drug barons, had been captured prior to having their faces blasted off by shotguns at point blank range. Taylor had been one of the first on the scene, had heaved his guts up when he saw three masses of bloodied pulp. The agents' families had been given bodies to bury. Whether they were the correct bodies was another story. Closed casket affairs.

Since that day, Taylor had seen things that no human being should ever see, serving in hotspots like Iraq and Afghanistan. Bad enough the fragmented bodies of military personnel having to be pieced together to make them even semi-presentable lying in their coffins, but when the suicide bombers strutted their stuff and the innocents got sucked in it was even harder to take. From the old, the infirmed and the young, to ordinary people going about their daily business, their lives gone in an instant. It was at times like these that Taylor's resolve would take a severe pounding.

Despite all of this, he still loved the job. And, he still had his ideals. Cynics would say these ideals were old fashioned in an ever-changing world. That the Cold War was long gone and that the need for Ryan Taylor's particular set of skills had gone with it. That low-key *espionage* had become religion-driven *vengeance*. That the world was in the grip of full-on terrorism and that the only way to see it snuffed out was to meet it head-on, in the foxholes and caves, the back streets and city centres, in the air, on land and in the water.

At times in his recent past, Taylor had become dispirited and disillusioned, but only because the very nature of his role – and a little directive known as The Official Secrets Act – had stopped him from kicking in some Fleet Street editor's door, or from abducting a BBC news producer, telling him how he and his like had prevented an airbus from taking out half of Canary Wharf, or how close that successful Olympic Games opening ceremony had come to eclipsing 9/11.

Despite that, the buzz he got from knowing he was doing his bit to keep the world safe from the bad guys normally stiffened the resolve, re-ignited the spirit. Only now, Taylor was feeling more than a little unappreciated. And it didn't mix well with the paranoia.

A couple of blasts of icy air straight from the mountains swirled their way into the doorway. Taylor shivered, and as he stepped back out on the pavement to zip up his jacket, he noticed an unoccupied phone booth along the road.

Ignoring strong urges to call April, he glanced at Frank Renner's note before feeding in some coins and tapping the keypad.

Three low purrs, then: 'Hello.'

'A business associate of mine gave me this number. I'm looking for a girl, tonight,' Taylor said, slipping his hand over the mouthpiece as a couple of police motor cycles roared past.

'This business associate, what is his name?'

'Come on, you know I won't tell you that. Do you have a girl or not?'

'Not tonight.'

The call disconnected, Taylor's spare coins rattling into the little cup. 'Oh, that's just great!' Taylor hissed. He snatched up the coins, re-fed them, dialled again.

Another few purrs-

'Hello.'

'Wait, don't cut me off again. I have money. I'll pay anything you want. Please.' Taylor tried to sound desperate, like the sickos he imagined used such services.

'Tomorrow. Nothing for tonight.'

'But I have to fly to Los Angeles first thing in the morning. It must be tonight.'

Taylor could almost hear the man mentally counting the money. Finally:'One thousand dollars, payable to the girl beforehand.'

'No problem. Where is your place?'

'We come to you.'

'Listen, I don't want my wife finding out. She's here in Geneva with me.'

Silence.

'Hello?'

'Go to The Reigart Hotel and book a room, then text me the room number. The girl will be there at 7pm. You must pay the money to her when she arrives. Do you understand?'

'No problem.'

The call disconnected.

CHAPTER THIRTY-SEVEN

It had been almost five minutes since he'd killed Christopher Halliday. And during those five minutes he'd blinked only about four times, breathed in and out maybe every twenty seconds, so intense was his concentration.

Waiting played a huge part in his life. Patience, and the ability to maintain concentration, were the main reasons he was so good at his job. They were the reasons governments were willing to pay him top dollar to secure his services.

An hour ago, his finger had hovered over the trigger as the woman climbed the steps to her front door. But that would've been far too easy, so precise were the Kern 4 x 24 telescopic sights. In the end, Francine Halliday had done exactly as she'd been told. She'd knelt on her kitchen floor facing him, to be shot like her dog. He'd told her to kneel and she'd obeyed. It had felt good. Like being God, deciding who lives or dies.

He loved his work. It was everybody's dream - being paid well for doing something they loved. And, so far, today had been a profitable day. Especially since the demise of the Americans' original choice of assassin. God bless the CIA.

A brief break in concentration to dab away snaking trails of sweat from temples and both cheeks. A quick look at the watch. Ten minutes since the last kill. *Any minute now.*

Faint stirrings of police sirens in the distance. As well as barricading the back-door exit to ensure only one way out, he had taken the liberty of calling Geneva's emergency services the moment he'd killed Halliday. He'd painted a picture of random gunfire and people dying. He'd made it his business to know where the police station was, how soon the cops could be mobilised, and how long it would take them to arrive at the scene. New York would be around four minutes, London the same. Geneva, he'd estimated ten.

As the police car draws closer, the shooter notices the faintest of shadows cast on the edge of the front door.

Crouching low, he blinks a couple of times to clear his eyes. He eases his shoulder into the rifle butt, melts the scope snugly into his eye socket.

His breathing quickens. It is always the same. He cannot control it. Adrenalin pumps through his body, tingling every nerve ending and crashing head to foot like Californian breakers.

He grips the cold barrel tightly, tensing the muscles in his hands, arms, neck. He exhales slowly, relaxing the same muscles.

He is not even aware of the police car broad-siding into the street, though no doubt his target will be.

His finger caresses the trigger. There is the tiniest of noises as the finely honed mechanism twitches under pressure.

A half-smile and lick of the lips as a tall man appears in his crosshairs. A quick glance at a photograph of MI6 man, Brian Ricker, earlier received as an email attachment from his latest client.

Code name: *Federici*, killer for hire, holds his breath and squeezes the trigger.

CHAPTER THIRTY-EIGHT

It was almost seven o'clock. Taylor had left half a dozen messages on Brian Ricker's mobile. No response. Nothing.

There was a knock at the door.

Before Taylor could react, his date for the night breezed in. Dressed in a cropped red leather jacket, white blouse stretched across her ample bust, black high-heels and the tiniest of shiny micro-skirts – also black - the stunning blonde dropped her little shoulder bag on a chair before seductively walking towards him.

'Well, well,' she purred, maintaining eye contact with Taylor as she slipped behind him, lightly trailing the back of her hand across his left shoulder and down his arm to the tips of his fingers. 'Now what do we have here?'

Taylor's mobile rang. He turned his back on the girl to answer it. 'Brian? Where the hell are you?'

'Taylor, is that you?' the voice said.

Taylor didn't recognise it, although he identified the accent straight away as English. 'Who is this?' he asked.

The girl walked round in front of him, motioning towards the bathroom as she took off her jacket. Taylor pushed the door open for her.

'A friend. I heard you might need one right now,' the voice said.

'You know what they say, a friend in need,' Taylor replied, completing the code.

'There's a little English bar on Junckers called *Strange Brew*. Meet me there in half an hour.'

'Can we make it an hour? I've something to take care of first.'

'One hour. Don't be late.' The call ended.

Right on cue the girl stepped out of the toilet, adjusting her excuse for a skirt as she entered the room. She was carrying her shoes.

Taylor estimated her at around five three, maybe four, and barely on the right side of legal. 'What's your name?' he asked.

'What would you like it to be?' she replied, slipping her arms round his waist. He backed off, holding her at arms' length.

She frowned. 'What's the matter, you don't like what you see?'

'I don't have much time.'

'But I'm all yours till morning, baby. Now if we can get the money out of the way first?' she said, turning to pick up her bag from the chair. 'Do you need a receipt?'

Taylor laughed. 'No, but I'll tell you exactly what I do need. I need you to take me to Javier.'

'Scheisse!' she spat, 'I knew it! You are police, aren't you?' She gathered up her jacket and bag as she spoke, slipped her shoes back on.

'No, I'm not a cop, but please, listen to me,' Taylor said as he grabbed her by the arm.

'Are you kidding? Javier would kill me if I led you to him. He is very unstable. He will probably kill me anyway when he finds out I have not made any money tonight.' She laughed nervously, pulling her arm free.

'I wouldn't worry about that. I'm going to put him out of business for good. I made a promise to a friend and I intend to keep it.'

She shook her head. 'I wish you good fortune, but nobody messes with Javier.'

'I'll take my chances. You don't sound so upset about it?' Taylor said.

'Are you kidding? I hate the fat excuse for a man! He makes so much money from us, lets us keep so little. I hope he dies horribly,' she said, with venom.

Taylor peeled off a couple of hundred dollars and pressed the money into her palm. 'I suggest a change of profession,' he said.

She headed for the door, at the same time stuffing the notes in her bag. 'You are very cute. I would have given you one for nothing. Never mind.' She shrugged before continuing, 'Go to 3160 Rue de la France. It's a ten-minute taxi ride.' She stopped at the door, turned and smiled. 'Good luck,' she said.

***

Taylor asked the taxi driver to wait for him. Twenty minutes should do it. He had no plans to actually kill this pimp, or anything as remotely drastic. He'd promised Franck Renner he would put an end to his operation and that's exactly what he intended to do. It was amazing how persuasive Ryan Taylor could be standing behind a gun, pushing the right buttons.

Taking the steps to number 3160, he noticed the front door of the house was damaged at the top lock, as if someone had jemmied it open. And recently, Taylor assumed, inhaling the heady smell of shattered oak as he reached the top step. He drew his gun, pushing against the heavy door with his boot. It swung in a couple of inches, creaking against its hinges. Taylor put his shoulder against it, nudging it open the rest of the way.

He stepped into almost total darkness, save for a thin sliver of light spearing across the floor from a room halfway along the hall. As Taylor edged towards the room, he could hear the sound of a television or radio set on low volume.

Counting to three under his breath, he crashed this door in with the sole of his boot. It slammed against the inside wall, embedding the handle into the stud partition, jamming it fast.

Taylor's momentum carried him a couple of steps inside the room. His initial reaction was to reach into his pocket for a handkerchief to quell the unbelievable stench.

The corpse had been so only a very short time, much too short to exhibit signs of decay. As for the smell, Taylor's thoughts flew off at a tangent as he suddenly felt sympathy for the people who earned their living clearing up this type of mess on a daily basis. He could only imagine the additional smells another couple of days might add.

Clamping the handkerchief against his nose and mouth, he moved around a sumptuously expensive leather sofa on which Javier had drawn his final breath.

Dressed only in a white t-shirt which looked about five sizes too small, and a pair of grey boxer shorts, the pimp's final expression would not have looked out of place in a horror movie.

Red-rimmed eyes seemed to stare right through Taylor. A mixture of white powder, vomit and nose effluence covered the mouth and lips, trailing down the neck and chest, most of the front of the t-shirt catching the fall-out as if from an erupting volcano.

Taylor noted dark staining on the man's boxers where he'd wet himself, along with God knows what else, and little patchy puffs of powder all over his bare arms and legs where he'd coughed them up.

He stooped to check Javier's face as closely as his stomach would allow. The eyes were puffy, the cheeks coated, dry and dirty. At his side lay half a bag of something Taylor guessed was heroin.

This man had taken a drug overdose, that much was clear, but he hadn't taken it voluntarily. This was a hit. Sometimes it wasn't about knives or guns. Sometimes the killer might afford himself a little *artistic licence*. It would all depend on the level of sadistic pleasure he craved.

Some might say, and Ryan Taylor reckoned it was hard to disagree, that it was just another low-life getting exactly what he deserved.

Careful not to leave any trace evidence of his visit, Taylor made himself scarce. It was a good outcome for all concerned, except, of course, for the unfortunate victim.

CHAPTER THIRTY-NINE

'How far to the Strange Brew pub?' Taylor asked.

'About two hundred metres, sir,' the taxi driver said. 'It's not far past the church. Go to the top of the road. The place is down Junckers, on the right.'

'Thanks. Can you stop here, please?' Taylor said. He wanted to check out the pub from a safe distance. He paid the driver, remembering to tip him well. He recently read somewhere that people who tip well are always remembered more for the size of their tip than the size of their nose.

The church clock read 7.55pm.

Taylor walked briskly up the hill, pausing at the top. The pub was about fifty yards down Junckers, slap-bang in the middle of a large, cobbled pedestrian area. Half-a-dozen young saplings planted in heavy tubs sat out front framing the entrance. A couple of wooden benches were fixed to the wall under the windows, and Swiss and British flags fluttered on poles either side of the door. The place seemed to be in a decent area and, from the outside, looked clean, tidy and well looked after. Taylor wasn't interested in clean and tidy. Safety was more the order of the day.

Two old-timers were sitting on one of the benches, completely oblivious to the world or anyone on it as they battled out a game of poker. On the other bench, a frisky young couple were enjoying a different kind of game. The couple had attracted the attention of a handful of kids on bikes. The youngsters sniggered as they took turns to ride past the amorous couple, each one venturing closer to them than the one before. Inevitably, there was an exchange between the young man and one of the bikers. Taylor was too far away to catch any of the dialogue, but he deduced fairly quickly that what was said must have been a tad juicy when the man felt he had to tear himself away from his girlfriend long enough to give chase to the cackling teenagers.

Taylor glanced at his watch: 8.02pm. He hated being late, but felt he had earned the right in this case. After all, he *had* been busy.

He stepped back around the corner out of view. So far, he hadn't seen anything untoward and quickly began to consider his options, replaying the earlier telephone conversation in his head. The caller had spoken with a Northern accent. Taylor hadn't had any prior contact with Leo Mannheim, but he knew he hailed from the North West. The Controller of MI6. Was he in Geneva? It made sense. It was only a short hop across the water. And Mannheim *had* promised to help them. At least that's what Brian Ricker had told Taylor. But then where was Ricker? What had happened to him? Was this a fit-up, a clearing away? Had something happened to Ricker? Was Taylor next? Would Leo Mannheim, or whoever he was, have organised a special welcome? There was only one way to find out. He paused, preparing to make like a sitting duck.

Good timing, Taylor mused, as a taxi pulled up to the kerb some thirty yards behind him and a young couple, maybe early twenties, got out. Taylor knew from their attire that they were going out for the night as they strolled up the hill towards him, hand-in-hand.

'Excuse me, you speak English?' Taylor said.

'Yes,' the man said politely.

'My wife is waiting for me in a pub near here. But I have such a terrible memory I can't remember the name. Can you save my life?' Taylor laughed. 'All I know is that it's an English pub and it's near here. I think it's on the street up ahead.' He pointed up towards Junckers.

The couple lapsed into another language to discuss his request. Taylor recognised the language as German.

Eventually, the man responded: 'The Strange Brew pub? Is this the one you are looking for?'

'Yes, of course. Thank you,' Taylor said. He pointed up to the left. 'This way?'

'No, it's the other way. Down to the right. Please, why don't you walk with us, we are going to have dinner in the restaurant next to the Strange Brew. We'll show you exactly where it is. We wouldn't want you to get into trouble with your wife,' the man laughed.

'Thank you so much,' Taylor said, having eased his sitting duck problem through safety in numbers.

CHAPTER FORTY

Taylor thanked the young German couple before walking past the card playing pensioners and the young lovers, up to the front entrance of the pub. Both couples were too engrossed in their various activities to notice him.

Reaching the entrance, Taylor was forced to stoop below a solid oak beam with the date, 1895, branded into it. *Just how small were people in those days?* The present owners had killed two birds with one stone by sticking a row of brightly coloured union flags on the beam. As well as letting everybody know the nationality of the present owners, the stickers gave people of above average height advance warning of a potentially painful head knock.

Thankfully, the ceiling inside had been heightened somewhat since 1895 and Taylor straightened as he entered the bar. Soft, easy listening music was playing in the background. The lighting was low. There were only five people in the pub, not counting the young man and woman who were serving behind the bar.

Taylor scanned the area as his eyes became accustomed to the light. Two older men were sitting at the bar. He could see from their posture and their familiar demeanour towards the barman that they were locals. A couple sitting in a private booth to Taylor's left were holding hands and gazing into each other's eyes. Taylor would be aware of any movements by keeping the couple in his line of vision as he made his way to the only other occupied booth on his right, near the door.

The man sitting there certainly looked the part and confirmed this by nodding at Taylor.

'You're late,' the man said. Taylor immediately recognised the voice as the one he'd heard on the phone an hour earlier.

Taylor didn't respond. He eased into his seat, again glancing across at the lovers before meeting the man's stare.

'Don't worry, we're alone,' the man said. 'Drink?'

Taylor shook his head.

The man studied Taylor's face. 'You look like hell,' he said.

'I've had better tours,' Taylor responded. Another glance towards the couple.

'Leo Mannheim,' Mannheim said, extending a hand.

Taylor scanned the bar as they shook. Then over his shoulder, back towards the door through which he had just entered.

'What's wrong?' Mannheim asked, noting his discomfort.

Taylor leaned in. 'Well sir, I'm sitting here in a foreign country with the Controller of MI6 and there's not one secret service agent in sight.'

'Oh, they're here. Not far away. They're just not right here.'

'Sorry, sir. It's been tough,' Taylor said.

'No need to apologise. I can't imagine what you've been through already.'

'Comes with the territory, I suppose. Brian Ricker? He's dead, isn't he?' Taylor cut to the chase.

Mannheim's sombre expression confirmed it.

'There's no easy way to break the news, son. I'm sorry.'

Taylor sighed. 'What happened?'

'Federici happened. And not only Ricker. Bavard, the hotel manager, the young hotel receptionist, Chantelle something-or-other, and another couple, a man and wife. God knows where they fit in.'

Taylor shook his head sadly before Mannheim continued. 'I swear MI6 didn't issue the order. But this man is no more than a killer for hire. I know for a fact the CIA has used him in the past.'

'Has to be the Americans? Makes sense,' Taylor said. 'Somebody's panicking, tying up loose ends. The man and woman you mentioned, they were the parents of one of two girls killed by a hit-and-run driver. And you can add at least another three to his list. Both the other girl's parents and her grandfather.'

'But what had they to hide?' Mannheim asked.

'They were maids at the hotel serving the US contingent at the summit. After they were killed, somebody from the States sent both families money, according to the hotel receptionist Ricker spoke to.'

'To buy their silence.'

'Fat lot of good it did them. And it ended up costing the receptionist her life, along with Bavard.'

'These maids, what have they stumbled onto?'

'Another local girl, a prostitute, was murdered during the summit. She was a friend of one of the maids.' Taylor chose to omit the finer details about the women or their families. He saw no point in putting any more innocent people in the firing line, especially not the young autistic boy, Luke Giroud, or Franck Renner. And he considered drug dealer Javier's death to be collateral damage, no more.

'You think this girl, this prostitute, was killed by the Americans, and you have no idea why?' Mannheim asked.

Taylor shrugged.

'Her family, surely they must know something?'

'Been there, sir. Dead end,' he lied.

'That's too bad, son. Much as I hate to say it, we're in a bit of a pickle here.'

As Taylor questioned, silently, the use of the plural in Mannheim's last sentence, Mannheim leaned back in the chair, rubbing his brow. Taylor braced himself for the bullet in case it was a signal. The way things were going for him it would have come as no surprise.

'Sir, my wife and son. Brian said they were being taken care of?' Taylor said, as if only just realising that particular arrangement might now be under threat.

'No need to worry. They're being looked after at a secure location. I can personally guarantee their safety,' he said, frowning. 'Wish I could do the same for you.'

'What exactly *are* you able to do, sir?' Taylor's tone contained obvious frustration. 'Where do we go from here?'

Mannheim didn't answer. He stared at Taylor as if he were searching for a sign telling him what he should do with his 'rogue agent.'

Producing a padded envelope, Mannheim laid it flat on the table and slid it across in front of Taylor. 'It's very obvious the answer to this whole mess is in the States. Go and do your job, son,' Mannheim said.

Taylor realised he was probably bound for Washington DC.

Mannheim leaned forward to speak quietly. He tapped the envelope. 'In here, false passports, US Drivers' licences, and a list of MI6 contacts in Washington. And bank account details with a Visa debit card and pin number. There's ten thousand dollars lodged in the account. It's for kit or equipment – necessary kit or equipment,' he stressed. 'Our people will keep an eye on the balance and top it up if need be. All I'll say is, don't go on any shopping spree. There's a recession on.' Mannheim said, resisting the urge to smile.

'Thank you, sir,' Taylor said, slipping the envelope out of view.

Mannheim shook his head. 'I only wish I could do more.'

CHAPTER FORTY-ONE

Fort Augustus, Scotland

It was early morning and Joe was already out in the expansive garden of his new home. The garden was the one thing about the property that he was not entirely happy with; mature trees needed pruning, overgrown bushes shaping, and sprawling lawns had numerous bare spots where the grass required re-sowing.

Joe had been awake since before 5am, had showered, then grabbed some muesli with his coffee and was now outside, prowling around. He had made a promise to Brian Ricker, a promise to protect Brian's friend Ryan Taylor's family with his life, if need be.

Since the moment Ricker, then a scrawny twelve-year-old, first walked into karate instructor Joe Li's dojo on the south side of Glasgow, an unbreakable bond had developed between the little Japanese and the sickly boy, often bullied at school and largely ignored at home. Ricker had become the son he and wife Mai had never been able to have. There was no doubting Joe played a major role in turning the frail, introverted boy into the confident, well-adjusted teenager, able to look after himself, on to the secret service man, trained to kill in the blink of an eye.

And it had been Joe and Mai, of course, who had helped to guide Ricker through the long rehab process following the incident where he'd taken a bullet in his spine.

Ricker had made a point of advising Joe about unmarked cars that would appear in front of the house from time to time, though more as a way of protecting the baby-sitting secret service agents within than anything else.

Half an hour ago, at around 6am, a blue car had pulled up across the street. Joe had noted two men in the front seats. He'd watched one unscrew a thermos and fill a couple of cups before handing one to the other man. Puffs of steam misted the windscreen as the men nestled down in their seats, preparing for the long haul.

Tugging open the door of his little shed, Joe picked up a soft hand-brush and swept away some cobwebs spread across a selection of tools he'd inherited from the last owner; a rusty pick, a spade with a split shaft, a hedge trimmer with a lump of insulating tape around the cable, a shovel with half a head which looked like something from an *Andy Warhol* exhibition, and what looked like it used to be a very decent yard brush (with the emphasis on *used to be*). Joe smiled as he held up a brand-new set of garden shears, still in the wrapper. Judging by the state of the bushes in the garden, he could understand why.

Thanks-a-bundle, Joe mused as he stared at the motley collection now lined up outside against the shed. He repeatedly tested the strength of a little fold-away chair he'd found in a cupboard under the stairs. Satisfied he wouldn't end up in a heap, he forced the feet of the chair down into the grass and sat facing the kitchen.

Joe Li's thoughts drifted back to one week ago. A sodden April and Jake Taylor had arrived on his doorstep from Glasgow in the middle of a downpour. Brian Ricker's friend had got himself into a spot of bother and there was a chance the friend's family could be in danger.

Should only be for a few days, Brian had assured Joe. Joe had agreed without hesitation or further explanation. *Your friends are our friends, Brian. And they can stay here for as long as they want.*

Joe and Mai had taken a real shine to little Jake Taylor, her smothering him with giant cuddles, and him reading endless stories and nursery rhymes while marvelling at the pure joy and wonderment etched on the kid's tiny face.

April and Mai had become firm friends almost from the get-go, both sharing an unyielding passion for all things culinary. It was the last thing sixty-three-year-old Joe Li needed. He'd always been a fit man, as you'd expect of an eighth Dan black belt. Lately though, Joe's waistline had begun to thicken. Irresistible dishes coupled with the onset of old age and a changing metabolic rate were all in the frame.

In the past, a gruelling training regime – Joe used to work out like a madman - would have been enough to ensure any weight gain was minimal. Mai Li would watch on with disdain as her husband punished his body again and again, desperate to burn away the extra calories.

More recently, however, Joe had curtailed most of the exertions, bowing graciously to his advancing years. Problem was, this week he'd had to contend with wife and accomplice, both seemingly hell bent on using him as a kind of gastronomic guinea pig for their collaborative creations. Joe figured he had two choices - the power to say no, or the resumption of his legendary Karate training regime. The regime was a no-no, leaving the other option, also involving exercise, albeit much less extensive - the simple, but seemingly difficult, shake of the head.

'Mister Joe! Mister Joe!' A small voice cut through the early morning mist. Jake had already christened his new friend. Initially, the child had been a little wary of the strange couple in the big house. Two days on, and they had become like the grandparents he never had. Ryan Taylor's folks were long gone. April's parents had also died some years earlier, her father lost prematurely to cancer and her mother to a hit-and-run driver. The little boy had hardly let Mister and Mrs Joe out of his sight for the past week. This morning, he had woken even earlier than normal, run through to his hosts' bedroom, and discovered one of his new friends gone. Five minutes later, he was toddling unsteadily out through the French doors in the lounge, escaping into the garden area behind the house.

'Mister Joe!' Jake's face bore a little worried frown as he realised that his quarry had vanished. Joe was peeking out at him from behind a shrub. He covered his mouth, trying hard not to laugh and give away his position. Jake was too smart for that as he spotted his adopted grandfather's shoes under the shrub and sneaked quietly in behind him. 'Boo!' he shouted at the little man, who pretended to be startled.

'Come on, shorty. Let's go and see who's up,' Joe said, scooping up the wee boy in his powerful arms. Jake giggled at being upside down and seeing the world from that angle as Joe stole a glance at the blue car on his way to the house. By their comfortable looking position, it looked to him like the occupants were already in a deep sleep. Joe smiled as he quietly pulled the door close behind him. 'Shhhh.' He put his finger to his mouth and laughed when Jake mimicked him.

'So that's where you are!' April Taylor was pouring herself a coffee when Joe and Jake entered the kitchen. Jake giggled as she tickled his tummy with her free hand. 'Would you like a coffee, Joe?'

'Coffee, and only coffee, would be nice. Between you and my wife I doubt if I'll be able to button my trousers by the end of the week.' Smiling, he rubbed his belly.

'Sorry.' She made a face.

'I'm joking.' He beamed a wide smile as he gently lowered Jake to the floor. 'You know he is a very special little boy. You should be very proud, both of you.'

'Thank you.' April just about managed a smile before she was forced to steady herself using the back of a chair. Fast as lightning, Joe grabbed her arm as she threatened to keel over, guiding her down onto the chair. Rubbing the back of her hand, he asked if she was okay.

'I-I'm fine. Just a little tired, I guess.' She swallowed hard, as if about to throw up.

'I'll fetch my wife-'

'No, please. Don't disturb her. Really, I'll be fine.'

He took over the coffee making duties and within a few minutes she was sipping the sweet liquid, the colour returning to her face.

'Who am I kidding? I'm not fine at all,' April blurted out, fighting back tears. 'I'm-I'm terrified I've lost him.'

Joe folded his arms, pausing for a few seconds to choose the right words. 'You know I've never asked Brian what he does for a living. Now that's not to say I don't know what he does. I do. Maybe it's a bit like sticking your head in the sand. Who knows? But it's the way Mai and I deal with it. The job is what he is good at, what he chooses to do. How could anyone try and take that away from him? Brian's like a son to me, to us. When he suffered a serious injury some years ago, at first it was as if our world had ended. But the days, weeks and months rolled by and eventually he recovered enough to go back to work. We realised we'd been there for him every step of the way, encouraging, cajoling, and where necessary, sympathising, when the situation arose.' He paused. 'What I'm trying to say is-'

'That I'll find a way to deal with the situation. Make the best of whatever happens.' April leaned across to pat him on the hand.

'You are already much luckier than a lot of people. You love Ryan and he loves you, this is clear. And you have this one.' Joe pointed to the little boy, blissfully unaware, sitting in the corner of the room playing with some wooden building blocks Mai had rushed out to buy within an hour of receiving the call from Brian Ricker.

'Thank you, you and Mai have been so kind to us,' April whispered, then turned to greet Mai who was pulling her robe closed as she shuffled into the kitchen in her giant teddy bear slippers. 'Sorry, I hope we didn't wake you.'

'No, not at all,' Mai said kindly. 'But you know I was missing a gorgeous boy about so high.' She held out her hand. 'Has anyone seen him?' Shrieks of delight filled the kitchen as she stooped to tickle the boy. 'How would you like to try some of Mrs Joe's special treats?' Mai said, rubbing noses with Jake.

'Oh no,' Joe Li groaned, rubbing his belly.

'Jake! Be careful, sweetie. I have hot food here.' April gently scolded her son. 'Maybe Mister Joe can take over?' She beckoned towards Joe. 'Here you are, Mister Joe. Jake loves pancakes for breakfast. This one's nearly done. You just need to flip it over after a few seconds.' She handed him the frying pan and spatula, watching in admiration as he expertly flipped the pancake, catching it square on, and returning it to the heat for the last few moments.

'I'm really impressed, Mister Joe. You're an expert,' April said. The pancake landed on the side plate beside another five previously made. 'Tuck in,' she said.

'Perfect!' Mai said. 'Couldn't have done them better myself.'

Joe closed his eyes, gritted his teeth...reached for the plate.

Jake was making himself comfortable, piling cushions on a kitchen chair. With Mai's help, of course. He was now perched unsteadily on top, elbows on the table, waiting to be served. Four small plates, a spreading knife and a tub of maple syrup in front of them, they were preparing to tuck into their delicious breakfast.

Nobody noticed a second car pull slowly into position across the street.

Mai Li loved a right good soak in the bath more than anything in the world – well, maybe it came a close second to her recipe book. Now that she had finally retired from looking after the paperwork in her husband's gym, she felt she had earned the right to pamper herself from time to time. Long hot baths, scented candles and expensive fragrances were now her main vices.

Afterwards, she glanced at her naked reflection in the full-length mirror, strategically placed away from the harsh looking natural light that flowed into the large bathroom. *Pushing sixty and still got it*, she mused. Admiring her small slim frame, she giggled, thinking back to the time when she would use it to mesmerise the hell out of her beloved Joe. They had been together for over forty years. Childless, but happy. No regrets.

'No regrets,' Mai whispered to her reflection.

Back inside the master bedroom and ready to enjoy some

serious pampering, Mai sat down on the edge of the bed and started to gently towel dry her long dark hair. Humming quietly to herself as she brushed, she sensed a movement to her right. She turned slowly, smiling broadly, expecting to foil her husband's pathetic attempt at a practical joke. Instead, she was looking into eyes she didn't recognise – a stranger's eyes. The little Japanese woman froze, the man's strong hand roughly clamping over her mouth before she could even think of screaming. She was no match for his superior strength and her life was ended in a split second when the blade flashed across her tiny neck. The man lowered her lifeless body to the floor, her blood mushrooming across the cream-coloured carpet in her now not-so-private chamber.

Downstairs, April had spent the last twenty minutes or so with a smile on her face. Whenever she felt low, she would relax with a cup of tea and sit and watch her son at play. She'd marvel at the array of emotions and facial expressions Jake could exhibit watching his favourite Disney show starring his namesake with *the Neverland Pirates*.

Mother and son were in the lounge and Jake had insisted on rifling through her handbag until he found the DVD in question. 'Jake, you'll wear it out if you're not careful!' She'd protested when he held the DVD up with a smile. As usual, he got his way.

As the credits rolled up at the end of the show, April noticed Joe Li pass the window outside, a yard brush and shovel in his hand. She noted the serious look on his face and the speed of his stride as he headed towards the front of the house. Jake saw him too and bolted through the kitchen and out the back door despite his mother's protestations. As she started after her son, April sensed something behind her, felt a sharp pain in her side. Her first instinct was to run towards Jake, but she managed no more than three steps before her legs gave way under her. Her head struck the floor. Hard. White became grey, then black...

Joe Li had seen the other car parked down the street a few feet behind the blue one. Though now in his sixties, his eyesight was still as good as any twenty-year-old's. His hearing was not too shabby either, and when he'd heard a couple of muffled cries coming from the direction of the street, his senses ramped up to full alert.

Joe had arrowed his newly found set of garden shears he'd been holding into the turf at his feet, then lifted a couple of things on the pretence of doing a little tidying-up at the front of the house.

As he reached the front gate, he looked inside both cars. The one at the back was empty, while the blue car sported two unruly, art nouveau-like splashes of red, one on the side window and the other catching most of the windscreen. The occupants were smothered in blood with chunks of brain and splinters of bone stuck to the windows.

'Mister Joe! Mister Joe!' Jake called out as he emerged into the garden. He turned a three-sixty before spying Joe at the other side.

Giggling loudly, the toddler put his head down and took off in Joe's direction. Joe had little choice but to meet Jake head-on and roughly sweep him off his feet before dumping him on his backside in between a small cluster of bushes in the middle of the garden. Jake's bottom lip trembled and tears filled his eyes as he watched Mister Joe dart towards the kitchen.

One of the men walked into the garden, gun drawn. Before the man could react, Joe swept the gun from his hand with the speed of a striking cobra. A left-handed reverse punch then struck him squarely in the throat, the fatal blow compressing his windpipe. His body heaving and shuddering for oxygen, the man's face and lips slowly turned blue. He fell onto his back, desperately clawing at his throat until death provided release.

Joe had the weeping Jake back in his arms in a matter of seconds, running full-pelt for the sanctuary of his little shed.

The bottom of the door jammed half-way in the turf. As Joe tugged at it in his haste to get him safely inside, he accidentally bumped the little boy's head with the edge of the door. This provoked an ear-splitting, high-pitched squeal.

'I'm sorry, Jake,' Joe whispered, holding him tightly to him. 'Please don't cry. You'll be safe here.'

Joe did his best to soothe the child as he contemplated his next move. He knew nothing about these men, or their reasons or motives for invading his home. But he did know one thing. He knew everything about the human body, what made it tick, what disabled it or shut it down temporarily, and what put it out of action forever. He had just killed a man for the first time in his life. He'd always had the power within him to do it. As did his pupils. How does that saying go? With great power comes even greater responsibility? *Well screw that*, mused Joe Li. When these men made the decision to enter his home, uninvited, they'd crossed the line. As far as he was concerned, they were fair game.

Satisfied that the boy was out of danger for the moment, Joe's attention switched to the people inside the house. He prayed he wasn't too late. Before pulling the shed door over, he forced a smile for Jake's benefit and started towards the house. He sensed two sudden movements to his right: one was a blackbird taking to the air, the second, the sound of a gun being primed for action. Joe wheeled around, his hand landing on the garden shears he'd earlier speared into the ground. He took aim and sent them flying through the air like frenzied helicopter blades, the point of one slamming into the man's neck close to his Adam's apple. As the blade sliced through his spinal cord on its way out the other side of his neck, the sudden shock of the blow jolted enough strength to the man's trigger finger to squeeze off a round. Joe felt a searing pain in his right shoulder as the bullet thudded home, the force of the impact throwing him hard against the shed. Inside, Jake yelped with fright as the shed lurched off its foundations, scattering tools, empty plant pots, half full bottles of anti-freeze and engine oil and an array of nails, screws and various items of ironmongery from the many rows of shelves. As he lay stunned, fighting to catch his breath, Joe was heartened by strong screams coming from inside the shed, indicating that the lad had escaped serious injury. Bracing against the incredible pain in his shoulder, Joe dragged himself to his feet. He picked up the weapon the second man had dropped as he died, stepped over his body, and again headed for the house.

Joe Li hated guns and the damage and misery they were capable of inflicting. He'd had his fill of them whilst on national service back in Japan. He vowed that when he returned to civvy street he would never again handle one unless it was under exceptional circumstances. He figured this qualified.

As he entered the kitchen, a third man, attracted by the commotion outside, appeared in the doorway. Joe reacted first, squeezing off a couple of rounds. With his right hand useless due to the bullet jammed in his shoulder, he had to make do with the weaker left. One bullet split the door frame near the man's head, the second making a neat hole in the middle of a picture hanging on the wall. The man, stunned by the sudden attack, lifted his gun to take aim when Joe Li fired a third. He screamed in agony as he lost a kneecap, then was silenced forever by the fatal fourth bullet, a direct hit through the left eye.

As the body fell to the floor, Joe heard a man's voice in the distance, coming from the garden. Outside, the last man had little Jake in a headlock, his knife pressing against the pale skin of the boy's neck.

'It's up to you, old man,' the man said, 'You decide if he lives or dies.' His grip tightened on the knife. Jake whimpered as the point of the blade broke the skin.

'Wait. Please. Don't. He is only a child. He does not deserve to die,' Joe Li said, lowering his gun.

The man raised his, took aim.

CHAPTER FORTY-TWO

Dulles International Airport, Washington DC: 8.00am

Taylor breezed through customs as Victor Andrew Hudson, attracting hardly a sideways glance. Before leaving for the airport in Geneva, he had gone for a subtle change of hairstyle and a pair of gold-rimmed spectacles with clear lenses – Taylor possessed perfect vision – and he was good to go.

After grabbing some bacon and eggs with a cup of strong coffee in a cafe near the airport, Taylor slung his case on the back seat of a waiting taxi and climbed in beside it.

'Where to, buddy?' asked the driver, stifling a yawn. He pushed a pencil behind his ear before laying down Washington's version of *The Racing Post* on the passenger seat.

Taylor reached into his pocket and thumbed through the pages of a little diary in which he had taken a few *Google*-inspired notes during the flight from Geneva. His finger trailed down the page. 'Holiday Inn, please.' He had written down *unremarkable* and *middle of the road* next to it.

'DC or Wood County?'

'Sorry?'

'There are two.'

'Oh, eh...DC.'

'No problem.' The driver squinted at Taylor in his rear-view mirror. 'You English?'

'That's right,' Taylor lied because it suited him, and because he'd been drawn into a sort of plummy, home counties accent, for whatever reason he knew not.

'You here on business?'

'Yep.' Taylor intentionally clipped his reply in an attempt to stop the driver slipping into his routine.

'What is it you do?' the driver then asked. He was in the mood.

'Business statistics.'

Conversation killer.

Taylor paid the driver twenty dollars out of the five hundred he had withdrawn from an airport cash machine. He knew any card transactions would be closely monitored by the Secret Service. Mannheim had even admitted as much. They would have expected him to draw cash as soon as he landed. It made sense. It was no big deal, in Taylor's opinion, as it would merely confirm his arrival on US soil. His plan, going forward, was to continue to take cash randomly from a number of city centre machines. He had no intention of handing the card over as payment for a hotel room or a meal in a restaurant. He'd even given the taxi driver bum information as to where he was staying in DC. Taylor had watched the taxi round the corner after dropping him off at The Holiday Inn. Then he'd walked the three blocks to another unremarkable, middle-of-the-road hotel: The Helix.

CHAPTER FORTY-THREE

Next morning, Taylor tugged open the blinds and stared out at a glowing sun rising over Washington, hovering on the horizon like a giant, hazy blood-orange. His room on the hotel's top floor rewarded him with stunning views of the city. In the distance, along towards Pennsylvania Avenue and the White House, the Washington Monument seemed to spear a thousand feet into the air, dividing the city into two neat parts: on the right, the Smithsonian Institute and the FBI building, on the left, the Vietnam Veterans' Memorial situated close to its more illustrious cousin, the Lincoln Memorial.

Taylor's gaze switched to the street directly below as random movements attracted his attention: an electric milk float silently swept past, the only evidence it was there, the light clinking together of glass bottles; an early morning jogger dressed head-to-toe in mp4, headphones and shiny bright lycra, picked up the pace, striking out for home; a fox, omnivorous and resourceful, disturbed by the arrival of the weekly garbage truck during a final forage among the contents of somebody's upturned bin, darted for cover, squeezing through a tiny hole in a wicker fence. The hole looked to Taylor as if it might struggle to accommodate an average sized rat never mind a fully grown dog fox. Then he recalled one of those middle-of-the-night National Geographic programmes he and April had slumped down on the couch to watch, or rather stare at, during a brief respite from their foul-tempered, teething-driven baby son's onslaught. Some guy had carried out a study of the growing phenomenon that was the urban fox. How the animal had had to constantly adapt to its changing surroundings, to continually evaluate situations to survive. This animal had evolved to the point where it could now be referred to as a distant cousin of the common-or-garden country fox. This version would eat literally anything and live anywhere, from under an old shed at the bottom of a garden in the suburbs, to behind a rusty, corrugated sheet in the corner of a city centre building site. And this version was doing everything to ensure continuation of its kind. In London alone some boffin had studied the urban fox for a year, somehow reaching the conclusion that there were at least 28 of them to every square mile of the city.

Taylor laughed when he saw one of the burly garbage truck workers aim a hefty kick or three at the pile of rubbish strewn all over the road, cursing as he did so. Taylor's smile grew even wider when he saw the fox push its head back out of the hole. He could've sworn he'd seen the animal stick out its tongue at the worker as he struggled to gather up the mess.

Taylor's smile faded. A cold shiver eased its way up his spine as the events of the past week or so crept into his brain. At this very moment he was no better than the urban fox, reviled and despised, to be hunted down and shot without mercy.

His attention returned to those famous Washington landmarks and, just for a moment, instead of the White House and the Lincoln Memorial, he saw Glasgow's Kingston Bridge over the River Clyde, with the Mitchell Library providing a magnificent backdrop. On the other side, an image of the space-age type architecture that made up the Science Centre seemed to hover over the Potomac, with the SECC, Armadillo and the brand-new Hydro concert venue also looming large in front of him like ghostly apparitions from a past life.

I wish...

Taylor started as the room phone rang out. Gathering his thoughts, he stared at the phone for a few seconds before answering. Lifting it to his ear, he slipped his hand over the receiver, remained silent. The call hovered for three seconds, then disconnected.

'Dammit!'

In three minutes, Taylor had stuffed everything in his bag and was legging it down four floors to the point where he knew he could pick up the bolted-to-the-building, slightly rickety, fire escape stairwell. Earlier, at 4am, he'd made it his business to take a walk around, to plan for such an exit before he eventually settled down to grab some sleep.

The stairwell led him to a delivery yard at the back of the hotel, where he hopped aboard an idling fruit and veg truck and slung his bag on the passenger seat. Crashing the gear stick, Taylor floored the pedal and powered the truck towards the exit amid burning rubber. The startled driver appeared from an open door near the hotel kitchen, almost losing all ten toes in a vain attempt to jump aboard his truck.

Taylor glanced in the mirror in time to see the furious driver swing a heavy boot into the dirt and lose his footing before thumping down hard on his tail bone.

Ouch!

He hung two hard lefts and a right within a couple of hundred yards until he found his way onto a main freeway, heading for the other side of the city. *This is not good*, he thought.

Great choice, Ryan! This thing sticks out like a clown at a wake. Not only was the truck bright yellow, it had the biggest and cheesiest cartoon character he'd ever seen emblazoned on the side: tomato head, lettuce belly and spring onion legs with radish shoes, veggie boy was also shown kicking a field goal using a sprout for a ball!

Taylor took heart when he passed an identical truck, then another, the driver waving his arms and flashing his lights at the runaway Brit. A mile or so down the road, another veggie boy was taking an off ramp, while yet another blasted his horn at Taylor before heading for his next drop.

Any notion of concealment in numbers soon wore off when Taylor considered not how many veggie boys there were in the whole of Washington, but how the company identified them. His bet was on helicopter friendly numbers - big ones - covering the whole of the truck roof.

But he still felt ahead of the game. His brain raced into overdrive as he considered the sequence of events: the truck driver's 911 call; the exchange of information; the alert hitting the local area; some eager young cop, fearless, and probably peerless, behind the wheel of a car, hunting his quarry to the ends of the earth.

Taking that thought into consideration, Taylor abandoned the vehicle among some bigger ones outside a truck stop diner in the Georgetown area of DC.

On his way to the main drag, which, according to a battered old sign outside the diner, was a mile away, he felt movement in his bag. Familiar movement.

Silent vibrate.

'Crap!' Taylor said. Leo Mannheim had given him the mobile back in Geneva. He had meant to make sure it was switched off after he landed at Dulles airport. He thought he'd done so. He hadn't. He'd been GPS tracked. Taylor swore again as he fumbled through the bag. The phone display said: *Private Number.* No surprise there. Eventually, he hit answer just before the call ended, jamming the phone against his ear.

'Hello.'

'Taylor?' a male voice replied. Confused, Taylor recalled the last part of his conversation with Leo Mannheim back in Geneva: *I'm the only one in MI6 who knows this number.* Taylor had no idea who was on the other end of the phone, but he knew one thing. It wasn't Mannheim.

'Who is this?'

'My name's not important. What is important is that you confirm who you are.'

The voice was easy to tag: American, but could be from anywhere.

'I'm five seconds from hanging up.' Taylor saw no point in prolonging the agony.

'I'd think very carefully about doing that. Especially if you want to see your family alive again.'

The man's words took Taylor's breath away like a blow to the solar plexus. He spent a few seconds trying to steady himself as his legs turned to jelly. Leaning on a rusty old 'A' board sign set outside a small cafe for support, he pulled in a long breath. 'Okay, I'm listening, but why should I believe you? My family is safe. They're being looked after by friends,' Taylor said as calmly as the situation would allow.

'You're right about one thing. Your wife and son *are* safe, at least for now. Whether they stay that way depends on you.'

'I need to know. I need to speak to my wife.' Taylor's voice broke with emotion, the mere mention of the words *wife and son* giving the situation credence, making it a million times more *personal*.

'Not now,' the voice said. 'We'll be in touch.'

'Wait!' Taylor called out in vain. The call had dropped out.

Taylor stared at the screen in disbelief. The whole gamut of emotions rushed in and out of his brain over the next few seconds: fear, rage, sorrow, disgust, confusion; then fear and rage again...

He stuffed the phone in his pocket before slumping down on a chair at one of the cafe's tables. He struggled to banish the heavy fog enveloping his brain as it threatened to stifle all reasonable thought processes.

As he began to consider his options, such as they were, he jumped when a voice came from nowhere. 'Sir, can I get you anything?'

The waiter had sprung at him from inside the cafe, like a spider sizing up its prey. He stood poised, notebook at the ready.

'Eh...coffee. White...Two sugars.' Taylor held up two fingers as he battled to find the words.

'Any food, sir?'

Taylor shook his head then sat up as the phone kicked off again. The waiter scurried off.

Taylor stared at the display: Unknown Number.

CHAPTER FORTY-FOUR

'I take it you heard that last conversation?' Taylor said, crushing the phone as he spoke.

'We heard.'

'You assured me they were safe. You gave me personal guarantees.'

'I'm sorry. We messed up.'

'Tell me you know where they are.'

Leo Mannheim's silence said everything.

'What happened?' Taylor was finding it hard to keep control.

'We've had some security issues lately. Been testing some processes with low level information. I didn't like what was coming back so I gave the order to have April and the boy-'

'Jake,' Taylor interjected. 'The boy's name is *Jake*.'

Mannheim grunted. 'I'd arranged to have April and Jake moved to a more secure location later that day.'

'That day? When exactly did this happen?'

A short silence. 'A couple of days ago.'

'A couple of days!' Taylor shouted at the phone. He stood, waved the waiter away when he arrived with his coffee. The waiter left the coffee before wisely retreating. 'Wait!' Taylor barked again at the phone. He caught the waiter's attention before he reached cover behind the little counter area at the back of the cafe. Taylor held up his hands in apology and made an exaggerated play of slipping ten dollars under his coffee cup. The waiter stayed where he was, nodding an acknowledgement. Taylor slung his bag over a shoulder and set off for the main drag. He again put the phone to his ear. 'When did you plan on telling me? When their bodies washed up on some remote Scottish beach somewhere?' Taylor was breathing hard as he pounded the street. He felt sharp pangs of guilt stab his heart again and again for getting the people who mattered most to him into this whole sorry mess.

'I took the decision, Ryan. There really was no point in telling you. What could you have done? I thought it best that we wait for them to make contact. It is the smart play.' Mannheim paused. 'Are you still there? Taylor?'

Taylor said nothing. He knew Mannheim was right. He was already formulating a plan, a plan designed to provide the building blocks, lay the foundations without which he felt he would never be able to rescue his wife and son. 'Another of Brian Ricker's rock-solid contacts bites the dust,' Taylor said with more than a hint of sarcasm, then regretting the statement almost as the words left his lips.

'The couple, both of them, were killed,' Mannheim said quietly. Taylor felt bad enough until he heard the next part. 'The woman had her throat cut in her own bedroom. The man took a bullet between the eyes. But not before he killed three of them. We think he gave his own life to save the b...eh, Jake.'

Taylor exhaled loudly. 'It just never ends, does it?' he said, his voice barely a whisper.

'All I can say is, I'm sorry,' Mannheim said. 'What are you going to do?'

'Whatever it takes.' Taylor forced a half-hearted smile. 'There's one good thing. My family's still alive and I aim to keep it that way.'

'The ball's back in their court, son. They'll want you to give yourself up for your family.' Mannheim stopped short of expressing an opinion on what would happen if or when Taylor did just that.

'How secure is the line, sir?' Taylor asked.

'It's bomb proof, that I can guarantee. Our guys are the only ones who'll hear everything.'

'Okay, I'll need to hang onto this phone, at least until they get back in touch. I may disappear for a while after that. I have, *plans.*'

'Do whatever you have to. Remember, you're not alone. We've some good people working on this as well. People I can trust.'

The phone went dead.

When he'd first heard of the abductions, Taylor felt the uncontrollable urge to hurl the phone as far into the nearby Potomac as he could. Now he was glad he didn't. His unfolding plan might just include a request or two for information not to be found on any normal website. He had kept that particular door ajar. Taylor still felt some connection, despite everything, with Mannheim and his precious Secret Service. The Controller could have quite easily washed his hands of everything. For him it would have been the smart move. Why run the risk of making an enemy of your strongest ally, the biggest, most powerful administration since the Roman Empire?

Taylor frowned as he walked towards the main drag. A bus came into view and he filed in behind a short queue, preparing to ride into town. One thought kept gnawing away at him; he couldn't quite fathom out why any of the US agencies could stoop so low as to kidnap innocent civilians for blackmailing purposes. CIA? FBI? Or Homeland Security, which was set up in the wake of 9/11 as a more aggressive entity to bolster the fight against terrorism in all its shapes and forms? Taylor wasn't convinced. It wasn't the American way. But if not these agencies, then who?

The bus pulled up at the stop at the exact moment Taylor's phone rang out again. He stepped back out of the queue, allowing the bus to move on. Looking around to confirm he was alone, he answered.

'Taylor?' It was the same voice as before.

'Yes.'

'If you want to see your wife and son alive again, you'll do as I say.'

'Go to hell!' Taylor said, flicking the end call display.

He swallowed hard.

In for a penny...

As he waited for the next bus into town, he began to feel mildly sick.

CHAPTER FORTY-FIVE

Taylor had spent the past two hours since he checked in to yet another cheap hotel googling so hard that the glare of the screen nipped his eyes and made his head ache. He'd exhausted every possible combination of words within United Nations G-20 Summit Geneva 2014 that he could think of. It was as if the summit had been wiped clean. *Sanitised.* As if it had never taken place. Finally, he gave up on that idea, deciding on a change of tack. He remembered reading an article on phone phreaking. He also remembered thinking it was a load of codswallop: *phone phreaking* - the art of information gathering. *Yeah right.* Only now, Taylor was so desperate he was ready to put the theory to the test.

A picture of The White House flashed up on the screen. He jotted down the phone number below the image.

'Hello, White House administration.' The woman sounded pleasant enough.

'Hi there. To whom am I speaking?'

'My name is Janice. How may I help you today, sir?'

'Hi Janice. I need to ask you a question?'

'That's what we're here for, sir?' Already, she sounded mildly pissed off. *Promising*, thought Taylor.

'If your boss tells you he wants something done like, yesterday, but he doesn't tell you exactly what it is he wants, or even how to get it, what do you do? What would *you* do?'

'This, boss, I'm assuming he's not stupid?'

'No. In fact, completely the opposite.'

'Then I'd relax.'

'Really, how so?'

'Well, I'd say he has enough trust and confidence in his people that he feels he doesn't need to go into detail. He knows the job will get done.'

'You're saying I should simply *do my job*?'

'I'd say so.'

'I'm impressed. I hope the big boss, y'know, the president, also realises how lucky he is.'

An audible sigh...then, 'Thank you. Listen, I'm really busy. Can you-'

'Oh, yes. I'm sorry.'

'That's quite all right, sir.' Another sigh. 'Now tell me, what can I do for you?'

Perfect! Taylor imagined her face getting redder by the second.

'I suppose I should really get to the point. And, thank you again, you've been very patient.'

'Thank *you*,' she replied, curtly.

'My name is George Buchan and I work for a London-based, current affairs periodical, UK Today, perhaps you've heard of us?'

'No, Mr. Buchan, I haven't.' Ice cold.

'Oh, right. Okay, then I'll get straight to it, tell you why I'm calling, shall I?'

'Please do.' More ice, now also heavy on the sarcasm.

'Once a month, as well as our regular features, we do a more in-depth report and analysis of the politics, lifestyle and working conditions in one of our neighbouring European countries. You follow?'

'Mm-hmm,' Janice half-grunted, sounding as if she were losing the will to live.

Taylor pressed on. 'Now you may ask why I'm ringing you about this European country, especially when you are where you are and I am where I am.'

'The thought had crossed my mind.' Full-on sarcasm.

'It's because we're featuring Switzerland this month, Geneva in particular.' Taylor listened carefully for a switch in her attitude to barriers-up defensive. Any change, however small, would tell him that information regarding what had happened at the summit had leaked its way like wild fire from department to department.

'Please, go on.' Still cold, no change detected. So far so good.

'So, we were fully intending to run a special feature on Swiss politicians following the recent Geneva summit, but we found them even duller than our own. That's when somebody came up with the bright idea of doing a special feature on one of the visiting country's politicians. Then it was a question of which country. We get enough of German and French politics over here, more than you can shake a stick at. No, it was unanimous. Everybody wanted to do a piece on the US delegates. It would be a combination of Swiss culture and American attitudes.' Taylor grimaced. He hoped she would buy it.

'And what sort of information would you require, sir?'

'A list of the US team that attended the summit? I believe there were ten, not counting the president himself? If we were able to write a little biographical piece about each of them? That's all. Nothing heavy, more or less a quick resume of their careers to date.'

'I'm sorry, sir, that information is classified. Goodbye.' She hung up.

Taylor shook his head, cursed, then realised his mistake. 'Idiot! Keep it short. Build up the information.' He lifted the phone again and chose another number. As he waited for the connection, he began to consider some phone phreaking dos and don'ts.

Play the sympathy card. Rile them first if you have to, and then hit them with the sob story. They feel so guilty they'll practically tell you anything. Only works with certain types, though. You can forget a jobsworth.

'Hello, thank you for calling The White House. How may I help you?'

A woman's voice, perhaps a little crusty and experienced for Taylor's liking. *Jobsworth*?

'Hello, and how are you this morning?' he said, brightly.

'My health is not in question, sir. How may I help?' the voice rumbled.

He disconnected, counted ten seconds, and re-dialled.

The same greeting. Again, a woman's voice, but this time younger, maybe mid-twenties, he estimated.

'Hi there. I hope you're well today.'

'Yes, I am. Thank you for asking, sir.'

'You're new?' Taylor took a shot.

'I'm temporary, sir. Maternity cover with the chance of a permanent job, depending on how things work out.'

Perfect. 'Hope things go well for you. I thought I hadn't heard your voice before.'

'Thank you, sir. You call often then?'

'I work for a British based magazine. We tend to do a lot of stuff on US politics. Janice usually helps me out with the details.'

'Sir?'

'Janice, in admin.'

'Oh yes, I know who she is. Don't really know her.'

'She's really nice. I feel like I know her so well. Her husband's Tom and they have two kids, Aaron and Victoria. Same name as our daughter.'

'Really? How old?'

'She...she would have been sixteen.' Taylor lowered his voice. 'She was killed in a car accident.'

'I'm so sorry, sir.'

Taylor knew by her tone he'd reeled her in.

'Thank you,' Taylor said.

'How long ago did it, you know?'

'Six years, three months and twenty-seven days.'

'Sir, I have another couple of calls coming in. What information do you require from us?' Her voice wobbled with nerves. Taylor sensed impending panic, as if she would do anything to get him off the line.

'I'm looking for a copy of the list of US delegates who attended the UN summit in Geneva this year. My magazine's main topics this month are US politics and Switzerland. This way we can double up?'

Keep it basic.

'A minute please, sir.'

No flat refusal. At least, not yet. Then: 'Can you let me have your email address?'

Bingo!

Taylor had already requested of Leo Mannheim that the powers that be set him up to receive emails on behalf of his fictional employer: press@uktoday.co.uk

Taylor scanned the document. He did his best to clear his thoughts of everything. Of Jake and April, of Troy and Maddie Williams and Brian Ricker, of Federici and Fontaine, the Secret Service, the CIA. Everything.

Taylor's finger trailed down the computer screen, pausing under each name in turn. As he whispered the name, he closed his eyes, searching the dark recesses of his mind for a link, a trigger to send him in the right direction. His brain turning into a mish-mash of all of the above, he swore. He tapped enter to forward the file to Leo Mannheim before slamming down the lid of the laptop. As he nestled back in his chair folding his arms, Taylor imagined the sort of instructions Mannheim would add to the file before sending it on its way to the 'geeks' in *Intelligence*: *I want to know all there is to know about these people. I want to know if they like ogling eight-year-olds. I want to know the last time they stole from the pick 'n' mix at Woolworths. I want no stone unturned. You understand?*

CHAPTER FORTY-SIX

Las Vegas, Nevada

'He hung up? Vinny, you're kiddin' me, right?'

'No, boss, he told me to go screw myself.'

The big man behind the desk shook his head, laughed heartily. 'We have his wife and son and he tells *us* exactly where to go. Now that takes balls.'

'What are you going to do now, boss?' Vinny asked.

The big man wasn't listening. He was already working out his next play.

'Boss?'

'Huh? Eh...listen, Vinny, why don't you go give Red a hand? There's a problem with the sprinklers.'

'Sure, boss.'

As Vinny left the room the big man settled back in his chair, began tapping keys on the laptop in front of him. An image of the British Secret Service agent, Ryan Taylor, flashed up. 'Okay, Mr. Ryan Taylor,' he whispered. 'Let's see what you're made of.'

Maxie Royce really was a big man in these parts. And not only in stature. Early fifties, six-four and nigh on twenty-five stone, Royce was one of Las Vegas's major players. Construction, real estate, casinos, betting, prostitution, drugs, even gun-running. If it was there Royce was into it. The legit stuff – the construction, the real estate - was straightforward and up-front, more or less. Most of the rest of his portfolio had been lawyered so tightly over the years, you could peel away a dozen layers and not even come close to pinning as much as a parking ticket on Maxie Royce.

Royce had begun life in a trailer park along the coast, through the state line into California, the product of a quick bang in a school toilet. His mother had only just turned fourteen when she lay down to give birth to him, alone, in the squalid festering conditions of the *family* trailer. Fortunately, a neighbour had heard the girl's screams and cared enough to call 911, the medics getting there in the nick of time to save the baby's life, but too late to prevent his mother bleeding to death. Reports of the child weighing as much as twenty pounds were perhaps greatly exaggerated, though there seemed to be no doubt that his sheer size had been a contributory factor in the girl's untimely death. The 'proud' father, a year older at fifteen, counted himself out of the affair, smirking and shrugging and denying all knowledge of anyone and anything.

Granny came through for the kid, in her eyes at least, choosing to name him after her then pimp, Maxie Drexler, before neglecting him almost to the point of starvation. Only the actions of the same good Samaritan neighbour again saved the lad's life.

Maxie was then taken into care where he bounced around various homes and foster families, some good, some not so good, until he found himself approaching sixteen and running drugs for a local punk on the streets of Vegas.

Brash and street-wise, Royce soon worked out ways of 'improving' operations, usually involving his taking charge of them one way or another. The day after his eighteenth birthday he committed his first murder, cutting his boss's throat over a disagreement about short wages. A meagre five dollars. But then five dollars or fifty thousand, the result would have been the same. Maxie was used to getting what he wanted. By negotiation, by force, either way.

At twenty, he celebrated reaching his first million by hiring a private detective to find his no-good father, by then a homeless drunk who spent his days shuffling about the streets of Sacramento, digging in trash cans for scraps, praying daily for sweet release.

Maxie Royce was delighted to grant dad his wish. Payback was recovered in full when he drove his old man far out into the desert, before leaving him staked out and naked, staring into the mid-day sun, with a colony of hungry red ants for company.

Granny was next on the list. And finding her proved just as easy for Maxie as actually killing her. By then an alcoholic and heroin addict, and still living in the same run-down trailer park, Lena Wysocka's only function in society, other than providing sexual relief for money for sad and lonely males, was to steal anything not nailed down to feed her drug habit. It was a whole lot more than she used to do for her precious grandson and Maxie was only too happy to point this out to her as he strangled her to death with her own filthy scarf.

Two down, one to go. Widowed since her mid-twenties, Vera Nolan had moved a couple of times since Maxie had last seen her. By the time his detective tracked her down she was still alone, but comfortable, in a nice house in a decent part of Sacramento. Ironically, Vera was working for the IRS, had done for years. The nature of the business Maxie was in meant crossing swords with that particular government department on a regular basis. However, rather than spit fury at them and throwing toys out the pram like most of his mobster associates, he preferred a more diplomatic approach. The events of the past five years totally vindicated his actions, his expensive accountants ensuring he made more money than most can only dream about.

Vera Nolan almost dropped the vase she was carrying when her young ex-neighbour turned up at her door. Cold, calculating Maxie Drexler sobbed rivers of tears as he hugged the woman who had twice saved his life.

More than thirty years on, Vera was living even more comfortably in a wing of Maxie's sprawling mansion back in Vegas. Drexler had been changed in favour of Royce, Vera's maiden name, as he considered her his rightful mother. And, mindful of the esteem in which he held her, the former IRS employee felt protected by being put in charge of only his legitimate businesses. Vera knew about the other stuff, or at least some of it. She would have to have been pretty stupid not to. Stupid she most certainly wasn't and she was well aware of Maxie watering down his dark side for her. Vera preferred to let him think he was diluting any danger to which she may be exposed. She knew it helped him sleep at night.

These days, Maxie was banking well over fifty million a year. Even he had no idea of the extent of his wealth.

'Vinny told me about the phone call. What happens now, boss?' Red Summers waited until he and Royce were alone before asking the question. One of the few men in Vegas who stood taller than Royce, Red relied on his boss for almost everything since he'd been taken on as hired muscle more than ten years ago. Now in his early thirties, the bodyguard was one of only two people in the world that Maxie fully trusted. The other was Vera Nolan.

'You leave the thinking to me, Red,' Maxie said as he tapped the side of his head. He kept Red Summers close at all times, advised him on everything, from what he should wear to when he ought to go to bed. The big man would always obey orders without question, and by habit.

'Don't worry, Red, let me take care of things. You go get some shut-eye.'

Having sent Red Summers to his room out by the pool, Maxie waited until Vera retired for the night at around 11.30pm before making his way past the two guards at the front of the house, then down a few steps to the summer house.

The room in which he was holding Ryan Taylor's family was huge, and palatial, and far enough detached from Vera or indeed anybody else for that matter. The guards at the front were part of a 24-hour contract, there to protect the estate's occupants, nothing else. They hadn't an inkling that there were special guests living on the estate.

Maxie had given Red Summers explicit instructions to ensure April and Jake Taylor were well looked after. He had no intention of harming either of them. It was more than could be said for the rest of the organisation, especially slimy rat, Carlo Fachetti, soon-to-be Don of the Fachetti family since the death of his grandfather six months before. Maxie and Don Fachetti had been tight, a fact that had always stuck in Carlo's craw. When the situation with Ryan Taylor arose, Carlo had purposely jumped the gun, as it were, sending four of his best men to Scotland to kidnap Taylor's family. The consensus among the families was that Carlo had done this to undermine Maxie Royce. Everybody knew this type of thing was Maxie's bag. There was no one better. Cool, calm, straight talking, he always got the job done.

Fachetti had lost three of his men to the skill of Joe Li, providing the catalyst for dozens of unwanted reports of terrorism landing on Scotland's doorstep. Luckily, MI6 had been unable to establish the identities of any of the dead men, but nevertheless the pressure heaped upon Fachetti from the rest of the families for endangering the organisation's existence was too much to bear and he was forced to stand aside, allowing Royce to take over. Maxie was convinced Fachetti would currently be monitoring the situation, however, itching to step back in if he sensed weakness.

So far, Maxie had had no contact with April and Jake Taylor since they were brought to his mansion two days ago. He had planned to keep it that way and have the matter wrapped up in hours rather than days. Ryan Taylor's refusal to cooperate had derailed that particular plan. Maxie now felt that he would have to personally intervene to get the job done.

Royce didn't know if it was because of his relationship with Vera that he felt the urge to knock the door out of respect before entering the room.

It was true he was no stranger to female company. Before Vera had come into his life, he tended to treat women very badly, no doubt fallout from his crappy upbringing. He'd hurt them, not in a violent way, but psychologically. As if he needed to humiliate them. To dominate them, make them feel inferior. Unsurprisingly, nobody had managed to get really close to the man, but now at least, thanks to Vera's influence, he would display some affection, show some mark of respect.

He pushed the door open and stepped inside. The main lights were out, and in the far corner of the room a baby's cot was bathed from above in the gentle orange glow from a nightlight. He could see the little boy's chest swell and subside with each peaceful breath. As he walked towards the cot, he heard footsteps coming his way. Sidestepping April Taylor's flailing arms, Royce nimbly spun her around, sending her crashing into the wall next to him. Two heavy objects fell from her hands, the impact sending them careering across the room. As she slumped to the floor unconscious he reached for the light switch.

The harsh light frazzling his brain, he took a couple of steps before bashing his shin against something solid. *Ow!* A heavy tripod-style footstool rolled away from him and across the slippery tiles before neatly coming to rest upside down in the middle of the floor. Royce smiled when his brain cleared enough to be able to work out what had just happened: the tripod, doubling as a trip hazard, had become a onepod, the other two solid oak *weapons* sliding below the cot out of harm.

Maxie grimaced when he heard the child stir and then splutter into life. 'Hell,' he whispered.

CHAPTER FORTY-SEVEN

Almost five minutes had elapsed since April Taylor was knocked unconscious. Stirring, she fingered a bump the size of an egg on the back of her head. 'Jake!' she cried as she swung her legs off the plush sofa on which Maxie Royce had laid her.

'He's fine,' Royce said. He was leaning over the cot staring at the little boy who had eased himself back to sleep.

'Get away from him!' She shot to her feet too quickly, just as quickly dumping down on her backside as she felt her head swim, her legs turn to soft chocolate.

'Now hold your horses. You took quite a bump there,' he said, reaching across to steady her.

'Don't touch me!' She tugged her arm away. 'You stay away from me, from us!' Staring defiantly at him, she winced as she again ran the tips of her fingers over her injured head.

Maxie noted the waver in her voice. He held up his hands. 'I'm going to sit over here. Okay?' He backed across the other side of the room and perched on the edge of an easy chair.

Refusing to take her eyes off him, even for a second, April shuffled across the sofa towards her son and placed herself between him and Royce. In her haste she nudged the bars of the cot. Jake stirred a little, made a bad-tempered face, and continued sleeping.

'I suppose you'll want to know why you've been brought here,' Royce said.

'I already know the reason,' April snapped. 'I'd much rather you told me why you found it necessary to murder my friends.'

Royce sensed the apprehension in her voice, though he felt she was doing her best to try and hide it. He found himself with a quandary. Does he go all out and butt heads with her, knock her confidence a little, therefore making her feel vulnerable and more likely to cooperate? Or does he empathise, try and get round her that way?

Thing was, Maxie Royce wasn't big on empathy.

'By all reports your friends could take care of themselves.'

'Joe was only trying to protect us. He gave his life for-for my son.' She struggled to get the words out.

'It was, unfortunate.'

'Unfortunate? You heartless bastard, I wish it had been you!' she shouted.

Royce had lit the blue touch paper.

'There's no doubt that would be on a few people's wish lists,' he said, folding his arms.

'I wonder why.' She narrowed her eyes.

He paused for a moment. 'You got balls, I'll give you that.'

'Wait till you see the size of my husband's when he tracks you down.'

Royce sniffed. 'I don't suppose telling you I wasn't directly involved with you and your son's abduction is gonna get me off the hook, is it?'

April thought for a moment, as if trying to process this information. Eventually: 'Tell it to someone who cares.'

'Why don't you tell me the reason?' Royce said.

'What reason?'

'The reason you think you know why you're here.'

'It's obvious, isn't it?' she said. 'You're using us to get to Ryan.'

'And what do you think will happen if he doesn't play ball?'

She didn't answer at first, then when she tried to speak nothing would come out. She turned her head away before composing herself.

'That would be up to you,' she said, weakly.

Royce was rocked back on his heels. He was beginning to look at her in a different light, though he was trying hard not to. He kept telling himself it was just business. Only this time it wasn't working. Maybe he was getting soft in his old age, but he admired this woman's strength in adversity. With all the decks stacked against her, and in his line of business he was a master of manipulating the odds, she refused to shed even one tear. She was still trying to be strong for her child.

Ten years ago, Maxie Royce would have done such a good job on this woman, by the time he had finished with her she would be looking for razor blades to slice her wrists. Then, job done, he would have sat down to a hearty meal with a glass of Chablis, read a few pages of his latest book – his favourite was true crime – and grabbed his full quota of undisturbed sleep.

April Taylor continued to stare at him. As Royce looked too deeply into her eyes for comfort, for the first time in his life he felt compelled to make a snap decision. And not the kind of decision he was used to making. It felt strange to him, but good strange.

Then the dark side began to creep back as he contemplated setting up an *arrangement* whereby all parties might benefit.

All parties, bar one.

CHAPTER FORTY-EIGHT

'I'm sending you the list back right now. Our people have trawled every secure site they could find, looked under every rock. They're in among the dirty washing. Anything dodgy, it'll be there. Sometimes it takes a little while to tease it out.' Leo Mannheim was talking on a secure line, or so he'd been assured. He was sitting at his desk studying hard copies of the information he was about to email to Ryan Taylor. Mannheim had seen absolutely nothing out of the ordinary in any of the files. There were a couple of minor indiscretions linked to one of the delegates, but tantamount to a speeding ticket rather than anything as grand as a homicide. There had been suggestions of impropriety regarding expenses on another senator's foreign trip. Another had been left bankrupt in an earlier life, courtesy of too many unfortunate visits to the racecourse. By all accounts, the man had got his life back on track, pardon the pun. These cases apart, nothing else sprang forth.

Mannheim felt the need to stay positive for Taylor's sake. Who knows, maybe Taylor would pick up on something his team had overlooked.

'Thanks, sir. I assume by your last sentence there's not much to go on?' Taylor said.

Mannheim put his hand over the receiver, cursed, said, 'Do your job, son. If our people uncover anything else, anything at all, I'll get it over to you right away.'

'Appreciate it, sir,' Taylor said. He sat back in his chair, a rueful look on his face as the email pinged in.

'I take it they haven't called back,' said Mannheim, referring to the abductors of Taylor's family.

'They will. They need me. As long as I'm alive, April and Jake are safe.'

'You sound confident.'

'I am, sir. So long as I can keep out of Federici's way.'

'About that, I've put out some feelers across the pond. Unofficially, of course. Apparently, the CIA made an initial approach to Federici to carry out the contract on Troy Williams.'

'But that's not so unusual, sir. These guys can be difficult to contact at the best of times. Fontaine must have been their next choice.'

'That's as maybe, but the approach to Federici was made two days before Liebermann was assassinated.'

Taylor's brow furrowed. 'Then everything was in place before Troy even got there? And nobody will officially admit to this?'

'Right. And that's not all,' Mannheim continued. 'We've heard Federici is working for another client at the same time.'

'Sir?'

'He's effectively doubling his fees for taking you out. My mole says that some consortium based out of the west coast of America also wants you dead,' Mannheim said.

Mannheim said nothing more for a few seconds, then, 'Take an hour or so to study the information I've sent. I'm hoping something jumps out at you. If not, it's probably prudent to look elsewhere. It might now be the right time to broaden your horizons, son.' Mannheim had become the realist.

'Got it, sir. Thanks.'

Taylor hung up, lifted a pen, and began to take notes on the back of a pad. On a blank page he scribbled the name: *Walter McMichaels*.

CHAPTER FORTY-NINE

It had been over an hour and a half since Taylor spoke with Leo Mannheim. Since then, he had scrutinized every dossier on every person present at the summit, except President Wilson Travis himself. And his eighteen-year-old son, John, whose name Taylor didn't know had even been on the guest list. Maybe the kid was being groomed for the top job a la the Bush family? The thought fleetingly crossed Taylor's mind, but only fleetingly. He had more important things to consider, for instance, why some west coast US consortium would have any interest in wanting him dead.

Taylor closed the lid on his laptop. He'd already made the decision not to waste any more time on the Geneva list. He began to think that whatever had taken place in that hotel in Switzerland had nothing to do with any of the people on that list. Taylor was ready to head straight for go as per Leo Mannheim's suggestion. The only problem he envisioned was actually getting to Walter McMichaels. As he turned the writing pad over to locate the page on which he had written the Chief of Staff's name, he also flicked past a list of Leo Mannheim's Washington contact telephone numbers and email addresses that he had offered up during their meeting in Geneva.

Taylor placed his finger under the first number, memorised it and dialled. As the phone purred in his ear, he slid his finger over to the right of the page for validation instructions.

'Hello, Peter Parker here.' A male voice cut in. Taylor shook his head in a *they're getting younger every day* sort of way as he imagined a kid of around sixteen on the other end.

'Do you know why they call my ninety-year-old grandad, Spiderman?' Taylor said slowly and clearly as instructed. He realised his voice was about to be validated by the geeks.

'Because he can't get out of the bath.' A fake, computer-generated clown's voice followed by hysterical laughter almost shattered Taylor's eardrum.

'Sorry about that,' Peter said. 'I really ought to adjust the volume a little.'

'More like a lot,' Taylor said, biting his tongue.

'One second… Okay, that's cool. Validation is complete. All you need to do is email your query to number three on the list along with the subject's name. Oh, and don't forget to add exactly what you want.'

Taylor trailed a finger down the list of email addresses, underlining the third with a pencil. 'When will I get the information?' he said.

'Twenty-four hours. No more. I'll be in touch.'

'Thanks.'

'Later.'

Taylor smiled. He'd only just made the connection with Peter Parker and Spiderman.

Sliding open the laptop, he selected new email and entered the third address from the list. He typed in FULL DOSSIER REQUIRED in the main body of the email, along with the name *McMichaels, Walter John, Chief of Staff* in the narrative line.

As the message zipped across town, via wherever, to Peter Parker, Taylor felt his mobile phone vibrate in his pocket.

He took a couple of deep breaths before hitting accept.

CHAPTER FIFTY

Taylor slid his finger across the phone's screen, then, trying hard to control his breathing, covered the mouthpiece with a cupped hand.

Ten seconds passed. He daren't move or utter a single word, closing his eyes in deep concentration. He'd read somewhere that shutting off one of the five given senses tends to sharpen the others. Close your eyes, concentrate, and your hearing improves ten-fold. That was the theory. Taylor wasn't so sure, but he was willing to give it a go. What had he to lose?

Concentrating hard, he thought he could make out one or two background sounds. He was convinced he could hear his son laughing and gurgling. Not close, but perhaps in an adjoining room. Maybe this thing does work. He knew there was somebody there, waiting, listening. The laughing and gurgling stopped, as if they had never happened. Taylor began to question his sanity.

'No more games.' A gruff voice that Taylor didn't recognise broke the silence.

'I'm not in the playing games business,' Taylor said, trying to cap his anger. 'Why don't you meet me and I'll explain?'

'Don't know if you've noticed but you're not exactly in a position to make demands.'

'Okay, what is it you want from me?'

'I'd say that's pretty obvious. We have something precious of yours. Two things. It's you for them. That's the deal. Plain and simple.'

'How do I know you won't kill them anyway?'

'You don't. You'll need to take my word for it.'

'I want to know they're still safe.'

'You'll need to take my word for that as well.'

'No deal. I speak to April now.'

The call ended.

Taylor sat in silence for a full minute, his stomach churning. The phone rang again. Taylor recognised the caller. 'Sir, did you get a location?' he said.

'No. They tell me the phone must be linked to some kind of scrambling device. I'm sorry, son,' Mannheim said.

Taylor heard the buzz of another incoming call and cut Mannheim off.

'Hello.'

'Ryan? Is that you?' April Taylor said calmly.

Taylor sighed. Immediately, he felt as if the weight of the whole world had been removed from his broad shoulders. 'April, it's so good to hear your voice. Are you okay? Is Jake-'

'We're fine, Ryan,' she cut him off. 'Please don't worry. We're being well looked after.' April Taylor had the knack of making the best of any situation. When Royce had told her she would be speaking to her husband, right away she was considering the quickest and easiest way to ensure that Ryan remained sharp, focused, with any feelings of rising anxiety kept to a minimum. The only problem with that notion was that Taylor knew his wife inside out. He knew all about her making the best of a bad situation. He knew all about her calming influence. But this was different. Never before had she, had they, been placed in such a position of danger. Taylor was certain that even she would find it impossible to stay calm and positive, given what had happened, unless she was telling the truth. The thought warmed his insides.

'I'm coming to get you, honey. It won't be long. I promise. Give my love to Jake.' Taylor spoke the words with feeling because he knew time was short. The point of the exercise was to establish that she and Jake were still alive. With that done Taylor expected a swift change of phone friend. Or indeed no phone friend at all as the call dropped out. If he was right the phone should kick off in-. Exactly on cue.

'Satisfied?' Royce spoke first.

'Thanks.'

'Save it. You now have to do exactly as I say to keep things the way they are.'

'Better get on with it then,' Taylor said, tight-lipped.

'I'm guessing your Secret Service guys are hanging on every word. And they'll have already told you they can't trace the call.'

'Go on.'

'Thought so. Okay, first things first. They'll have to find somebody else to bug. This arrangement is strictly private. If I get a sniff of anything, I'll pull the plug and that'll be the end of it. Understood?'

'Understood.'

'Good. Now we're getting somewhere. We'll be in touch in a few days.'

'Wait!' Taylor stared at the phone. The display indicated that the call had terminated.

Another thirty seconds passed before Mannheim was back on the line. Briefly, Taylor described his previous conversation.

'Don't worry,' Mannheim said. 'We'll be with you all the way. Some of the latest technology we have-'

'Forget it, sir,' Taylor cut in. 'I'm not taking any chances. How easy was it for his people to scramble a phone line? I'll call you.'

'Now wait a minute, son. I-'

'Can't hear you, sir. Bad line.'

CHAPTER FIFTY-ONE

Taylor hailed yet another cab, instructing the driver to take him to Peter Parker's choice of meeting place. Or at least close to it.

Leo Mannheim's contact in DC had sent the request by email four hours before. Taylor hadn't thought much of the tone of the email: *I have your information. Meet me at Meridian Hill Park at Noon today. Joan of Arc statue. Don't be late. Peter.*

Prior to the meeting, Taylor had used the morning to visit another MI6 contact. The guy had kitted him out with a little *insurance* - hand-gun shaped insurance. Not special, but effective.

On his way to his midday rendezvous, Taylor batted random thoughts back and forth. He very much doubted that any of these 'intelligence analysts' actually ever met anyone face-to-face during their rather sad and lonely existence. These guys were the old bookworms of the pre-computer era with their floppy hair, knitted sweaters and heavy rimmed glasses. Yes, technically they may well be field agents, but it was a very loose term. These days their main aim was to collect, analyse, assimilate, and distribute information. Give them a hard drive and a cloud and they'd prevent a war. Hand them a gun and they'd more than likely lose a toe.

That said, Taylor felt he had no choice but to accept Peter Parker's unusual invitation. That's not to say Taylor was simply going to *walk in the front door.*

Taylor got out of the cab a couple of hundred yards from the park. Entering via one of the main gates, he bought a glossy programme from an attendant, then tagged along with a motley team of teachers and pupils and a dozen or so stragglers of various types as they began a tour of the park. As the entourage moved past a small pavilion, behind which a couple of junior teams were playing baseball, Taylor's hand landed on a black Fedora hat someone had left on a park bench. As he scooped up the hat, he noticed a pair of heavy-rimmed sunglasses inside it. Quickly, he put on both hat and glasses. After glancing at his reflection in a window of the pavilion, he decided to discard the hat – an extra from The Blues Brothers would be the one person the world and its wife would remember – and lost himself among the crowd.

As the multi-lingual tour guide slipped into his well-worn routine, Taylor opened the programme and scanned the index. The Joan of Arc statue was the fourth item on the list. He carried on down until he reached the bottom entry: *Map of the park*. He dug a fingernail into the page and swivelled to his right, shielding his eyes from the sun as he estimated how far away Joan of Arc was. A row of tall oak trees around three hundred yards away obstructed any view of the statue which, if the map was correct, should be tucked in close behind.

Taylor noted the time: 11.33am. The tour guide was finishing off his description, in French, of the first landmark.

Realising there was little chance of the party reaching the *Maid of Orleans* on foot before midday, Taylor had begun to consider alternative options until an open top bus appeared on the scene. Things were looking up. Everyone climbed aboard, heading for landmark number two.

Three minutes to midday and the bus was trundling past the oak trees towards item number four. As they rounded the last tree, Taylor was slipping the dark glasses to the tip of his nose, peering over them, scanning the area in question. Thirty-foot-high trees lined both sides, under which and next to a pathway, sat a row of fixed park benches. All of the benches that Taylor could see from his position on the bus were vacant. Around fifty yards away and slap bang in the middle of the 'amphitheatre' was Joan of Arc herself, jet black and on horseback, with a sword in her right hand. Standing atop a small musicians' platform set up behind the statue was a figure, a man. Taylor aged the man at around twenty-five. He was tall, maybe six-two, with sandy hair, cropped short. Wearing a navy Puffa jacket, jeans and beige-coloured desert boots, Peter Parker, or whatever his name was, turned towards the bus. Taylor watched him nervously rub the palms of his hands together as he watched the vehicle come to a halt some thirty yards from the statue.

Teenagers, teachers and the rest disembarked and flooded towards Joan of Arc, following the tour guide as if he were the Pied Piper.

Parker took the wooden stairs to level ground. His gaze swept across the gathering until it settled on the most likely candidate.

Taylor pointed at a spot somewhere in the middle of the crowd. *Never get separated from the herd.* The pair stood shoulder-to-shoulder as the tour guide flicked through his notes before beginning his talk on all things Joan of Arc.

Taylor leaned in towards the younger man. 'Why here?' he whispered.

'It's my local park. I saw Don Mclean here last fall. Awesome.' Parker turned to smile at the MI6 man. But it was a nervous smile thought Taylor. Fear? Trepidation? Definitely.

Taylor took another look around the area. Lots of trees and benches. No tall buildings. That was good for him. Not so good for an assassin.

Taylor had already checked out everyone on the bus. Nobody gave him cause for concern. He leaned in again. 'Why not respond by email? Why face-to-face?'

Parker didn't answer at first. He stole a look right, then left. Taylor noticed a bead of sweat quickly form on his cheek. 'Orders,' he said, almost like a ventriloquist, hardly moving his lips.

'Whose orders?'

'My boss.' Parker raised his hand to scratch the stubble on his chin. Taylor noticed the hand shaking like an alcoholic on a desert island with only salt water for a companion. 'He ordered me to meet you face-to-face. He said I'd to actually hand you the report. Because the information was of a confidential nature. I tried to tell him these emails couldn't be more secure, but-'

'He ever had you do this before?' Taylor interjected.

'No, sir. But then I'm not really a field agent. I get, uncomfortable.'

You don't say.

Taylor turned to look Parker straight in the eye. He was used to seeing raw fear. He could smell it. He had encountered it many times before in all its various guises. It could never be masked or hidden. This was another example, up close. He would need to act fast.

'I suggest you tell me exactly what is going on here,' Taylor said. He let his jacket fall open slightly, enough to let Parker have an eyeful of gun.

'I-I can't. They're listening.' A couple standing next to them reacted to Parker's voice notching up a little.

Taylor ignored them. Wheeling the analyst around, he ripped open his jacket and his shirt. 'Great!' Taylor hissed, interrupting the tour guide mid-flow. Parker's chest was decorated with a map of twisted wires and white suction pads.

In seconds, an empty ring formed around the men, with people almost falling over themselves in their haste to get out of there.

Taylor ripped the equipment from Parker's chest and grabbed the collar of his shirt before pulling him in face-to-face. 'Where are they? Where the hell are they?'

'I-I don't know! They told me to meet you here, at the statue! Stay close to the statue, they said! Please, I-'

'Shut up!' Taylor shouted as he strained to listen.

'But-'

'Be quiet!' he shouted again. 'Listen, damn you!' Taylor had detected a faint ticking noise.

'I hear it!' a kid near the front shouted. 'It's coming from there!'

He was pointing at the statue, or rather at an area under the horse's rump.

Pandemonium followed as Taylor pulled his gun and fired two, three, four shots in the air. Everybody turned and ran, some tripping, tumbling and crawling for their lives. Everybody, except young Peter Parker who appeared numb - frozen even - staring into infinity like a rabbit caught in headlights.

As Taylor grabbed at Parker's jacket, pulling him one way, he fought to wrench himself free and, in his panic, took off straight for the statue.

'No, wait!' Taylor called out after him. He was forced to let Parker go when he heard the bomb's pre-ignition kick in.

An almighty blast blew Joan of Arc apart, turning her into thousands of tiny concrete projectiles. Dozens of them cut Peter Parker into pieces, firing parts of him as much as fifty yards in all directions. People lay on the ground screaming as warm body chunks rained down on them.

The last thing Taylor heard before he passed out was an unbearable ringing in his ears. The last thing he felt was pure nausea, courtesy of an overwhelming stench of burning flesh.

CHAPTER FIFTY-TWO

The young man in the smart suit acknowledged the two CIA agents standing guard at one end of the corridor. As he made the short walk to the gallows, or so he imagined, he saw another two flank the room door like bookends. His basic instinct was to run as fast and as far away from there as he could. But he knew running wasn't an option. People don't run from the CIA.

Yesterday, he had assured his boss he would tackle the on-going problem that was British Secret Service agent, Ryan Taylor. Now he was on a salvage mission. Carter Munroe damned his luck at receiving the email that would change his life, or what was left of it.

Munroe had confidently strolled into his boss's office, had run the plan past Walter McMichaels with a confidence and self-assurance that belied his years. McMichaels had given him his place, listened well, even provided a little free guidance. In the end McMichaels figured it was worth a shot. If anything did go wrong, there would be a ready-made patsy to carry the can.

Munroe had then taken it upon himself to add a little seasoning to proceedings, no doubt with a view to fast tracking his career with the agency. He had decided at the last moment that simply setting Ryan Taylor up for an assassin's bullet wasn't enough. *What if I could do the job myself? Where would that get me? A little improvisation was surely to be encouraged, was it not?*

Unable to sleep a wink last night, Munroe was dreading the call after the event. That call had come this morning less than five minutes into his working day. He'd vomited his breakfast, the little he'd been able to eat, down the toilet before leaving the safety of his office at CIA headquarters and taking a cab to the hotel.

It is a not-so-well known fact that the CIA regularly takes block bookings in random hotels, especially around Washington DC. Block bookings under fictional names. To deflect the heat. Usually when it had something to hide. Today it most certainly did have something to hide.

Carter Munroe could taste the bile crawling into his throat as he eventually summoned the courage to rap on the door.

'Come in!' McMichaels barked. His voice sounded throaty, gruff, wounded even, like a bear cornered in its lair with a thorn stuck in its paw.

An ashen-faced Munroe entered the room. McMichaels was sitting behind a desk in the corner, leafing through the contents of a buff folder, refusing to avert his gaze.

'Sir, you wanted to see me?' God only knew why but Munroe's voice was steady and even, for now.

'Sit down,' McMichaels said, peering over his glasses, indicating towards a chair placed strategically, or so Munroe imagined, in the centre of the room. Munroe found himself checking for a trap door in the floor before he sat, his hands crushing the arms of the chair.

For a full minute McMichaels said nothing, but continued flicking over pages, occasionally glancing at his young colleague.

He closed the folder, placing it carefully down on the desk. He removed his glasses and sat them on top of the folder, linked his hands together, and eased back in his seat.

'You know what this is?' McMichaels grabbed the folder and waved it over his head before slapping it back down on the desk. His glasses shot across the desk to the edge, perching half-on, half-off.

'No, sir.'

'This, is a blow-by-blow account of the events of yesterday afternoon. It doesn't make great reading, Carter. One dead, fifteen injured, four seriously.'

'Sir, I-'

'Let me finish.'

Munroe bowed his head.

'It wouldn't have been so bad if the principal target had been taken out as well. Though he soon will be. They tell me he's still unconscious.'

'Sir, I-' Munroe was once again halted, this time by a raised hand.

'I thought I could trust you, Carter. You assured me you had things in hand. The target. Out in the open. That's all you had to do. A goddamned bomb in the middle of a park? Surrounded by teachers and schoolchildren. Where in God's name did that come from?'

'Sir, there shouldn't have been anybody on site at that time, except our guy and the target. Somebody on the park staff took a late booking.' Munroe shook his head. 'Sorry about the statue, sir,' he said sheepishly.

'I couldn't care less about the statue,' McMichaels growled. 'This is a gigantic mess. People want answers, son. The President wants answers. What do I tell *him*?'

'Sir, you can trust me. Please, let me sort it out.'

'How do you fix *this*?' McMichaels reached across the desk and picked up the morning edition of The Washington Post. He tossed the paper across the room at Munroe who caught and refolded it before placing it back on the desk.

'I've already seen the news, sir,' he said, limply.

Munroe had read the lead article. In fact, he'd read it four times and still hadn't felt any better after each reading. Whilst it wasn't exactly Woodward and Bernstein tearing down the Nixon administration through their aggressive Watergate investigations, the modern-day Post journalist was still a force to be reckoned with. This version could also not be silenced and had no fear of government departments and their shady offshoots either. Today's edition of the paper had reported the facts, first of all. Nothing controversial there, but then they had seen fit to go on and *speculate*. Walter McMichaels hated words like *speculation* and *spin*, especially from the media. In his view media speculation only served to put the wrong ideas into the wrong heads. McMichaels had considerable clout within this administration, of that there was no doubt, but even *he* could do very little about the newspapers, especially this newspaper.

The article had begun by scratching the surface of terrorism, which was exactly the way McMichaels and the CIA had originally intended to play it, but had then swung the focus towards gross negligence displayed by certain government organisations. And if that wasn't bad enough, the journalist had finished off his article by suggesting that the whole thing may have been a plan to carry out a contract killing, engineered and acted upon by government agencies and/or persons unknown, close to the White House. If only he knew how right he was. But then, as more and more people seem to be getting involved, maybe he did.

A sombre Walter McMichaels then pulled back, deciding to go easy on Carter Munroe. He went through the motions, telling Munroe he was disappointed with what had happened and the way that it had happened. Then he amazed Munroe by also shouldering most of the blame for the debacle. 'Maybe you weren't ready for this, Carter,' he said. 'I really shouldn't have put you in this position. It's on me, it's my fault.'

Little did Munroe realise, but McMichaels had already worked out his get-out-of-jail card even before Munroe had knocked on that door. As soon as he had put himself forward for the job, the young man might as well have stuck his head above the parapet. The outcome had Walter McMichaels preparing to take aim.

The media release would go something like this: *Carter Munroe had been battling depression for the past year. We have reason to believe he was behind yesterday's incident at Meridian Hill Park. Munroe is dangerous and we appeal to anyone who knows of his whereabouts to turn him in as soon as possible. Washington DC, and its fine citizens, cannot feel safe until he is apprehended.*

Carter left that hotel room feeling as though a huge weight had been lifted from his shoulders. Yes, his career would suffer, but the important thing was he still had his precious job. He would take a sideways step for a year or two, then push on. *People have short memories, he mused. If I can only ride this out, I can come back even stronger. The world hasn't heard the last of Carter Munroe.*

The black limousine that McMichaels had told Munroe would take him back to the office pulled up at the kerb. The back door swung open and, as he climbed aboard, Munroe smiled instinctively at the man in the seat next to him. The man known as Federici did not return the smile as he grabbed Munroe by the head and easily snapped his neck.

From the window above, Walter McMichaels watched the limousine pull away. He closed the blinds before slumping down in his chair, head bowed. Reaching into his desk drawer, he cracked the seal on a bottle of scotch and downed a hefty mouthful.

CHAPTER FIFTY-THREE

'Why the guard?'

'Dunno, maybe the guy in there's the one that planted it.'

'Can't be much of a bomber if he gets blown up by his own bomb.'

The women exchanged respectful smiles given the events of the previous afternoon.

Nurses Leona Davis and Rebecca Watson had only just begun their shifts in the intensive care unit at The George Washington University Hospital. As soon as they had set foot in the building, they had been informed by security that they would be required to attend a short meeting in one of the hospital's conference rooms prior to beginning work. There had been no need for anyone to explain the reason. This type of thing was common procedure following such an incident.

The nurses had changed into their uniforms and were making their way via intensive care to the meeting room on the level above.

Davis and Watson filed into the room, nodding towards some of their colleagues before taking their seats near the back. There were around forty or so people in the room, including three sitting at the front table, about to take the meeting.

Davis and Watson already knew William Traynor, the hospital's head of administration, as one. Tall and anorexic looking, Traynor had become known by some of a golfing persuasion as 'the walking one iron'.

The man next to Traynor was probably early sixties, proudly wearing his policeman's uniform. He must have been an important man as the uniform looked as though it weighed a ton due to the amount of gold braid hanging all over it.

The third man had on a sharp suit, charcoal black, with a white shirt, red tie and shiny black shoes. He was early forties, well built. His face displayed very little emotion. He looked like a guy who couldn't comprehend the meaning of the words *no* and *can't*.

Traynor sat between the other two. He stood for a few seconds, waiting until there was complete silence before he began. 'Ladies and gentlemen, thank you for attending this meeting at such short notice. It is not our aim to keep you long this morning. We all have important jobs to do. As a result of yesterday's incident, there are some seriously injured people in desperate need of the level of care that this hospital, above all others, can provide.' Traynor felt no need to hold back on the politics. It was in their blood, these people. Any opportunity. He continued, 'As you might expect, it is our wish that we get these people out of intensive care and into the other wards as soon as possible to continue their recoveries.' Traynor turned to his left, indicating towards the man in uniform. 'Washington Police Department Commissioner, Brendan Mulroney, is going to say a few words.'

Mulroney nodded at Traynor as he stood. He also acknowledged a couple of reporters standing against the wall at the back of the room. 'Thank you. Firstly, I'd like to echo Mr. Traynor's words and also convey my best wishes and those of my colleagues at the Washington PD to the injured and their families. Secondly, I want you to know that this type of incident, these pre-meditated explosions such as the one that took place at Meridian Hill Park, discounting the events of 9/11 of course, are as rare in this city as hen's teeth. Nevertheless, we were lucky yesterday, you know that?' He paused for effect. 'It could have been a whole lot worse. I believe that what this cowardly act has done, or will do, will strengthen the resolve and kindle the fighting spirit of the people of this great city.' More unashamed politics. 'I would ask you, ask each and every one of you, to work together to act as guardians for each other. Because working together will ensure that evil can never win.

Thank you.' He sat back down, enjoying not only the head nodding his speech had provoked, but also dreaming of the juicy headlines sprawled all over the evening editions.

'It's the week before the elections. And with strong rumours all over City Hall about some MI6 rogue agent. Honey, it's like a dream come true.' Mulroney had told his wife that morning, in private.

But not everybody in the room was feeling the love. Shaking her head, Leona Davis turned to Rebecca Watson. 'Watched the Channel 7 version this morning. Same crap,' she whispered.

Traynor stood to thank the commissioner and introduce the man on his other side. 'Special agent, Lance McAlpine, from the FBI.'

McAlpine rose to speak. Deadpan. He chose not to acknowledge Traynor in any way, looking for all the world like he was aiming to go straight for the jugular. 'To date, we have suffered one fatality and fifteen more casualties, some serious. Others at the bureau might describe these stats as *light* given how many people were actually at the scene. I will let you judge that statement for yourselves. I have my own thoughts.' He made a strong fist with his right hand, bumping it gently against his leg as if it were a mechanism to suppress rage. As if he wanted to beat the living daylights out of the guys who bullied his little brother. He continued: 'Our enquiries are on-going, as you would expect, and still at a very early stage. Be warned, both the FBI and the CIA have people in and around the building and the immediate vicinity, going about their business. Some you will identify, most you won't. These people are highly skilled operatives and must be allowed to carry out their work. If there is any interference by any individual it will be severely dealt with.'

McAlpine's icy stare chilled the gathering.

Feeling decidedly uncomfortable, Traynor leapt to his feet.

'I'm not done.' McAlpine shot Traynor a *special* look. Traynor eased back down onto his chair like a scolded schoolboy. McAlpine continued: 'Some of the injured are unconscious. And, chances are, if they're going to come to, it'll be in your presence.' More stares. 'In the event that this does happen, you must say nothing to them about this incident. Make sure they are comfortable, yes, but that's it. Do whatever it is you people do best, but what I don't want from any one of you is speculation or opinions. Remember they may have information locked away in their heads that could be crucial to this case.' McAlpine dug into his pocket and pulled out an envelope containing a couple of hundred business cards. He held up one of the cards between two fingers. 'Somebody wakes up, call this number then report it to your superior.' He held up a warning finger. 'Try and be clever and you'll end up in jail, I promise you.'

'Sir, one of the patients in intensive care? There's a man guarding the door. I assume the guard is one of your men? And the patient? Is he the one that planted the bomb?' Not exactly the shy type, Nurse Davis almost had to shout to get her message to the front. She wanted to make sure everyone in the room heard her.

McAlpine's expression didn't change, though his face flushed with rage. 'No comment, and, no comment,' he hissed.

CHAPTER FIFTY-FOUR

'How's our handsome boy?' Rebecca Watson asked as she breezed in the room. Tucking strands of wispy blonde hair under her hat, she performed a quick check of her make-up. In case her handsome boy wakes up.

'Don't you mean *my* handsome boy? I saw him first.' Nurse Leona Davis trailed her fingers down Ryan Taylor's cheek before walking around the bed to monitor the equipment attached to him.

'Leona, I was kidding,' she lied, 'He's a killer.'

'We don't know that. He can't exactly speak up for himself right now, can he?'

'There's a gorilla on the door and everybody else has a name. Doesn't that tell you something? He is cute, though, I'll give you that.' Rebecca cocked her head at the stricken MI6 agent.

'Why am I always attracted to the bad guys?' Leona shook her head as she finished off her checks. 'My mom's right, why do I bother?'

'Because that's what we do,' Rebecca said, giving her friend a quick hug.

Medium height, flame-haired with temper to match, and pretty rather than beautiful, twenty-eight-year-old Leona Davis had had her fill of wasters and no-users. A couple of short-term relationships were preceded by another she'd constantly referred to as *the one*. Best friend Rebecca had been there for her each time to help pick up the pieces, especially when lazy layabout, *the one,* had decided to hit on her when Leona was otherwise engaged paying her last respects to her cancer-stricken father at the local hospice.

Rebecca had also gone out with her fair share of scumbags and sleaze balls over the years. A year younger than Leona, she was tall and slim, bordering on model-like. And she was the nicest friend anybody could ever ask for, or so Leona would tell her, usually when she'd had a little too much to drink.

'He's had a right bang on the back of the head and some bleeding from the ears. Apart from that, he's fine. Cuts and bruises, but no broken bones. And the scans have come back clear. He's going to have one almighty headache when he wakes up, though.' Leona dabbed Taylor's forehead with a flannel as she spoke.

'Looks like we'll find out who he is soon enough. You coming?' Rebecca looked at her watch as the minute hand on the clock on the room wall flicked to the top. 'It's 5 o'clock and there's a pizza out there with my name on it.'

'Oh, I put in for a little overtime. I'm on till nine.'

'You're kidding, right? You never do overtime,' Rebecca said, hands on hips.

'You know, with the holidays coming up and all that...'

'Wow, that is just nonsense, sister! You want to be here when he wakes up, don't you?'

'Is it that obvious?'

'Maybe a little,' Rebecca laughed. 'Ok, hon, now you be careful. And remember what that FBI agent said. We've to call in if he comes to.'

'Yeah, yeah. I know.'

'Though I suppose, with chuckles out here.' Rebecca nodded towards the big guy standing outside the door.

The best friends hugged again before Rebecca left, smiling at the guard as she slipped past.

No response.

CHAPTER FIFTY-FIVE

Relatives of the bomb victims had come and gone all day in the intensive care unit, every one of them running a gauntlet of tight security, TV cameras and newspaper reporters. Leona Davis watched the last of the reporters and their equipment cram into vans and head for the exits. She sighed with relief along with the rest of the hospital staff as they vanished into the darkness.

It was heading for nine o'clock and approaching the end of her shift and Leona was going through some final checks. The members of staff who had volunteered for overtime were beginning to drift away. This would leave, more or less, the usual complement to see the patients through the night. A few of the less seriously injured people from The Meridian Hill Park bombing had been moved to recovery wards. Only three of those involved still remained: a twelve-year-old schoolgirl, who had made good progress throughout the day and whom the doctors expected to move tomorrow; an elderly teacher, who actually came through the nightmare relatively unscathed, only to suffer a heart attack on the way to hospital; and, of course, not forgetting *John Doe*. And Leona certainly wasn't forgetting him, though not to the detriment of her quality of care for the others. She was too much of a professional to allow that to happen.

As ever, Leona had followed procedure, liaising with members of the nightshift staff leading up to the imminent changeover. Before she left, she wanted to take one final look at *John Doe*. She didn't exactly know how or why she was so fascinated with this particular patient. Part of her hoped that he would wake up on her watch, yes, but another part, the raw, vulnerable one, wished that he could stay on her ward forever. That way the expectancy, the wonderment would always remain. Disappointment could never be an issue.

Leona pulled up a chair and sat down at Taylor's bedside. Placing his hand in hers she clasped it tightly. Somehow, she sensed a strength flooding from him. She smiled a contented smile.

Fancying herself as quite the medium, she believed all sorts of special powers flowed through her as they had her mother and grandmother before her. Rebecca was sceptical to say the least and Leona knew this, but her friend was too much of a sweetheart to cruelly scoff at the notion.

'Please, wake up. Please...' Leona whispered.

The clock *clicked*: 9pm.

As she rose to leave, she felt Taylor's hand tighten on hers. She tried to pull away, but the sudden movement only re-affirmed his grip. His eyes sprang open, his gaze darting all over the room. His breathing ramping up like a runaway express train, he sat up and began tearing the wires and tubes from his chest and arms. The noise from emergency alarms and buzzers filled the room.

'Wh-where am I?' Taylor heaved between breaths.

'Just take it easy. You had an accident. You're in the University Hospital. I'll get help.' She made to get up.

'No! Stay! Please!'

'But-'

'Stay for a minute, please?' Taylor realised he was crushing her hand and let go, holding his hands up apologetically. 'I'm...I'm sorry. Give me a minute, will you? Please?'

'Would you like some water?' She raised her voice in a half-hearted effort to alert the guard. She couldn't say why but she was glad when he didn't react. Then the words of the FBI agent rang in her ears: *Don't try to be a hero. You might end up in jail.*

'Thank you,' Taylor said. His hands shook as he struggled to regain his senses.

Leona handed him a little cone-shaped paper cup full of water before switching off all of the bedside equipment. She stood halfway across the room, her attention nervously flitting between Taylor and the door.

'Please don't be afraid. I'm not going to hurt you,' he said as he rubbed his aching head with both hands.

'Do you remember what happened?'

'Everything. I remember everything,' he gasped.

'People are saying you're the bomber.'

'No, I was the target. Was anybody...was anybody?'

'Killed? Yes, one man.'

Taylor bit his lip. 'Parker. He took the full blast. I remember.'

He swung his legs off the bed, wobbled as he tried to get to his feet.

'Whoa, wait. What are you doing?' She raced across the room to steady him before he went down.

'I-we have to get out of here. It's not safe.'

'Look, it's fine,' she said, pointing at the door. 'There's a guard outside.'

'Listen to me.' Taylor grabbed her by the arm, leant in close. 'They're going to send somebody here to kill me. You have to get my clothes. We have to go now.'

'Wait a minute. You're not making sense. You can't go anywhere. You're not in a fit state. Let's get you back into bed.'

'Look, nurse. We're in danger. They'll kill us both. You have to help me.'

'And I'm saying it's fine,' she said.

'The guard?' Taylor said, staring into her eyes.

Leona walked to the door and swung it open. No guard. She walked out into the corridor. No other nurses or doctors either. She stepped back into the room and closed the door behind her.

'That's strange,' she said, scratching her head. 'I can't see anyone on the ward. It's empty.'

'Listen carefully. I work for MI6. I'm a British Secret Service agent. Don't ask me why this is happening because it's a long story and I don't have the time to tell it. All I know is a man, a killer, is on his way here and if we don't do something quick, both of us will end up dead.'

'Wh-what do you mean?' She spluttered the words. She didn't quite know why, but she was beginning to believe the stranger. 'What do we do? I mean, I've never-'

'Ok, what's your name?' Taylor asked, only just managing to fend off a huge wave of nausea as he got to his feet.

'Leona,' she said, her voice barely a whisper.

'Okay, Leona. Can you get me my clothes? I can't exactly go out like this, can I?'

She laughed nervously. Yanking open the bottom drawer of a bedside locker, she pulled out the clothes Taylor had been wearing and laid them on the bed, along with a white plastic bag that jangled when it was put down. Taylor snatched up the bag and rifled through it, quickly transferring some of the contents to his trouser pockets. He found his mobile phone right at the bottom and sighed with relief when he realised it was still operational. *Don't suppose there's a gun in here as well?* He stopped short of actually saying the words.

Taylor's brain went into overdrive as he got dressed. Time for an assessment. The situation wasn't ideal to say the least. Bad enough he was a sitting duck in a deserted hospital ward, still groggy, with an almighty headache, and unarmed, he also had the problem of having to protect an innocent member of the public. This young nurse was terrified, and understandably so. She had lapsed into a trance, her eyes glazing over. Of course, she had never before been placed in such a position, but he had to snap her out of it if he wanted to make sure she stayed alive.

First things first, get her to safety. 'Leona, is there a store cupboard on this floor, preferably one with a lock?'

Confused she shook her head.

'A store cupboard. Is there a cupboard on the ward?' He put his hands on her shoulders, shook her ever so gently.

She pointed to her left. 'It-it's two doors along.'

'Can you lock it from the inside?'

'I-I don't know. Yes, I think so.' She closed her eyes, as if to engage her brain.

'Good. Now I want you to listen carefully, okay?'

'Okay.'

'I want you to get in that cupboard, right now. I want you to lock it from the inside, sit on the floor and don't make a sound or move a muscle until I come back for you. You got that?'

'Y-yes, but what about you?'

'I'll be fine, I promise. You ready?' He guided her to the door.

She took a deep breath. 'I'm ready.'

'Good girl. Okay, let's do this.'

As he opened the door and stepped out into the corridor, the ward was plunged into total darkness. Taylor reacted quickly, pushing her back into the room. He whispered, 'Don't make a sound. Get down on the floor.'

He sat down next to her, their backs against the wall next to the door. 'Don't they have emergency generators to maintain the power?' he said.

'They would have kicked in by now. Something's wrong,' she whispered.

'The hospital must surely have emergency lighting?' As he said the words, a pale, luminous white light above the door came alive, bathing them in a gentle glow.

Taylor heard the slightest of noises out in the corridor. He grabbed Leona by the arm and pulled her across the room, forcing her under the bed in the nick of time before the door was crashed in.

Leona thrust her hands over her ears and screamed as loudly as her lungs would allow. The figure standing in the doorway squeezed off two rounds in the general direction of the source of the scream, one of the suppressed bullets thudding into the bed, the other clattering against the bed frame and spinning harmlessly across the room.

Taylor took his chance. He leapt from the shadows, kicking the gun from the man's hand. It flew into the corner as the two men squared up in the half-light.

Trading a succession of thrusts and punches, each one expertly parried, the men battled for their lives. Taylor opened up his adversary for a straight right, but missed. As he followed through with the punch, the man stepped to the side and smashed his forearm into the back of Taylor's head, hitting the spot where the blast had wounded him. Taylor fell to his knees, struggling to stay conscious. The man saw his chance and stooped to retrieve the gun. Taylor responded by reaching out an arm and tripping him. He crashed headlong into a medicine trolley as he fell, pulling it over on top of him. Leona screamed again as instruments from the trolley showered the floor close to her.

Taylor grabbed Leona by the arm and dragged her out from under the bed, roughly pulling her to her feet. As the dazed assassin scrabbled on the floor for a few seconds until he could work out exactly where his gun was, Taylor and Leona were already out into the corridor heading for the stairs.

'You have a car?' Taylor shouted as they hurried down to ground floor level.

'It's in the staff car park. This way.' She gulped out the words between choppy breaths. 'Oh no!'

'What?'

'I forgot the door was chained at night! It's alarmed as well! We can't get out!' She began to shake with fear, no doubt imagining the assassin coming down the stairs. 'We're trapped here!'

'We'll see about that!' Taylor snapped. He wrenched a fire extinguisher off the wall and, picking his spot, fired the bottom of it into the lower glass section of one of the double doors.

Then he kicked out all the shattered glass from the bottom section. 'After you,' he said.

Leona crouched to crawl through first, crying out as she tore her knee on a ragged piece of glass protruding from the frame. Taylor was poised to follow when he heard heavy footsteps gathering momentum in the stairwell. Still holding the extinguisher, he popped the pin. There was a sudden rush as he covered the floor tiles near the bottom stair with foam. Discarding the extinguisher, he bent to make his escape, a bullet ricocheting close to his head as he exited. Taylor turned around in time to see the assassin slip on the foam and hit the floor heavily. The roar of a car engine close to him made Taylor turn around again. Leona Davis was behind the wheel of her little yellow Volkswagen. He raced round to the passenger side and wrenched open the door. 'Go!' he shouted.

As they sped away from the hospital, Taylor turned to see the hired killer stride out into the car park, holster his gun, then turn and disappear into the gloom.

CHAPTER FIFTY-SIX

Crash!

Walter McMichaels was in the basement retreat of his house, doing the thing he seemed to be doing a lot of lately. *Drinking to forget.* This time he was drinking whisky to try and obliterate from his mind the earlier events of the day. That was until he felt compelled to launch glass and contents against the wall as a response to some unexpected news received by telephone call seconds earlier.

Ryan Taylor was really pissing him off.

'It's one bloody man we're talking about here!' McMichaels roared down the phone. 'Is this guy a bloody super-hero or something? Do we need to call in the National Guard?'

'This man, Taylor, he is a worthy adversary. And intelligent. He is able to *improvise* like no other I have ever faced.' Federici's voice was calm and soothing, like the personable foreign language teacher everyone remembers from their schooldays. The reality was far from that.

'Are you telling me you're not up to the job? You were supposed to be the best,' McMichaels barked.

'I am the best. This man has been extremely fortunate to survive this long. But his good fortune *will* run out.'

'I hope so, for your sake.'

'Please do not threaten me, sir. I do not appreciate this.'

'And I don't appreciate incompetence in any way, shape or form on my watch, which is why Carter Munroe was added to your list. Don't have me add your name to somebody else's.'

There was silence for a few seconds. Eventually: 'Your wife's name is Helen, but close friends and family know her as Nell. She likes to go to coffee mornings in town every Monday where she meets the same group of ladies. She has lunch with your daughter-in-law, Trudie, on Wednesdays at Nico's, an Italian restaurant in the centre of the city. Nell's car is black, a sporty looking BMW. She has had on-going problems with the a/c and is so fed up with this, that she has threatened to take the car back to the dealer, Hilltown Luxury Cars, to demand a refund. Your son, Thomas, is an accountant in the city, working for the firm Close, Handley and Miller. He has been sounded out about a partnership with the firm, though this has more to do with his connection to you, rather than any outstanding talent he possesses. His sons – your precious grandsons – are called Jack and William. They are aged ten and eight and named after past presidents, Kennedy and Clinton. The boys are special to you and share your love of baseball, especially the Washington Redskins. You try not to miss a match with your son and grandsons and can often be seen playing with them on weekends at your local park. Unfortunately for you, this park has an abundance of secluded spots and boasts many areas suitable for an assassination attempt.'

'Listen, you sonovabitch! You come anywhere near my family and I will see you destroyed. I will end you!' McMichaels, hardly believing what he was hearing, blasted back.

'I could have taken any one of them out in the blink of an eye. If you do decide to send another after me, I will kill him first, then every member of your family, one by one. Free of charge. You will never hear from me again. I will kill everyone closest to you. I will bury their bodies under the White House lawn and there is not a thing you can do about it. Now be assured, I will find Ryan Taylor and I will kill him and our business will be concluded.'

'I understand.' Walter McMichaels' voice had become small, the contemplation of the destruction of his entire family too much to bear.

'Then I shall proceed as arranged,' Federici said.

'The nurse, Leona Davis. I can easily find her address-'

'She and Taylor will never go there. That would be folly in the extreme. No, I have a plan to flush her out. She will go the same way as Taylor, agreed?'

'Agreed,' McMichaels said before ending the call. He leaned back in his easy chair and stared at the ceiling. His mind drifted back what seemed like a hundred years.

A product of Yale where he achieved top grades, the young Walter McMichaels became a successful criminal defence lawyer, courted by some of the finest law practices in DC. But politics was in his blood. He was a confirmed Democrat, had even played a significant role in getting Jimmy Carter elected to office. On the day of his wedding, McMichaels confided in his new wife, Nell, telling her of his special dreams and ambitions. Of what he was going to do to change the world, to make it a better place for everyone, regardless of colour, creed, religion. Of how he would always be his own man, prepared to do the right thing for the good of the nation.

Disgusted, he closed his eyes as tightly as he could, ashamed of the whore he'd become.

'Nonsense, pure nonsense,' he whispered, tears tracking down his cheeks.

CHAPTER FIFTY-SEVEN

'Oh my God! Oh my God, what am I doing? What the hell am I doing?' Leona Davis kept repeating the words. She perched on the edge of the bed, rocking back and forth. She clenched and unclenched everything. Muscles she didn't even know she had. Her gaze darted around the room, her whole body jumping at the slightest noise.

Taylor had booked them into a nondescript motel room in a nondescript part of town. Signed the register Mr. And Mrs. Harvey Moon. The yellow Volkswagen was tucked into a dimly lit corner of an overspill car park at the rear of the motel.

'Take it easy-'

'Don't you tell me to take it easy! That-that man back there. He-he wanted to kill me.'

'I did try to tell you that.'

'Don't! Don't even-' She waved a finger at Taylor. 'I-I have to go home. I-'

'You can't go home.'

'But I haven't done anything. They don't know who I am. I can go home and-and forget what happened. This has nothing to do with me. It's you they want. You're the bomber.'

'Believe me, they'll be waiting for you at home. And by now they'll know exactly who you are as well as everything about you. They'll know how much money you owe and to whom, the last time you flossed. They'll even know the name of your first rabbit. And, by the way, I'm not the bomber. I didn't plant that bomb.'

'Why should I believe you? I don't know you from Adam.' She covered her face with her hands. 'Why me? What have I done?'

'Nothing. You've done nothing.' Taylor sat down beside her. 'Look, I can fix this, I promise. But I need you to keep calm for now. At least until I can figure things out. Okay?'

She shrugged. 'What choice do I have? Wait, I-I could go to the police,' she said cautiously, visibly brightening at the thought.

'I considered it. You could tell them exactly what happened-'

'Then it's settled. I drive to the police station and tell them what happened. I'll explain to them how this man appeared and tried to kill us. They'll be cool with that, right?'

Taylor didn't answer. He was still poring over options.

'Right?' She pressed the issue.

'No, it's too dangerous.'

'But why?'

'I can't tell you why. It really is best you don't know. This is my problem. I didn't ask for it, but, hey-ho, it's mine. And too many innocent people have lost their lives along the way. I can't, I won't be responsible for another one.'

'But what can I do?' she pleaded.

'Tomorrow. I'll start fixing this tomorrow. You'll soon have your life back,' he said with a new-found confidence.

Leona Davis forced a smile onto her pretty face. She couldn't quite figure out why or how, but somehow, at that very moment, she felt safe with this man. If he was telling the truth about the bombing – and she now felt strongly that he was – then he hadn't asked for any of this. He hadn't asked to be blown up; he hadn't asked to be rushed unconscious to her unit in her hospital; he hadn't asked to lie that way for hours on end; he hadn't asked to be attacked and shot at by some maniac. And he certainly hadn't asked to assume responsibility for some woman he didn't even know. Her thought processes continued: This, stranger, had taken responsibility for her all right; he'd only just saved her life.

'How's the leg?' Taylor asked. They'd stopped beside a general store on the outskirts of the city where he'd bought a surprisingly well stocked first-aid box along with a bottle of mild disinfectant. He'd then rather expertly cleaned and dressed the nasty gash in her leg she'd suffered while escaping.

'It's fine. You'd get a job on my ward any time,' she said, warming.

'Get some rest,' he said, crossing the room and pulling a spare blanket from a shelf in the rickety wardrobe in the corner. 'I'll take the chair.'

He took off his shoes before squirming around and moulding himself into the chair, trying to get comfortable. Job done he tugged the blanket up to his neck.

Leona kicked off her shoes and shimmied up the bed until she reached the pillow. She lifted her legs and pulled the top cover across her. 'Y'know my mom would go ape,' she said.

'Oh yeah, why's that?'

'Bad enough I admit to her I spent the night in a seedy motel room with a strange man. It would be worse, much worse, if I couldn't even tell her his name.'

'It's Ryan.'

'Ryan. I like that.'

CHAPTER FIFTY-EIGHT

Leona Davis had been alone in the motel room since Ryan Taylor left more than an hour before.

She had slept surprisingly well, despite everything. Could be something to do with that feeling of security she'd lain down with.

She hadn't heard any of Taylor's morning routine, only stirring when he'd handed her a cup of strong coffee on his way out the door.

He'd been quite clear with his final instructions. *Stay in the room, keep the blinds closed and don't answer the door. I'll tell whoever's on the desk you've come down with the flu. That should keep the staff away, but just to be sure I'll tell them I'd appreciate it if you're left alone. I've hired the room for another night to keep them off your case. Don't call anybody and, I'll say it again, don't answer the door.*

When she'd asked him where he was going and how long he was going to be, he'd given her his stock reply: *Best you don't know.* Then he'd said, simply: *Trust me.*

Leona had drunk the coffee, showered and dressed. She'd fixed her hair as best she could and put on a little make-up to make her feel better. Or maybe she did it to look good for her new friend. She didn't know anything about him, aside from the fact he wasn't a bomber, or so he'd told her. She'd noticed he wasn't wearing a wedding ring, but then how many guys actually did these days?

She'd switched on the TV – he hadn't mentioned anything about that – and ended up channel hopping until landing on a re-run of a Jerry Springer show.

Some tattooed non-entity had cheated on his girlfriend with her best friend. He'd been caught red-handed, had denied everything saying he'd sleep-walked into the best friend's room, taken off his clothes and climbed into bed with her. Of course, the best friend had been so tired and confused and unaware of what was happening, the fact that they were both in bed, naked and wrapped around each other was neither here nor there. The obligatory lie-detector test had been taken and as Jerry delivers the inevitable verdict, all hell breaks loose on the set. The girlfriend's two barrel-cheated brothers launch an attack on the tattooed non-entity. Jerry's bodyguards are pulled in and are trying in vain to restore order. Jerry's staying well out of the way. The studio audience whoops and hollers and the show's technical people bleep out so many swear words, at one point it becomes one long continuous bleep. And in the middle of it all, the two friends are hugging each other and crying. The best friend is saying she's so, so sorry.

Then this guy in the audience pipes up and asks the tattooed non-entity why he hadn't simply told the truth. That he'd slipped on a bar of soap and accidentally penetrated her best friend. Problem solved! The place erupts with laughter before the credits roll. Leona loves this show.

She picked up the bedside clock. Taylor had been gone almost three hours, Jerry Springer is long gone, and the only thing mildly interesting to her on the TV is some British reality show about people visiting strangers' houses, eating their hosts' meals and cattily grading their culinary efforts. Leona would never admit to anyone she enjoyed such shows, except to herself. Or maybe her mother.

She picked up her handbag from the floor and began to rummage around, coming across a scrawled piece of paper, instantly recognising it. It had been there for some time. She flattened it out on her knee. Some months before, Leona Davis had suffered an early 'mid-life' crisis, declaring to her mother and best friend, Rebecca, her intention to drastically alter her outlook on life. She'd considered writing a *bucket list,* then had decided to postpone this until she was at least forty. *Plenty of time. Nothing as final as a bucket list right now. Maybe a few advisory points to get in some practice for the real thing.* She'd then scribbled down some random stuff on the piece of paper: ditch the reality shows, all of them; try and drink some tea; be courteous when driving; stay cool when you meet a cute guy; join a gym and run a marathon for charity (she'd scored this one out, then felt guilty and had rewritten it); have at least one technology free day a week; overcome my fear of water – swimming in the stuff, not washing - and spiders.

She shivered at the thought of the last entry before refolding the paper and returning it to her handbag. As she reached in, her hand brushed against her mobile phone. She pulled the phone out and stared at it. In a few logical, sequential movements, her thoughts skipped along from her ward at the hospital, to the likely gossip spreading like wildfire among the staff, growing arms and legs, to the official spin William Traynor would most probably throw in. From there it was on to Rebecca – *my God, Rebecca! What must she be thinking? Am I dead or alive? Oh, sweet Jesus, my mom! Rebecca will have definitely called her! They must be worried sick!*

Leona's thumb hovered over the telephone emoji as she contemplated ignoring Taylor's advice. One *quick call to my mom. One minute to tell her I'm okay. That's all. Then Rebecca. One minute each. What harm could that do?*

CHAPTER FIFTY-NINE

Taylor had spent the time since he left Leona Davis engaging a couple of local contacts from Leo Mannheim's list. He had firstly called a man known simply as Vic, arranging to pick up a small handgun with suppressor. Nothing fancy. A Beretta, or maybe a Walther. Taylor had no preference. To him a gun was a gun and the same principle applied. Point and squeeze. Nothing to it.

After what had happened with Peter Parker, Taylor was more than a little apprehensive about risking his life on the strength of another of Mannheim's contacts. But then, what choice did he have? He needed a gun and he couldn't exactly walk in off the street somewhere and buy one. Not without a licence. Not here. Maybe in a more gun-friendly state such as Oklahoma or Texas, but not here.

He'd agreed to meet Vic in the basement of Murphy's Bar in Scotia Street, on the east side. It wasn't ideal as he'd have to enter through a side door from a secluded lane. Wide open with too many windows, thought Taylor. No hiding places, and no cover. Sitting duck sprang to mind.

The pick-up itself had been simple: Vic, or whoever he was, was sitting at his kitchen table tucking into bacon and eggs. Taylor identified himself first off. Vic grunted, wiped his mouth with the back of a hand, reached across the table and slid over a brown package. Taylor thanked him, slipped the package in his pocket, and left. He'd then spent twenty minutes randomly flitting in and out of shops, bars and cafes until he was satisfied that he wasn't being followed. Eventually, he found a quiet place to inspect the goods. A Walther PPK, with a suppressor and a couple of spare clips. Not bad. Not bad at all.

Taylor's second phone call that morning was to code name: UPTON. He had totally missed a tiny addendum to Leo

Mannheim's list advising him to *look this guy up when you land.*

It had taken Taylor about five seconds of conversation to realise that Upton was the code name of ex-MI6 agent Ronnie Moran, a fanatical West Ham United supporter. Moran was now what is known in the trade as a *sleeper.* As the name suggests, sleepers are - on the surface at least - inactive for the most part, until they are prodded into life to assist an operative in difficulty. Ryan Taylor definitely qualified.

Sleepers fall into four broad categories; those that carry out such a role by choice, usually geeks or bookworms – people who would faint when somebody in their proximity suffers a paper cut; those 'retired' or 'moved aside' to accommodate a more capable agent; those not able to continue with their duties due to age or injury, or both; or those whose bottle had either crashed during a mission, or is being tipped to crash.

Taylor knew Ronnie Moran pretty well. He'd worked with him on a couple of low-key tours in the Middle East and had liked the Londoner from the get-go. He had never had cause to doubt his abilities. But then low-key forays into Saudi Arabia or Qatar were perhaps not reliable gauges to support such an observation.

Five years ago, Moran had possessed the required courage to parachute at night deep into Afghanistan along with another three agents - two of them SAS - for three months of special ops on a top-secret covert mission among the mountains and foxholes in the north of the country. Kitted out with thermal suits, night vision goggles and breathing apparatus, they'd jumped into blackness at 50,000 feet. They'd hurtled through thin air at speeds close to 500 miles per hour, the HALO (high altitude low opening) arrangement necessary to nullify the chances of being picked off by Taliban snipers on the way down.

Halfway through the mission, the team was pushing northwards towards the city of Mazar-i-Sharif when, on the outskirts, it encountered small pockets of resistance. Anyone involved in this type of warfare will tell you that he would rather stare into the whites of his enemies' eyes; that he hated facing the opportunists, the cowards who hide behind their human shields. Women, old people, children, these bastards will use every dirty trick in the book. Nothing was off limits for them.

Moran had accidentally killed an eleven-year-old girl, the same age as his own daughter, catching her in the crossfire. Despite reassurances from the rest of the team that the same could have happened to any one of them, Moran had taken the girl's death so badly that, for the rest of the mission, for all intents and purposes, he'd downed tools. A joiner or an electrician chucking it halfway through a job was bad enough. For one of the members of an elite fighting force deep inside enemy territory calling it quits had the potential for disaster.

Somehow the team managed to get out of Afghanistan in one piece, but it was to be the final tour for Ronnie Moran. Rightly condemned, although also sympathetically, by the other members of the team, Moran was faced with a *take it or leave it* option regarding his future. In all honesty he hadn't put up much of a fight, opting for a foreign posting where he could work on developing a skill-set markedly different to the one he'd originally been trained to use.

Taylor hadn't seen Ronnie Moran since the unfortunate incident and, as such, hadn't had the opportunity to commiserate with his friend. He didn't know Ronnie's family, aside from the fact he had a wife and daughter. And he didn't know what had happened to them after Afghanistan. Taylor was genuinely pleased to hear his friend's voice and was hopeful that he had found his true calling. He would soon find out.

Moran had suffered the nightmare scenario - every special operative's dread - aside from the loss of his own family. He'd killed a child. Accidentally, yes, but she was dead. Her family still had to bury her, grieve for her.

Taylor allowed his thoughts to flow naturally to his own family. He'd felt a whole lot better after he'd spoken to April. He was confident she and Jake wouldn't be harmed for as long as he drew breath. He would just have to make sure he continued to do so. Simple.

Taylor paused to check the address Ronnie Moran had given him. According to his notes he was standing right outside the building. He'd expected said building to be located down a side street and slap-bang in the middle of one of the seedier areas. It was. A street full of betting shops, bars, takeaway houses, pawn shops, run-down cafes with what looked like a hotel at one end. At least that's what Taylor assumed it was. It boasted a crumbling facade and dirty windows with cracked panes and flaky paintwork. The illuminated sign no longer illuminated and most of the letters were missing, ghostly imprints left behind: *S   HO   L.* Taylor filled in his own version: *SHIT HOTEL.* Then he noticed a little sign at ground level, hanging off some rusty railings: *SPUR HOTEL – Vacancies. I'll bet*, he mused.

The door he was looking for stood out as it was freshly painted dark green and was clearly marked with the number. It was set between a Chinese takeaway and a betting shop. An old punter was standing in front of the shop, leaning against the plate glass window, pulling hard on one of those home-made roll-up cigarettes. Taylor found himself staring at the man. Grey straggly hair and three-day-growth, the man wore a grubby shirt that looked as if it had been ironed once using a cold brick. His trousers had been good quality maybe ten years ago, but were now shiny and stained, and his shoes, which had never been quality at all, were dirty and scuffed to hell. He looked back at Taylor with the haunted expression of a man who couldn't sink any lower; a man who used to be somebody; a man whose life had been turned upside down and then all the way round again; the one man in the world looking forward to Armageddon.

Taylor stepped forward to push open the door when he was stopped in his tracks.

'Didn't your old mum ever tell you it's not polite to stare?' It was a familiar voice with a familiar accent.

Taylor turned back towards the old man, the only other person around. He smiled. 'Ronnie? Ronnie Moran?'

'The one and only.'

CHAPTER SIXTY

'Becks, I can't spend too long on the phone. It's too dangerous.' Leona blurted out the words as soon as her friend answered.

'Lee, are you drunk?' Rebecca sniggered.

'Drunk? What are you talking about? I was nearly killed.'

'What? Why would you say such a thing?'

'Because it's true, stupid.' Leona's short fuse was smouldering. She continued, 'What's wrong with you? What are they saying at the hospital?'

'That you called in sick this morning. A stomach bug, they said.' Rebecca hesitated as she tried to recall the conversation with the woman on the reception desk.

Leona froze. 'Oh my God,' she said quietly.

'What happened, Lee?'

'The guy. He woke up as I was getting ready to leave.'

'Traynor said he'd been moved to a prison hospital. The guard went with him.'

'That's BS, Becks. The guy's British. He's some kind of a spy or something.'

'Are you sure, Lee? The talk among the staff is that when he woke up, he confessed everything. He admitted he'd planted the bomb in Meridian Park.'

'But that's crap. He saved my life!'

'Crap, how?'

'Ok, listen. The lights went off in the ward. All of them. I've never seen that happen before. Then this-this other guy burst in the room. He had a gun and started shooting. There was a fight and then me and Ryan-'

'Ryan? This guy's Ryan now? What the hell, Lee, you're scaring me. If this is a joke, it's not funny in the slightest. I swear I'll never speak to you ever again.'

'Then why don't you go and check the room? It was all shot up. A trolley was knocked over.' Leona's eyes grew wide. 'Listen, go downstairs and look at the broken glass in the double doors leading to the car park.'

'Lee, I came in that door this morning.'

'And?'

'The doors are fine. They're fine. And I was in that room less than twenty minutes ago. There's already another patient in there. The room's okay, Lee.'

Leona pressed end call. She felt the overwhelming urge to throw up, eventually managing to stave it off. Switching the phone off, she dropped it into her bag like a hot potato.

CHAPTER SIXTY-ONE

'Coffee?' Moran said. He and Taylor were standing in the little galley-style kitchen that served the entire first floor.

'Black, one sugar,' Taylor said. He continued to stare at Ronnie Moran in full disguise as if he could not comprehend how much the man he remembered had changed. As if this old guy had swallowed Ronnie whole and only opened his mouth to let his voice come out. The Ronnie Moran in Taylor's head was mid-thirties with neatly trimmed sandy hair and the fresh complexion of a guy ten years younger. The Ronnie Moran standing next to him looked as if he had days rather than decades to live.

'It really is me, Ryan, you do know that?' Moran smirked as he spooned sugar into a cup and handed it to Taylor. Taylor shook his head. Smiled.

After coffee, Taylor followed Moran out of the kitchen and they made their way to the end of a long corridor. As they walked, Taylor began checking the doors. 'Lodgers?' he asked, counting ten doors, plus another facing them at the end of the corridor.

'Nope, only me. MI6 rent the whole floor. Most of these rooms are empty. I use a couple for storing stuff.'

'What kind of stuff?'

'See for yourself,' Moran said, pulling a key from his pocket and unlocking the eleventh door. He felt along the wall for the light switch and then stood back to allow Taylor to enter first. As Taylor pushed his way inside, the lights popped and fizzed a couple of times before kicking in, which was just as well as every window had been bricked up. The room was huge and square with unusually high ceilings, like a small factory unit, which, essentially, is what it was. The entire room, aside from the terracotta tiled floor, was painted the brightest white Taylor had ever seen. And, as well as the slightest whiff of paint, suggesting that decorating works had probably been carried out within the past two to three weeks, Taylor was aware of what he thought was a smell akin to burning rubber, or maybe plastic.

Along one side of the room sat a row of tables and only one chair – one of those padded, hydraulically-adjusting, swivel types on wheels that Taylor guessed Moran used to quickly roll from one area to the next. On each table sat three dummy heads on metal stands. The dummy heads – eighteen in all – were draped in wigs and toupees of all colours and types.

Taylor walked over to the nearest table to take a closer look. Pieces of false skin – prosthetics, rubber, silicon – he had no idea which, were neatly positioned side-by-side in strips on one of the table tops. They looked like tiny, miserable rashers of thinly cut bacon from a discount store. Another table was laid out in a collection of beards of all types, including a glass display case full of false moustaches. 'Where did you get all this stuff, Ronnie?' Taylor said.

'I make it myself. The beards, the moustaches, the skin.' Moran lifted a rasher of freshly made skin, pulling it and stretching it between his hands. He handed it to Taylor then jerked his thumb over his shoulder towards what appeared to be a fancy domestic slow cooker sitting on a sturdy looking stainless steel trolley similar to the type of gurney you might find on a hospital ward. A tiny orange light on the body of the slow cooker flashed in and out every few seconds. Taylor heard intermittent bubbling and popping in time with the flashing light.

'This is where we make these bad boys,' Moran said, pointing at the *skin* Taylor still held between his hands.

'We?'

'Me and Diane. She helps me out here sometimes. You never met Diane, did you?'

Taylor shook his head.

'My wife. Thank God for her and Jess-' Moran's voice suddenly cracked.

Perfect, thought Taylor. It would save him asking after Moran's wife and daughter. It was quite clear the business in Afghanistan with the girl being killed and the uncertainty with the job had not done any lasting damage on the home front.

'I'm glad things are working out for you, pal.' Taylor meant what he said. 'There's only one thing, though.'

'What's that?'

'Going to take off that bloody make-up? Every time I look at you, I think you're going to peg out!' Taylor laughed.

'And that's exactly the impression I wanted to give. Pretty effective, eh?' Moran said, at the same time peeling off layers of grey wrinkled skin from his neck, cheeks and under and above his eyes. Then he carefully removed the fake stubble before slipping off the straggly wig. His blond hair had been flattened during the process and he bent to look in a mirror as he fluffed it up, rubbing some life into it. Throwing clear water over his face from a little bowl sink, he dabbed himself dry with a couple of paper towels. 'Tell you what, it's a lot quicker coming off. I'll take the stuff off my hands later, if it's all right with you?' Moran beamed an infectious smile, almost identical to the picture of him Taylor carried around in his brain.

Taylor took a sip of coffee as he turned to survey the rest of the room. He pointed to an area in the far corner covered by four or five painters' dustsheets. 'What's over here, Ronnie?' he asked.

Moran wandered across the room and tugged at the corner of one of the sheets. 'Wait till you see these.' Moran began pulling sheets off like an excited kid tearing open Christmas presents as Taylor's jaw dropped nearer the ground with each unveiling. Before him were a number of metal racks, propping up an impressive collection of almost every type of uniform imaginable: freshly laundered Metropolitan PD uniforms in various sizes with assorted badges depending on rank, and complete with nightsticks, tear gas canisters, handcuffs, tasers and even genuine police-issue guns and holsters; DC fire-fighters' uniforms with boots, hi-viz jackets and trousers, helmets, breathing apparatuses; also paramedics' uniforms with carry-cases full of gear. There were examples of almost every occupation known to man: doctors, nurses, joiners, plumbers, electricians, construction workers; there were sharp suits for city bankers and high flyers and more casual garb to suit architects, draughtsmen and civil engineers; almost half of one rail was taken up by creations more likely to be worn by tramps, vagabonds and down-and-outs, much like the way Ronnie Moran was currently dressed.

'I'm impressed. But where did you get all this stuff?' Taylor asked.

'I'd like to say I created all of it, but no, it was provided.'

'These are all genuine uniforms, aren't they? Any idiot could see that.'

'Maybe so.'

'Oh, I get it. No names, no pack-drill.'

'Correct.'

Taylor grinned. 'No Red Indian headdress?'

'Eh?...Oh, right. Nice. Never heard that one before,' Moran said sarcastically, picking up on the *Village People* reference.

'A few female outfits in your collection as well, Ronnie? You got something to tell me?'

'Very funny. No, this lot's not just for my use. Other people use the *facility* as well.' Moran tapped the side of his nose.

'And Mannheim pays the rent.'

'He does.'

'You're telling me some other agencies of an American persuasion use this facility?'

'Maybe.'

'And these, agencies, pay for this service?'

'That's right.'

'How would you feel about some Scottish guy hiring someone of your expertise for a few hours?'

'I shouldn't think there would be a problem with that.'

A flicker of a smile crossed Ryan Taylor's face. Not for long.

'I'm in big trouble and I need your help, Ronnie,' he said.

'I know, Ryan. Word gets around fast over here,' Moran said, placing a comforting hand on Taylor's shoulder. 'Who's the mark?'

'Walter McMichaels.'

Moran's eyes grew wide. 'The president's chief of staff?'

'The very same.'

Moran shrugged. 'In for a penny.'

CHAPTER SIXTY-TWO

Federici closed the lid of his laptop and went over some final checks before leaving his hotel room. Not that such things were necessary. The best killers in the world were meticulous in their preparation. All of them. These guys never took unnecessary chances. That's why they landed the top gigs.

He crunched another couple of antacid tablets to fend off the dying embers of the indigestion he'd suffered through the night. There had been a few episodes over the past couple of weeks and he put it down to a combination of adrenalin rushes and the increased workload playing havoc with mealtimes. Maybe he'd also cut down on the spicy curries in the future.

Down on the street, he hailed a cab. Sliding across the back seat, he made a big play of eyeballing the driver via his mirror, pausing ten seconds for effect before barking the address.

The ploy worked, the driver deciding against uttering a single word during the journey, until he announced the fare when they got there. The killer peeled off one crisp Ulysses S. Grant and pressed him into the driver's hand. Big tip, no chit-chat. Everybody happy.

Federici was what behavioural experts would call a *sociopath*. Puerto Rican by birth, he had had the kind of upbringing one might have expected: an alcoholic father who would often beat his son black-and-blue for the thrill of it, and a whore-bitch mother, evil and rotten to the core. Federici had sought solace in orphanages and foster homes. He'd been abused socially, physically and sexually, teased and bullied to the point where he had never been able to call anybody friend. As such, he had hit his mid-teens hating everybody and everything. Naturally bright, he had turned his back on anything remotely academic in favour of his first love; the thing that gave him his buzz. He kept himself in good shape for killing people. But he had rules; no drugs, no drink, no smoking. And sex, the rougher the better. He would slap the whores around, picturing his mother's face in each of these women. One unfortunate victim suffered a broken jaw and nose and a fractured skull following one particularly frenzied attack. He still remembered laughing out loud at her pathetic pleadings for him to call an ambulance. He'd been tempted to strangle her to death in his car and be done with it, only relenting because he had been keen on continuing her suffering. He'd decided in the end to dump her at the side of the road before driving away.

Then he'd read about some bloody good Samaritan who'd stopped to help the woman. He was so angry he'd driven round the area for hours in his car in some futile attempt to find the 'bastard Samaritan.' Eventually, he'd taken his anger out on some stray cat, crushing its skull under his wheels before going home somewhat happier.

At the age of twenty-one, Federici had fulfilled his first mob contract, the killing of some young woman about to enter the state's witness protection programme. The job had called for stealth and secrecy. No problem. He'd cut the woman's throat from ear to ear after stabbing her guard in the eye when he answered the assassin's knock on their hotel room door.

Other types of contracts followed and it wasn't long before he found himself operating in the big leagues, offering his *specialist* services to so-called legitimate organisations such as the FBI, CIA and MI6. He'd even done some killing around Europe for Interpol.

One might be excused for thinking *for hired killer read sociopath*. There was no doubt that Blake Fontaine had also been a sociopath. He *was* a hired killer, but the difference between Federici and Fontaine and the likes of Taylor and Troy Williams was basic and clearly defined. All four of them killed people, good and bad, deserved or otherwise, that was true. It was a basic pre-requisite of the job. But while Ryan Taylor would do his utmost to isolate his target and minimise damage, a man like Federici wouldn't lose a second's sleep over taking out a dozen more people. Or a hundred. Or even a thousand.

Sociopaths are defined as lacking moral responsibility or social conscience. They are mostly loners, unable to forge relationships unless their partners are of similar ilk. Moors' murderers, Myra Hindley and Ian Brady, and evil husband-and-wife duo, Fred and Rose West, are prime examples. And it follows that the vast majority of serial killers are sociopaths. So how does one pigeon-hole the likes of Federici and Fontaine? Perhaps under the heading: *Legalised serial killers?*

Federici stood outside the door. The woman on the other side most probably didn't need to die. She had been drawn in to the mix through no fault of her own. That said, it was clear by the conversation he had earlier listened to that she knew nothing of note. But then, *he* knew nothing of note either. There was no need. He was simply there to do what came naturally. The hows or whys didn't concern him.

He tipped some of the contents of a bottle onto a handkerchief, returning the bottle to his pocket. Scratching the door with his nails, he stepped forward when he heard her come to see who or what was outside. Prior to the door opening, he looked along the street both ways. No witnesses. As she opened the door, he thrust the handkerchief over her mouth and nose and stepped past her. He slid his forearm across her neck from behind and gently pulled her inside, kicking the door closed.

She put up little resistance, grabbing weakly at his hand and arm as the chloroform kicked in. Dragging her into the bathroom, he laid her down on the floor next to the bath. He slipped the bath plug in and turned both taps. As the bath filled, he removed all of her clothes, folding them neatly and placing them on the toilet seat.

He turned off the taps and tested the temperature before lifting and gently easing her into the bath: too cold would probably wake her up, while too hot would mark her skin, a fact that wouldn't be lost on some smart-arsed pathologist.

He removed a new shaving blade from its dispenser and placed it between the thumb and forefinger of her right hand. Holding her hand tightly, he swept the blade across her left wrist, once, twice. Changed hands and repeated the process. The sudden sharp shock brought her round, but only briefly as he reached into his pocket for the chloroform-soaked handkerchief. In seconds she was unconscious again. He draped her arms over the sides of the bath to make sure the blood loss would be quick and significant. Waiting by the door, Federici watched as copious amounts of blood fizzed from the wounds, splattering the floor as her heartbeat cranked up to cope with the sudden evacuation.

He stood there watching, drinking in every single moment, until her body heaved and shuddered.

Then she was still.

CHAPTER SIXTY-THREE

It was gone seven by the time Taylor's cab swung into the motel car park. He paid the driver, closed the cab door and turned to face the room he and Leona had stayed in last night. The blinds at the front were still drawn as per his final instructions to her before leaving this morning, but the door was ajar, ever so slightly so, but ajar. He didn't need to be Einstein to figure out what had gone down. He would stake good money on it. He rattled out half a dozen likely outcomes in his brain in as many seconds. All of these outcomes did not end well for Leona Davis. But why the open door? A message for Taylor: *Wherever you go I know I can find you. I can outsmart you. There is no hiding place.*

As he neared the door, Taylor pulled his gun and flicked off the safety catch. He felt his stomach churn at the thought of what he might find inside.

His senses stretching to breaking point and beyond, Taylor picked up on a sudden noise behind him. He swivelled. A petite blonde woman around mid-forties, or so Taylor reckoned, stood at the other end of the barrel. Although he had never seen her before, he was pretty sure he knew who she was. Her eyes were wide, panic-stricken. Taylor relaxed his grip and lowered the weapon as slowly as he could. He managed to catch the woman with his free arm as she fainted.

He swore under his breath. It was all he needed. He lowered the woman to the ground, then took off his jacket to cover her. He felt her wrist for a few seconds to find a steady pulse. Her breathing was slow and rhythmic. She would be fine. Time to see what was waiting for him in the motel room. He pushed the door open using the gun barrel, pausing to steady himself, and stepped inside. A familiar, chemical-type smell met him inside the door. *Chloroform?*

The television was on, tuned to one of the many news channels, and some weather girl was telling the good people of Washington DC that they were going to get some sunshine tomorrow with a few outbreaks of rain. Taylor's gaze was drawn to the little rug under his feet. He stared at the manufacturer's tag, noticing it had been turned the other way. Returning the gun to the waistband of his trousers he hunkered down to take a closer look, lifting a corner of the rug. He squatted even lower, looking directly at an area where the light shone brightest against the wooden floor. Trailing three to four feet into the room, the light picked out a thin coating of dust and grit, the same as he'd found under the rug. He closed his eyes in anguish as his brain arrived at a logical conclusion. There had been a struggle, during which the rug was kicked across the room. Someone had put it back with the logo facing the wrong way. The killer was covering his tracks. Or rather, the killer-elect. Confirmation was surely only moments away.

Taylor recognised Leona's black work shoes. They had been placed neatly together, OCD-like, laces tucked inside, close to the television.

The bathroom door was closed. Taylor knew what was coming. The main event. As he moved towards the door he reached for his gun, the noise of splashing water coming from the bathroom providing the prompt. *Enough.* He lifted his foot and smashed the door in. There was a scream.

To his astonishment it was a man's body that was lying face down on the floor next to the bath. Taylor had seen many dead men before in his line of work, in many different situations. He knew instantly that this man was dead. He knew it by the way the body was positioned. He bent to feel for a pulse. The skin on the man's neck was cold. It had happened some time ago, that much was clear. Taylor couldn't care. Establishing time of death was a job for the city coroner. Taylor planned on being somewhere else when this exercise was taking place.

Leona Davis was shivering in the bath, naked and disorientated, as if she had just woken up. She had screamed loudly at the suddenness of the door going in before eventually realising where she was and what she was. She thrust her left arm over the northern areas, right hand due south. Her eyes darted around the room as she blinked hard, trying to shake off the effects of the chloroform.

Taylor put his gun away and waved a large bath towel in front of her, at the same time diverting his eyes to protect whatever modesty she had left. Leona climbed shakily out of the cold water and eased into the towel, nudging all the way into his arms. She began to cry when she saw the body at her feet. It was clear to him by the look on her face that she had no idea what had taken place.

Taylor held the sobbing girl while he tried to figure out exactly what had gone down. He had worked out maybe ninety percent. He looked around the small bathroom as he tried to establish the remaining ten.

Leona's clothes had been neatly folded and placed on top of the toilet lid. There was a black holdall sitting against the wall, its drawstring pulled tightly closed. Taylor had no need to rush to open up the holdall. He knew the kind of stuff it contained, or rather he could make an educated guess: chloroform, gun, knife, gloves, gaffer tape, strangling wire, and other items too horrific to contemplate.

The entrance rug, the shoes, the neat pile of clothes, they all pointed to one thing, he mused. People who intend to commit suicide generally leave order and tidiness behind. They may vacuum and clean the house, remove their spectacles, turn off the TV, neatly fold any suicide note. He'd even heard of one woman sending her entire wardrobe to the dry cleaners before doing a Superman impression off the local suspension bridge. Taylor considered Leona Davis incapable of suicide. Which left the only other possibility: an act of deception.

So far so good, Taylor thought. But there was one vital component missing. The man had taken her by surprise, drugged her with chloroform and dragged her to the bathroom where he'd laid her on the floor. He'd then run the bath and, while it was filling, he'd gone back into the room and straightened the rug. Her shoes? Leona hadn't been wearing them when she'd answered the door. Taylor had remembered seeing them lying toe-to-toe under the TV when he'd left this morning. The man had placed the shoes together and tucked in the laces. Then he'd gone back into the bathroom, turned off the water, stripped Leona and folded her clothes. He'd put them on the toilet seat. He'd then lifted her into the bath. Then what? What was missing? No blade. No buckets of blood. Something had happened directly after he'd put her in the bath and directly before he'd been able to find a razor blade. Something major. Something serious enough to take his life. Taylor eased past the still stunned Leona and picked up the killer's holdall. The contents were more or less the same as he'd earlier envisaged. Among the other stuff was a small pack of razor blades. He returned the holdall to the floor and turned his attention back to the body. Dressed head-to-toe in black, the man looked muscular, lean and fit. A lot like the man who had attacked them back at the hospital. Taylor had fought hard for his and Leona's lives in the half-light. The identity of the attacker had been way down the list. Now it was at the top.

With the body heading into early rigor, Taylor struggled to turn it face-up. The man was maybe late twenties, early thirties. He had a neatly proportioned face with a strong jaw-line, black hair and mahogany eyes which were open, staring, glassy, the moment of his death frozen in time. His skin was pearl white, almost flawless. Was this man sadistic killer, Federici? Taylor had no way of knowing for certain. The only tenuous links he could think of were the man's dark hair and skin colouring in keeping with the killer's Latino name.

Taylor noticed an abrasion and slight swelling at the right temple, indicating that he had dropped like a stone, hitting his head on the floor. But there were no bullet holes, no blood. He checked the lips. They were grey-blue. He lifted the top lip at one side to examine the gums. Pale, barely pink. *If I didn't know better...*

'Heart attack.' The voice came from behind, startling him, interrupting his thought processes. Leona, half-way along the road to pulling her world together, had watched Taylor go through the same checks she had done herself many times before, in other situations.

'I'm no expert, but then *you* are. You okay?'

She was perched on the edge of the bath, her lips tightening over her mouth. 'I'm sorry,' was all she could say.

'For what?'

'I used my phone. Is that why he-?' She was unable to finish the sentence.

'They must have tracked the phone. I'll tell you one thing. You are the luckiest girl in the world. What odds would you get on a man of this age keeling over from a heart attack?'

'Is this the same man who attacked us at the hospital? Is it over?'

'Truth is, I don't know,' he said. Taylor knew it was far from over for him, but if he could make sure Leona and her family were taken care of...

'Damn!' He'd forgotten all about the woman out in the car park.

CHAPTER SIXTY-FOUR

Helen Davis stirred on hearing a familiar voice guide her back to the here and now. Her first instinct was to reach up and hug her daughter. Then tears from both women.

As Taylor watched, naturally thoughts of his own family came to the fore. He had no idea where they were, or even if they were dead or alive. He had to assume they were alive. In the cold light of day, it made sense. Why kill them and risk total retribution from a man backed into a corner with nothing to lose? A man who would do everything in his mortal power to exact terrible revenge, inflict hurt and misery on those responsible. Taylor thanked God for leverage. *Leverage*. It meant that as long as he stayed alive, they stayed alive.

Feeling better through some reenergised positivity - or whatever the books said it was - he afforded himself a rueful smile as he watched the two women celebrate their extraordinary slice of luck, although Helen, as yet, had no knowledge of how close to death her daughter had come. Taylor couldn't help but stare at the two of them. He was right. This woman *was* Leona's mother. Helen was a slightly chunkier, middle-aged version, but there was no doubt, her daughter was the image of her.

As they continued to embrace, Taylor noticed the mother stealing glances in his direction. He figured she would be looking for answers from him. And quickly. And why shouldn't she? Her precious daughter had been holed up with a strange man in a dingy motel for the best part of 24 hours. And her daughter wasn't exactly looking or feeling peachy on it. Helen Davis would at least want to know who this stranger was and why this was happening.

Of course, Taylor couldn't tell her too much. It was for her and her daughter's own good. But he would have to come across with something. Strike a balance. Enough to placate her, but not enough to get both of them killed. How he was going to explain the dead man on the bathroom floor of her daughter's motel room would be a tough one. He would figure it out as he went along.

'Stupid,' Taylor said, louder than he intended.

'What? Ryan, what is it?' Leona said. Taylor noticed how, as she spoke, she kept her body between him and her mother, indicating that she didn't fully trust him. Who could blame her?

'I need you to help me. Your mum will be fine for a minute. That's all it will take. Can you find me a couple of pens, preferably with black ink? And a piece of paper?'

'I have pens in my bag. I think my notebook is in there as well. Why?'

'Perfect,' he said, ignoring the *why* for now. 'Can you bring them through?' He motioned towards the bathroom.

Leona followed him in carrying the pens and notebook when a blinding flash made her jump. Then another.

'What are you doing?' she said.

Taylor was standing over the body, using his mobile phone as a camera. 'Something I should have done when I came in,' he said. 'I can email photographs of this guy to HQ. Maybe he'll come up on one of our databases.'

'And these are for fingerprints?'

'You're good,' he said, smiling. 'Quick on the uptake. With the systems they have now the techs can scan photographic images of fingerprints. Eh, would you mind?' He lifted up the man's arm. It cracked a little due to the rigor. 'Sorry.'

'It's fine, I've only come across it a couple of million times before.'

Taylor liked this girl. She had spirit. He liked spirit in a woman. Then he shrugged off the notion realising he was heading down the *April* path once again. First things first.

He watched as Leona unscrewed the body of a couple of pens before cracking the refill near the nib end. 'Hold his fingers up,' she said.

Squeezing the broken refills onto a little saucer, she dabbed a little of the ink across the tips of the man's thumb, forefinger and middle finger. She repeated the process with the second pen until all five fingertips were inked. Then she held the paper in her hand as Taylor rolled each fingertip across it one-by-one before repeating the process. The slightly more faded second prints would, in all probability, be the most successful as they tended to stand out better. When he had finished, Taylor let go of the man's hand. It would have been comical given a different situation as the arm stayed where it was, up in the air, as if he were calling a waiter or signalling at a bus to pull over. Leona pushed the arm back down.

Taylor examined the prints. 'Mmmm, not bad. I think these should do.' He placed the piece of paper on the floor and flashed off another half a dozen photographs. After he'd finished, he scrawled up the paper and thrust it in his pocket. 'Can you wipe the ink off his fingers? And get rid of these?' He indicated towards the pens and broken refills.

'Sure.'

'Thanks.'

Taylor spent five minutes tapping the screen of his mobile before hitting send. He imagined the information zipping across the pond to Leo Mannheim's unit in England. He slipped the mobile into his pocket.

'What now?' she said. 'Will someone else come for us?'

'If this is who I think it was they'll be waiting for him to call this in. He always worked alone.'

'By *this*, you mean...?'

Taylor ignored her question. 'We have to get away from here, soon. All of us. I suggest you go and break the news to your mum.'

After she'd left the room, Taylor rifled the dead man's pockets. His wallet contained some credit cards printed in various names, and around five hundred dollars in cash. No passports – they would most probably be in a safe back at the killer's hotel room. He pocketed the cash and tossed the wallet into the holdall. He turned the body back over the way it had been found, picked up the holdall and threw it on his shoulder.

The mobile phone in his pocket kicked off.

CHAPTER SIXTY-FIVE

'Hello,' Taylor said.

'Glad you're still with us, son. I was beginning to worry as I hadn't heard from you,' Leo Mannheim said.

'Thanks, sir. I take it you weren't told of the bomb?'

A short pause: 'The explosion in the park? You were involved in that?' Mannheim said.

'A bit too close for comfort.'

'But that's not Federici's style. Too public, too many people.'

'I think it was on orders from closer to home, sir. If you know what I mean.'

'Some bloody glory hunter, no doubt.' Mannheim spat out the words with venom.

'Aye, sir.'

'You're not damaged, are you?' Mannheim said.

Taylor smiled at the use of the word *damaged*. It was common among special forces. As if he were a luxury car or a speed boat or something.

'A little the worse for wear, but otherwise okay,' Taylor said. The more he spoke with Mannheim, the more he realised that his boss hadn't called in response to the email. Then he thought: a simple exercise like setting up a mobile phone to receive electronic data would be lost on somebody *old school*. 'Sir, you didn't get my email?'

'Email?'

'I sent it a few minutes ago. I thought you had called to respond.'

'Son, me and technology don't usually see eye-to-eye. I'll call you back.' He disappeared.

265

Taylor smirked. 'Tosser.'

As he stepped back into the next room, he heard another mobile jingle go off. It was Madonna's *Like a Virgin*. He arched an eyebrow at Leona. Her mother, now sitting up on the sofa, shook her head. 'May I?' Leona said, holding aloft the phone.

'No problem,' Taylor said.

'Hi, Lita. How are you?' Leona said. She put her hand over the mouthpiece, whispered to Taylor something about it being one of her friends.

Leona Davis didn't say another word for two minutes. During the call her expression changed a dozen times, none of them for the better. At the end she dropped the phone on the floor and slumped down on the sofa, curled up in her mother's arms, sobbing her heart out. Helen Davis turned to give Taylor the most venomous, hate-filled look he had ever seen.

'What's wrong, baby? Leona, what's the matter?' Helen said.

'It's Becky. She-she's dead,' Leona said between short, choppy breaths.

'What? But how?' Helen's face immediately turned ashen. She closed her eyes, tears trailing down her rosy cheeks.

Taylor knew how, and why. Suicide. Not. The same deal as was on the table for Leona Davis. The killer had used Rebecca and Leona's friendship to turn it into a suicide pact. Neat and tidy. No clues. He knew the detectives would invariably take the easy way out. It was human nature. Why burden an already overburdened workload?

'Grab your things,' Taylor said as he imagined the beating of the jungle drums regarding Rebecca's *suicide*. 'Both of you. We have to get going. Now.'

Helen fired more daggers in his direction as she helped her daughter to her feet. Taylor picked up Leona's bag and handed it to Helen. She snatched it from him, said nothing. He picked up his bag and the killer's holdall and led them to the door.

'Wait.' He put up his hand to stop them. 'Stay here for a minute. I need to get us some transport.'

He peered across the car park until his gaze settled on an old works pick-up truck in the corner. All of the other vehicles in the vicinity were either new or no more than a couple of years old at most. At least that was the impression Taylor was forming. Hotwiring was an art that was dying out fast, killed by constantly updated immobiliser systems. The old works pick-up was no palatial ride, but it was inconspicuous and would do just fine in the circumstances. Beggars couldn't be choosers.

Pulling up outside the door, Taylor leant across the seat and waved at the women to join him.

CHAPTER SIXTY-SIX

Taylor headed south-westerly, down Interstate 95 from Washington DC for an hour or so until he hit Fredericksburg. His knowledge of the American Civil War was limited to a couple of John Wayne films and an old documentary he'd seen as a boy, narrated by Charlton Heston or Henry Fonda or whoever. That said, Taylor did recognise the name, *Fredericksburg*, and he was delighted to spy a huge illuminated sign barely inside the city limits that lit up two or three lines about The Battle of Fredericksburg, which ran from December 11th to the 15th, 1862. The result was a famous victory for the confederate general, Robert E Lee. Taylor immediately thought of his late grandfather and how he used to entertain the family on special occasions with an uncanny rendition of the Al Jolson song.

Taylor hummed a few bars before glancing to his left. The two women were sitting next to him on the double seat, asleep in each other's arms. He was spending the quiet time over the last fifteen miles or so trying to work out some answers to Helen Davis' inevitable questions.

Taylor had felt his mobile vibrate in his pocket a couple of dozen times during the fifty-mile journey along Interstate 95. He knew it was Leo Mannheim but daren't risk answering while he was driving. With infra-red surveillance cameras sited all over the place in the US, Taylor was not prepared to take a chance on getting pulled over by the cops. Mannheim would need to cool his jets until Taylor got his passengers to safety.

Hilltop Falls Motel. The sign was not so well placed and dimly lit, and missing a couple of bulbs. The motel itself could barely be seen behind a row of tall trees. It would be easy to miss. So much so that Taylor almost missed it himself, swinging a right onto the off ramp at the last second. Perfect.

The women were tossed against each other and woke up with a start. Breathing hard, they dug their nails into the seat as they stared into the darkness.

'Sorry,' Taylor said.

'Where are we going, Ryan?' Leona asked. She could almost hear her mother's face squeak next to her as the skin around her mouth tightened, Leona guessed because she was being too familiar?

'Another motel room I'm afraid. I'm going to make sure you get settled in and then head back to the city,' Taylor said.

'Don't you think you've done enough already?' Helen shot back.

'Mom, this isn't Ryan's fault. He's trying to help us,' Leona said.

'And he's doing such a good job. Rebecca's dead, you almost joined her, and now we're all on the run from God-knows-who or what.'

'Look Mrs. Davis, I'm only trying to do the right thing here. I didn't ask for any of this. I'm sorry your friend is dead, Leona, but maybe she wouldn't be if you'd done as I asked this morning.' Taylor already had the words out there by the time he realised what he was saying.

Leona burst into tears. Helen pulled her in close.

'Oh bravo! Well done,' Helen said. 'Now it's *her* fault.'

Taylor crunched to a halt in front of the check-in and pulled up hard on the handbrake, the ratchet mechanism chattering like a one second burst of machine-gun fire. 'I'm sorry, I shouldn't have said that.' He leaned to the side to try and catch Leona's attention. 'Look, the people we're dealing with here. They're not normal. These people will kill you without thinking twice about it. Last night, they knew everything about you, Leona. Everything. They knew about your friendship with Rebecca. You couldn't have done anything to save her. It's not your fault. And I've been drawn into this. It's not my fault either. It's not anybody's fault. They have my family. I have a wife and son and they have them, both of them. Somewhere. I have no idea where they are, but I will find them. I have to.'

All three sat in silence, the women as if they were taking their time to digest the information, and Taylor because he felt embarrassed at spilling his guts in such a manner.

He reached into his pocket and drew out the five hundred dollars he'd taken from the dead man. He handed it to Helen Davis. She grunted something that sounded like a thank-you. 'You must stay here,' Taylor said. 'A day, two at most, I promise. I'm going up to DC now and I aim to sort your situation out by tomorrow afternoon, latest. There are one or two things I need you to do for me. No phones. No calling family or friends. No calling anybody. These people have the most sophisticated GPS tracking systems on the planet. All you have to do is switch on your phone and they'll find you. And you must stay here. Don't leave your room. I'll call you here, tomorrow night, on the motel phone.' He stopped to take a breath. He was satisfied with almost everything he'd said. He wanted to get across the danger factor more than anything else. Judging by the look on their faces, he had achieved that. And, he'd done so without giving them any real information. As ever, the less they knew, the better.

'I'll help you get settled in,' Taylor said, clicking open his door.

'Won't they be looking for three people?' Helen said.

'Yes, you're right. It'd be safer if the two of you checked in together without me.' He pulled the door close.

'Come on, Leona.' Helen pushed Leona towards the door. Leona glanced back at Taylor as she stepped out, opening the door wide for her mother. They walked arm-in-arm around the front of the pick-up, heading for the motel reception.

'Good luck,' Helen said to Taylor on the way past. She even managed to raise the semblance of a smile.

CHAPTER SIXTY-SEVEN

Taylor swung onto Interstate 95, heading back towards DC. On their way down to Fredericksburg, he'd noticed a little 24-hour diner off the main track on the other side of the road, about 5 miles out of the city. It was now gone 11pm. It had been a long day and he was starting to feel a little weary; good time for a couple of mugs of strong coffee.

As he took the exit for Wally's Diner, Taylor heard his mobile phone buzz again in his pocket. Crunching gravel, the pick-up laboured into a space in front of the diner. Taylor managed to catch the call before it hit message options.

'Hello, sir. Sorry I couldn't speak earlier,' he explained.

'No problem,' Mannheim said. 'I wanted to make sure you got the news personally.'

'Sir?'

'Our people did a rush job on the information you sent. The photos drew a blank. And we ran the prints through all the main databases, came up with nothing there either. Then it got interesting. Last week, one of the analysts was working on another case involving a middle-Eastern man on the run across France and Belgium. There was some talk about him being one of these bloody suicide bombers, y'know the type of bastard who'd appear at your shoulder, smile at you, tickle your kid's chin before he blows everybody to kingdom come? Anyway, as you'd expect, Interpol were taking charge of the investigation. Our man got friendly with some subordinate in the technical department in Lyon and he picked up a link and a codeword to a database that nobody in MI6 knew existed. He ran the prints. Lo and behold, he came back with a positive id. Puerto-Rican, Juan Pablo Martinez, aged 15, in Spain supposedly visiting a sick uncle, was done for assault with a baseball bat. He did some short time and then disappeared off the radar. Nothing special in that I know, but when you consider his mother's maiden name was-'

'Federici.' Taylor finished it for him.

'Indeed,' Mannheim said.

'Thanks, sir,' Taylor said. He felt like rolling down the window and shouting to the heavens. Instead, as always, he was considering his next move. At least he now had some breathing space. For how long remained to be seen.

'And that's not all,' Mannheim continued. 'You'll probably not believe this, but I heard a little whisper that this guy, Federici, died of a-'

'Heart attack,' Taylor cut in once again.

'You really must tell me how you do that, son,' Mannheim said.

'Sorry, sir. You could say I had a professional second opinion on it.'

'Eh?'

'Nothing, sir. Lucky guess, I suppose.'

Mannheim grunted. 'So where do you go from here?'

'Well sir, I think it's time for the main event.' Taylor hoped that his boss would be on his wavelength. He didn't want to come right out and say the name, Walter McMichaels.

Mannheim *was* on the same wavelength. 'Sounds like a plan. Let me know how we can help you.'

As soon as they'd ended the call, Taylor was again prodding the phone's screen. 'Ronnie? It's tomorrow. I'll be at yours for 8am.'

Ronnie Moran acknowledged and Taylor rang off.

He walked into Wally's Diner and ordered coffee to go. He planned on getting to bed no later than midnight. Tomorrow promised to be another big day. The time for really growing a pair had come. Taylor hoped he wasn't biting off more than he could chew. He would soon find out.

CHAPTER SIXTY-EIGHT

Taylor had slept surprisingly well given his itinerary for the rest of the day. He'd risen at 6am, eaten breakfast and gone over some final checks. The plan was starved of time, full of holes and extremely risky, much like his life during the past couple of weeks, but every hour, minute and second spent away from his family made his situation increasingly intolerable. Lately, he felt as if he were constantly swimming up to his neck in quick-drying cement, with two medicine balls tied around his ankles. And with Rebecca Watson already dead and Leona Davis' and her mother's existence at serious risk, he'd made up his mind it was time to take things to the next level.

At 7am he'd slipped a new clip into the Walther. Although he hadn't planned to actually use the weapon, he wouldn't hesitate if he didn't like what he was hearing, Chief of Staff to the President of the United States or not. Taylor was fast turning into that man who had nothing to lose. He wanted answers, and fast. He hoped to God that, face-to-face with Taylor and his Walther PPK, McMichaels would say all the right things. If not...

Taylor slipped the suppressor into his pocket. He would make a big play of ensuring McMichaels saw him screw the thing on to the end of the gun. McMichaels had to be convinced he intended to use it. And Taylor would use the plight of April and Jake to further galvanise him. To make it impossible for McMichaels to deny him. At least that was the plan. And that was the easy part. Getting up close and personal with Walter McMichaels would be much more difficult.

At 7.15am Taylor made a five-minute phone call to Leo Mannheim for a rush on some information vital to his plan.

By 7.30am he was nosing the pick-up towards some temporary gates set up outside a new office block complex close to Ronnie Moran's workshop. Half a dozen vans were already waiting in the compound and the gates were still locked. Taylor assumed by the nervous tapping of steering wheels and general feeling of unrest in the air, that one of the security guards hadn't shown up for work this morning. Taylor got out of the pick-up, shook his head and threw his hands in the air, slamming the door and stomping off in mock disgust.

At 8am Taylor met Ronnie Moran out in front of his workplace. The Londoner, this time out of disguise, was easily recognisable.

Upstairs in his kitchen, Moran set out two mugs on the worktop, spooning coffee into them. As he reached into the fridge for the milk, he flicked the switch of his kettle. As the kettle rumbled in the background, Moran pulled up a chair, sat and folded his arms.

Taylor leaned back against the worktop. He watched Moran's face run a gamut of emotions as he outlined the plan. At the end, Moran only had one question to ask. 'The gun? You're not actually going to use it, are you?'

'What, are you on drugs? Kill the second most powerful man in the world in his own back yard?' Taylor heard himself say the words. It was a surreal moment for him, as if he had stepped away from his body to say them. His training had prepared him well. The buzz-words, the phrases; prepare for the worst; predict; prioritise; engage; take action. And, if all else fails, take lives.

'Okay, let's do it,' Moran said, displaying a little too much bravado for Taylor's liking. Taylor tried to banish from his mind the reason Moran was kicked out of special ops and redeployed to Washington. He tried really hard, but it kept flashing back in there. Along with the questions were the inevitable doubts; what if Ronnie shuts down mid-way through? What if I'm left there high and dry, trousers down? What if-? Enough!

Taylor considered the flip side. Thought of the positives. He had received good vibes from Ronnie since they'd met again. He seemed energised and focused on his work. His family were with him and they meant everything to him. Taylor reckoned Moran would want to do right by them. There were wrongs being done to one of MI6's own and he would want to be there to help put them right. He would want to make his family proud of him. All of the above were great motivators.

And, he and Ronnie had the most important thing in their armoury; the thing that countless armies over the centuries had used as a most powerful tool. Often vastly outnumbered, unskilled and with inferior weaponry, these armies had used this tool to defy all odds to win the battle. They had the element of surprise.

CHAPTER SIXTY-NINE

'Hello.' Thomas McMichaels answered the phone. Ronnie Moran thought he sounded a little pissed off already.

'Mr. McMichaels?' Moran said.

'Yeah, eh, look, if you're calling to try and sell me something, we don't need anything-'

'Oh no, sir. My name is McGruther and I work for Global Communications.'

'Our phone system is fine, thanks-'

'You misunderstand me, sir. All I was going to say is that we've discovered an intermittent fault within a branch of our telecommunications systems and our diagnosis is telling us it's coming from your property. It's affecting other properties in the area.'

'I'm not even with Global.'

'I realise that, sir, but we all use the same lines. Different companies charge different rentals.'

'Don't you think I know that?' McMichaels snapped. 'Anyway, the line sounds fine to me.'

'As I said, sir, it's intermittent.'

'Okay, so what do you want me to do?'

'If you can allow one of our engineers access to your home to check it out? Shouldn't take too long.'

'Aw what, really?' A frustrated McMichaels looked at his watch.

'Sir?' Moran said.

'It's just that, well I really need to go to work. My wife's already left for school with the kids. She's got one or two things she needs to do and won't be back till around twelve. Can it not wait till then?'

'Sorry, sir. I can't guarantee an engineer for the rest of the day. And the fault can reoccur at any moment.'

'You've got to be goddamned joking,' McMichaels whispered under his breath.

Moran tried not to laugh, although it was probably more to do with nerves than anything else. 'Sir?' he asked.

'Nothing. I'll call my office to tell them I'll be a little late. When can your guy get here?'

'We've someone about five minutes from you. The engineer's name is Furillo. Appreciate this, sir, and don't worry, we'll have the fault fixed before you know it. You have a nice day now.'

Five minutes later, a Global Communications van pulled up outside Thomas McMichaels' home. Ronnie Moran was wearing an Elvis-style wig, complete with sideburns you could land an aeroplane on. Moran figured that potential witnesses, even McMichaels himself, would only be able to tell the cops they saw someone who looks exactly like Elvis. Only the obsessive compulsive among us would be able to recall fine detail. Moran would take his chances. He checked his name badge was affixed properly, grabbed his bag of genuine tools, and headed up the path to the front door.

'Global. Name's Furillo,' Moran said, flashing his badge as soon as the door opened.

'This is a complete pain-in-the-ass, you know that?' McMichaels said, determined he was going to get his point across. 'I suppose you better come in.' He stepped away from the door. Moran wiped his boots on the mat and stepped inside. 'So where do you need to check?' McMichaels said.

'Right here,' Moran said. His gun was pointing at McMichaels' chest.

McMichaels turned white. He held his hands up to his face.

'Relax, you won't get hurt so long as you do exactly as I say.

Now sit down.' Moran waved the gun towards an easy chair facing away from the front window and any interested neighbours.

'Please, please don't hurt me! It's money, right? It has to be money. Let me open the safe for you. It's right behind that picture.' He pointed at an expensive looking, portrait-style painting that hung above an ornate fireplace. Moran didn't know a whole lot about art, but he knew he wasn't looking at only a couple of grand worth of painting. He thought for a second that maybe he was in the wrong job. How much easier and more profitable would a job on the dark side be? He'd only been in the door five seconds and already he knew where the safe was. He could rifle the contents in minutes and nab the painting as well, plus anything else that takes his fancy. Maybe a hundred thousand dollars, give or take, for five minutes. Not bad work if you can get it!

'Listen good,' Moran said. 'The next five minutes are going to be the most important five minutes of your life so far. Mess it up and it'll be a trip to the morgue. Now tell me you understand.'

'But-'

'Tell me you understand.'

'Yes, I understand.'

'That's better. Now here's what I want you to do. I want you to call daddy and tell him that young Jack had an accident this morning. He was bouncing on that big old trampoline you have in the back yard.' Moran motioned towards the trampoline which he could see from the window. 'He fell off and hit his head. He wasn't moving and you couldn't bring him round. You called the paramedics and they've taken him to the Children's National Medical Center, on Michigan Avenue. You know it?'

'It's close by,' McMichaels croaked.

'Good. Tell him you called mom and that she's going to meet you there. Tell him to hurry. You got that?'

Moran listened in as Thomas McMichaels carried out his instructions to the letter. McMichaels' voice wavered and wobbled all the way. Moran reckoned the authenticity of the call would not be called into question by Walter McMichaels. He concluded that the difference in reaction between somebody jamming a gun in your face, or fearing that your son had been badly hurt in an accident, would be infinitesimal.

Thomas McMichaels put down the phone. He cried out when he felt a sharp jab to the neck. He felt his legs go funny. Then he was unconscious.

Moran put the syringe back in his bag. He looked at his watch: 9.10am. *Should be good for a couple of hours.* He pulled out his mobile and punched in Taylor's number. Taylor answered on the first ring.

'You're on,' Moran said.

***

Taylor took a deep breath. He figured, taking into account reaction time and distance from the White House to the hospital, he had maybe half an hour tops before McMichaels Snr. arrived. Earlier, Taylor had donned one of Moran's authentic doctor's whites, complete with name badge and other accoutrements. He was conscious of the fact that McMichaels would have seen enough snaps of him to know what he looked like and hoped that Moran's alternative hair colouring and rushed make-up job would fool the politician long enough to allow Taylor to lure him away from the secret service men. This part of the plan worried Taylor more than any other, aside from what Ronnie Moran might or might not do. He could only hope that they would buy his story.

The element of surprise.

Taylor had spent the past half-hour wandering about the Children's National Medical Center, making sure plenty of people saw him at reception, along the corridors, in the elevator, ordering coffee in the canteen. The place *was* huge and Taylor reckoned staff would come and go there all the time. He wasn't worried about anybody asking nosey questions about who he was or where he worked previously. He figured he had enough in his armoury to easily field such questions.

Taylor's main concern was in case something bad went down in accident and emergency before Walter McMichaels arrived. He also prayed that nobody would ask him anything remotely medically related during the next half hour. The sum total of his knowledge in that area could probably be written on the back of the proverbial postage stamp.

Taylor, as Dr. Matt Hewson, decided on one more tour of the building. He looked at his watch again before he went inside. As Thomas McMichaels' house was only five minutes drive from the hospital, he expected Ronnie Moran to be close by. Moran's next involvement threatened to be the one real glitch in the plan. The success of the operation was dependent on such a fine line as the period between McMichaels being parted from his guard detail and Taylor and Moran getting him away from the hospital.

Twenty-five minutes after Taylor received Moran's phone call, a police motorcycle rider's siren and flashing blue lights blazed a trail along Michigan Avenue, heralding the arrival of the Chief of Staff's sleek black limousine.

'Bloody hell,' Taylor muttered. He was standing at the entrance to accident and emergency when he saw the entourage thundering his way. He could hardly believe his eyes. He hadn't considered such an entrance. 'Stupid!' he spat, realising that he should have. After all, this *was* the Chief of Staff. The man could move mountains on a whim.

Taylor would have to move fast, otherwise he could lose the situation. Hospital staff, orderlies and people waiting to be seen in A & E, all alerted by the commotion, were beginning to spill out onto the tarmac area in front. Taylor pushed his way through the crowd to the head of the welcoming committee. He watched the motorcycle cop flick off his lights and siren before riding on past with a wave for the limo driver. Taylor heaved a sigh as he watched the motorcycle head for the exit. A few moments before the limo pulled up, he turned to face the staff, hands in the air. 'Okay folks, show's over. Go back to your posts. I'll take it from here.' He tried to sound as calm as he could, moving towards them, herding them back inside. It seemed to work pretty well, most turning to obey, though a couple of persistent individuals managed to slip past, probably thinking some visiting celebrity was making a grand entrance to kiss some babies, shake a few hands. But when a middle-aged man in a grey suit stepped out into the sunshine, they immediately lost interest, turning to go back about their business.

McMichaels was tall, six three, and slightly stooped, but he was also a man who had clearly looked after himself. He was sporting a deep tan, as if he'd flown in from the Med that morning.

Taylor stepped forward to greet McMichaels. He was aware of the two secret service men, one at each side of him, sizing him up, watching for something out of the ordinary. Taylor had been in their position many times before. He knew exactly what they were thinking, how they were feeling. They would be watching his eyes, looking for signs of an imminent threat. Taylor knew these guys were the best in the business, simply because they had been assigned to protect this man. It would take real courage to carry this off.

Taylor stole a rapid glance at each agent before he spoke. Both wore Raybans the colour of night. He doubted they would remove the glasses anytime soon. It was part of the effect. Dark suits, white shirts and blue ties with black, patent leather shoes so shiny you could see your face in them, they stood at Walter McMichaels shoulder like a pair of solid oak statues. Muscles straining under their jackets, one was a little taller than the other, though both were over six feet.

'Gentlemen, welcome to the Children's National Medical Center. Mr. McMichaels, my name is Dr. Hewson and I'm looking after your grandson.' So far so good, thought Taylor. He thrust out his right hand, exchanging a firm handshake with Walter McMichaels.

'When can I see my grandson, doctor? How-how is he?' McMichaels said, visibly upset.

It was plain to see from McMichaels demeanour that the sudden news, however false, regarding his grandson had shaken him up. Taylor almost felt sorry for him, until he recalled his own plight.

'Jack received a nasty bang on the head, sir. Knocked him out cold. But he's awake at the moment and feeling very sorry for himself.' As he spoke, Taylor was aware of the agents' attention being drawn away from him. This was good as it could only mean they were buying his story.

McMichaels pulled in a long, slow breath. 'That's great news, doctor. Is my son here yet? Can I see Jack?' he said, calming.

'Yes to both questions, sir, of course you can. Mr. McMichaels is in with your grandson. I'll take you there now. Follow me.'

Walter McMichaels and the two men tracked Taylor into the waiting room. Taylor made to lead them all out towards the A & E ward before stopping abruptly at the exit door. 'Sorry guys, but you'll have to wait here,' he said.

Expressionless, the men stared at Taylor before turning their attention to McMichaels.

'It's fine, doctor,' said McMichaels. 'That okay with you guys?' he said, giving them their place.

The taller man grunted an acknowledgement.

'Lead the way, doctor,' McMichaels said.

Taylor walked briskly along A & E to the end of the corridor, pushing open a fire exit door which led to a set-down area at the rear of the hospital. He held the door open for McMichaels.

'Where are we going, doctor? Was that not A & E we've just come through?' McMichaels asked, a hint of concern in his voice.

'We've opened a new section at the other side of the lot, sir. It's much more comfortable there for young Jack.' Taylor saw from McMichaels' reaction that he was again buying the story.

The element of surprise.

Once they had passed through the exit door, Taylor spotted an ambulance parked in the bay close to them. He heard the driver's door open and saw Ronnie Moran as Elvis walk past him to open up the back doors as if he were about to deliver another poor soul to the hospital.

Taylor took a good look around as he walked on. There was no one to be seen. It was now or never.

He clamped his hand over McMichaels face and immobilised him with a knee to the side of the leg before easily wheeling him around and guiding him into the back of the ambulance. He jumped in beside the stricken McMichaels before Moran slammed the doors shut.

Moments later, Moran was behind the wheel, tearing along Michigan Avenue, lights and siren accompanying their escape.

CHAPTER SEVENTY

Taylor and McMichaels sat facing each other in the back of the ambulance as Moran gunned it into the suburbs of DC. As the traffic began to ease, he moved the vehicle into the slow lane and flicked off the emergency procedures. Taylor let go of his seat when he felt the speed subside. He eased back against the side of the ambulance. McMichaels stooped to rub his leg where Taylor had kneed him. Both men hadn't taken their eyes off one another, hadn't said one single word during the getaway.

'Sorry about the leg,' Taylor said.

'I'll live,' McMichaels said, straightening. 'There was no accident, was there?'

Taylor shook his head. 'Hurting kids? It's not my style,' he said.

Relieved his precious grandson was unharmed, McMichaels pulled in a long breath, then said, 'You're Taylor?'

'That's right.'

'And your friend?'

'Not important.'

'I'll say one thing. You got balls. They were two of my best men back there,' McMichaels said.

Taylor shrugged.

'Where are you taking me?' McMichaels asked.

Taylor continued to stare at him. Didn't answer. Things weren't going as well as he'd expected. He was unable to detect the slightest hint of fear, dread or even mild apprehension coming from Walter McMichaels. It didn't make sense. For a man with so much to lose. Or did he?

'I assume you're looking for answers from me?' McMichaels said, calmly.

Again, Taylor didn't respond.

'You're wasting your time,' McMichaels snapped.

They slowed almost to a halt, then took a slow careful right before trundling along what felt to Taylor like a minor road, maybe even a dirt track. They carried on at fifteen miles per hour for ten minutes or so, swinging left and right, until the vehicle took a steady left, then straightened as it came to a halt.

The ambulance lurched and bobbed as Moran climbed out and rattled the door close. Taylor heard Moran's footsteps on the ground outside as he moved round to the back doors.

The doors flew open and Taylor jumped out. He looked along the road they had come, saw nothing but tall trees spearing into the sky. A few yards to his right, behind some unkempt gorse bushes, he could hear the hustle of a little brook. Turning, he realised that they had travelled as far as they could, the road, such as it was, petering out not far from them, swallowed up by trees, weeds and bushes. On his left and backing against the trees, giving the impression it was preventing them from falling down, sat a rather run-down excuse for a wooden shack. It looked to Taylor as if it had been used as a stop-over point or a half-way house for generations of fishermen or hunters. Maybe a hundred years ago. Now, it looked as if a gentle breeze might well be enough to take it out.

Referencing his choice of premises, Taylor made a face at Moran before turning to help McMichaels down the steps at the back of the ambulance. Grabbing an arm each, they guided him up the wooden steps to the front door.

Moran produced a tiny key from his pocket and reached over to unlock the door. As he pulled it towards him, the strong retaining spring took him by surprise, the door slamming back against the wooden frame. The resulting cloud of dust kept them outside for a few seconds as they stepped back to allow the air to clear.

Inside the shack it was dank, dark and musty. Among the many dusty webs above their heads, spiders scurried for safety as the strangers entered their domain.

Everything inside was dark oak coloured, the only light filtering as best it could through two windows, one at each side of the door. Another door to the left was lying open, sunlight reflecting off a grimy wash hand basin and toilet. On the other side of the room yet another door was closed. Presumably, this led to a bedroom. Taylor felt no desire to investigate further.

Taylor indicated to McMichaels to sit on one of four chairs beside a large oblong table set dead centre of the room. 'Not exactly the Ritz, I know,' Taylor said, again making a face at Moran who shrugged. Taylor pulled up a second chair at the other side of the table facing the door. McMichaels didn't even flinch as, behind him, Moran creaked open the door to take a final look along the track. Satisfied they hadn't been followed Moran allowed the door to snap shut before nodding at Taylor. Still no reaction from McMichaels. Moran stayed on his feet, leaning back against the door.

Taylor stared at McMichaels for fully sixty seconds, searching for even the most miniscule of signs; he saw no darting looks, no repeated blinking, no pupil movement, no twitching, no laboured breathing. Nothing.

In a past life, back at Strathclyde Police HQ in Glasgow, Detective Sergeant Ryan Taylor had been a natural in this type of stressful, one-to-one situation, when rapid gathering of information, together with a signed statement was essential for securing a conviction; when the time for pressing a charge was drawing close; when the last thing the Glasgow detectives needed was some scumbag they knew was guilty, walking free to re-offend before the day was out.

His stock in the force rising, Taylor had been hankering after a career advancement when, out-of-the-blue, he was recommended by a superior officer - a guy with *connections* - for *special duties*.

Taylor took to these duties like a duck to water. He had loved being a policeman, but he absolutely adored his role in MI6. At least he had until recently.

As Taylor stared into Walter McMichaels' eyes, he felt suppressed anger and frustration bubble close to the surface. He had done nothing wrong. *Nothing*. And yet he was supposed to be guilty of committing unlawful murder, of taking bribes, of corruption. On top of that, he was running for his life from everything and everybody. He was endangering innocent people simply by being in the same room. His family had been taken and a close colleague and one of his best friends murdered. And Troy Williams' daughter, Maddie, had been on the list, a twelve-year-old. If Taylor hadn't flown to Tel Aviv, she would also be a statistic.

Under the table, Taylor balled both fists in readiness. He knew that McMichaels had all, or at least most of the answers. It was making him angrier by the second that this man was sitting there knowing why all of this was happening. Worse, he was *allowing* it to happen.

Taylor gritted his teeth, trying to calm down the furnace stoking up inside of him. He tried to imagine he was back in Glasgow, staying in control, keeping calm. Letting the suspect lose his temper, shoot *his* mouth off if he chooses.

All the time Walter McMichaels continued to stare at Taylor. As if daring him to do his worst. Bizarrely, Taylor's thoughts then turned to the game of poker. He considered himself to be a pretty useful player. As he continued to watch McMichaels, Taylor would stake his life on him being an expert poker player. Either that, or he was witnessing the finest acting performance he had ever seen.

'This won't do you any good, you know?' McMichaels was the first to speak.

Promising, thought Taylor. First round to the good guys.

'Tel-Aviv. A summit meeting in Geneva. The connection?' Taylor kept it smart, short, choppy. For now.

'What makes you think there is one?'

'Okay, you want to play it that way? Fine by me.' Taylor leant forward, elbows on the table. 'Maddie Williams is kidnapped. Those responsible blackmail Troy Williams, saying they will kill Maddie if he doesn't go to Israel and take out one of their top ministers. Why?'

'Why don't you tell me?' McMichaels held out his hands.

'After Liebermann is dead, and, by the way, Troy didn't kill him, all hell breaks loose. Troy, Maddie, Brian Ricker of MI6. All killed.' Taylor decided to include Maddie in his death list. He doubted that they were still looking for her, but wouldn't take the chance. It could only be of benefit. 'Then, before Ricker died, he figured out that the reason for all this might have been due to something that happened during the Geneva summit earlier in the year. It was a forgettable, low-key exercise for both MI6 and you guys. And Liebermann-'

Taylor stopped mid-sentence. As he'd been speaking, his attention had been stolen by Ronnie Moran's constant fidgeting. This was why he preferred to conduct such interviews on his own. Taylor pressed on, his icy stare firmly fixed on McMichaels. At last, he could sense uneasiness in those eyes. A couple of twitches, one or two extra blinks of the eyes, a sudden short breath.

Taylor's mind was racing. Liebermann had definitely attended the summit. Taylor's thoughts switched to Liebermann's deputy, Moshi Rabinowitz, back in Tel Aviv, and how he reckoned he was so close to spilling his guts before Federici's not so timely intervention.

Then a light flicked on in Taylor's brain. Not a forty-watt bulb sort of light, but a hundred million candle power search-light. Another part of the jigsaw had just slotted into place.

Liebermann had seen something during the summit. Something important. Something significant. Something to do with the US contingent. And something to do with Stephanie Renner. Taylor would bet anything that Liebermann had witnessed something important enough to compel him to resort to blackmail. And the way Rabinowitz had described his boss, blackmail was something of which he was comfortably capable.

The thought was taking Taylor into the unthinkable, taking him into unfamiliar territory. For the first time since he was a youngster, he was experiencing pure terror. Except he wasn't six-years-old and it wasn't because of next door's dog. And, as he continued to stare at McMichaels, he could almost taste raw fear as it transferred back and forth between them.

Beads of sweat were forming on McMichaels' forehead. His pupils were dilating. Darting glances. More sweating. Involuntary body movements.

Then Taylor began to feel sick. If he'd been alone, he would've been on his way to the toilet by that time. In the presence of Ronnie Moran and their illustrious guest he had to keep it together. He took a couple of slow breaths to steady the nerves, to concentrate on controlling the feeling of nausea. He tried to think more about confirming his thoughts and fears, rather than on contemplating how much of a game changer that confirmation would prove to be. If he was right, it was huge.

'Here's how I think it went down,' Taylor said, grasping his chance. 'Liebermann witnessed the murder of Stephanie Renner by one of the US delegates at the summit. After he got back to Israel, he decided he could make a lot of cash by blackmailing the killer, or friends of the killer.'

McMichaels' face became redder by the second. His hair, his shirt, they were running with sweat, dark patches mushrooming from his armpits and across his back. He looked as though he might pass out at any second.

'Pure and utter nonsense!' McMichaels could only blurt out. 'Way off the mark there!' His voice grew louder.

Taylor glanced up at Moran. It was plain to see he didn't like where this was going.

'Really? Then why don't you fill me in, tell me how it really went down?' As he finished the sentence, Taylor reached into his inside pocket and pulled out the Walther, making a big play of carefully screwing on the suppressor as planned. Done, he raised the weapon, training it on a spot in the middle of McMichaels' forehead. 'Who was it? Back in Geneva? Who killed the girl? And before you answer, consider this.' He paused, leaning in closer. 'I have nothing to lose,' he said as calmly as he could.

McMichaels swallowed. 'I can't tell you. You don't understand. They'll kill my family.'

Confirmation enough? Probably.

What happened next would certainly seal it. McMichaels muttered something like, *I'm sorry*, as he reached across the table. Before Taylor could react, McMichaels clamped a hand over his and squeezed. The bullet jerked McMichaels' head back as it ploughed a hole in his forehead, ripping its way out the other side, instantly spraying a shocked Ronnie Moran's shirt with a shower of blood.

Moran stood rooted to the spot, stunned, unable to speak.

Taylor dropped the gun on the table. He kicked his chair back and shot to his feet as the body slumped heavily to the floor.

CHAPTER SEVENTY-ONE

'Oh my God! What the hell happened, Ryan?' Moran held his chest, backed hard against the door. He kept looking down at his once light blue paramedic's shirt, most of it now stained deep red. Taylor didn't reply. He was too busy staring at the crumpled body on the floor.

Taylor had already slipped into reaction mode. Literally, within a minute of Walter McMichaels' body hitting that floor he had formed a plan in his mind to try and rescue the situation. Moran's reaction, on the other hand, was purely personal and merely served to vindicate MI6's decision to remove him from front line duties.

To further complicate things, as well as what to do about Ronnie Moran, there were a couple of side issues to be resolved, namely Leona and Helen Davis.

First things first. 'Ronnie, listen to me.' Taylor walked over to his colleague, purposely blocking his view of the horrific scene. He roughly grabbed Moran's shoulders, preventing him from edging to one side to continue staring at the corpse. Taylor shook hard. The move seemed to work, Moran's attention snapping back to the big Scot.

'Ronnie!' No response. Taylor continued: 'You were never here. You played no part in this. You haven't seen me since we were in the unit together. You got that?'

Nothing.

'Look, McMichaels' son was the only one who saw you. You were in disguise. He'll never remember you.'

'But what about you? What will you do?' Moran eventually gasped. His attention darted from Taylor to the body and then over his shoulder as far along the road as he could see.

'I'm going to sort things out here,' Taylor said. 'I want you to take these clothes off and change back into your civvies. Leave the clothes and your box of tricks in the ambulance for me. Okay?'

'Yeah, okay. What about...?' Moran's colour was returning to near normal as he pointed at the body.

'Leave it to me,' Taylor said.

'This is not good, Ryan.'

'Ya think?' Taylor even managed to force a smile. Not for long.

'It wasn't your fault. He did it. He pulled the trigger,' Moran said.

'Yeah, well, doesn't really matter now, does it?'

Moran disappeared into the ambulance, then reappeared dressed like a tourist, complete with light rain jacket, t-shirt, shorts, walking boots, skip cap and fake Nikon around his neck.

'I've left some stuff in the back for you. Nothing complicated,' Moran said. 'Ryan, listen. I wish I could-'

'It's fine, Ronnie,' Taylor cut in. 'Thanks, but you have to think of your family.'

'What did McMichaels mean when he said they would kill his family? Who was he talking about? What really happened in there? What would make somebody do something like that?' Moran's head was now clear enough to proffer a few probing questions.

Taylor shrugged. 'I wish I knew,' he lied.

Ronnie wished his friend good luck and they hugged briefly before Moran headed off on foot.

As Taylor watched Moran round the bend, he suddenly felt very alone.

Well, it's probably not every day one reaches the conclusion that the President of the United States is a murderer.

CHAPTER SEVENTY-TWO

Taylor stood on the steps to the shack for what seemed like an age. He couldn't shake an image he had formed in his mind; an image of the most powerful man in the world with his hands around Stephanie Renner's neck. Stephanie morphed into April and then to Jake...he shrugged off the notion.

The stakes had changed but the rules were the same as far as Taylor was concerned. As long as he stayed alive his family would stay alive. If that were to change, if he were to be captured or killed, it was game over. It was time for action, one move at a time.

He went into the back of the ambulance and rummaged around in drawers and cupboards, under seats. Opening his holdall, he fired in a selection of drugs and syringes, sticky tape, rubber gloves, bandages, swabs, lanolin wipes. He zipped up the holdall and placed it on the passenger seat. On the dashboard he found three pens, a tiny notebook, and a couple of disposable cigarette lighters – one full, the other half-full. He opened a little zip pocket on the holdall and dropped the items inside, all except one of the lighters which he stuck in his pocket.

Taylor examined the area behind the shack; it was nothing more than a tangled mass of weeds, bushes and thick undergrowth. Back inside the shack, he shook his head at the sight of McMichaels' body lying beside a growing pool of blood. He walked past the body into the toilet. A sad little toilet roll covered with spiders' webs was sitting on top of the cistern. A rickety looking cupboard, which no doubt used to be called a *vanity unit* about fifty years ago, hung above a filthy basin. Taylor opened the doors. A huge spider scurried into a dark corner. On the top shelf of the unit sat some old disposable razors, a toothbrush, a tube of toothpaste that was so out of date it had gone as hard as a brick, and a little box of dental floss. The bottom shelf was home to a rather grim looking, dark purple mouthwash.

Taylor swung the doors shut and decided to try his luck in the bedroom. A rusty head-board and bed-frame, on which sat an old mattress, had been pushed into the corner of the room. A little chest of drawers sat against the opposite wall. All of the drawers were empty, save for a family of spiders and various little bugs the likes of which Taylor had never seen before. He made to go back into the living area when he noticed something sticking out from under the bed.

Result! The thing turned out to be a large sheet with a moth-eaten double duvet sitting on top of it. He dragged both out into the living area and hauled the table and chairs to the back wall of the shack, well away from the centre of the room. Next, he laid out the duvet on the spot the table had sat and rolled McMichaels' body onto it. Taylor reached across to close the politician's eyes before covering the body with the sheet. He returned to the ambulance for the roll of sticky tape. Folding both sides of the duvet across the body, Taylor put his knee on top to hold it while he tore off a couple of short strips of tape with his teeth, eventually using them to keep the duvet in position.

Lifting the corpse's legs with one hand, he used the other to roll the tape around them half a dozen times. He repeated the process at chest height before smoothing down the end of the tape and shoving it in his pocket.

Taylor did a quick tour outside one final time before propping open the door and grabbing hold of an end of the duvet. He dragged the body down the steps and across the ground to the back of the ambulance. He swung open the doors and quickly heaved the body up the stairs and into the back. Then, he took off the doctor's uniform and stuffed it in the bag containing Moran's bloody outfit before changing back into the clothes he had been wearing prior to the operation. Slamming the doors closed, he once again walked around behind the shack. He broke off a dozen or so branches from a dead tree. The branches were thin, hard and brittle – perfect for what he had in mind.

Back inside the shack, Taylor ripped out a few pages of an old yellowed newspaper he'd found in the corner of one of the rooms. He rolled the pages tightly into conical shapes, twisting them and tying them into circular knots like little paper wreaths. Stacking the paper on the floor near the back of the shack, he snapped the tree branches into smaller lengths, placing them in a criss-cross formation on top. He reached into his pocket for the lighter, flicking at the tiny wheel with a thumb. In seconds the newspaper caught fire, taking with it a few of the dead branches as they crackled into life.

Back at the wheel of the ambulance, Taylor waited until he was certain the place was going to be totally destroyed before he started the engine. After a minute or so, rhythmic puffs began to escape under the door like Indian smoke signals. Through a window he watched as a bright orange glow rose steadily, quickly gaining energy.

Taylor had purposely set the fire at the back of the shack, giving him more time to get as far away as he could before somebody called the fire brigade. As the shack and everything inside it was bone dry, he reckoned he might only get a few extra minutes before the sirens went off. Flooring it towards the main road, Taylor glanced in his mirror in time to see long plumes of smoke curling around the trees and bushes and stretching for the sky.

He hoped he had done enough to ensure the incident would be put down to bored teenagers, rather than some guy setting a fire to obliterate damning prints and blood evidence. Time would tell.

CHAPTER SEVENTY-THREE

As soon as he hit the main drag, Taylor headed south-west down Interstate 95 and that familiar route towards Fredericksburg. He hadn't forgotten about Helen and Leona Davis, but had to take care of a couple of vitals before he could even consider calling them.

He figured he would make quicker progress and have a better chance of going undetected if he hit the ambulance's riot buttons; a sort of reverse psychology. Would a cop car stop a speeding ambulance? And wouldn't other road users just move aside? Sweeping into the fast lane he hit the switches, the soaring squeal of the siren deafening him, the twirling light bars illuminating the road ahead.

After thirty minutes, and having made good progress, Taylor switched off the siren and lights when his first mental checkpoint from last night come into view: *The Everglades Trailer Park*. The place sounded as if it should be in Florida rather than DC, he remembered thinking the previous evening.

Slowing to around fifty, Taylor waited until he passed the park entrance before flicking his indicator. A further two hundred yards up the road he slowed to take a careful right, edging the vehicle past his second mental checkpoint - a wooden sign made out of mock driftwood which read, in white painted capital letters: *FISHING PERMITS FOR SALE*. Taylor reckoned the sign hadn't been up long and had been purposely aged. The edges were clean and polished and the stake it was attached to freshly painted. Taylor prayed the body of water was deep enough to conceal a little more than just fish.

He guided the ambulance into a long straight drive thronged by a dozen giant oak trees on each side. The trees were set about fifteen feet apart and the space between each was taken up by tangled masses of gorse and berry bushes, their branches chopped short before they encroached on the drive. The drive itself was only about twelve feet wide and the oak tree branches below the height of twenty feet looked as though they had been recently lopped. The branches above this height had been allowed to fuse and twist together over the years, creating a tunnel effect. As Taylor reached the top, the row of trees came to an end and the drive opened out into a clearing of some two acres square, trees hemming it in on all sides. The grass in the clearing was newly mown short and stubbly and had been bleached almost white by the sun. Taylor began to piece things together. New sign, lopped branches, mown grass. Somebody was either renovating existing or building new.

In the far corner of the clearing, Taylor spotted a narrow pathway and guided the ambulance towards it. Jumping out, he stood at the mouth of the path for a couple of minutes, checking he wasn't being followed. He didn't plan on being away for too long, but locked the ambulance anyway. The last thing he needed were ramblers or tree-huggers sticking their noses in.

Taylor walked along the path for around fifty yards in almost total darkness, dense foliage all around him. Then he remembered he was carrying one of those little pocket/key-ring torches. He recalled Jake proudly handing his daddy the torch to use *for his work*. Taylor had made a big thing of hooking it on next to his keys. He doubted the thing even worked. It did, and surprisingly well.

He shone the torch above his head, picking out a number of bulkhead lights screwed to tree trunks with numerous lengths of conduit carrying the cables. Flashing the torch along the path in front of him, he noted the bushes and branches had been trimmed right back and any potentially dangerous surface roots dug up and disposed of. The developers had restored the path's surface using hardcore and chunks of turf. It became clear to Taylor that the area where he had left the ambulance was designed to be a car park. The fishermen would park up, grab their equipment, and take the short walk through the trees. But to what? The other end of the path would provide the answer.

The lake was as narrow on one side as the length of a football field, but stretched in the other direction as far as the eye could see. Like the clearing Taylor had just left, it was surrounded by trees. The water was still and clear. A dozen wooden jetties, each with an identical mooring point, stretched out into the lake. A huge modern building sat on the water's edge close to the jetties.

Taylor knew nothing about fishing, but he knew enough to assume the building could house dozens of small boats. A quick calculation of jetties times moorings made one hundred and forty-four. It was going to be one hell of a place. He reckoned the building hadn't been up that long as he caught a waft of newly cut wood and chemical treatments in the air. As with the driftwood sign, the builders had tried to age the construction, to give people the impression the facility had been there for some time.

Over to Taylor's right, close to the trees, were the beginnings of another building. Judging by the area covered by the foundations and the number of pallets of bricks and roof tiles stored nearby, this building was not going to be insignificant either. Taylor reckoned this had to be the socialising area. Meals and drinks for fishermen, their families and friends.

All of this held no interest for Taylor and what he needed to do. It was quickly back to the job at hand. The water was clean and clear, which was bad. The place was deserted, which was good. The owners had planned it well, catered for many people; bad. It looked like it wouldn't be open for business anytime soon; good.

Taylor started when he heard a car engine fire up not far from him.

Tracking the sound, he ran towards the edge of the trees on his right. As the car pulled away, he cut a right, arriving in seconds at another dirt track he hadn't been aware of. He ducked back into the undergrowth as the blue sedan trundled past. Taylor blew out his cheeks when he saw the young couple inside straightening their clothing, mortified at being disturbed during a spot of hanky-panky.

Taylor carried on along the track for a couple of hundred yards until it joined Interstate 95, insignificantly, not far past the trailer park. 'This will do just fine,' he whispered under his breath.

*****

The ambulance pulled back in off Interstate 95 and rolled carefully up the track towards the edge of the lake. Taylor reckoned the quick fix would be to submerge the ambulance in there. He stepped over to the edge of the water to try and gauge roughly how deep it was. The first ten feet or so looked to gradually step down. Beyond that, who knows? He had decided to leave the body inside. If he tried to submerge it independently, its natural gases would lift it to the surface within a couple of weeks. If he could get the ambulance out far enough, into deep enough water, it could be many more weeks before it was discovered, if at all. And even if somebody did snare it with their line, Taylor wouldn't need to worry about fingerprints. The water would take care of that problem.

Taylor left his holdall, Moran's case, and the bag containing the bloody clothes on the bank. Tipping the contents of the holdall on the ground, he used it to ferry back and forward piles of rocks which he proceeded to bed down into the sandy bank along with some lengths of timber he assumed were left over from the work on the jetties. Confident he had enough rocks to do the job, he bent to check the take off angle, tossed the holdall on the ground beside the other stuff, and jumped into the driver's seat.

Taylor knew he was only going to get one go at this. He put the vehicle into reverse, retreating as far as he could on stable ground. There had been some overnight rain and the track looked soft in places. Despite that, the vehicle managed around fifty or even sixty yards before the back wheels started to lose traction. He took one final look around before flooring the pedal. The vehicle gathered speed quickly as it was designed to do, bouncing a few times on the uneven surface. Taylor battled to stay on the track as he upped the speed. Steering the front wheels expertly towards the man-made ramps, he threw open the door, leapt out and rolled clear. The wheels hit the ramps hard, sending the vehicle into the air before it crashed down onto the glassy surface, yards out into the lake. He got to his feet and dusted himself down. He heard the engine splutter into silence, watched the ambulance gurgle and list to the left, then settle back to the right.

In seconds the vehicle was halfway submerged and dropping nicely. Taylor bent to pick up the items he had emptied from the holdall when the pressure of the water around the ambulance produced a sudden belch, and it stopped.

Taylor froze for a full ten seconds until, in one steady movement, it slipped below the surface, bubbling and thrashing as it vanished from sight. He blew out his cheeks in relief as he continued to watch air bubbles rise to the surface for a full two minutes before peace was restored. Job done he chucked the rest of his stuff back into the holdall. All except the mobile phone. He had kept it switched off since before the business with McMichaels. If he felt uncomfortable at carrying it then, it now felt abhorrent to have it anywhere near him. Taylor doubted he had another friend left in the whole wide world. He doubted whether MI6 would, or even could contact him after this.

Sending up a final prayer that the Vegas people who had his family were on the ball, he switched the mobile on and stuffed it in his pocket.

Pouring a little lighter fuel over the bloody clothes, he found a quiet corner out of sight and torched them. Then he slung the holdall over his shoulder and lifted Moran's case. In no time he was standing at the edge of Interstate 95, his intention, to thumb a lift to Wally's Diner.

If he was right about the Vegas people, he was about to do another sitting-duck impression.

CHAPTER SEVENTY-FOUR

Taylor waved goodbye to the truck driver who had given him a ride. Lifting the holdall, he walked up the short drive to Wally's Diner.

The diner was maybe a third full. He chose a booth next to the window where he could get a good look at everybody coming in.

He nodded at the fat man behind the counter – Wally, he assumed – and sat down as the waitress appeared beside him. Taylor had spotted her when he walked in. Young, slim and pretty, she wore her dark hair pulled back into a clasp, a scraping of make-up to colour her cheeks, and a sensible skirt – an inch below the knee – and flat, comfortable looking shoes. Her name badge said: *Lindsey*.

By contrast, the other two waitresses looked like they had crawled through mountains of foundation, blusher, hairspray and lipstick, and then jumped off wardrobes into skirts and uniforms that were at least four sizes too small. And they were chewing gum. Taylor was willing to bet any money *his* waitress didn't plan on joining Wally's company pension scheme.

'Sir, what would you like today?' Lindsey said, smiling sweetly.

'Coffee please, black,' Taylor said. 'And some scrambled egg and toast.' Bizarrely perhaps, he felt hungry.

She scribbled down the order. 'Can I suggest the pancakes and maple syrup for afters, sir? We have the most delicious on the planet right here at Wally's.' Another sweet smile accompanied the gentle sales pitch. Oh, she was good.

'Why not? Let's go for that.' He was sold. Better still, he happened to love pancakes. 'Been busy today?'

'It's been steady, sir. By the way, you can have as many coffee refills as you wish. We only charge for the first.' Another smile.

'Thank you, I might take you up on that. You been working here long?'

'A couple months, sir. I'm doing it for a little extra money. Y'know, till I go back to college.' Yet another smile.

Taylor pointed towards the owner. 'How's Wally treating you?'

'Lyndsey! Table six!' Wally barked as she prepared to answer.

She made a face that said everything. 'Excuse me, be right back with your order.'

Taylor did a lot of thinking as he wolfed into the food. The girl had been one hundred percent right about the pancakes. They were the best he had ever eaten. Staring out of the window, his gaze fixed on the drive. He reckoned it wouldn't be long until he saw some *developments*. The short time he had at his disposal before anything happened would give him the opportunity to go over things again. He had made some observations and assumptions concerning the involvement of all the major players in this whole sorry mess. He knew by peoples' actions and reactions whether those observations and assumptions were on the money. Moshi Rabinowitz's reaction to Liebermann's involvement, which turned out to be nothing more than simple blackmail. This had led to the question of what Liebermann was actually blackmailing anybody about. Walter McMichaels' reaction to fairly gentle and controlled questioning regarding said Liebermann and blackmail had, of course, been the most startling, pushing McMichaels towards the most violent suicide; violent enough to prevent him even considering options; and violent enough to surely confirm his president's guilt.

Taylor had spent most of the past twenty minutes watching Lindsey take all kinds of crap from all kinds of people. She seemed like a sweet kid who was only trying to get on in life and now here she was, having to endure foul-mouthed crap from behind the counter from a fat, greasy low-life, jealous jibes from lazy, no-nothing hussies disguised as so-called waitresses, and even more rude comments and gesticulations from customers - people who really ought to know better.

Taylor had never before sat for so long in such a place. He couldn't believe some of the things he was witnessing. And he couldn't get involved, much as he'd like to. Lyndsey kept smiling sweetly, no matter what nonsense was coming her way. It made him angry. He doubted he could take any more.

His attention was drawn to an SUV, black as night, with tinted windows. Taylor continued to stare at it as it pulled up into a bay only a few yards from where he was sitting. He could see the shady outline of two guys in the front seats. They looked big, really big. The driver's door swung open and a huge foot planted itself on the ground. Then the foot went back inside and the door was pulled shut. One of the rear doors then swung open and another big man stepped out.

The man appeared to have eyes only for Ryan Taylor. Taylor reckoned he was the main man. *The big guy had probably told the others to wait in the motor, told them to blast me to kingdom come if I so much as lift a hand to scratch my nose.*

Showtime.

CHAPTER SEVENTY-FIVE

Taylor glanced towards the SUV, then felt for the gun in his pocket as Maxie Royce walked up to his table. The gangster was wearing light shoes and slacks with a white t-shirt and navy blue, sleeveless jumper with big white diamonds on the front, as if he'd only just stepped off the eighteenth green.

'This free?' Royce said.

'Thought you'd never get here,' Taylor said. 'Knock yourself out.' He calmly sipped his coffee.

'Name's Max Royce. I assume you're Taylor?' Royce got straight to the point, as if he'd spent his life doing so.

'That's right.'

Lindsey appeared at Royce's shoulder like the good waitress she was.

'Can I get you something to drink before you order, sir?' she asked.

'Coffee, black, please,' Royce said, making eye contact with her. Smiling, he tapped his ample belly. 'Better make it just coffee, honey.'

'Hey! Table 4!' Wally shouted at her and she scuttled off.

'Who rattled his cage?' Royce said, jerking a thumb over his shoulder.

'I'll say this,' Taylor said, ignoring Royce's question. 'You don't exactly look like a Mafia boss.'

Royce threw his head back, laughed. 'I'm not even Italian. There is no hardcore Mafia anymore. Not here anyway. Now we have organised gangs. A few are Italian, some are Irish, one or two Russian. There's even a guy I know who's from Mozambique.'

'You have my wife and son?' Taylor's voice remained calm and even.

'I have them. They're safe. I give you my word on that and I'll take you to them right now.'

'How do I know you're not lying? That you've killed them already and you'll kill me as soon as I stand up?'

'I guess you'll just have to trust me. Seems to me like you don't have a whole lot of other options,' Royce said as Lindsey appeared with his coffee. He thanked her.

'What have you heard?' Taylor thought he might as well find out what was out there.

Royce looked over his shoulder, put his elbows on the table and leaned in. 'I know all about the stunt with McMichaels. You got balls, I'll say that.'

'Apparently so,' Taylor said. 'The story's out there already?'

'No,' Royce said. He leaned in even closer. 'I said I know about it. If you were a journo and called the White House to request an interview, you'd be told McMichaels was taking some time off.'

'They're not releasing the story?' Taylor said. 'But what about his family, his son?'

'You know how it is. Whatever the establishment wants the establishment gets. I take it he's well hidden?'

Taylor felt his face flush. 'You could say that. But why keep it under wraps?'

Royce eyeballed the rest of the people in the diner again in case somebody was getting interested. 'You mean you haven't worked it out yet? You must have turned the screw on McMichaels. What kind of secret service man are you?'

Taylor had asked the question to serve a purpose. It had served that purpose. He needed no further confirmation.

'What now?' Taylor said, holding out his hands.

'We fly to Vegas by private jet. Then, once you're reunited

with your family, I have a business proposition for you. One that suits your particular skill-set down to the ground. And, if it works, it just might solve your little predicament. It's entirely up to you. What do you say?'

'Sounds intriguing. By entirely up to me you mean we'd be free to go if I didn't take you up on your offer?' Taylor said.

'Absolutely, although I don't know how far you'd get.'

Taylor knew Royce was right. He couldn't possibly just take off with April and Jake. The authorities know Walter McMichaels had been kidnapped. They also had a good idea as to who had done the kidnapping. What they didn't know yet was that they were looking for a body. God knows what would happen when that part came out. And, either way, Royce knew he had Taylor over a barrel. On a positive note, if there could be such a thing, Royce had let slip that his business proposition might prove advantageous to Taylor if it succeeded. It was a no-brainer. 'Looks like you have yourself a deal, Mr. Royce,' he said.

'Then what are we waiting for?' Royce slid to the end of his bench seat, stood. He bent his head towards Taylor. 'What about our mutual friend, McMichaels?'

'Don't worry about him, he'll be fine,' Taylor lied.

'I get it. Your own little insurance policy?'

'In case you have a change of heart when we get out of here,' Taylor said.'

Royce laughed. 'Smart move. No need though, I gave you my word.'

'You'll forgive me if I say I've had it up to here with people and their promises,' Taylor said, raising a flat hand above his head.

'Fair enough. Then let's go,' Royce said.

Taylor peeled off a couple of notes, a twenty for the food and drink, which he placed under his coffee mug, and another fifty of MI6's money which he pressed into Lindsey's hand as she arrived to begin clearing the table.

Taylor leaned in towards Royce. 'Do me a favour. Give the girl a huge hug as if you mean it. Call her by her name. Tell her you'll see her soon,' Taylor said, nodding towards Lindsey.

'Eh?'

'Just do it, please.'

Royce wrapped his giant arms around the girl, lifting her off her feet. He kissed her on both cheeks. 'Lindsey, you take care. I'll be back to see you again in a little while,' he said. He put down the girl, kissed her again, this time on the forehead, and shrugged at Taylor on his way out.

The look on Lindsey's face was priceless as she tried to fathom out what had just happened. She opened her hand. The sight of the crisp fifty took her breath away. She looked at Ryan Taylor, then fat Wally.

Taylor walked over to the counter and beckoned Wally over. Wally grunted as he wiped his hands on his apron. Taylor whispered into his ear. Wally turned all colours before Taylor was finished with him. Taylor walked back to the booth to lift his gear, winking at a bemused Lindsey on his way out the door.

When he got outside Royce was standing by the SUV with the rear door open. 'Ok, what went down in there?' Royce asked.

'I told him he should be honoured as he'd just had the privilege of welcoming Don Christobelli - you - from Chicago into his diner. Told him if he didn't change his attitude towards your niece, Lindsey, you would come back with some friends, chop him up and feed his fat arse, piece by piece, to your dogs.'

'Hmmm,' Royce said. 'Might not be too far from the truth.'

'Before we leave for Vegas, I need to ask another favour,' Taylor said.

CHAPTER SEVENTY-SIX

On the way to Shannon Airport in Fredericksburg, where they were scheduled to pick up Royce's refuelled Lear Jet for the flight to Las Vegas, Taylor pled the case for Leona and Helen Davis getting back their lives. With Walter McMichaels temporarily out of the way, or so he believed, Royce agreed to hustle one of his contacts in Washington – no names - to drop any interest he might have in ordering contracts on the Davis women. To his credit Royce acted immediately, calling his man on the phone. The high-profile contact confirmed, following Federici's demise, that this was not on the agenda.

Taylor then called Leona to give her the good news; to tell them to go home and get on with their lives. She and her mother cried tears of joy and relief before Leona asked Taylor if that was it. Was it really all over? To allay her fears, he had lied through his teeth, telling her that he was travelling to the airport as they spoke, that he would be reunited with his family back home very soon.

With one important problem out of the way, Taylor did his best to turn his attention to what lay ahead of him in Nevada. He had never before been to Las Vegas, his knowledge of 'Sin City' restricted to the stuff he had seen on TV shows such as CSI and Robert Urich's Vegas.

The five-hour flight by Lear Jet, which would normally set a person back several thousand dollars, was extremely comfortable and enjoyable for Ryan Taylor, especially given what was waiting for him at the other end.

He had politely declined Maxie Royce's offer of a few relaxing hands of poker during the flight in favour of getting some much-needed shut-eye. His body ached to high heaven. He felt as if he had been awake for a week and had been forced to run a marathon over rocks in bare feet every single day of that week.

Taylor's immediate plan was to ditch thoughts of rogue presidents and chiefs of staff until he had confirmation that April and Jake were safe. Then he would tackle these problems. Exactly how he would do this would have to come to him. At the moment he had no idea. He found himself intrigued by Maxie Royce, and whatever it was he wanted done. He wondered what interest Royce had in the people in power at The White House. Yes, Royce had asked questions about Walter McMichaels, but Taylor hadn't felt pressure to confirm whether or not the chief of staff was safe and sound and tucked up in bed waiting to be released. Taylor got the impression Royce didn't give a toss as to whether McMichaels was alive or dead. It was Taylor's last thought before his exhausted body finally succumbed to sleep.

Taylor felt the gentle bump of the jet's tyres on the tarmac. Straightening his seat, he glanced at his watch: 10pm. He was so exhausted and disorientated that he had no idea if it was morning or night. A quick glance out of the window at some of the bright lights of Vegas confirmed that it was the latter.

'You looked as if you needed the rest.' The voice came from behind Taylor. Royce unclipped his seat belt and slid into the seat next to the Scot.

Taylor again stared at his watch: 'Four hours. Not bad for me.'

'I know what you mean. I'm not the best of flyers either,' Royce admitted. 'There'll be a car waiting on the tarmac. It'll take us to my estate on the outskirts of the city. Your family is there. You hungry?'

'Starved.'

'I'll get one of the guys to call ahead. Rosa, my housekeeper, will rustle something up for us. Steak okay?'

'Perfect, thanks.'

'No problem.'

The jet taxied to an exclusive corner of the airfield at the same time as a stretch limousine rolled in out of nowhere; the car looked to Taylor like the real deal, as long as a luxury coach and again black as coal, tinted windows all over, bulletproof glass, shinier than a still lake under a full moon, powerful looking guy at the wheel.

Taylor stood at the top of the steps for a few seconds before disembarking. He found himself staring out across the city at ten million neon lights. His gaze cut to Royce's two bodyguards who were sandwiching their boss as he hit the tarmac. The guys were good, that was as plain to Taylor as the nose on his face. They were aware of everything around them, prepared for anything. He was glad things had gone like clockwork back at Wally's Diner. He doubted he'd have survived had they gone wrong. On a positive note, he mused, if this is Royce's usual standard of babysitting, he needn't worry too much about his family. He was glad they were all on the same side. For now. But if that should change...

One of the guys opened a rear door for Taylor and he climbed in. He sat facing Royce and his bookends. The first thought Taylor formed as he looked around was something about being able to play a game of tennis in the car. There was a big, square marble table about a foot thick in the space between them; pearl white with grey flecks. Beautiful. Expensive. A big square in the middle had been expertly hewn out and this now housed a dozen bottles of booze; whisky, brandy, vodka, gin, Bacardi rum, Morgan's spiced, and a selection of fine wines.

Royce hit a button at his side and a secret compartment slid out from under his armrest. The front section of the compartment was refrigerated and contained a bucket of ice. The back section had enough room to hold a dozen glasses of all shapes and sizes.

'Drink?' Royce said.

'You don't do things by halves, do you?' Taylor said, selecting the bottle of vodka.

'You're learning. By the way, I have Martini as well,' Royce said, smirking. The blank expression of his guards didn't alter.

Taylor narrowed his eyes before eventually getting the joke. 'Shaken, not stirred,' he said, with a hint of Sean Connery thrown in.

CHAPTER SEVENTY-SEVEN

The journey from the airport to Royce's estate took only ten minutes and skirted the very edge of Las Vegas. Royce admitted it had been chosen as it was away from the razzamatazz. As Royce explained the set-up to him, Taylor reckoned the real reason was more to do with the location being easier to secure. High ground was a brilliant leveller. The mansion was perched right at the top of a hill. Any tall trees had been cut down and the entire estate was littered with search lights and roaming cameras, all attached to towering lampposts.

Royce even had a secret underground bunker. He explained to Taylor that the cops would do a shake-down of the place every six months or so. Royce had a mole in the police department who would tip him off any time this was going to happen. He'd then shift the hot stuff into the lead-lined bunker until the coast was clear. The arrangement worked a treat. And when Royce told Taylor the bunker was stocked with food and supplies, bedding and laid-on entertainment, was heated and ventilated, and could easily cater for human beings, Taylor felt another wave of contentment slide over him. Although the thought of April and Jake being held against their will was abhorrent, if Taylor could choose a place for it to happen, it would be right here, inside Royce's fortress.

The limousine cruised into the drive, its headlights picking out a tiny sentry box standing alone outside imposing wrought-iron gates. Taylor heard an exchange between the sentry, he assumed, and the driver. The sentry stepped out, walkie-talkie in hand. Taylor figured he was radioing another security guard somewhere on the hill. The sentry gave the driver the thumbs-up and the gates creaked open. Taylor shielded his eyes as he tried to look up at the house itself. The way the lights had been positioned made it impossible. It was a near perfect hideaway. As well as the lights and cameras, there were the gates and perimeter fence which were both electrified and painted with special anti-climb paint, as were the gutters and parts of the roof. The house had motion sensors, infra-red night vision equipment as standard, and an arsenal any SWAT team would be proud of. The only imperfection Taylor could identify was the obvious one, the human one. As with anything, it was vital to recruit the right staff. Staff that refused to be bought at any price.

The limousine crawled slowly up the twisting drive before pulling to a halt inside a roped-off section close to the house. Taylor got out and took his first real look at Maxie Royce's mansion, set over three levels and, like the man himself, super sized. In fact, everything seemed super sized; the roof tiles, the flashings and gutters, the stones used to construct the walls, the windows, and the flagstones that made up the many patio areas around a swimming pool which had been cut into a deep valley below the house. The pool itself looked as big as a Scottish loch. And there was even room for a summer house close to the pool.

'What do you think of the place?' Royce said, putting a friendly hand on Taylor's shoulder.

'As I said, you don't do things by halves. Actually, I was wondering why you didn't just land that old jet of yours around here somewhere. I'm sure you have a spot in the corner.' Taylor pointed into the distance, shaking his head.

'Not bad, is it?' Royce said. Taylor had stopped listening. He was scanning every dark corner, every doorway and every pathway around the house, as if expecting his wife and son to appear from the shadows.

'Follow me, there are a couple of people you might want to see,' Royce said. He led Taylor past the security checkpoint at the very brim of the hill, acknowledging the two guards sitting inside as they stared at banks of monitors, scrutinising every movement in and out of the estate.

Royce and Taylor walked down some steps towards the entrance to the summer house. Now Maxie Royce was a big guy, and his bodyguards were no midgets either, but the man standing guard by the entrance door eclipsed everybody. Taylor's senses were stretched to the limit when the man turned to face them as they arrived.

'Hi, boss. Good trip?' Red Summers said.

'Yeah, was okay, Red,' Royce said. 'Red Summers, this is Ryan Taylor.' The two men shook hands. 'How's our guests?' Royce continued.

'Yeah, fine boss. April was hungry earlier so I brought her a couple sandwiches and some coffee. Jake's been asleep since gone eight, so, yeah, we're all okay.'

Although Taylor had only just met Red, he couldn't say why, but he instantly liked him. Whether he detected something genuine in his voice, or maybe it was because of the way he used their names; it wasn't *the woman* or *the kid*, it was April and Jake, as if he'd struck up a friendship with them, despite the situation.

'It's all yours. I'll leave you to it. Come up to the house when you're ready to eat. Rosa will see to it you're looked after,' Royce said, before he and Summers headed out. Royce wheeled around as he hit the top step. 'Oh yeah, and when you all come up to the house, pretend you flew in tonight, will you? All of you. Vera doesn't know your family has been staying. If you tell her you're here on business, she'll understand. She's used to people dropping in and out.'

'No problem. Vera your wife?' Taylor said.

'Not exactly. I'll explain later, okay?'

Taylor thanked Royce before turning to face the door. The sudden feeling of utter elation was indescribable and it made him fuzzy headed. He drew in a long, slow breath as he turned the door handle.

CHAPTER SEVENTY-EIGHT

'Red, I meant to ask you earlier if you could have someone look at the toilet cistern. I had to fiddle around with it to get it to work.' April Taylor had her back to the door when she heard it click open behind her. She was leaning over the side of the cot, staring at her little sleeping boy. 'Red?'

'Now is that not a sight for sore eyes?' Taylor said.

April froze, then let out an almighty shriek. She galloped across the room, launching herself into his arms.

'Oh my God! Oh my God! Oh my God...' she repeated again and again as she hugged and kissed and hugged and kissed the life out of her husband. 'I can't believe it! You're here!'

Taylor held her head between his hands, as if he couldn't quite believe it either. He was sure he saw the merest hint of a tear form at the side of her eye before it was swept away. It was typical. Even now she was putting on a show for him, determined that he didn't see her drop her guard. He felt so proud of her. She was made of so much sterner stuff than he. Taylor kissed her tenderly on the lips. 'I was so scared I'd lost you, lost both of you,' he said, his voice wavering. 'Some tough guy, eh?' he sniffed.

'More like amazing,' she said. 'And I wouldn't let anyone say any different. I knew you would come through for us, Ryan.'

Taylor kissed her again and broke off to walk over to the cot. Once again, he felt tears well up as he bent to stroke his son's hair. As he stood there, both hands on the side of the cot, a more serious look cast on his face. 'April,' he said. 'When this is over, I'm out. I can't do it anymore. It's not fair on you, on him. I mean look at him. How could anybody want to hurt-' His throat felt like it was closing up. Not letting go of the cot, he eased down on to the chair next to it. April snuggled up to him and they hugged again.

***

Taylor walked into the bathroom and splashed some water on his face and around the back of his neck. April had boiled a kettle and made some coffee. She handed the mug to him as he walked back in. They sat together, linking arms. Immediately, he sensed she would want some answers and, as before with Leona Davis, he would need to box clever when he considered which ones.

'You look absolutely done in, Ryan,' she said, stroking his cheek.

'It's been a little fraught.' He forced a smile as he looked over the place. 'No need to ask how they've been treating you here.'

'It's been okay,' she said. 'The guys have been really nice. Red and Arnie, in particular. Jake really likes Red.'

'What about Maxie Royce?'

'He frightened me at first. Then, I don't know. It's funny, but he seemed to change. He's not nearly as bad as he likes to make out.'

'He has a proposition for me.'

'A proposition?'

Taylor shrugged. 'Didn't know if he'd mentioned anything to you?'

She shook her head. 'At first he was horrible. He said they wanted you to give yourself up to save us. I think he was saying that to scare me. Certainly worked, though I tried not to let on.'

Taylor smiled. 'I bet you did.' Then he frowned as he recalled that first telephone conversation with Royce. 'At first?'

'Yes, then he assured me that he wouldn't harm a hair on our heads. Or on yours. Gave me his word.'

'And he won't go back on his word,' Taylor whispered.

'Sorry?'

'No, it's just-, he mentioned that before. He says he never goes back on his word.'

'You're not saying you trust this man, Ryan, are you? After all, he is holding us here against our will.'

'Royce told me he wasn't the one who ordered the kidnapping. And we *are* still alive. All of us,' Taylor said.

'But we're still being held here.' April pointed at the door.

Taylor tilted his head. 'Have a look.'

April snatched the door open and poked her head outside.

'Well?' Taylor said.

She flew back into the room, closing the door. 'What are we waiting for? There are some blankets for Jake in that cupboard in the corner. I need to get my jacket.' She bolted into the bedroom.

'April! April, stop!' He grabbed her arm. 'Hold on a minute, please.'

She wrenched her arm free. 'What are you talking about? You said they were letting us go.'

'No, I said we were free to go.'

'And the difference is?' She stood, hands on hips.

'The difference is, we can't. Not yet anyway.'

'You're saying that this isn't over? And by how much is this not over, Ryan?' She had always been as sharp as a tack.

Taylor didn't answer. The look on his face was enough.

'Oh my God. They're still after us, aren't they? Who, Ryan? Why?' she said, gritting her teeth.

'Baby, this thing goes higher and wider than you could imagine. All I'm saying is that we'd be safer here, for the next few days at least. You know I won't let anything happen to you, to Jake.'

Taylor felt a wave of nausea pass over him as he uttered the words.

CHAPTER SEVENTY-NINE

The smell of grilled steak filled the air as Taylor and his wife walked into Royce's kitchen/diner with a still sleeping Jake safely ensconced in his buggy.

In keeping with everything Royce owned, the area was the size of a hotel conference room – a very big hotel conference room.

Royce and four of his guards were standing over by a huge picture window, heaped plates in hand, looking out across Las Vegas. Royce had described to Taylor some of the stunning views from this window on their way from the airfield. And with its six-inch thick, bulletproof glass, there had been no compromise on safety. Taylor reckoned the view was the most spectacular he had ever seen, the lights of the city stretching as far as the eye can see.

A Hispanic looking woman, Rosa, Taylor assumed, was scuttling back and forth carrying huge cuts of meat from an industrial looking piece of catering equipment to a chunky wooden dining table. The table was littered with every size of plate, every condiment, and there were two large bowls, one full of French fries and the other containing enough tossed salad to feed half the city.

Taylor aged Rosa at around sixty. Short and dumpy, her dark hair was streaked with grey and scraped back from her face into a short pony tail. Her ebony eyes twinkled under the piercing lights and she had a squeaky-clean look about her with her shiny cheeks and white apron.

'Senor, Senora, please, eat.' Rosa said with a huge welcoming smile as she banged a couple of steak laden plates down on the table.

'Gracias,' Taylor said. 'Fantastico.'

April said thank you. 'Show off,' she turned to whisper.

'Aw, he is so beautiful, no?' Rosa said a little too loudly for April's liking as she fawned over the child. Jake screwed up his face, grunted a couple of times, and continued sleeping.

'Thank you,' April said, smiling.

Taylor spread a few fries and some salad over the steaks, April put the brake on the buggy and they pulled up seats next to the table.

Taylor put up his hand to acknowledge Royce before getting in about his meal. Royce mouthed: *enjoy*. Taylor didn't know if it was because he was absolutely ravenous, but this was possibly the best steak he had ever tasted. Clearing his plate in no time, he kissed April on the forehead, grabbed a small glass of white wine from a silver tray, and wandered over to the window. Three of the guards, including Red Summers, had already joined them at the table. The fourth made his way over as well when he saw Taylor coming, nodding at the Scot on his way past.

'Looked as if you enjoyed that,' Royce said. 'Finest prime cuts in the US. All the way from Texas.'

Taylor nodded. 'Okay, Maxie,' he said. 'Let's cut to the chase. What's the deal?'

Royce got as far as opening his mouth when something over Taylor's shoulder caught his attention. 'Vera, over here. I want you to meet a business associate of mine.'

Taylor turned to see a tiny, silver-haired lady walking towards them. She was wearing soft slippers, a heavy towelling bathrobe, and a smile almost the same size as she was. 'I'm sorry,' Taylor said. 'I hope we didn't disturb you.'

She reached out a hand. Taylor was surprised by the strength of her handshake. 'No, don't be silly,' she said. 'I'm used to people around the house.' She made a face at Royce. 'Comes with the territory.'

'And you wouldn't have it any other way,' Royce said. 'Ryan, Vera, Vera, Ryan. Y'know, this little woman here saved my life, twice. She's one in a million.'

She tutted loudly, shook her head. 'Don't listen, I think he's had too much to drink already.' She tipped an imaginary glass towards her lips. Royce reached across and wrapped his arms around her. She was like a tiny fly caught by a giant spider, but still managed to wriggle free. 'Maxwell! How many times have I told you not to do that?' She pretended to hate the attention. 'You don't know your own strength.' She winked at Taylor.

'So what business are you in, Ryan?' she asked.

Before Taylor could respond, Royce chipped in for him. 'Renewables, Vera. Wave power. It's the future. Ryan's company is looking at submerging some turbines in San Francisco Bay. I'm thinking of investing.' Royce glanced at Taylor.

'Yes, I read somewhere that something like 400 billion gallons of water rush through the mouth of the bay every day,' she said. 'How exactly does it work, Ryan? Can you explain?'

'Ryan's company-' Royce began to speak.

'Is your name Ryan?' she said, cutting Royce dead. Taylor tried not to smirk. There he was, this successful billionaire businessman, one of the most powerful men in the US, and he'd just been backhanded into touch by Tweety Pie's granny.

She stared at Taylor, expecting an answer.

'Tidal power uses the ebb and flow of water. It's driven by the gravitational pull of the moon and sun.' Taylor paused. 'And the great thing about tidal power as opposed to wind power is that it's completely predictable. Given the green light, I believe we could supply electricity to most of San Francisco, right out of the bay.'

Vera continued to stare at Taylor for a few seconds. Eventually, another big smile. She winked at him from the side Royce couldn't see. 'Good luck with the project,' she said.

'See what I mean, one in a million,' Royce laughed.

'Now who do we have here?' Vera spied the sleeping boy and broke off to do some fawning, and to introduce herself to April.

'Do you think we got away with it?' Taylor said as he watched the women embrace.

'Nice try, but no cigar.' Royce shook his head. 'At least she likes you, I can tell. Where to God did you get that wave crap anyway?

'I read a lot,' Taylor shrugged. He leaned in towards Royce. 'Is it true? Did she save your life?'

'Damn straight. I don't know what I'd do without her.' Royce's smile vanished for a while. Then, as if realising he had lowered his guard, he brightened. 'Listen, about the other thing. Not here. Get a good sleep and we'll talk in the morning. You and me. No crap.'

'Fair enough,' Taylor said. He picked up a second glass of wine and watched on as Vera and April chatted away like long lost sisters.

CHAPTER EIGHTY

Taylor rose at 5am. He and April had gone to bed bang on midnight. Both had been so tired they'd gone out like a light. April was still asleep and, going on past performance, would remain so until at least 8am, unless the munchkin had other ideas.

After showering, Taylor crept through to the living quarters and unzipped a red and blue holdall one of the lackeys must have left there while he and April were in Royce's diner. Taylor had been far too tired to investigate before they went to bed. He assumed the holdall contained a few clean clothes, maybe some toiletries. He headed straight for the bulges in the side pockets, pulling out a couple of pairs of socks, a six pack of cotton boxers, an electric shaver and toothbrush, along with shaving foam and a big tube of toothpaste. Inside the main compartment he found three pairs of footwear: plain black shoes sporting the thickest leather soles he had ever seen, tan Timberlands and white Nike Air trainers, all UK size 9 - Taylor's size. Underneath the footwear was a three-pack of Moschino t-shirts, along with two cashmere pullovers and a couple of pairs of Dolce & Gabbana jeans. Draped over the back of a chair was a navy leather Burberry jerkin-style jacket. Taylor had seen a similar one advertised in the window of a boutique in Carnaby Street the last time he'd been in London. It was one of those shops with no tags, where if you had to ask the price of something it was assumed you couldn't afford it. He reckoned the jacket would set back somebody stupid enough to pay it around two grand. Shaking his head, he slipped the Burberry back over the chair and dusted down his old, but comfortable Gap jacket. Old habits...

6am: For the past half hour, Taylor had been sitting on a chair between April and Jake, sipping strong coffee and staring into space. He'd done his best to try and prepare properly for his meeting with Royce. *What's done is done. We can't turn the clock back. We must now look ahead.* Or similar.

He slipped quietly out the door and up the steps to the side of the pool. Nodding at one of the guards, he made his way back towards the kitchen/diner to see if there was anything on the go. It was early, but you never know. Bingo! He followed the aroma of freshly cooked bacon along the corridor like the Bisto kid. Pushing open the door into the diner, he wasn't surprised to see Maxie Royce already seated, tucking into bacon, eggs, tomatoes and lightly browned toast. At his side sat Red Summers. Red put down his knife and fork. Taylor watched him reach back with his right hand, feel the waistband of his trousers when he heard the door open. As soon as he saw Taylor, he smoothed down the back of his pullover and continued eating. Taylor could clearly see the tell-tale bulge under the pullover.

'Come over and join us,' Royce said. 'Rosa, bring more!'

The acknowledgement came, in Spanish, from the kitchen.

'You sleep well?' Royce said.

'Like a baby.'

'I take it they're still asleep?' Royce jerked his thumb in the direction of the door.

'Yep.'

Rosa scurried in with another heaped plate and laid it down in front of Taylor. He thanked her and began to eat.

They all sat in silence until Red had finished.

'Red, give us a few minutes, buddy, will you?' Royce said.

'Sure, Maxie. I'll go see if any of the guys are up yet,' Red said, smiling at Taylor as he rose.

Taylor and Royce sat in silence until they'd both finished breakfast, then Royce suggested they pick up their coffees and go to his office at the back of the diner, away from flapping ears. The office was regularly scrutinized for listening devices, though exactly where these devices would be sited was anyone's guess; the room was about the only small thing in Maxie Royce's life, with a desk and two chairs, no windows or air vents. It didn't even have a telephone. It was a room designed to shut out the world. Royce would spend more hours inside this eight-foot by eight-foot box than anywhere else, for an occasion such as this, or if he simply wanted somewhere to do some clear thinking.

The door clicked shut.

Taylor sat and waited for the play. Royce kicked it off. 'I heard you had help for the McMichaels thing?'

'He was a sleeper. Nobody important. A driver, nothing else.'

Royce put up his hands. 'I get it. You're protecting him. That's fine. You're a stand-up guy, I get that, too. Well, this isn't about him.'

'Then why mention it?' Taylor said.

Royce shook his head, smirking. 'Okay, let's start again. Some people I know have an interest in wanting you dead.'

'Go on.'

'The same people who decided to take your wife and son hostage.'

'Your, *associates*.'

'Barely that. As I said before, we're just glorified gangs with gang leaders. We all do our own thing.'

'Which is why I'm sitting here talking to you and not encased in a block of concrete in the middle of some bridge support,' Taylor said, trying to lighten the mood.

Royce threw his head back and laughed. 'I think you've been watching too many gangster movies. Though technically, yes, you're right. We hired a guy to kill you, that's true. And, yes, I was part of that, absolutely.'

'What's changed?' Taylor said.

Royce eased back in his chair. He continued to watch Taylor. Taylor knew he was about to find out exactly how far Maxie Royce was prepared to go with this. A man in Royce's position didn't get there by being flippant and careless. He got there by placing his complete trust in only a select few. Vera, Red, maybe another one or two of his men. That might be about it. Eventually Royce spoke: 'I've changed. Things that were important to me years ago. Money. Power. Well, maybe I have enough of both.' Royce leaned in closer to Taylor, hands clasped together. 'Lately, I've been thinking, all this, who am I going to leave it to? I have no children, no woman in my life. I'm not a faggot in case you were wondering. I've had women from time to time. Not the right women, if you know what I mean?'

Taylor nodded, unsure as to exactly where this was going.

Royce continued: 'It's just that, when I saw what you have. Y'know, the wife and kid?'

Taylor fidgeted uncomfortably. He was feeling a little irritated as he recalled Royce telling him last night that their meeting should contain no crap. Yet here he was, already neck deep in it.

Royce sensed the feeling. 'Okay Ryan,' he said. 'I'll get to the point.'

Taylor nodded, said nothing.

Royce went on to explain some of the finer details of his unfortunate upbringing, and how Vera had been involved, possibly as a way of highlighting how he had come from nothing. How he had reached that point in his life where he wanted more. He wanted to be a family man. Man's basic instincts. *To protect, nurture and provide.*

Royce continued: 'Now I don't want to get too deep into some of the business dealings we do here from day to day. All I'll say is I've done some things I'm not proud of. There is an organisation I'm part of called *The Firm*. Drugs, prostitution, other stuff. I have five of the biggest casinos in Vegas.' He studied the floor for a second, as if ashamed of his admission. Brightening, he continued: 'I also have businesses I am proud of that are whiter than white; construction, motor parts, real estate, restaurants. I even own a TV production company. I have good people running these companies, but Vera oversees everything. She likes to get involved. Sure, she knows about the other stuff. She's not stupid, right? She doesn't say anything about them, but I know she hates them. I see a look in her eyes sometimes, as if she despises me for it. It tears me up. She's been like a mother to me.'

'What do you need me for?' Taylor said. Now he had an inkling as to where this was going, but was still puzzled as to what he could do to help.

'I hire the best accountants in the business to look after my legitimate companies and, because I pay them a higher rate than anybody else, and on time, these guys leave nothing to chance. Because of them the staff, the bills, the suppliers and the taxes are paid on time. It costs me five million a year to save ten times that amount.'

'Maxie, you're talking, but you're not telling me anything,' Taylor said.

Royce took a long breath, said, 'I need to be clean, Ryan. I want to ditch the bad stuff.'

'Then do it. Get rid of it all.'

'It's not as simple as that. When you're in, you're in. You don't just pull out of one of these, *arrangements*. Each organisation relies on the input and support of all the others. The Firm needs unity and stability, and serious cash to make sure the drugs keep coming over the border from the likes of Colombia and Venezuela. The more drugs The Firm buys the better price we get. And the cheaper they are, the more money everybody makes. It's simple economics. The same principle applies to the casinos. The Firm needs serious cash to keep the gaming commission onside, as well as pay off the public spirited, upstanding members of the Las Vegas police force.

'Okay, I see that,' Taylor said. 'But why me, what can *I* do?'

Royce lowered his voice. 'I hate to say it, Ryan, but I'm looking at a dead man. Whether it's been pure skill or good fortune, or a combination of both that's kept you alive, I don't know. I *do* know that, whatever it is, it's going to run out. This, plan, if it works, it might just save your bacon.'

'I'm listening,' Taylor said. At the moment he didn't have a whole lot of other options.

Royce pulled his chair in even closer. 'The girl who was killed in Geneva? I'm assuming you found out how it happened. Through McMichaels?'

Taylor nodded. 'Something might have come out in conversation.'

'Yeah, well did you know it's happened before?'

'You mean, the president-?'

'Seems that our beloved President Wilson Travis has a weakness for hookers. Not so strange in itself when you look at our country's past history, though somehow I doubt if Kennedy personally choked women to death during his years in office.'

'How many?' Taylor said, open-mouthed.

'Four that we know of. Not murders per se. Usually sex, the rougher and kinkier the better, apparently. I guess this one went a little too far.'

'My God!' Taylor said a little louder than he intended. 'But how? Why does he get away with this? You can't tell me it's only because he's the president.'

Royce shrugged. 'Ordinarily, you would be right. But when you have the clout of the most powerful firm in the country behind you...'

'The president's on your payroll?' Taylor sounded astonished.

'Not exactly.'

'Then what exactly?'

'The Firm bankrolled his presidential election campaign to the tune of seven hundred million dollars.'

'Why him?'

'If you google Wilson Travis, Wikipedia will tell you he came from a prosperous Ohio family. That his father was a lawyer and his mother once worked as an aide to Gerald Ford. It's all lies. Wilson Travis died at birth. The man you know as the president grew up on the wrong side of the tracks as Thomas Handley. He got into all sorts of trouble when he was a kid, running numbers, stealing cars, pushing drugs. He was a punk, but he was also a brilliant student. He sailed through school and ended up winning a scholarship to Harvard. They wanted him so badly his place was funded entirely by endowment funds and federal and state grants. Immediately after he graduated, Handley disappeared off the radar to be reborn as Wilson Travis, complete with first class Harvard law degree, birth certificate and social security number.'

'Courtesy of The Firm?' Taylor said.

Royce sighed. 'Don Facchetti arranged it. Handley ran a few errands for the old man. The kid ran rings around everybody, made a real name for himself. Earned a few bucks in the process. Facchetti saw the raw potential, cleaned up the kid's background and identity, and, with his new found knowledge of the law, gently guided him into politics. Travis went on to become the youngest senator in history. At that time The Firm was having some problems getting gaming licences approved, as well as suffering losses nearly every day with shipments of drugs being seized and prostitution rings busted all over the place. Don Facchetti called the gang leaders together for a meeting and proposed that we all contribute to a fund, a war chest set up to take over the presidency of the United States. It was so easy in the end. Travis' sheer freshness and talent made mincemeat of his rival for the Democratic nomination. And the Republicans were in such disarray it was inevitable that Travis would become the next president. Walter McMichaels was already in place at the White House. We only needed his ass to collapse and we were ready to take on anybody. Didn't take much. A mix of cash and some well-placed threats on his family and he was onside.'

Taylor's heart bumped in some extra beats at the mention of McMichaels and his family. He had no intention of highlighting the fate of the chief of staff. He had nothing to gain by doing so, most probably get himself very dead. 'So, in the main The Firm always gets its way?' Taylor said, moving on. 'And Travis and McMichaels run the administration?'

'Not *in the main*, Ryan. *Always*,' Royce said, shrugging. 'The gaming commission sits in The Firm's pocket, people look the other way when the drug shipments arrive from South America, and the police don't go near the whore houses, unless they're booked in for an appointment.'

Taylor looked pensive. 'I can see why they would want to protect the gravy train at all costs.'

'There's so much money involved that lives don't matter anymore. Guilty as charged.' Royce held up his hands. 'I'm headed straight for Hell, I know that. But maybe I can balance the scales some before I get there.' He forced a smile.

'All right, I'm in. Let's go over this plan of yours,' Taylor said as if he really did have a choice. He extended a hand. They shook.

'Might as well tell you about the added complication,' Royce said.

Taylor's eyes narrowed.

'The original Don Guiseppe Facchetti who brokered the deal for The Firm died last year,' Royce said. 'The old man was real smart, always willing to listen to different viewpoints for the sake of the business. I got on really well with him. His son, Angelo, was cut from the same cloth as his old man, but he'd no love for the business. Angelo was a speed freak and got himself killed in a car accident ten years ago. When Guiseppe died, everything passed to Angelo's son, Carlo, Guiseppe's grandson.'

'And?'

'And he's a lunatic.'

'Fantastic,' Taylor said.

'Worse, I gave old Guiseppe my word I'd do my best to look out for Carlo. To make sure he wasn't harmed. And-'

'And you never go back on your word, right?' Taylor cut in.

'Right. But if the plan works, Carlo shouldn't suffer. At least not physically.'

CHAPTER EIGHTY-ONE

On his way back to the summer house, Taylor's heart skipped some more beats as he picked through the bones of the meeting with Royce while they were fresh in his mind.

Over a week ago, as his troubles in Tel Aviv were mounting, he had questioned his decision to go there. He recalled feeling as guilty as hell, especially with what had happened to his friend, Troy Williams. Now, on a purely personal level he was glad he had made that trip. Given this new information, Taylor was certain that if he hadn't gone to Israel, he, and most probably his family as well, would already be dead. Either McMichaels, through the CIA's network of assassins, or Royce's Firm would have made sure of it.

Taylor knew Royce's motives were legitimate. Absolutely. He was dirty and now wanted to be clean. Royce had said as much. If it were untrue, Taylor and his family would be dead, and President Travis and The Firm would be overseeing the appointment of a new chief of staff. The arrangement would carry on as before.

The way Taylor saw it, Maxie Royce's decision to get out of the rat-race was the one and only piece of good fortune to come his way. If Royce's plan worked, he would get what *he* wanted and it followed that Taylor's situation might not be too shabby either. The main losers would be the other organisations within The Firm, but with loose cannon Carlo Facchetti at the head of the second largest member after Royce, it worried Taylor that Facchetti might resort to all kinds of stuff to restore order.

Royce knew about the move on McMichaels, though not yet the aftermath. Taylor had to assume that Carlo Facchetti also knew. If Taylor's assumption was correct, how was Facchetti going to react? And if Carlo knew Maxie Royce was also harbouring the British secret service man everybody wanted to eliminate, as well as his family...

Taylor calmed himself by poring over the merits of fortress Royce, until he got to the *Achilles heel* - the staff. All the security systems in the world would make no difference. One key person on somebody else's payroll was all it would take for the house of cards to collapse.

Taylor walked through the door of the summer house. Jake was awake, standing up and grasping the bars in his cot. Beaming the biggest smile in the world for his daddy, the little boy reached up for a well overdue cuddle.

Next door, April turned off the shower and bent to squeeze the excess water from her hair. She heard familiar whoops and shrieks of laughter before excitedly throwing on a robe and sneaking over to the door she'd purposely set ajar while she took her shower.

She stood there for a full five minutes, stifling giggles as she watched the men in her life lark about on the floor. The gentleness and sincerity, the unbreakable bond between father and son that April Taylor felt whenever she watched them, never ceased to amaze and delight her.

Suddenly her concentration was broken by the strange look that came over Ryan Taylor's face. A look so intense she had never before seen it. It was fair to say she didn't much care for it. Her concentration was again broken, with events happening outside the probable cause. 'Ryan, what's going on? What's that noise?' she whispered.

Taylor didn't answer. He turned to face his wife. His look hadn't gone. Not by a long shot. In fact, it had become even more intense.

The sound of gunfire tended to have that effect on him.

CHAPTER EIGHTY-TWO

Taylor snatched Jake up in his arms and handed him to April. The sudden movement alarmed the boy and she had to move fast, hug him tightly to quell tears. Taylor ran across the room and pulled a gun and a spare clip from his holdall. He slipped the clip into his back pocket. Pausing, he turned to face April. 'Stay right here. Lock the door. I'm going to check things out.' He kissed her full on the lips and Jake on the forehead. 'Don't worry,' he said. 'I'm not going to let anything happen to either of you.'

'Come back to us,' was all she could say.

Taylor nodded and was out the door in a second. She flicked the lock and backed hard against the wall, aware of her heart almost leaping out of her chest. Holding her son in as close as she could, she began to fear she might smother him.

Taylor eased along the wall from the door until he hit the bottom of the stairs leading to the poolside. He estimated as many as ninety to a hundred rounds had gone off in the distance, he assumed close to the main gates. He identified the sounds as coming from a mix of automatic and semi-automatic weapons. Whoever was breaching Maxie Royce's community had arrived prepared for a battle.

Taking the steps four at a time, Taylor then raced past the pool and ducked into the middle of a small collection of thick, but neatly manicured bushes.

Earlier, as he'd always done when assessing risk on a job, he had scoped out the estate. Assuming something was going down, he'd identified the bushes on the hill as the place to be when it was happening. Although he hadn't expected to come under attack, he was as prepared as anybody could be in the event that things kicked off.

Taylor crouched down to ground level where the foliage was lighter. He shuffled through the undergrowth on his belly until he reached the spot where he would find the optimum position. He shook his head as he surveyed the scene playing out below him.

A pair of black SUVs were nosed close to each other across the entrance to the estate, effectively blocking any escape attempt. Taylor noticed all the doors of both vehicles lying open, indicating that there probably had been at least four men in each, the rest of the room inside taken up, no doubt, by firearms. Four of Royce's men were spread-eagled on the ground, two outside and two inside the gates. The men hadn't stood a chance. Like the US forces at Pearl Harbour during World War 2, they had been caught early morning with their pants down and cut to pieces before they'd even been able to draw their weapons. Their bodies were no more than a mish-mash of bloodied pulp with circles of creeping crimson framing their heads.

The invasion team was dressed all in black with balaclavas protecting their identities. Not that any of them looked in the mood to leave witnesses. Taylor counted eight in total. Each one was packing a semi-automatic rifle, most probably a Heckler and Koch or similar, and a handgun secured in a chest holster. They meant business all right.

Taylor continued to observe the team as it huddled for final instructions before the inevitable assault on the house. The next couple of minutes would tell him everything about the task facing Royce and the rest of his men.

Taylor's worst fears were confirmed as he watched the team split into four pairs and set off for the next part of their mission. The way they acted and moved worried him. They looked lean, strong and fit. Definitely military. Probably mercenaries. And, judging by what he had so far seen, Taylor was willing to bet they were well used to working together. If they had been sent by one or all of the remaining members of The Firm to wipe Royce and his cronies off the face of the Earth, they were going about things the right way.

Taylor had seen enough. He figured he had maybe three minutes at most before they were on top of him. As he retraced his steps back to the summer house, he glanced over to his left towards the main house. Red Summers and half a dozen of Royce's men were armed and lying-in wait outside the front of the house. Unfortunately, they were in full view and bunched too close together, like the Clantons about to face the Earps at the OK Corral, a mismatch that didn't end too well for the former.

Taylor counted seven men, plus the four already dead made eleven. He realised he was looking at Royce's entire defence detail, apart from the man himself, and Vera. And Taylor couldn't imagine her as a gun-toting Ma Baker. They were in the deep stuff, up to their necks.

'Red!' Taylor shouted. He waved his hands. 'Spread out! Take cover and shoot anything that moves! Eight men, three minutes!'

Summers acknowledged and the men dispersed, finding cover behind statues and bushes.

Taylor ran back to the summer house and thumped the door with his fist. 'April, we have to go! Bring Jake!' he shouted.

The door opened and April appeared, the boy in her arms. Taylor grabbed him. 'This way.'

They ran down some steps to their right and along a short corridor towards a grey door facing them. The metal door was covered in tamperproof curved headed bolts, two inches in diameter. It looked as if it could repel a tank attack. On their way from the airport last night, Taylor had listened to Royce describe his impregnable underground bunker. He was now challenging Royce to prove it.

He tugged at the door, grunting as he struggled to open it.

'There are five locks on the inside. Nobody can get in here unless you let them in,' he said to his wife. 'Don't worry, I'll be right back.' He kissed her and Jake and prepared to push the door closed.

April put her hand on his shoulder. 'But what about you, Ryan? Please, stay here with us,' she pleaded, but knew it wasn't an option. She had seen that look of determination many times before.

Taylor waited until he heard all five locks click into place before leaving.

As he reached the bottom of the stairs leading to the poolside, the deafening onslaught kicked off again. He heard footsteps above him as he hit the top step. Reaching out to grab a rifle muzzle as it crossed in front of him, Taylor yanked the muzzle downwards, driving the butt up into the man's gut as hard as he could. The man's trigger finger locked, and he fired off a dozen random rounds before he dropped to his knees, doubled over in agony, the breath knocked out of him. Bullets ricocheted all around them and Taylor yelled out as he felt a sudden searing pain at the back of his thigh.

Recalling the team had paired off at the bottom of the hill, Taylor expected the second man to appear at any time. He heard a rustle in the bushes from which he had earlier observed them. His left arm encircling the stricken attacker's neck, Taylor hauled him to his feet, his right hand yanking the rifle from the man's grasp.

An adrenalin-fuelled second man flew out of the bushes. Before he realised what was happening, he had cut his colleague to pieces. Taylor felt the bullets thudding into the man's head and torso as he crouched behind him. Reaching for the gun tucked into his waistband, Taylor let go of the dead man and dived to his right, flipping the gun over and firing off three rounds as he went down. The first tore into the man's shoulder, the second skimming his cheek. The third bullet ploughed through his left eye, spraying the poolside with blood as it ripped out the back of his skull.

Taylor sensed further danger from the left. He rolled to his right and as he landed, once, twice, three times, bullets from the third man's gun tracked him, pinging in all directions as they blasted off the hard ground. One of the deflected bullets caught

Taylor in the upper arm near the shoulder. Grimacing, he gripped his gun tightly and lowered his head to minimise the target. Half a dozen retaliatory shots in number three's general direction hit paydirt. The man dropped his gun before clawing at his throat. Gurgling sounds filled the air, indicating Taylor had hit something vital. The body tumbled into the pool, clouding it black-red within seconds.

Taylor felt his arm. It stung like hell, however on closer inspection, it was barely grazed. He winced as he fingered the round backside of the bullet lodged in a muscle below his right buttock. He looked at his hand. It was wet but not dripping wet. He had been lucky. The ricochet had taken most of the propulsion out of the round. If it had been a direct hit anything could have happened. The best outcome would have been a *through and through* where the bullet passes through soft tissue, avoiding muscles and tendons. The next best would have been some muscle and tendon damage with the risk of infection higher if the bullet doesn't re-emerge. The worst option would have been damage to the main femoral artery. *Game over.*

The sound of gunfire began to subside until it became firstly sporadic, then eerily silent. Taylor held his breath as he backed against the wall of an outbuilding, midway between the main house and the summer house. From there he would get a good view...

'My God,' he muttered as he surveyed the scene. He counted ten bodies in all, five of Royce's men and three of the assault team, shot to pieces and scattered around the front of the house. Red Summers and Maxie Royce were nowhere to be seen. The main door to the house was wide open.

One of the injured black clad assailants on the ground, on hearing the approaching footsteps, moaned as he tried to raise his gun. Taylor hardly broke stride as he shot the man twice in the head on his way past.

Pausing outside the door, Taylor released the spent clip, letting it fall at his feet before pushing the replacement firmly home.

Inside, his instincts guided him left. Passing through Royce's TV lounge, Taylor tried to visualise the layout. He was almost certain there was an upper floor, a mezzanine area at this side of the house.

He was right. A door opened up to reveal a wide sweeping stairwell. As he hit the bottom stair, some shots rang out from above followed by a woman's cry. *Vera?*

Taylor ran up the stairs, only pausing at the top when he heard another shot and another cry. There was an open door at the end of a short corridor. A pleading voice grew louder the closer Taylor got to the door. Then a familiar voice chipped in. Maxie Royce's.

Taylor could see about half of the room from outside the door. Another one of the assault team was lying on his back. Half of his face was missing, most of it moulded into the wall next to him. Red Summers was lying next to the dead man, his back propped against the wall. Maxie Royce was kneeling at Red's side, holding a white towel against the big man's stomach. Red's breathing was quick and choppy, as if every breath was agony. Taylor saw the look on Royce's face, the deep red stains on the towel. This was bad. And in the background, a woman was whimpering. Vera.

Red saw Taylor first. Although he was so obviously badly injured, he managed a quick movement of the eyes to indicate to Taylor the position of the last man.

Taylor stepped inside the room and squeezed off one round.

CHAPTER EIGHTY-THREE

An hour after the siege on the house Taylor decided to step outside for some air. He needed some time to clear his head, plan where he was going to go from here. He had called April on the bunker telephone, mainly to reassure her, but more importantly, to tell her to stay exactly where she was, at least until they got things *squared away*.

A doctor had arrived on the scene within minutes, giving Red Summers some oxygen and making him as comfortable as he could before further help arrived. As they were waiting for an ambulance, the doctor examined Taylor's injuries. Taylor already knew the damage to his arm was not serious, the medic taking his time to clean and bandage the wound. The bullet in the leg was a little trickier. It had been lodged in a muscle just below the skin's surface and, given the choice of a visit to hospital or treatment on the spot, Taylor had opted for the latter, asking the doctor to 'dig it out and patch me up'. There was no way he was going to leave April and Jake alone here after what had happened.

The doctor had given Taylor a couple of injections around the area, numbing the pain before expertly removing the bullet and cleansing the wound prior to bandaging it up. He'd then handed Taylor a tub of antibiotic tablets to fend off infection, with the instruction: *finish the course*. The doctor had been dressed in the cleanest whites Taylor had ever seen. Early forties, smartly groomed, Gucci shoes, Vacheron Constantin watch, this guy was top notch. Even his leather carry-case and chunky equipment bag looked as though they had come out of a Louis Vuitton store. Taylor could only imagine how much all of this was costing. And when two green-suited paramedics appeared within twenty minutes of the initial call to whisk Red away to some private medical facility on millionaires' row,

Taylor had mentally added another zero to his estimate. Then the thought came to him that not one of the medics had broached the subject of the two dead men in the room, lying under tarpaulins. He added yet another zero.

Taylor watched as firstly Royce, then Vera, hugged Red as the medics prepared to take him outside. It was heartening to Taylor that, although Royce was clearly one of the bad guys, at least he had some sort of moral code when it came to close friends and family.

Red stopped the medics as they reached the door, thanked Taylor before exchanging a weak clasping of hands.

Royce hadn't said much since the attack. After Red had gone, he and Vera sat facing each other, her taking big gulps of brandy and him tenderly rubbing the back of her hand.

Taylor noticed a neat, round bruise had formed at Vera's temple It was where the last man had been jamming his gun before Taylor's bullet ended his involvement in the matter.

As he walked out into brilliant sunshine, Taylor could hardly believe his eyes. All of the dead bodies at the front of the house had gone. Every drop of blood on the stonework had been scrubbed and hosed clean, the only sign that anything untoward had taken place, a whiff of strong disinfectant hanging in the breeze.

The three men Taylor had taken out at the poolside were gone, including the one left floating in the pool itself. And the door of the outhouse he had used for cover was open. Inside, a number of scrubbing brushes, squeegees and bags of chemicals were poised for action. A couple of guys were already draining the pool in preparation. One of them gave Taylor a knowing nod. Taylor acknowledged before walking over to the top of the hill to take a look down the long drive towards the main entrance. Same story; bodies gone, and all traces of death cleared away. In the distance Taylor could see a couple of sentries standing next to the checkpoint outside the gates. Another couple of Royce's men were roaming the grounds. Yet another two were pulling up at the main gate, ready for work.

It was business as usual, and there wasn't a cop in sight.

CHAPTER EIGHTY-FOUR

'How's Vera?' Taylor asked. He'd come back inside to find Royce locked away all alone in his *thinking room*.

'A bit shaken up. She'll be okay, thanks to you.' Royce paused. 'And you were right,' he said.

''bout what?'

'This place. The protection, the systems. All this,' he said, raising his eyes. 'All this makes no difference if you have a traitor in the ranks.'

'Who was he?' Taylor asked.

Royce waved a dismissive hand. 'A guy. Only been with us a couple months.'

'How'd you find out?'

'He was up to his eyeballs in gambling debts. I make it my business to know these things. Red spoke to him last week but he assured him he was dealing with it. I even gave the guy an advance on his wages. Then he was seen picking up a little extra last week at the track. Now I know where that came from. How stupid am I?' Royce balled his fists.

'Was this guy on the gate?' Taylor asked. It would confirm how he was thinking.

'Mm-hmm. First one to get plugged. Fat lot of good the money did him.'

Taylor shrugged before asking after Red.

Royce brightened. 'I spoke to somebody at the hospital. The bullet lodged in his small intestine, missed all the important stuff. They're going to cut away the damaged section. He'll be out in a few days.'

'That's good news,' Taylor said. He leaned in close. 'Tell me, Maxie. This business with you wanting to go straight and everything, does this mean cutting your ties with the law?'

'I don't follow,' Royce said, looking puzzled.

'Well, I know if I'd just taken part in a gun battle back in my hometown, I'd expect the place to be swarming with cops and media people by now.'

'Oh, yeah. Well, let's say we have an, *understanding*.'

Taylor lifted an eyebrow. 'You might want to keep that understanding, for a while at least.'

'I think you're right.'

'So what happens now?' Taylor asked. 'Facchetti's not exactly going to roll out the welcome mat. Plan B?'

Royce scratched his chin. 'Facchetti knows me. He'll be having kittens as he'll expect swift retaliation. In the past that's what he would've gotten. I'd have sent an exocet missile straight through his front door. I'd have made him disappear. Then I'd have cut his wife's throat and drowned their kids.' He spat out the words. 'But I won't do that. Mark my words, Facchetti's time will come all right. But it'll be on my terms.' A big finger tapped his chest. 'When I'm ready.'

'It all sounds very neighbourly, I'm sure,' Taylor said, heavy on the sarcasm.

Royce's expression softened. 'One thing I've learned in this business, Ryan.'

'What's that?'

'Never act on impulse. Give it a little thinking time first. Best chance you have of arriving at the correct decision. You agree?'

Taylor thought carefully, folded his arms. 'Personally, I'd go with the exocet.'

'Which is why you do what you do, and I do what I do. Nothing personal, but you react like a wronged employee. It's natural. Me? Everybody expects me to do the right thing, the smart thing. The thing that'll make sure they keep their jobs, that they have food on their tables, clothes on their backs.'

Bristling, Taylor stared at Royce. 'That's all good and well,' he said, 'But you're forgetting one thing, aren't you?'

'What?' Royce said, instantly regretting his last statement.

'I'm not your employee. You and your cronies made a choice when you brought my family into this. You went and got me involved. Now I get that you want out, and that you're trying to clean up your act. But in the absence of any doubt, be assured I'll do whatever it takes to protect April and Jake.'

Royce's face creased into an uncomfortable smile. 'Fair enough. I'd expect no less. Listen, we'll meet back here at five o'clock. It'll give us both a little time to cool off.'

Taylor rose to leave. He got as far as the door before Royce spoke again. 'You know, Ryan, if it hadn't been for you, we'd all be dead. I owe you, big time. If we can get through the next couple of days-'

'The heat off and a relaxing flight back to Scotland, Maxie. That's all I want,' Taylor said. He turned to face Royce. 'You wouldn't really have cut his wife's throat and drowned their kids, would you?'

Royce looked pensive for a second. 'Try me.' His face broke into a wide smile.

CHAPTER EIGHTY-FIVE

Taylor had lain awake until 4am. He'd dozed off and woken up again at his usual time, deciding to lie where he was on the sofa, get as much rest as possible. He was going to need it.

At 9am, he dragged his aching body to the bathroom. Leaving the bandages on his arm and leg in place, he gave the rest of his body a quick wash, brushed his teeth and carefully towelled dry. As planned, he and Maxie Royce had re-convened at 5pm last night to discuss how they moved forward on the plan to ensure both got what they were looking for; Taylor, to be able to get his family home safely, and Royce, to begin building the blocks towards a cleaner future.

Taylor looked at his reflection in the mirror as he got dressed. He retrieved his gun and holster from the wall cabinet into which he had placed it last night, well away from tiny inquisitive fingers. He slipped the suppressor into a little side pouch on the shoulder holster before clicking the holster into place. He did some final checks on the gun then buttoned it in securely.

As he stared into that mirror, he couldn't help but feel massive reservations about Royce's plan of action.

Royce had called a meeting with the other families in the Firm, with one obvious exception - Carlo Facchetti. The meeting was set for 11am in one of the luxury suites at The Imperial Hotel, owned by Royce himself, on Las Vegas' famous strip. During the meeting, it was Royce's intention to inform the members of the Firm of his desire to go legit and to outline the measures he would be prepared to take to attain such status. Taylor felt that this baring of the soul would leave the businessman vulnerable and isolated and ripe for some Firm alliances, possibly with Carlo Facchetti at the helm, to sweep in and snuff Royce out completely. Taylor reckoned Royce would be taking a gigantic gamble, not only with his businesses, but also with the lives of April and Jake. Taylor had told him so in no uncertain terms. He'd asked Royce to hold off until he'd dealt with Facchetti. *After that*, Taylor had said, *you'll soon find out if the bastard has any allies.*

Taylor went on to tell Royce that his desire to be clean could bring everything tumbling down, and that it was not his intention to get caught up in that.

Royce being Royce, the planned meeting at the Imperial Hotel at 11am it was.

Then Ryan Taylor had been forced to look at options, unbeknown to Maxie Royce. Taylor's initial remit, one that he intended to follow, was to get face-to-face with Carlo Facchetti. Then what? Who knows? Because of Royce's pig-headedness, he would have to play it by ear, an arrangement that Taylor despised. Inevitably, it would end up with somebody getting killed.

Taylor returned from the house at 9.45am with two slices of lightly buttered toast, scrambled eggs and coffee for April, and a kid's portion of porridge oats for Jake. He had tried his best to eat some cereal and toast with his coffee, the twist he felt in his gut only allowing meagre portions of each to pass down his throat.

He laid down the tray at his wife's bedside, kissed her on the forehead. He bent to kiss the still sleeping Jake, stroked his hair and inhaled deeply before heading for the door. Royce had a car sitting out front, leaving for the strip in ten minutes.

'Be careful, Ryan,' April said, sitting up in bed and wiping the sleep from her eyes.

'Remember what I said,' Taylor whispered, waited for the response.

'I know. After you leave, go to the bunker and stay there until you get back.' She knew by the look on her husband's face that there was no point in arguing.

CHAPTER EIGHTY-SIX

'Good morning, Mr. Royce. The suite is ready for you now. Coffee and light snacks are only moments away. Shall I show your guests up as they arrive?' The man stepped forward as soon as Maxie Royce's feet hit the welcome mat.

Royce, as ever flanked by a bodyguard on each side, shook hands with Richard Greencroft, his manager at The Imperial Hotel. As always, Greencroft looked and acted the part, oozing sheer class and professionalism, and Royce was shrewd enough to pay him accordingly.

'Yes Richard, please do. And how is Victoria? Keeping well, I hope.' Royce always made it his business to know his staff. It made for a contented workforce.

Greencroft beamed. 'My wife is very well, thank you, Mr. Royce. And Vera?'

Royce gave him the thumbs up as the lift doors closed before he and his bookends rode up to the sixth floor. He would spend the next few minutes before the meeting reading through some notes and checking a few calculations he had spent most of last night jotting down. He hoped his figures would make sense to the gathering. If they weren't convinced, he still had his ace card to play. If that failed, who knows.

From the comfort of the suite, Royce heard the lift doors slide open. The first of his guests was arriving.

***

Taylor walked the five blocks from The Imperial Hotel to the rather expensive looking Cafe Mocha which was situated slap-bang in the middle of the strip. As he scanned the cafe, he couldn't help but think that the name the owners had chosen undersold it by a long way. Back home in Glasgow, a classy joint such as this would be located in Royal Exchange Square, right next to the Gallery of Modern Art and called Chez Maison or Le Grande Cuisine. A quick glance at a menu sitting atop one of the plush outside tables confirmed that the establishment was set up to sell far more than coffee and doughnuts, and charging an arm and a leg for them as well. Judging by the large number of people sitting both inside the place and at the outside tables, it would suggest that maybe the owners were doing something right.

Taylor walked up to the counter and ordered a milky latte with a sugary doughnut, shook his head at the amount he was asked to pay, paid it anyway, and strolled back outside to sit at the only vacant table, two rows back from the sidewalk.

Directly across the road, the second biggest hotel on the strip – after The Imperial – reached for the sky. The Marrakesh Hotel and Casino Emporium housed over six thousand rooms and, despite the name, had always boasted strong Sicilian *family* links. The current custodian was the Facchetti family.

Adjusting the position of his seat until he had the hotel entrance in his line of vision, Taylor opened his hardback, stole another brief glance at a recent photograph of Carlo Facchetti concealed within the pages, and settled back to enjoy his expensive coffee.

***

Royce's flunkies stood side-by-side and arms folded outside the double doors of the sixth-floor suite. Inside, six members of one of the world's most powerful alliances sat around an enormous rosewood table: Sean Bonner, Vernon Wallace, Maxie Royce, Per Hansen, Nicholas Van Heuren and Teddy Capaldi. Five of the six looked decidedly wary of an, as yet unnamed, seventh man sat directly to the right of Maxie Royce. Most of the formalities out of the way, Royce glanced around the room before opening his leather ring binder. He flicked over a few pages, pulled out some sheets, setting them down in a neat pile beside the binder.

Royce kicked it off: 'Gentlemen, thank you for attending at such short notice.' He motioned to his right. 'I'm sure you are all aware Firm rules allow a member to invite a potential investor to attend a meeting.'

'Aye, but giving prior notice, Maxie.' Irishman Bonner was the first to make his point. 'Just turning up here, it's not right.'

'You know, Sean. You're right,' Royce said. 'I'll ask the gentleman to step outside while we debate the point.'

The stranger made to stand.

'Wait,' Teddy Capaldi piped up, as Royce had expected. 'I don't see a problem with this. I'm sure Maxie is not about to discuss the finer details of our business in front of Mr-'

'Langdon, Frank Langdon,' Royce said.

'In front of Mr. Langdon.' Capaldi nodded at Langdon before scanning every face, resisting the temptation to smirk at Bonner. He continued, 'And it's fair to say we're all interested in fresh investment, right?'

As he'd expected, Royce was now able to throw it open. 'Gentlemen?' he said.

Bonner threw his hands up, shook his head. Wallace shrugged as if either way was fine by him, Hansen nodded, and Van Heuren gave no indication, effectively carrying the motion by majority.

The reason for Capaldi's intervention was two-fold: one, Teddy happened to be Royce's main ally, and two, he did not much care for ex-IRA terrorist, Sean Bonner, and his cohorts. Three years ago, Capaldi had been the only member to vote against Bonner joining The Firm, the reasons unclear at that time. It soon emerged that there was history between the two regarding the hostile takeover of an ailing hotel, close to the strip. Bonner's company had employed bully-boy tactics to beat Capaldi's to the punch and, fanning the flames, Bonner was now making serious money out of the venture.

Cleverly, Royce had always managed to play the two of them when it suited him. Today, it clearly did suit him.

Royce exchanged a brief glance with Dane, Per Hansen, before continuing. Hansen's reply by way of expression said it all: *you conniving bastard.*

***

Taylor watched as the black Lincoln convertible rolled up to the front of the hotel. The open-topped car seemed to go on forever and Taylor smiled at the irony as he realised it reminded him of the car in that grainy TV footage he had often seen of JFK's final journey all those years ago in Dallas, Texas. Was Taylor about to become a modern-day Lee Harvey Oswald? That would be up to Carlo Facchetti.

Facchetti got out of the car and gingerly climbed the steps to the hotel entrance. When he hit the top step, he turned quickly to face the people going about their business on the street below. Taylor could see he was spooked. Facchetti looked drawn and tired to Taylor, as though he hadn't slept for a month. He seemed rooted to the spot until his two bodyguards caught up and all three disappeared inside.

Taylor pushed his coffee cup and side plate into the middle of the table, pocketed Carlo Facchetti's photograph, and slipped the hardback under his arm. He dropped the book into a waste bin on the sidewalk outside the cafe before crossing the street and slowly climbing the steps to the hotel. Mindful of the ubiquitous nature of Vegas' surveillance culture, Taylor picked his way past the street cameras, keeping his head down. He pulled up his jacket collar as he stepped off the carousel into the hotel reception, effectively thumbing his nose at the watching security staff. He straightened as he walked up to the desk, certain that Facchetti's security team had already eye-balled him.

***

The members of the Firm were engaging in a Q & A session with potential *newbie*, Frank Langdon, the purpose, to ascertain how much money he was prepared to bring to the table, how he had earned that money, and how he felt about placing it among some *alternative* investments.

As Royce had earlier predicted, not one of the members had yet mentioned Carlo Facchetti by name, not only because of the stranger in their midst, but also because they would all know about the Italian's unforgiveable breach of Firm rules when he sent a hit squad to storm Royce's house. Broaching the subject would, of course, prove uncomfortable for every one of them.

Royce, watching the men closely, couldn't be sure that Facchetti was entirely without support within The Firm. He was confident he could count on at least three. Like Facchetti, Teddy Capaldi was of Italian descent, but that was where the similarity ended. The two families had been sworn enemies ever since their forefathers had waged war on each other back in Sicily over a hundred years ago. The prospect of making some serious money had allowed them to set aside their differences, but the tension between them was always there, bubbling just below the surface.

Capaldi was in Royce's corner, as were Per Hansen and Vernon Matthews, neither of whom had any time for Facchetti. Royce had always found Nicholas Van Heuren evasive and secretive, but he would bet any money that the Dutchman was far too intelligent to get himself involved with a low-life like Carlo Facchetti. Royce wasn't so sure about Sean Bonner. The Irishman had black, soulless eyes, like a shark, and Royce had never trusted him. *Bonner and Facchetti?* Yes, he could quite easily imagine this alliance.

Royce leaned back in his chair, sipping away at a glass of ice water as he witnessed his long-time associate, and confidence trickster, Nick Laverne, a.k.a Frank Langdon expertly field all sorts of questions on all things financial. Laverne was so convincing he almost sold Royce himself on the idea. By the time the Q & A session had finished and the show of hands taken, Langdon was given the go-ahead to deposit a hundred million dollars, thereby buying out Royce's interest in the three casinos he owned on the strip. Although the other members of the Firm would not profit from such an arrangement as existing money was merely being shifted rather than added to, the motion was passed unanimously as it meant fresh blood was being introduced to the alliance. Like the conman he was, Laverne had performed so plausibly that he had The Firm members eating out of his hand. Maybe they felt that Carlo Facchetti's days were numbered and that Langdon was a smarter, more switched on, user-friendly alternative to the Italian. Royce glanced at Sean Bonner. Even he seemed convinced. The plan was working.

And when Langdon carefully chose his moment to hint that he wouldn't be averse to throwing his financial clout behind the Firm's jewel in the crown, its drug involvement in Colombia and Venezuela, the members didn't even flinch when Royce cutely slipped in the fact that he would be bowing out of that particular activity. Especially when Langdon hinted that he may want to invest more money in it than Royce had ever done.

Going forward, the contracts would be agreed, drawn up and signed. Then Frank Langdon would again become Nick Laverne and bail out to the Bahamas with a handsome pay-off from Royce. Royce would reacquire the three casinos and sell them on under an assumed name. The Firm would then need to decide if they had the stomach to screw the South American drug lords or try and boost the under investment by bringing in even more fresh blood. Either way, Royce wouldn't give a toss. He would be well out of it.

As the meeting drew to a close, Royce's attention turned to Ryan Taylor. Due to Laverne's presence at the meeting, Royce had managed to evade the question of what had happened to Taylor and his family, along with potentially awkward references to missing US Chief of Staff, Walter McMichaels. Although McMichaels was not yet officially posted as missing, Maxie Royce's mole in the Senate had confirmed it. Royce knew that the rest of The Firm would also be aware of this.

***

Taylor walked right past reception and rode the lift to the fifth-floor, certain he had grabbed somebody's attention by the time the doors slid open.

He made his way towards the far end of the corridor, dipped under the camera set in the corner where ceiling meets wall, and pulled out a hand spray. Taking careful aim, he sent a couple of bursts of white paint into the camera lens. The monitor linked to the control room immediately delivered an opaque image of the corridor. The security man squinted into the screen. As he tried to focus on a blurry cocktail, Taylor took off towards the camera at the other end of the corridor. In seconds camera two was sabotaged before he hit the stairwell heading for the floor below, taking out another two on his way. He repeated the process on floors four and three before slipping into the communal restroom on three. He figured that when they came searching for their boss, five hundred rooms per floor times three floors would be a lot of checking. Taylor would be long gone by the time they found Carlo Facchetti.

Inside the restroom, Taylor flicked the lock on the cubicle door and slipped off his sweater, shirt and slacks. Underneath he was wearing the khaki uniform of a typical Marrakesh Hotel maintenance man. He reached into the pocket of the all-in-one suit to retrieve a chipped keycard attached to a blue plastic cord. The card would allow him entry to anywhere in the hotel and surrounding grounds. He passed the cord over his neck, straightening the keycard. It displayed a recent photograph, identifying him as: *Dalglish, Kevin.*

He checked his holster containing his gun and suppressor was neatly concealed below the suit, then stepped out of the cubicle and walked over to a wash hand basin near the exit door. Soaking his hands under the tap, he ran them over his hair, smoothing it down before jamming a wide brimmed cap over his head. A little goatee that Taylor carried in his pocket was tapped into place, completing the disguise.

He balled the clothes, tossing them into a laundry chute close to the restroom, and hit the stairs heading for the floor above. Emerging into the corridor, he spied the target room, Carlo Facchetti's secret office. It was only a few doors away. Taylor tapped the door, sensing the bodyguard's eye against the peep hole. The lock clicked and the door swung open. There was a sudden pump of compressed air as Taylor shot the man in the head. The man hit the ground hard. Taylor stepped inside the office and took aim. By the time the other bodyguard reacted, it was too late; he also fell heavily, taking out a small table on his way to the floor.

Carlo Facchetti stood alone among the carnage, a defiant look on his face.

CHAPTER EIGHTY-SEVEN

'Do you know who I am, you moron?' Facchetti snapped as Taylor pressed the gun to his head. Grabbing him by the scruff of the neck, he dragged the young mobster out into the corridor.

'One more word and I'll blow your head off,' Taylor hissed, the memory of yesterday's events still fresh in his mind. He spotted a couple leave their room at the far end of the corridor. Luckily, they headed in the other direction. He turned to face Facchetti. 'Your choice. Dead or alive, it's all the same to me.'

The threat seemed to have the desired effect. Facchetti didn't utter another word as he was led up the stairs to the level above. Taylor smirked as he sensed Facchetti staring up at each camera they passed. *I'm here! For God's sake, come and get me!*

Emerging into another corridor, Taylor pushed Facchetti towards what he knew was an empty room - Royce had pre-booked it late last night - and flashed his card at the sensor. It glowed green, clicked open. Taylor hustled the Italian inside.

Facchetti looked over his shoulder. 'Look, buddy. You're making the biggest mistake of your life. I-'

'Shut up,' Taylor cut in. He flipped the gun over. 'Sit down.'

Facchetti sank all the way down into one of his own plush easy chairs.

Taylor stood over him. 'The name's Ryan Taylor.'

The colour drained from Facchetti's face. Maxie Royce's message had obviously got out to the right people. 'But you're-'

'Dead? Do I look dead to you?'

'Taylor? Oh my God, look, it was just business. It's nothing personal.'

Taylor gritted his teeth. 'I swear, if anybody else tells me that-'

'Okay, wait. Look, I can give you as much money as you want. I have millions. Tell me how much. I'll wire the money right to your account. A million dollars, two million? Name it. Whatever Royce is paying, I'll double it.'

Taylor heard the nervous tremor in Facchetti's voice and shot back. 'You can give me twenty million and it'd be of no use to me. I'd be too dead to spend it.'

'Then maybe we can help each other,' Facchetti said. Taylor noted the obvious change in his tone. Bravado was replacing fear. 'I know you need me, or I'd already be dead by now.'

Taylor said nothing. He saw Facchetti's face light up, as if the makings of a business opportunity were looming large. 'You do something for me, and I'll give you more money than you've ever seen. And I'll guarantee you and your family go home safely.'

No response.

Facchetti continued: 'I have contacts. All I have to do is say the word and you're off the hook. I swear.'

Taylor heard the door click open behind him. 'You took your time,' he said.

'Royce. How in hell did *you* get in here?' Facchetti said, squirming in his seat when he saw Maxie Royce walk in with a huge smile on his face.

'I'm not the only one with traitors in his camp, Carlo. Let's get this over with, Taylor. We need to get out of here, now,' Royce said in a matter-of-fact kind of fashion.

Instinctively, Facchetti put his hands up as Taylor raised his gun. 'Wait! Noooo-!'

Two bullets thudded into the target. Royce looked down at his chest as if he could not believe his eyes. Blood trickled down the front of his jacket and from the edge of his mouth. He gulped in three or four short breaths before dropping to the floor at Taylor's feet.

Taylor felt Royce's neck for a pulse. 'Sorry Maxie,' he said, turning to face a shocked Carlo Facchetti. 'I assume that was the thing you wanted me to do?'

Facchetti was breathing hard. He stared between Taylor and the stricken Royce.

Taylor continued: 'You said you could get me and my family out of this mess. I've done as you asked. Now you need to come through for me. First, I want you to get on the phone right now and wire a million dollars to this account.' He handed Facchetti a piece of paper. A more relaxed Facchetti scanned the details. 'It's a Swiss account?' he said.

'That's right. I always come prepared,' Taylor laughed. He made a big play of slipping the gun inside his hotel uniform, made sure he was seen doing it. Facchetti was now almost fully relaxed as he got on the phone to his bank, asking the manager to transfer one million dollars as per Taylor's request.

While they were waiting for the manager to come back with confirmation of the transaction, Facchetti rose to step over Royce's body and walked across to the room's mini bar. 'I think a celebration is in order,' he announced as he cracked the seal on a couple of whisky miniatures, handing one to Taylor.

'Listen, why don't you come and work for me? I could use a man like you,' Facchetti said, raising the whisky.

Taylor waved his bottle, then downed the whisky in one go. 'I'm listening,' he said.

Facchetti, pleased that he had at least garnered a reaction, also drained the bottle. He thumped it down on the table next to them, his weasel face pinched and drawn as he worked out his play. 'I want you to be head of my security team.'

'You must have a guy in that position right now?'

Facchetti shook his head. 'Maybe I'll have somebody put a slug in his head. Maybe you?' He put his hand on Taylor's shoulder, laughed.

Taylor thought for a few seconds, then: 'No thanks, I already have a job.'

'I'll give you five hundred grand a year, plus expenses. A house in Vegas, car, free medical care for you and your family.

A membership for the friggin' country club, for Chrissake! Tell me, what do you want? It's yours.' Facchetti's eyes were wide with excitement. In his opinion it had been a great day so far with Royce dead and the way clear to push on with his plans for The Firm. The suckers would fall into line, especially with his main opposition wiped out. Facchetti was certain of it. And if they didn't, he would have this ruthless killer to *persuade* them. Facchetti was still buzzing from the way Taylor had taken out both of his top bodyguards. And then Maxie Royce. And, with this man in charge of his ongoing health and safety...

'Okay, we have a deal,' Taylor said, thrusting out his hand, then quickly pulling it away. 'But there are things I need to know to be able to do the job to the best of my ability.'

Facchetti exhaled quickly, as if it were his normal reaction to good news. 'Go on.'

'I need to know everything about the operation. Everything you're involved in. No secrets or lies. The whole shebang. If you expect me to protect you, I need to know exactly what I'm protecting you against. You have to trust me. Otherwise, no deal.'

A look of mild annoyance flushed Facchetti's face, but only for a moment as he considered Taylor's request. Taylor could almost reach out and touch the Italian's thought processes as he sat close to him: *if I refuse, I could end up on that floor beside Royce; this guy could be the answer to my prayers; my useless dad and crazy old grandfather – they thought I was a punk; I'd show them; I'd be top dog; but if I tell him everything...*

Then, Carlo Facchetti made the most important decision of his life, driven on by a dangerous cocktail of man's basic animal instincts: greed, anger, revenge, jealousy, hurt, torment, envy...

Facchetti spent fifteen minutes spilling his guts about the murky business he and his kind were involved in on a daily basis. He covered everything, from the Firm's connection with the presidency, to President Wilson Travis himself, and not forgetting Walter McMichaels' involvement. From the Firm's man on the board of the gaming commission, to sharing highly sensitive details of the many high-profile officers of the law, judges, senators and solid upstanding citizens of the US of A, who regularly frequented Facchetti's brothels; along with exactly what it took to get each of them off. The kind of stuff that could blow society apart. Bravado and sheer stupidity had Facchetti even sharing crazy things like an old ex-CIA agent's account of how he had stood shoulder to shoulder with the shooter on the grassy knoll as the man fired the head shot that killed JFK on that fateful day in Dallas.

Facchetti's mobile phone rang. It was his bank manager confirming that a million dollars had been transferred to the Swiss account.

Facchetti offered Taylor a handshake to cement their alliance.

Taylor ignored him, instead pulling out a mobile phone. He hit one on speed dial. Somebody answered. 'Did you get that?' Taylor said. 'Okay, good.' He hit end call.

'What? What's going on? Wh-who was that?' Facchetti spluttered.

'That was one of my boys, Carlo.'

Facchetti almost collapsed with fright when he heard the voice coming from the floor.

'He has it all recorded. I think he was saying something like, you're done.'

Maxie Royce rose like Lazarus to his full height, towering over Facchetti.

'But, I-I saw him kill you!' Facchetti's face was turning whiter by the second.

Royce unbuttoned his coat to reveal two slugs lodged deep into the bullet proof vest he was wearing underneath. He turned to face Taylor, rubbing his chest. 'You didn't tell me it would hurt so much.'

Taylor grinned. 'Thought it was better that way. More authentic.'

Royce held his ribs. 'Nice goatee, by the way,' he said.

'Thanks.'

Royce turned to face Facchetti, spitting the empty blood capsule on the floor at his feet. He took out a handkerchief and wiped the side of his mouth. He pointed to the coat, prodding his finger through the holes. 'More fake blood.'

'What do you want from me? Are you going to kill me?' Facchetti's voice was shrill and deep in equal measures, as if it were ready to break at any time, like the adolescent teenager he had been not so long ago.

Royce stepped forward. 'All that stuff you spouted, that's all the security I need to erase you completely from my life. You stay away from me. I don't want to ever see or hear from you again. If I find out you're messing with me in any way, your little confession is going to go public. They'll be taking bets on the strip as to how long you'd last. I'd say minutes rather than hours.' Royce indicated towards Taylor. 'And this guy's going home to live out a quiet life with his family. Same rules apply. If you don't want to end up in a shallow grave in the middle of the Nevada desert, you know what to do. Any questions?'

Like a broken man, Facchetti bowed his head.

'Any questions?' Royce said again.

The Italian shook his head.

'Okay, let's get out of here. This place makes me nervous,' Royce said, turning towards Taylor.

Taylor pulled out a syringe full of knock out drug and speared it into Facchetti's neck. Facchetti gasped a couple of times before slumping back on the sofa.

'Nice touch back there,' Royce said as they hit the stairs.

'What?' Taylor looked confused.

'A million dollars in a Swiss account. Neat. I'm impressed.'

'I'd like to say the money was for me,' Taylor said, 'But I'd be lying.'

'How so?'

'I had Facchetti wire the money straight to an account in trust for a little autistic boy called Luke. His family got mixed up in all of this. They're dead. They're all dead. All except him.'

Royce looked at Taylor for a while as if he wasn't buying the story. He waited for Taylor's expression to change. It didn't. 'You really are a nice guy, Ryan, aren't you?'

'Keep it to yourself. Otherwise, I'd have to kill you.'

CHAPTER EIGHTY-EIGHT

The first thing Taylor did when he and Maxie Royce returned to the mansion, after he'd checked in with April and Jake, was call Leo Mannheim via Royce's secure satellite link.

Mannheim was already able to tell Taylor that he'd received a communication from his CIA source in the last few minutes saying that all charges against him were to be immediately dropped. And as no further contracts were contemplated, the matter was now officially closed.

Carlo Facchetti had had to move quickly to let his contact at the White House know that his big mouth had screwed them. And that, due to some pressing business commitments, he was thinking of taking a lesser role within The Firm, a sort of sideways step.

Taylor had also done some side-stepping of his own during the call, neglecting to mention the unfortunate business with Walter McMichaels. He was certain MI6 would at least have been privy to the same information Royce had heard, which meant that Mannheim would definitely know that McMichaels was missing, and that Taylor was responsible. Taylor assumed that Mannheim's apparent lack of interest in the subject was probably due to the US and their indifference towards one of their own. Leo Mannheim knew something was rotten somewhere near the business end of the Washington administration, but he had the good sense to leave well alone. He knew McMichaels would turn up at some point in the future. Dead or alive, it didn't matter as the current US administration would know exactly how to handle the situation. The most important thing for Mannheim to consider was that any solution would be sought without the involvement of MI6 in any way, shape or form. In the meantime, US top brass would press for a decision to appoint, firstly, an interim chief of staff, then a successor to McMichaels, allowing the bandwagon to roll on as before, sinister shadows of corruption continuing to darken the corridors of power.

In the end, Taylor almost drew the meeting with his boss to a close having not actually said a lot more than: *Good Afternoon, sir. I had a problem over here, but with a little help from my friends I've managed to fix it. Is it alright if I come home now?*

Taylor still had some unfinished business to take care of and would need Leo Mannheim's help to ensure this was concluded satisfactorily.

CHAPTER EIGHTY-NINE

Two days later

Chicago, Illinois

For the first time since her husband died, Corinne Williams woke up alone in an empty house. The mourning period had all but passed and concerned friends and relatives had returned to their busy lives.

Natural progression was how one distant second cousin had rather thoughtlessly described the process.

Most of the government security agencies had flitted in and out of things since the news of her husband broke, but even they had lost interest during the past week or so, eventually pulling all surveillance measures along with the state-of-the-art paraphernalia that came with them.

There were no strange cars or vans parked out in the street anymore, no undercover agents walking dogs or fake telecoms engineers removing and replacing access plates from lampposts.

Corinne Williams' husband was dead, and so far, nobody had been either able or willing to give her a straight answer as to how or why it had happened. She had been assured that her daughter was safe and well and that she would be home soon. That news and that news alone was the only thing that was keeping her functioning, but with every passing day, every single second she spent without Maddie, dark thoughts trickled into her brain, twisting her gut, playing tricks with her mind. And with every unanswered call she made requesting news - any news - more and more demons marched into her head. Everybody had packed up and gone home, leaving Corinne Williams with a gaping hole in her heart.

Pulling back the duvet, she swung her legs off the bed and stood, splaying her hand out behind her to steady herself against the effects of a minor bout of low blood pressure. She bounced back down on her backside before reaching over and popping a little blister pack of pills lying on her bedside table, downing two with a hefty swig of water. Her head cleared after a few seconds and she tried again to get up, this time succeeding. She walked into her slippers and trudged over to the front window, tugging at the cord to open the blinds.

Down below, the street was deserted save for a cab which had rounded the corner and was making its way slowly up the road towards the house. Probably one of the neighbours getting home after a night on the town, she mused.

Natural progression.

Corinne put on a housecoat and went downstairs to the kitchen, flicking the switch on her kettle. She retrieved a mug from the drainer and added some instant coffee along with a couple of sugars to give her a little edge. As she stood there listening to the rush of the kettle, her doorbell rang. She glanced at the kitchen clock on the wall: 10am; postman...regular as clockwork...

She picked up a pen on her way to the door, preparing to sign for the special delivery.

'Hi mom,' said a tearful Maddie Williams as the door swung open.

Corinne gaped, open-mouthed, at her daughter as if she couldn't quite believe her eyes. The pen tumbled to the floor and she stepped forward to envelop Maddie in a huge hug.

'M-Mom, I c-can't breathe!' Maddie's tears turned to laughter as her mother released her death grip, but only for a second. Corinne put her hands on her shoulders and gently pushed her back. 'Oh honey. Let me look at you!' She cupped the youngster's face in her hands before stepping back and checking the rest of her body, as if she were counting fingers and toes. 'Are you alright? Are you hurt?'

'I'm fine mom.' Maddie stepped aside, glancing over her shoulder. 'Look who's here.'

Ryan and April Taylor stepped out from behind the Williams' cherry tree in their front garden. April was carrying Jake. 'Hi Corinne,' Taylor said. 'We couldn't visit the States without looking you up.'

A wide smile framed Corinne Williams' face as if all her Christmases had come at once. Then the smile turned to sorrow as she stepped forward to greet him. 'How can I ever thank you, Ryan? Thank you. Thank you for bringing my baby back,' she whispered in his ear.

April held out her free arm and Corinne leaned across to kiss her cheek before drying her own tears with the flat of a hand.

'April, it's so nice to see you.' Corinne could sense the look of pity in April Taylor's eyes. She came up with the perfect way of changing the subject. 'And this young man must be Jake. I'm so glad he got his momma's looks.'

Taylor made a face. 'What's a guy to do to get a cup of coffee in this joint?'

They were drinking coffee in the Williams' spacious lounge. The Taylors were sharing a chunky, brown leather sofa. Corinne was sitting close to them in a rather uncomfortable-looking, high-backed chair as if she were serving a penance for past sins.

Taylor watched his little boy who was sitting straight-backed on the carpet in the far corner of the room. He was playing with some building blocks that Maddie had found in an old toy box she'd forgotten she had. Maddie was taking a block at a time out of the box, handing it to Jake who would try and take a bite out of it before tossing it back to her. She would wag her finger at him in mock anger and he would whoop with delight. Then Maddie would giggle along with him.

'Maddie always wanted a little brother,' Corinne said thoughtfully, staring at nothing in particular.

The Taylors glanced at each other. Corinne continued staring into space. 'You know I never wanted Troy to leave,' she whispered.

'Corinne, I-'

'No, let me finish, Ryan,' she cut in. 'I hoped, we hoped, that we would get back together, but the job-' She began to weep.

Taylor put his hand on hers. 'You and that little girl over there,' he said, nodding towards Maddie, 'Were the only things that mattered to Troy. And he gave his life protecting her.'

Her mood darkened. 'But why did he have to die? Nobody can tell me. It's just so unfair.' She broke down, weeping.

April stood, gesturing towards Maddie to take Jake next door while the adults ironed out the grown-up stuff. She knelt down in front of Corinne, holding both of her hands tightly. 'Corinne, I am so, so sorry about Troy and if there was something I could do or say that would make him walk through that door, you know I would.' She motioned over her shoulder. 'But you still have that beautiful, intelligent, incredible child through there who absolutely adores you. She's a credit to both of you. You have to keep it together for her, if nothing else.'

On their way to the airport, Ryan Taylor leaned across the back seat of the cab to give his wife a peck on the cheek.

'What was that for?' she laughed.

He shrugged, his mouth turning down at one side. What he didn't tell April was how relieved he was that he hadn't been forced to go over the hows and whys with Corinne Williams. Given time, he was certain Maddie would cover this.

'Ryan, what's wrong? Why the sad face?' April said, concerned.

Taylor snapped out of his thoughts. 'I was wondering how Brambles was.'

Brambles was the family pet, a two-year-old cocker spaniel.

April inhaled sharply. 'I forgot all about him. I told them at the kennels I wasn't sure how long he'd need to be in. How sad is that? Poor Brambles. He'll be thinking we've abandoned him.'

Taylor's expression changed. 'We'll pick him up on the way home. Then I'll drop you all off at the house,' he said matter-of-factly, glancing sideways for a reaction. He wasn't disappointed.

Eyes narrowing, she said, 'Ryan, tell me you're not going away again? Oh, for goodness sake!'

He held up his hands. 'I need to go back to Geneva. One day. That's it. I have a couple of things to see to there. Nothing dangerous, I promise. Okay?'

April turned away from him.

'Okay?' he pressed.

She continued to look the other way. Eventually, she agreed.

CHAPTER NINETY

The Taylors landed safely at Glasgow Airport, picking up the hire car MI6 had laid on for them, and rescuing their dog from the kennels on the way home. Brambles acted a little huffily at first, probably miffed at being left for so long, but seemed none the worse for wear. Ten minutes in the house and he was back to his old self. It was more than could be said for April. Taylor was forced to suffer the silent treatment as he took a quick shower and packed an overnight bag, a brief cheek-to-cheek with his wife the sum total of their mutual affection before he breezed out of the house.

The flight to Geneva International Airport provided Taylor with a little thinking time, in spite of the rasping snores coming out of the fat guy sitting in the seat next to him. Taylor would check in to a cheap hotel for the night, rising bright and early to take a taxi to his first destination. He studied the address on the printed copy of the email Leo Mannheim had sent in reply to his second request. His first was to organise Maddie Williams' safe passage from Brian Ricker's contact in Amsterdam to O'Hare International Airport, in Chicago, and on to a tearful reunion. *Job done*.

Taylor grabbed a quick meal at the hotel and requested an early morning alarm call before heading to bed around 9.30pm. A 7.30am call would allow him to gather his senses, wash and shower and eat a little breakfast before calling a taxi. He'd already asked Google for confirmation of address details and approximate travel time to there from the hotel. He estimated arriving around 10am.

The taxi pulled up outside the Friends of Susan Blacker orphanage at exactly 9.55am. As he stepped out into the sunshine, Taylor shivered at the sight that met him: heavy black railings, walls made of pitted sandstone, all black and weathered; roof turrets with broken spires and missing slates; decaying, heavily painted sash windows, looking as though they hadn't been opened in a hundred years. Outside, rusty swings with broken chain links and an old climbing frame that looked as if it would crash to earth if someone sneezed on it. The only things that looked strong and resilient were a million bright green weeds crawling out of the ground, twisting around and suffocating everything.

Taylor had done a little research on the place, discovering that Susan Blacker had been a Swiss silent comedy actress in 1920's America, appearing alongside giants of the movie industry including Charlie Chaplin, Oliver Hardy and Ben Turpin. There had been talk of an on-going affair with actor/director Mack Sennett, an accusation that the feisty Ms. Blacker had always vehemently denied. Her later years were blighted by poverty and illness, courtesy of being bled dry by a ruthless manager, and she died cancer-stricken and penniless in a New York ghetto at the age of only fifty-seven. During the *good years*, Ms. Blacker had used her name and position in society to champion charities and lost causes of every type and description, but it was due to her selfless work in helping to raise the funding required to develop safe havens for abused and under-privileged children that she really came into her own. The building Taylor was now standing in front of had become Susan Blacker's favourite, her special gift for her own people, for the place of her birth.

The facility had so obviously suffered down the years through lack of investment. A bit like its founder, it had once been something.

Taylor eased open one of the gates and walked up to the front door. He was surprised to see a modern digital keypad had been fitted to the wall next to the door, hardly in keeping with the general appearance. The options detailed on the keypad were displayed in English, French and German. Taylor hit reception and pushed against the door when he heard the lock spring open. Inexplicably, he formed a mental picture of Miss Finderbarr, his first primary school teacher, sitting behind a desk on the other side of that door. *Irma Grese* had nothing on Bunty Finderbarr. The word on the street was that she used to be a man. Taylor shivered at the thought.

Pleasantly surprised, he brightened when he stepped inside. The decor was fresh and clean and a few new items of furniture were dotted around, the most striking of which was the brand-new wooden reception desk. Taylor wasn't an expert on wood, but even he knew the desk was the real McCoy. Mahogany, he guessed. And he could smell faint traces of paint, estimating works to have taken place within the past few weeks.

The budget had clearly not stretched to include the flooring as the carpeting, though clean, was threadbare in patches. At least they were making an effort and Taylor felt a whole lot better now for Luke Giroud than he had done stepping out of the taxi a few minutes ago.

A pretty young woman of around twenty-five greeted him at the desk. She was wearing an immaculate powder-blue pinafore with her first name, *Grendel*, displayed in red letters on a little brass effect name plate on her left breast. Her light blonde hair was pulled back from her face, twisted together and clasped at the back like thick strands of golden rope, and her pearl white teeth dazzled under the harsh lights. She stood with her hands delicately placed on the desk, her fingernails filed to perfection and shining a tasteful light flesh colour. Taylor took in a whiff of expensive perfume as he reached the desk. 'Do you speak English?' he asked.

'Yes, I do. I'm the facility manager, Grendel Sochaux. How can I help you, sir?' Her voice was soft and soothing.

The quick lift of an eyebrow indicated mild surprise at one so young and pretty holding such a position before Taylor got straight to the point. 'My name's Ryan Taylor and I'm here to see Luke Giroud.' He needed to know if Leo Mannheim had come through for him. He had.

'Of course, Mr. Taylor. We've been expecting you. Luke has been brought down to one of our lounges. He is calm at the moment and doing some art work. I'll take you through.'

She slipped out from behind the desk and led him down a wide corridor towards a large fire door. The door boasted two slim panels of toughened glass. As they prepared to enter the room, Grendel turned to face Taylor. 'It is our policy to ensure that visits are supervised at all times. This will not be a problem for you, will it, Mr. Taylor?'

Taylor shook his head. 'No problem.'

'Have you met Luke before?' Grendel asked as she prepared to swipe her entry fob across the sensor.

'Yes, I have. Briefly. Don't know if he'll remember me though.'

'I am sure he will.' She smiled. 'Luke is a very bright boy. Everyone here will be sad to see him leave.'

'He's leaving?' Taylor played along.

'Why, yes. An unknown benefactor has set up a fund for him. Nobody knows who or why. He is being moved to a modern facility on the outskirts of Geneva. It is a truly wonderful place. I have seen it myself.' Grendel's eyes shone brightly as she spoke. It was clear to Taylor that she was genuinely pleased for the boy. 'Luke will receive the finest standards of care at this facility.'

'I can tell you've taken a shine to Luke, haven't you, Grendel?'

'Is it so obvious? Yes, he is a delightful child, but this,' she raised her eyes, 'Is no match for where he is going. I hope the location of the new facility does not present a problem to Luke's grandfather.' She swept the fob against the sensor as she said the words. The door clicked.

'Grandfather?' Taylor asked, puzzled. He leaned on the door handle, preventing Grendel from pulling the door open.

She stepped back, surprised. 'Yes, he is a lovely man. He has visited Luke four or five times over the past few weeks. The boy so looks forward to the visits.'

'Johan? Johan Giroud?' Taylor plucked the name from memory. But Johan Giroud was dead. He had seen the man with his own eyes, sitting in his armchair. And he looked far from fit to visit, especially with a bullet in his head.

'Yes, have you met Mr. Giroud?' she asked.

Taylor's eyes narrowed. I wonder, he thought. 'Tall, white haired? He has a small scar, here, on his right cheek?' He pointed to an area under his eye.

'Yes, that is the gentleman.'

'When did he last visit?' Taylor asked.

'Three, perhaps four days ago.'

'Thank you, Grendel. I'll call you when we're finished.'

Again, she presented her fob before heading back to reception. Taylor pulled the door open a couple of inches. He stopped to pull in a couple of deep breaths. Knots like balls of lead began to form in his gut. This was a game changer. Potentially, it could blow everything apart.

Although Taylor had no idea how much information the *grandfather* had managed to extricate from the youngster's troubled mind, his gut was telling him just how much. According to Grendel it had been three or four days since his last visit.

So exactly where was Franck Renner now?

CHAPTER NINETY-ONE

Taylor exchanged polite smiles with the middle-aged lady left in charge of Luke Giroud. Luke hadn't heard Taylor enter the room. He was far too busy meticulously colouring in a book using a bunch of wax crayons. Taylor held the woman's attention for a few seconds, putting his forefinger to his mouth as he crept towards the boy. She acknowledged before pointing at an easy chair strategically placed next to a window in the far corner of the room. He watched as she picked up a magazine from a rack on her way past, placing heavy-rimmed spectacles on the end of her nose and easing into the chair. She turned the chair slightly until it was facing away from them. Looking out at the main street, her attention switched between the magazine and the people outside going about their business.

Taylor heard a familiar noise as he drew nearer the boy. Luke was deep in concentration, so-much-so that he was doing his humming thing, his body rocking ever so slightly, back and forth, back and forth, back and forth.

Not wanting to alarm the boy, he carefully lifted a chair back, as opposed to dragging it, and sat down facing him. He folded his arms.

'Hi, Ryan. How are you?' Luke said, not averting his gaze.

Taylor laughed. 'That's very clever, Luke. How did you know it was me?'

'I saw you coming.' Luke pointed at the window before his attention snapped back to his *work*, a bit like an uncoiling spring.

Taylor was astounded at the speed and precision Luke displayed as different coloured crayons were picked up and dropped every few seconds, every stroke barely caressing the paper, and never ever crossing a line.

He decided to give it a couple of minutes as he could see Luke was almost done with this particular masterpiece – a bowl of fruit. The last thing he wanted to do was antagonise the boy. He seemed to be happy and in good spirits. If Taylor wanted to get him to open up, he would have to be cute about it.

Excitedly, Luke slammed his latest crayon down on the desk and spun the picture round for Taylor to look at. Taylor was amazed at how yellow the bananas were, how purple the plums, how green and red the grapes, and so on...

'I want you to have it, Ryan.' He thrust the book into Taylor's hands.

Taylor made a big play of carefully studying it. 'I'm honoured, Luke. This is great work.'

Luke snatched the book back, flipped over the page. 'I'll draw you another one...'

'Maybe in a little while. Can I talk to you first, man to man?' Taylor added 'man to man' when he sensed disappointment in the boy's eyes. It seemed to do the trick, as if the boy was ready to act responsibly. Like an adult.

'Talk about what?' Luke said.

Slowly, Taylor slid the book away from him, placed it on the edge of the desk, at the corner. 'Remember I asked you for help back at the house?'

'Mm-hmm.'

'Well, I need your help again. You're the only one I can trust.'

'Am I your best friend, Ryan?' Tears welled in his young eyes.

Taylor felt a lump form in his throat. The words hit him like a bolt of lightning. As before, he hated the deception, and, as before, he really had no choice. He had to find out what Luke Giroud had told Franck Renner. And he had to find out fast.

'Only the best friend in the whole wide world,' Taylor whispered, his voice cracking a little with emotion. He glanced over at the woman. She was too engrossed in her magazine to give a damn.

'It's about Stephanie, isn't it? You want to know what happened to her?' Luke said.

Taylor could sense sadness in his voice. 'Did the man ask you about Stephanie?'

Luke balled his hands, placing them under his chin. Started rocking back and forth, back and forth, back and forth.

Taylor was forced to re-group. 'What was the man's name, Luke? Was it Franck?'

The boy nodded sharply, continued rocking.

'Why did you tell everybody he was your grandfather?'

'He told me to.' More rocking. 'He said if they found out his real name he couldn't come and see me again.'

'Do you want him to come and see you again? You like him, don't you?'

'He is a nice man.'

'You know what? I like him as well. Franck is *my* friend too.'

A faint smile.

'What if I told Franck he could still come and visit you? You'd know I was telling you the truth, wouldn't you? Best friends don't lie to each other, right?'

Luke shook his head. He sighed. 'Can I have my book back please, Ryan?'

Taylor smiled at the boy, reached over to ruffle his hair. 'Sure.' Then he slid the book across in front of him. Luke picked it up and flicked over a few pages. When he eventually reached the back cover, he pulled out a glossy magazine photograph that had been tucked inside, and laid it down in front of Taylor. Taylor stared at the photograph and back at Luke, waiting for a reaction.

Suddenly, Luke's face contorted with rage. He jabbed a finger at the photograph, hissed, 'I told Franck that this bad man hurt Stephanie. He said he liked her and that she was very pretty. Stephanie told me she was going to tell him she couldn't see him again and that she didn't like him anymore.'

Taylor sat stunned for a moment. He snatched up the photograph, studied it again, as if he expected the image to change. Immediately, his thoughts raced back to the moment he picked up the list of summit attendees Leo Mannheim had sent him back in Washington D.C. This man had been in Geneva. Taylor should have picked up on it as odd, but didn't. *Stupid*! The name should have leapt out at him. Why was he there? Taylor was beginning to mentally cross and dot the t's and i's. Franck Renner must be on his way to Washington. And he had at least three days' start. If Renner did manage to *access* his target, and Taylor had no reason to doubt he would, it could blow everything to smithereens. Taylor had to get to him before Renner killed the man who had taken his daughter's life: the president's son, John Travis.

CHAPTER NINETY-TWO

Before he could even think about heading back to Washington, Taylor had to make time to go to Franck Renner's home, though he knew actually finding him there would be a long shot.

A tall, willowy woman answered the door. Her hair was long, soft and fine, and tastefully dyed a hint of blonde. Her face creased as she spoke, but kindly, and in all the right places. Taylor aged her around mid-sixties. He imagined she would have been a real looker in her prime.

'Mrs. Renner?' Taylor said.

'Yes,' she said. 'And you must be Mr. Taylor. My husband said you might call. Please, do come in.'

Why would he expect me to call?

Taylor waited in the hall as Georgia Renner shut Huber and Bloch (the Renners' dogs) in the back room before showing him into the lounge.

Taylor started when the noisy African grey parrot whoop-whooped at him as he walked past the conservatory door.

'Sorry, he always does that,' she said, sheepishly.

'Yes, I remember,' he said, also sheepishly.

'Please, sit down. Would you like something to drink?' She pointed towards the kitchen, or so Taylor assumed.

'No, thank you, Mrs. Renner, I'm looking for your husband. I have to find him, and quickly.'

'I'm afraid you will only find Franck if he wants you to find him. I have no idea where he is.' She smiled, like the dutiful wife of some country vicar.

Taylor gritted his teeth. 'I don't think you understand, Mrs. Renner, your husband may be in danger.'

'He is well used to it.'

'Sorry?'

'Look, Mr. Taylor. My husband's employment is, was, different from most others. I stopped asking him about it a long time ago.'

'*Is*? You're saying he's still an active agent?'

She looked confused. 'No, I didn't mean, well, the truth is, I don't know.'

'You're not making any sense, Mrs. Renner.'

'Before our daughter disappeared and the cancer began to take hold, Franck was happy to spend his days in the garden, or on the golf course, or spending time with our grandchildren. He and Stephanie were so close-' Her voice wavered. She cleared her throat before continuing. 'Finding out what happened to her became the only thing he could think about. Late night telephone calls, secret meetings with former colleagues. Sometimes he would disappear for days on end. And with his illness I was so worried about him.'

'Did he say anything to you? Anything at all about what he was intending to do?' Taylor had a fair idea of what Renner was planning. He had asked the question in case the old man had unwittingly let slip fine details. Again, it was worth a try.

'All he said was that he would be back in a few days,' she said.

Taylor could have said the sentence with her, word for word. Now for the sixty-four-thousand-dollar question: 'When did he leave?'

'Franck left the house at 5.30pm on Monday.'

Taylor inhaled slowly. On his way to the Renners' home, he had called the airport. The next scheduled flight to Washington D.C. was not due to leave Geneva until 10am tomorrow.

By then Franck Renner would have had a full four days' head start.

CHAPTER NINETY-THREE

After Taylor left the Renner house, he booked the flight to D.C. and checked into the airport hotel before plucking up the courage to call April to tell her he was going to be staying over in Geneva for another two or three days. His explanation was certainly convincing, all to do with government departments, paperwork and the 'pain-in-the-arse' that were local holidays. Convincing as it was, it didn't stop April chewing him out. As ever, he hated telling her lies. And, as ever, he felt he had been left with no other choice.

It had crossed his mind to contact MI6. What also crossed his mind were the possible consequences of tipping off any of the agencies, at home or in the States. Taylor thought of two right off. Firstly, security around the president and his family would be cranked up so high that only a madman, or a grieving father, might seek to finish the job he started. There could be only one outcome, and it wouldn't end well for Franck Renner. Secondly, in such circumstances, somewhere along the line, the source of the information – the giver - tends to get pulled into the mix. And Taylor had had his fill of playing public enemy number one.

He'd even considered calling Maxie Royce, but given Royce's now probable fragile position within The Firm, Taylor was convinced he would prefer to distance himself from any assassination attempt on the very administration he was using to keep Carlo Facchetti to heel. Now if that administration were to be blown apart. What consequences would that hold for Taylor and his family?

No, this was a problem he would need to try and fix on his own. He prayed he wouldn't be too late. Hoped that Renner would be forced to bide his time, pick his moment. The only fly in the ointment was that Taylor didn't figure Franck Renner to be the patient type.

CHAPTER NINETY-FOUR

6am: Taylor couldn't say why but he was somehow compelled to switch on the TV as soon as he woke up. Call it intuition.

The first news channel he came to was Swiss and, as such, the presenter was speaking Swiss-German, a variation of standard German. Taylor understood some words. He didn't need to be multi-lingual to work out the gist of what had taken place overnight. A short banner headline rolled along the bottom of the screen: *Eilmeldung: Sohn US-Prasidenten getotet.*

Every few seconds, a recent college photograph of a smiling John Travis flashed up on the screen. Cursing under his breath, Taylor kept pressing the channel change button until he reached CNN. He tossed the remote on the bed and flopped down on a chair close to the TV.

A solemn looking female journalist, her hand crushing a microphone, was standing outside what looked like the A & E department of a hospital. Police and ambulance light bars swirled in the background. Again, banner headlines rolled underneath. In the top right corner of the screen was a smaller image of the same photograph Taylor had seen on the Swiss channel.

'...details are sketchy at the moment, but we are expecting an official release in the next few minutes. What I can tell you for certain is that President Wilson Travis' son, John, is dead. We know that the eighteen-year-old was taken to the Memorial Hospital's accident and emergency department behind me here at around 5pm yesterday. Then, a clearly distressed President Travis, together with the first lady, arrived a little before 5.30pm. At around 2.15am this morning the hospital issued a short statement to confirm the news that, at 1.55am Eastern time, John Travis had sadly lost his fight for life. The statement went on to say that everyone at The Memorial's thoughts and prayers were with the president and the first lady at this sad time. At the moment it is not known...'

Taylor snatched up the remote and killed the TV. He flicked the kettle switch on and shovelled a heaped spoonful of coffee into a cup. Maybe the sudden influx of the drug would sharpen his senses. It was worth a try. His brain felt like mush. But at least he was able to figure out one thing; the next few hours would be crucial for him and April and Jake as the world waited for the whole story to unfold.

As far as Taylor could see, the US administration had some choices to make. Does it hang John Travis' reputation out to dry, and with it the credibility of the presidency? Worse, does it then go the whole hog and torpedo Wilson Travis' reign here and now, along with the careers of everybody who had dipped his toe into the corrupt pool, including Maxie Royce? Taylor very much doubted if things would be allowed to go that far. He reckoned the powers that be would be more likely to close ranks, circle the wagons, limit the damage or whatever way one likes to look at it. Taylor knew the whole thing was a crock, but also that the smart money for most people was on maintaining the status quo. The Travis family would get over their loss, drain the country of its sympathy, dust themselves down, and carry on. It wasn't right, but this was the way it had to be. Bizarrely, the boy's death might even boost the president's ratings in the run up to the end of his first term in office. The sympathy card sure was a powerful one in these circles.

Taylor started as his mobile halted the silence. He recognised the voice straight away.

'I'm assuming you've heard the news?' Leo Mannheim sounded tired, as if the weight of his awesome responsibility was bearing down on him, crushing him into the earth.

'Yes, sir.'

Mannheim cleared his throat. 'I need to know, have we anything to worry about here?'

'No, sir.'

'I assume you're not in that country at the moment?'

'That's right.'

'And that's good to know. Keep in touch.'

The phone disconnected.

Taylor could almost sense some of that weight lifting from Mannheim's shoulders with the last statement. Spoken like a man who didn't understand what had gone down and didn't want to, either.

Taylor sipped his strong coffee. It seemed to be hitting the spot. The mobile rang again. He hit the button and waited to hear the voice. Silence for about ten seconds...

'What's wrong? They do not teach you how to answer telephones in England?'

Taylor recognised Franck Renner's voice right away. Renner's wife had obviously passed on Taylor's number. 'I hear you've been a busy man,' Taylor said.

'Surely you don't believe everything you hear?'

'Wouldn't you, in my shoes?'

'Point taken.'

'Okay, I'm all ears,' Taylor said.

'Stay where you are. I'll be there in a few hours. By that time, you will already know.'

Before Taylor could say any more the connection ended. He tossed the phone back on the bed and took an even bigger slug of coffee, easing back in the chair. He felt better. Renner didn't sound traumatised. He obviously hadn't been killed, or worse, arrested. And he hadn't sounded to Taylor like a man who thought he was about to be either.

Taylor drained the coffee and began to consider his options. He could do the conventional thing like everybody else, put the TV back on and wait for news to unravel naturally. After all, he did have a few hours to kill before Renner appeared. Or he could hurry things along a bit...

He picked up the phone and scrolled down his list of contacts until the name *Maxie Royce* shone in the display. Before he could hit the dial button, the mobile rang. Eerily, the caller just happened to be...Maxie Royce.

CHAPTER NINETY-FIVE

By the time Renner boarded his plane in Washington, Taylor had already called the airport in Geneva to find out the arrival time. He assumed Renner would have telephoned his wife around the same time as he'd called him. He also assumed Renner would have asked her where he was staying. By doing so it would be highly likely that he intended to go to the hotel first. Armed with the information, Taylor worked out that touchdown to arrival time at the hotel would take in the region of an hour, maybe a little longer, allowing for ten minutes at the luggage carousel and for climbing right into a taxi. He reckoned Renner should arrive around 8.30pm.

At 7.45pm, after a quick call to the airport to check the plane had landed in time - it had - Taylor crossed the street to order a coffee and to watch proceedings from a small cafe. At 8.45pm he saw a taxi roll up in front of the hotel. The driver got out and opened the back door for his passenger.

Franck Renner lifted his suitcase and walked up the steps to the hotel. Taylor watched for any lip movements or signals. He inspected the adjoining buildings, the cars down on the street, ordinary people going about their business.

Renner rode the lift to the fourth floor as Taylor ran up the stairs. Taylor hit the landing in time to hear the muffled ting coming from inside the lift prior to the doors opening.

Renner looked less than surprised to see Taylor standing there. 'You were outside checking up on me?'

They shook hands. 'Hope it doesn't offend you,' Taylor said.

'I would have been offended if you hadn't.'

Taylor opened the door and ushered him inside, switching on the kettle as he passed.

'No coffee,' Renner said, unzipping his suitcase. 'Let's have a drop of the real stuff.' He pulled out a bottle of duty-free Scotch malt and walked over to a serving trolley upon which sat coffee making facilities. He cracked the bottle and upended two cups, glugging obscene helpings into each. Turning to face Taylor, he smiled as he handed him a cup, sat the other one down on a desk between them. 'Now I have to go somewhere,' Renner said. 'It was a long flight and I always try and avoid aeroplane toilets. I read somewhere that they are a breeding place for all sorts of things from all sorts of places.'

'Help yourself,' Taylor said.

A couple of minutes later, Renner came back into the room and sat down opposite Taylor. Taylor indicated towards the TV in the corner as some breaking news flashed up on the screen. He lifted the remote and the sound kicked in: '...*the killer's name has, in the past half hour, been released to the media. It is believed forty-two-year-old Thomas Redburn managed to slip past college security before walking into the classroom and shooting John Travis three times in front of his lecturer and horrified classmates. Redburn was later shot dead in the college grounds by federal agents. There have been no reports of any other injuries...*'

Taylor hit mute and turned to face Renner.

'Please, first we drink, then we talk,' Renner said before they tapped cups and drained the whisky. All of it. A warm glow passed over Renner's face as he eased back in the chair. Taylor sensed a hint of regret in the old man's eyes which he probably wouldn't have seen had he not been looking for it.

'John Travis killed my Stephanie,' Renner said, bowing his head.

'I know. Luke showed me the photograph.'

'And you thought I was going to Washington to kill Travis?'

'Weren't you?'

'That was the original plan, although I had no idea how I was going to do this. It would have been difficult.'

'Evidently it wasn't.'

'Let's say Mr. Redburn had a bit of a helping hand.'

'I'm listening,' Taylor said, folding his arms.

'I have a contact working in one of the US government departments.'

'CIA?'

'It's not important. What is important is that he is always informative, and discreet.'

Taylor lifted the cup. 'May I?'

'Please, help yourself.'

Taylor walked over to the little table and half filled his cup with the malt. He offered the bottle to Renner, who declined. As Taylor sat back down, Renner continued: 'We figured that Travis hadn't suddenly become a rapist and killer. We thought that he must have had previous. We were right. About a year and a half ago, a young fifteen-year-old was brutally raped in the shower area at an exclusive school in Washington.' He stared at Taylor. 'John Travis' school. During his final year.'

'Like father, like son,' Taylor said.

'Pardon?' Renner looked confused, obviously not picking up on the reference to the president's penchant for hookers.

'No matter. The girl, it was Redburn's daughter?' Taylor said. He was getting the drift.

Renner nodded. 'Nobody saw or heard anything,' he said. 'The police drew a blank. The case simply fizzled out. Everybody went back to their business. Then, Katie Redburn, racked by inner torment, took her own life. On her way to school one morning, she walked right off the platform in front of a train. Tom Redburn had already lost his wife to cancer the previous year. Now his only child was also gone.'

'I get it,' Taylor said. 'You give Redburn the information and he does your dirty work for you.'

Renner frowned. 'Believe me, it was not like that. I went to see him. I told him about Stephanie and about how I was yearning for justice. His eyes were dead and lifeless when he opened his door. He was going through the motions. By the time I left he had real fire in his belly. His life had purpose once again.'

'You knew he would kill John Travis.'

'Yes, I believed he would. As you know it can be the hardest thing in the world to actually take a life, even under the most appalling of circumstances, even when the person deserves to die more than anybody else in the world.' He made the sign of a gun. 'To actually pull the trigger.'

'You said you gave Redburn a helping hand?' Taylor said.

'I gave him a gun, told him where to hide it, when to enter the college. My friend distracted security by allowing a stray dog to run loose in the grounds. It looks as if the rest of the plan went perfectly.'

'And the authorities tie up the loose ends by shooting him dead. How very convenient.'

'Mr. Taylor, this man had nothing left to live for. I did him a favour. He took full revenge for his daughter's death before drawing his last breath.'

'And for *your* daughter's?'

'I cannot say I am unhappy about that. I am only human.'

Taylor felt Renner's stare burn right through him as he sipped the malt. 'So, it's over. You have your revenge, I go back to my life, and the president loses a criminally insane son, but takes full advantage of the sympathy vote to guarantee his next period in office.'

'Alas no, Mr. Taylor,' Renner said. 'If only it were so easy. I'm sorry, I genuinely am.'

'How so?'

'Through my contact I took the liberty of tracking your progress over the past few weeks. I know about the kidnapping of Walter McMichaels, though not of his eventual fate.' He paused to allow Taylor to make a comment. None came, so he pressed on. 'I know of your trip to Las Vegas and your liaison with Maxwell Royce-.'

'I spoke with Mr. Royce only this morning,' Taylor cut in.

Renner's brow furrowed. 'Really?'

'He called me, sent me this.' Taylor punched a couple of buttons on his phone and handed it to Renner. Renner's expression turned serious as he stared at an image of his meeting with The Firm's Teddy Capaldi. 'Maybe you can explain this to me?' Taylor continued.

Renner sighed. 'I know about Mr. Capaldi and his role within The Firm. I know of his feud with Carlo Facchetti. And I know how delicate Facchetti's position would be if anything happens to you.'

'Then I'm assuming you know where Luke's trust fund money came from?'

'Yes, it was the money that interested me in the first place.' Renner held up a hand. 'Though not that I planned to try and steal it. That was never the intention.'

'What is the plan then, Mr. Renner?' Taylor said.

'Mr. Capaldi listened to what I had to say. That I had access to you. That you trusted me. As I said, Mr. Taylor, I am only human. The truth is, he offered me money to make his problem, namely Carlo Facchetti, go away. A lot of money. Money that will make a huge difference to my family. It's too late for me, but for them...I'm ashamed to say that I accepted. He said that if I can make your death look suspicious, something that can be easily organised, it would appear like so to the other members of The Firm. Facchetti would be dealt with accordingly and The Firm would continue as normal.' Renner's attention dropped to his empty cup. Taylor noticed the move.

'The whisky?' Taylor said.

Renner nodded.

'But how?'

Renner drew in a deep breath. He reached into his pocket, producing a tiny clear sachet containing what looked like a couple of ounces of brown powder. He held it up for Taylor to look at before stuffing it back in his pocket. 'Slow acting poison. Detectable, if one digs deeply enough, as it has to be. But they tell me no pain,' he said, apologetically.

'How long?' Taylor said, unscrewing the lid of the malt and refilling his cup.

'One day, maybe two. I am sorry.'

'So am I,' Taylor said as he eased back in his chair before taking another swig.

Renner's face lost its colour. 'You switched the cups?' he said, his voice barely a whisper.

'I think you could be doing with that drink now,' Taylor said, holding up the bottle.

This time Renner agreed.

CHAPTER NINETY-SIX

London's East End

Taylor was following instructions to the letter. He jumped into a taxi at Heathrow Airport, requesting that the driver take him to the front door of The Tickled Trout pub. He paid the man and got out before stooping to pretend to tie his laces. As the taxi pulled away, he took a good look around to make sure he wasn't being followed. Satisfied, he strode through the front door of the pub.

Inside, including the barman, there were around two dozen people, all of them glued to a big TV screen on the wall, a live football match between North London rivals Arsenal and Spurs providing the entertainment. Perfect, thought Taylor, when not one of them, except the barman, gave him a second glance as he walked up to the bar. Taylor noted the name on a badge on the man's chest: *Norman*.

'What'll it be, mate?' Norman asked.

'Guinness, please.'

'Extra cold?'

'Go for it,' Taylor said, his gaze diverting to the TV when he heard the commentator's voice rise in response to a close call in Arsenal's penalty box.

'Which team, mate?' Norman asked.

'Neither of these,' Taylor replied. 'You?'

Norman put his finger to his lips before mouthing the name, Chelsea, and something about how his lot would wipe the floor with both teams at the same time. He leaned across the bar as he began pulling the pint. 'You Taylor?' he asked.

Taylor nodded.

'The man said you'd be here about now.' Norman pressed a button on the floor behind the bar with his foot. Taylor heard the click of the door release mechanism. Norman lifted up a little hinged flap of bar top and gestured over his shoulder towards a door at the end of the bar. 'Please go through. I'll bring your pint in when it's settled. Can I get you a sandwich or something?'

Taylor shook his head. 'Guinness will do fine, thanks.'

He made his way along a short corridor towards another door at the far end. Tapping firmly, he pushed his way in.

Leo Mannheim was sitting alone in a corner on a faded red leather couch that had seen better days. A battered old dart board and a pool table straight out of the 1970's, complete with chunky, threadbare cushions and scratched veneer indicated to Taylor that he was meeting the Controller of one of the world's most powerful government organisations in the beer soaked and nicotine-stained games room of a run-down boozer in London's east end.

Mannheim himself, with a two-day growth, grandad shirt, jeans and braces and scuffed plimsolls, looked as much like the VIP he was as Mickey Rourke did Brad Pitt. Taylor had to look twice to make sure.

'Glad you made it, son. Take a seat,' Mannheim said as he edged across the two-seater before sipping a mouthful of whisky from his glass. 'Did you get yourself a drink?'

'It's on its way, sir,' Taylor said.

'It's here now,' said Norman as he appeared behind Taylor and handed him the pint. Taylor thanked him, walked over to the sofa and sat down.

'Cheers, Norman,' Mannheim said. He held up his glass. 'Send us in a couple of refills in ten minutes or so, will you?'

'Ten minutes it is, Alf.'

After Norman had left Taylor turned to Mannheim, said, 'Alf?'

Mannheim laughed. 'I told him I owned chip shops all over England. He thinks I'm an eccentric millionaire.'

'And what does Norman get out of the deal?'

'He hosts regular county darts and pool tournaments and I supply the fish and chips free of charge if he lets me use this room in return. It's a million miles removed from HQ, but it lets me take care of business away from prying eyes and flapping ears.'

Taylor waited what he considered was a respectful time before getting down to the job at hand. Although he felt relaxed and in a non-threatening environment, given what had gone down over the past couple of weeks, he only planned on spending as long as was necessary in present company. No longer. 'Sir, I'd really like to get back home to Glasgow.'

'Yes, of course. Sorry, I should've realised,' Mannheim said. He put down his glass and shifted round to face Taylor. 'Okay, son. Here's how it is. I wanted to meet you to make sure we were both clear on the way forward.'

Taylor screwed up his face. 'I don't follow.'

'I'll put it another way. Let's say we have one possible version of events, and the official version.' Mannheim's face reddened, as if he were a teenager flushed with embarrassment about to make a move on his new girlfriend.

'Yes sir, I understand. We're covering backs. That's my cue for some straight talking, right?'

'My favourite kind, son,' Mannheim said.

'And this would be a two-way discussion?'

'Within reason.'

'Fair enough, sir. Where do you want to start?'

'Franck Renner,' Mannheim said.

Taylor nodded slowly. 'What do you want to know?'

'Well, the way I see it, and you can stop me any time, I think this guy tried to turn you over.'

'Go on.'

'And he wound up dead for his troubles.'

'Pretty much.'

'Okay, his daughter is murdered in Geneva. Somehow, he figures out who's responsible and persuades some unhinged American to do his dirty work for him. With the help of the CIA, of course.'

Taylor frowned. Not because of Mannheim's cruel description of a bereaved father wreaking vengeance on the person who had murdered his daughter. But because everything was beginning to slot right into place for Taylor. The CIA man who was Renner's contact across the pond had helped arrange a double hit. US president's son, John Travis, followed by his killer. The CIA stepped aside to let the first one go down before stepping right back in to finish it. Renner had taken Capaldi's money and had agreed to remove the person who had been at the sharp end all the way through, the one who knew more than anybody else. Taylor himself.

The plan backfired when Taylor outwitted the Swiss ex-secret service man. But how did this fit in with the overall plan? Was Taylor supposed to die? Would that have put everything to bed? Was he to be his country's sacrificial lamb in the same way Troy Williams had been the Americans'?

'Something wrong, son?' Mannheim said in response to Taylor's worried expression.

'Uh, no sir. Over-thinking things, I guess.'

Mannheim stared at his agent. 'Who wouldn't be paranoid, given what's happened to you lately?'

There was a palpable silence before Taylor visibly started when Norman backed his way through the door brandishing another couple of drinks.

Mannheim thanked the barman and waited until he had left them alone again before he next spoke. And when he did, it was again typical straight-talking. 'Brian Ricker's unfortunate passing has left us with a vacancy in Scotland.'

'Sir, I-'

'No hear me out, please,' Mannheim interjected. 'You see, I don't want a straight replacement up there for you. I think your talents would be wasted. It's there if you want it, but there are at least another four or five less qualified people I can slot into that role.'

'Then what, sir?'

'For reasons that would become clear, I can't go into too much detail at this point.' Mannheim sidled forward in his seat. 'The powers that be are looking for me to head up a unit, completely off everybody's radar, to handle more *sensitive* situations. I want you to be my right-hand man.'

'How sensitive?' Taylor asked, expecting very little elaboration on Mannheim's part. He was right.

'Sensitive, in a worldwide sort of way. That's all I can tell you. Other than you'd have to be based down here and work out of HQ. And, you'd treble your salary. Basically, you sign up, and then we go over the finer details.'

Taylor could sense Mannheim studying his every move as he began to consider the pros and cons: wages, career advancement and improved lifestyle were countered by upheaval, uncertainty and potential danger. Words like *sensitive* and *worldwide* conjured up images of difficult covert operations played out against terrorist groups. Everything about it rang alarm bells.

No matter which way Taylor looked at it, one particular organisation kept creeping into his brain: *ISIS*

EPILOGUE

Two months later

Glasgow, Scotland

Earlier that morning, April Taylor had fought back the urge to tell her husband. She didn't quite know how, but fought it she had.

She'd risen earlier than normal and slipped into the bathroom before he and Jake had even opened their eyes. She'd followed the instructions to the letter and was now holding the little magic stick up in front of her. Her heart pounded as she waited, refusing to avert her gaze. Eventually the word *Pregnant* appeared in the box.

Somehow, April had managed to get through showers and dressing and baby-feeding and breakfast without breathing a word, although the huge grin plastered all over her face at one point had almost given the game away.

It was all she could do not to spill the beans, but she had made the decision to cross the t's etc. and confirm it all first. Sometimes home tests can get it wrong, or so she'd read. Hence the late morning doctor's appointment.

April's mood darkened as she began to contemplate, again, the prospects for the continuing good health of the family following her husband's decision to accept Leo Mannheim's offer to head up the new anti-terrorism unit in London. Even a trebling of his salary and the prospect of a vibrant, exciting new life among the glitz and glamour of the capital had not won her over. Not even close. Ryan Taylor's new position reeked of danger. He knew it, and now, through his demeanour, so did she. The phrase *out of the frying pan* had almost passed her lips during lively conversations between her and her husband on numerous occasions lately, each and every time they revisited the events of the past few months.

April, her heart rate quickening, chastised herself for even harbouring the thought that the timing of the new baby could have been better. Tears welled up in her eyes as she battled to put her positive spin on things. Fast forward to this afternoon: Ryan would be getting back after his meeting with Leo Mannheim at the Glasgow office just after lunchtime. She would already be home, armed with life-changing news. She smiled. It was working.

Taylor walked in the door bang on 1.45pm. 'Something smells good. Anything for little ol' me? I'm absolutely starving,' he said as he opened the fridge, searching for scraps. 'April, you there?'

'Just be a minute.'

'Okay.'

Two minutes later, April entered the living room, Jake in tow. 'I have something I need to tell you,' she said, 'But it can wait. You first. How did it go?'

'How did what go?'

She rolled her eyes, sighed. 'Did you get everything sorted out?'

'Yep, all done and dusted.' He sat down on the sofa, chewing on a stick of celery he had rescued from the bottom of the fridge.

'That's good, isn't it?' She paused, he nodded. 'When do you start?'

'Two or three weeks, maybe even a month.'

She also nodded. 'Bit vague, isn't it? You'd think that everything would be mapped out. Y'know, tight timelines, like the military operation it is?'

Taylor took another bite of his celery, sniffed. 'You think?'

'Ryan, what is going on? I swear to god, I'll-'

He raised a hand, grinning. 'Chill, love. Otherwise, you'll blow a gasket.'

'Blow a gasket? I haven't even started yet! You walk in the door, shrugging your shoulders, telling me nothing! You don't even know when you're supposed to be in London to start this thing, or when we need to be moving down there to join you!' She stood over him, hands on hips, as she vented her anger.

'Who said anything about London?' he said, looking up at her, smiling.

'Eh? Ryan, so help me-'

Again, Taylor cut her off with a raised hand. 'Okay, I'll tell you what. You sit down right here and I'll level with you.' He held her hand as she sat next to him. 'This afternoon I was getting ready to go in and meet Mannheim. Literally five minutes before the meeting, my phone rang. Lo and behold, it's none other than Maxie Royce.'

'Maxie? What did he want?' April said, her eyes narrowing.

He took a deep breath, huffed it out. 'He offered me a job, in Vegas, starting in three or four weeks. He's flexible.' He paused for a reaction.

'Wh-what about us, me and Jake?' she replied, her voice quivering.

'You and Jake need to stay here. But it's ok, you know I won't forget you, either of you. I'll keep sending the money.' He threw his hands in the air. 'For god's sake, you'll be coming with me. What did you think, I'd leave you both here?'

'We're going to live in Vegas?'

'We're going to live in Vegas. Well, at least for a while. If we want to come home, we can. It'll be up to us. There will always be a job here heading up our Glasgow office. Mannheim's promised me that if things don't work out.'

'And just what will Maxie have you doing, Ryan, kneecapping people for a living?' She frowned.

He laughed. 'Nothing like that. Maxie assured me it's completely legitimate. He'll go over the finer details when we get there. I mean, what's not to like?' He popped the last piece of celery in his mouth as he rose from the sofa. 'Anyway, what's for eating?'

'I'll put something on in a minute,' she said, pulling him back down. 'There's something I really want to know.'

'What?' he said, a puzzled look on his face.

'What gives you the right to make a life changing decision like that without running it past me first?'

'April, honey, I-'

'No, let me finish, Ryan,' she cut in, trying hard to suppress her smile. 'You decide the fate and future of four people off your own back, and no consultation with any of us?'

'I'm sorry, I thought that-' He stopped mid-sentence. 'Wait, you said four?'

'Yip.'

'You mean?'

'Yes, that's exactly what I mean.'

Ryan Taylor gave his wife the biggest hug ever before they both eased themselves back in the sofa. Jake, sensing something was in the air, also appeared for a cuddle.

'I'd say that calls for a wee drink, wouldn't you?' he said.

'Absolutely.'

'Diet coke?'

'Perfect!'

THE END

WATCH OUT FOR THE RETURN OF RYAN TAYLOR IN THE NEXT BOOK IN THE SERIES: DESIGNER BABY

About Andrew D Malloy

Andrew D Malloy was born in Cardiff, Wales, but brought up in Scotland. He lives in Denny, Stirlingshire with his wife Sue, children Dani and Stephen, and Ollie the border collie.

An avid reader and a fan of the crime and thriller genres, he achieved critical success a few years ago with his first two novels, Frantic and Bible John Closure, before co-authoring Memoirs of a Hard Man - The Danny Malloy story, an autobiographical account of his father's life and times in football.

After a long sabbatical, he is back with the first in a series of books featuring Secret Service agent, Ryan Taylor.

Books two and three in the series, Designer Baby and Under Burning Skies, are in the pipeline and should be on shelves before too long.

Connect with Andrew D Malloy

via the website - www.andrewdmalloy.co.uk,

via Facebook - Andrew D Malloy Author

via Pneuma Springs Publishing Author's page

Other Book(s) by Andrew D Malloy

Bible John – Closure – ISBN 9781907728167

The illegitimate birth of twin boys in 1945: the infamous Bible John slayings: two present day murders.
What is the terrifying link that connects all three?

During the late 1960s, the actions of a vicious serial killer prophetically dubbed 'Bible John' caused mass hysteria among the young women of Glasgow, holding them in a chilling, vice-like grip of terror. Then, inexplicably, in late 1969, almost as quickly as they had begun, the killings stopped.

It is 2010 and two teenage girls are dead, strangled. On the surface the authorities appear to treat the murders as unrelated but ambitious young policeman, DCI Mason Blackwell, has other ideas...and a vested interest. A personal link to the original murders compels him to delve deeply to try and establish a connection between generations.

Blackwell, his good friend and colleague, DI Theresa Bremner, and ex-Special Forces agent, Tom Logan, now a top criminal psychologist, join forces to form a special unit designed to track down the killer.

In an age of recession and budget cuts, an already depleted police force is then stretched almost to breaking point by the emergence of another killer – one who randomly executes wife beaters and child abusers.

The scene is set for a nightmarish journey for Mason Blackwell and his team as the crime count threatens to spiral out of control. Expect the unexpected as the story dramatically twists and turns, sending all concerned towards a violent and terrifying conclusion...

Lightning Source UK Ltd.
Milton Keynes UK
UKHW010644290822
408013UK00001B/249